ALSO BY TONY SPALLONE

Murder at Breeze Canyon

MURDERS IN THE HIGH DESERT

by
Tony Spallone

The reviews are in for Tony Spallone's first book, *Murder at Breeze Canyon*.

"This the author's debut novel, but it's crafted as if he's been at it for decades. Thought at least six different times that I was absolutely sure 'who done it,' but I was wrong every time, and stunned by the plot twist at the end. Wonderful book for a beach read or a late night diversion, but be careful, you won't want to put it down."

"Terrific in its development of characters, relationships and plot."

"... an exciting crime novel that kept me involved until the end. As the murders piled up I kept guessing wrongly who the killer was. The writing was so clear and real that I could easily picture each crime and the progressive investigation. I had to read it every free minute I had."

"The threads Spallone weaves! You will get to know each character well. You will think them interesting. You will get to like them, until you find out more. You will just notice the hints of loose threads and not see the cloth until the very end."

"Only a true cyclist could conceive of all the twists and turns Tony Spallone put into the pages of Murder in Breeze Canyon. What a ride! When I got to the end, breathing hard, I found myself doubling back, looking for clues I had missed. They were there, skillfully planted in a plot so fast paced it virtually compels the reader to, well, breeze by them."

MURDERS IN THE HIGH DESERT

MURDERS IN THE HIGH DESERT

Published in the United States of America by Long Walk
Publishing.
    www.TonySpallone.com / Tony@tonyspallone.com

Copyright © 2015 by Tony Spallone

This is a work of fiction. Names, characters, businesses, places,
events and incidents are either the products of the author's
imagination or used in a fictitious manner. Any resemblance to
places, actual persons, living or dead, or actual events is purely
coincidental.

ISBN-13: 978-0-9864271-1-4
ISBN-10: 0-9864271-1-X

Edited by Stephanie J. Beavers Communications
www.StephanieJBeavers.com / 610-247-9494

Cover design by Slobodan Cedic

DEDICATION

To Mark, Sheri, Ryan, Nicholas, and Lauren.

ACKNOWLEDGEMENTS

I am so fortunate my wife Patti encourages me to pursue my passion for writing. She is the sounding board for my stories, my ego booster, and soul mate, and deserves much of the credit for the story line in this tale.

Thanks to Rose Williams who is my unofficial editor, and John Williams, both of whom enthusiastically embrace my stories.

My editor, Stephanie Beavers, who assiduously cleans and tightens my manuscripts, and patiently works to educate me via occasional grammatical teaching moments.

I also want to thank my friends, extended family, and everyone else who enjoyed my first novel, *Murder at Breeze Canyon*, and especially to Maryanne, Leo, and John for their wonderful and continued support.

PROLOGUE

In the dim overhead light Gwen Willington fumbled through her purse for the front door key to her condo. It was nine o'clock. She was returning from a laughter-filled girl's-night-out dinner at Le Champignon Bistro in Santa Fe. She found her key and was opening the door when she was rushed from behind by a man wearing a ski mask. The man shoved her hard against the door and just as quickly wrapped his arm tightly around her neck, making it impossible for her to scream for help. He had been lurking in the shadows of a black pine tree at the front of the building. Gwen's purse dropped to the ground with a thud.

She scratched and clawed at the man's arms with all her strength and violently kicked at him with the heels of her shoes, trying desperately to escape his hold. But he was relentless in his grip. In a matter of just seconds he dragged her inside and pushed the door closed behind them. He had one arm still tight around her neck, the other around her waist.

Gwen fought for air, for one more breath of life and strength. After a minute, her struggle ended.

Dead!

The man relaxed his hold and let her slide through his arms to the floor.

After removing his ski mask, he cracked the door open to see if the attack outside the condo had drawn anyone's attention. He heard only a dog barking in the distance. Satisfied there were no witnesses, he retrieved Gwen's purse, then closed and locked the door.

Next he reached into his pocket and pulled out a small flashlight. He shined the light on Gwen's lifeless face, tilting his head back and forth as though studying a fine painting.

Beautiful. Too bad.

He retrieved a blanket from one of the bedrooms, rolled Gwen in it, then sat on the couch and dozed until just before midnight. When he awoke, he looked out the front bay window and saw that all but a few lights in the neighborhood had turned dark.

He heaved Gwen over his shoulder, left the condo, and dropped her blanketed body in the bed of his pickup.

CHAPTER 1

Angela Foster saw the flashing lights about a half mile behind her as she drove along Route 14, north of the Yiqua Indian Pueblo. The seldom-used state road from Santa Fe to Albuquerque ran parallel to heavily trafficked Interstate 25.

Where was he hiding?

It was twelve fifteen. The warm June Sunday had turned into a typically chilly desert night. Angela had just ended her four-to-midnight shift at the Indian Bend Hotel and Casino, "the Bend," and was on her way home, after cutting across the desert on a back road that took her to 14. By the end of her shift, she was so tired she hadn't bothered to change for the half-hour drive north to her apartment in Santa Fe, and was still wearing her skimpy black-and-gold waitress outfit. She upped the heat in the car to seventy-five to take the chill off.

She looked at the speedometer and realized she was running at eighty miles an hour. All she could do was slow down without using the brakes and hope the cop was after someone else. She held her breath.

It wasn't the first time she was hard on the accelerator, eager to get home, exhausted after a long night's work.

Pass me, please.

She slowed to fifty-five miles an hour and maintained that speed, but it was too late.

The flashing lights quickly caught up with her, and ten yards from her bumper flicked its headlights at her.

Dammit!

She turned on her signal and pulled onto the dirt shoulder, skidding to a stop. She watched the cop from her rearview mirror and saw him stick his arm out the window. He motioned her to go farther off the road, down a dirt pathway that was bordered by an occasional pine tree and leading to nowhere that she could tell.

He flashed his high beams again when he wanted her to stop.

Why tonight? I'm so tired.

After the desert dust settled, she saw the vehicle behind her wasn't a cop car, but a pickup with a red flashing light on top of the cab.

It must be one of the Yiqua tribal cops.

She knew the reservation cops occasionally used unmarked vehicles to nab speeders who raced on stretches of highways built across their land.

The driver turned off his flashers, but remained seated inside his truck. Angela noticed the interior cab lights were off. *What's he doing back there?* Finally, he got out. He walked slowly alongside Angela's car and shined his powerful flashlight on her face. She squinted and dropped her head away from the blinding light—just what he wanted her to do.

"Officer, how fast was I going?"

"I had you clocked at eighty." His voice was raspy. "Have you been drinking?"

"No, I just finished my shift waitressing at the Indian Bend. I'm on my way home."

"I know."

"What?"

"You're heading home? Where's home?"

"Santa Fe."

He kept his blinding light on her face. "Let me see your driver's license."

Angela looked away from the intense light as she dug through her wallet to hand him her license. She noticed he was wearing blue vinyl gloves. "Angela, do you have any drugs in the car?"

"No, I don't do drugs."

"Stay here and keep your hands on the steering wheel," he ordered, and walked back to his vehicle.

She watched him in her rearview again as he stepped back into his truck and sat for several minutes. *This is ridiculous. He's taking forever.* She got out of her car. "Officer, hello. Officer? What are you doing? Can you just please give me a warning so I can go home?"

"Get back in your car!" he ordered from his open window.

She froze.

He shined the flashlight at her again.

She cupped her hand to the side of her face to shield her eyes from the blinding light.

"I said, get back in your car. Now!"

Angela retreated to her car, frightened by his angry tone. Inside, she put her hands back on the steering wheel.

The man was walking back toward her, but she was unable to see his face. She leaned closer to the rearview mirror to try to see what he was doing.

When he returned to her car, he shined the flashlight pointblank at her.

"You're blinding me," she said. "Can you put that light down?"

He kept it on her. "You know going eighty on this road is like having a death wish. You've got mule deer crossing the road around here at night. You hit one of those at high speed and you're dead."

"I know. You're right. I promise I won't speed again. Can you just let me off with a warning?"

"I probably could, but your taillight's out, too. That's a problem. I'm afraid I can't overlook both offenses. Besides, I believe you're under the influence of drugs. What do you suggest we do about that?"

"I don't know what you mean."

"I'll show you. Step out of the car."

"Why?"

He opened the door. "Because I think I know what you can do for me."

She squinted from the light but caught a glimpse of him. He was wearing a ski mask under a baseball cap. The word *POLICE* was stitched on the cap.

"Why are you wearing a ski mask?"

"I'm working undercover."

Angela was scared. She tried to close her door. "I'm not getting out."

He yanked it open. "Get out of the car. Now!"

She tried to turn the key in the ignition, but he grabbed her wrist.

"Stop it. You're hurting me. Let go," she yelled.

He wrenched her out of the car.

She was nearly hysterical. "What do you want? I don't understand why you're doing this to me."

"Stop resisting. I'll make it quick. Get out and walk around to the other side of your car."

She continued to argue. "I don't know what you think I am, but I'm not going to—" He grabbed her by an elbow and pulled her to the other side of the car where they would not be visible from the road.

"You know, Angela Foster, my report might say I found drugs in your car."

She challenged him through her sobs. "No way. I told you I don't do drugs. I've never even smoked pot."

"Sorry, but I found drugs on the front seat next to you."

"What drugs? You're making that up. I don't know what you want me to do, but I need to go home. Now, let me go, please, or…"

He shoved her against the car, turned off his flashlight, and set it on top of the car. "Face the car, spread your feet, and put your hands behind you. I'm going to search you. Do you have anything on you that will hurt me? Needles? Anything sharp?"

"No. Stop it. You're hurting me."

He clamped handcuffs on her.

"Stop it!" she screamed. "I told you I don't have anything on me. Where do you think I could hide anything wearing what I have on?"

The man removed his gloves and stuffed them in his back pocket.

"Oh, my God. I don't believe you're doing this. What do you want from me?"

"You know."

"No I don't!"

Starting at her shoulder, he frisked her. His bare hand lingered on her neck, under her hair. Then he patted her back and shoulders and moved to her behind—holding his hand there far longer than he should have. He reached around to her thighs, then up to her breasts. "Keep your feet stretched wide."

She struggled against his force and tried to turn around, but he kept her pinned to the car, his body tight against hers.

She was powerless to escape. "What are you doing? Stop it! Stop it!" she screamed.

"Angela, no one will hear you out here."

She sobbed. "Please stop."

"I'm going to say this once only. Look straight ahead. Do not turn around. Do you understand me?"

"Yes," she sobbed. "I won't. I promise."

He pulled a few feet away from her.

She heard the sound of a zipper and shrieked, "Oh, my God!" She turned to run from him, but he grabbed her and yanked her back against the car.

She felt a sharp sting on the back of her arm. Within seconds, she was numb and lifeless. He caught her as she collapsed, and lowered her gently to the ground, groping her as she lay gasping for air. Her eyes were open wide, but unseeing. He closed them. She felt his hands all over her, but she couldn't fight, or scream, or move, or open her eyes.

"Now, that's better. Such a good girl," he said. "Wait for me here. I'll be right back."

He walked unhurriedly to his pickup, stopped momentarily at the driver-side window, and retrieved a blanket from the bed of his truck. He unfolded it and placed it alongside Angela's car. He picked Angela up by her elbows and dragged her onto the blanket.

"She's heavier than she looks."

CHAPTER 2

Patrolman Harvey Eldridge of the New Mexico State Police was on his normal nightly patrol of Route 14. He passed what looked like an abandoned car about twenty-five yards off the roadway.

Eldridge turned on his flashers, made a U-turn on the narrow two-lane road, and headed back to check the vehicle. He pulled up behind it and shined his cruiser's side-mounted floodlight on the vehicle. He checked his computer's license plate recognition database to determine if the car was stolen, belonged to a wanted person, or if it was the object of any other police database search. The results came back negative. With his flood light lighting the way, he approached the car with caution, hugging the driver's side until he was able to look inside the car. It was empty. He saw the doors were unlocked and noticed the key was still in the ignition. He popped the trunk and found it, too, was empty. He walked around the passenger side of the car, then went back to his patrol car to fill out an Abandoned Car tag. The preprinted message on the red tag read "This vehicle will be deemed to be abandoned if not removed within 24 hours of the time below. Towing and storage expenses will be at the owner's expense." He wrote "3:00 a.m. June 5" on the time line and signed his name.

* * *

Sergeant Shiloh Youngblood was home on leave after a nine-month deployment in Afghanistan with the 3rd Cavalry Regiment of Fort Hood, Texas. Powerfully built and standing six feet tall, the round-faced twenty-five-year-old had departed his pueblo a year earlier as a boy and returned as a man. His jet-black hair, in a buzz cut now, was a far cry from the ponytail he wore when he enlisted. A hero of the war, he received a Purple Heart for injuries sustained in combat and was awarded the prestigious Silver Star Medal, the third highest award in the armed forces after the Medal of Honor and the Distinguished Service Cross.

His citation read:

Ambushed by the Taliban on a nightly patrol in Kandahar Province, Afghanistan, U.S. Army Sergeant Shiloh Youngblood and his squad were surrounded by the enemy and pinned down by heavy fire. Sergeant Youngblood and three others of his squad were wounded by shrapnel from a grenade blast. With the use of only his right arm Sergeant Youngblood exhibited great gallantry to single-handedly kill six Taliban fighters and to enable all seven of his squad members to escape.

Although fully recovered from his wounds, Shiloh was unable to sleep this Sunday night, his first night home. The nearly nine hundred inhabitants of his Yiqua Pueblo had greeted him by holding a parade and a hero's welcome, with speeches from the pueblo's governor and friends, and a food fest, music, and dancing until dark. But the long flight home combined with the excitement of seeing his family and friends kept him from getting much-needed sleep.

Though it was 1:30 Monday morning, according to Shiloh's body clock—still on Afghan time—it was ten hours later in the day. He would need a few days to adjust to the time difference and to turn off both the excitement of his return and the anxiety of his tour of duty.

Shiloh put on a light jacket to ward off the coolness of the desert night, and walked through the sleeping village, soaking up the sights and smells so beloved and so familiar to him. As he walked to the edge of town, he saw headlights from a vehicle bounce across the high desert and then suddenly go dark. He calculated the vehicle to be two miles out, in the middle of the Yiqua reservation, and well off Route 14.

What's going on out there?

Curiosity got the best of him and he decided to investigate. Aided by the light of a half moon, Shiloh walked into the desert toward where he last saw the lights of the vehicle. After thirty minutes he spotted a pickup and saw a man moving about the truck. He dropped to his haunches behind the edge of a slight rise ringed with rabbit brush and sage, and watched.

What's he doing?

A heavy cloud covering crossed the western sky and mantled the half-moon. The driver of the pickup looked up and then peered into the darkness to see if anyone had followed him. He saw only the wide expanse of the New Mexico desert, the distant lights of Santa Fe, and the dim lights of a few adobes in the Yiqua Pueblo. He said something, but Shiloh was unable to make out his words.

The man opened the tailgate. It dropped with a clank. He looked up again, said something else, and removed a pick and shovel. He leaned them against the pickup.

Unable to see what the man was doing, Shiloh lifted up for a better view.

The man caught movement out of the corner of his eye, but did not let on that he had noticed. He walked to the passenger side of the pickup, hidden from Shiloh's view. Through the open window, he retrieved a flashlight, then donned a ski mask and a baseball cap. He casually returned to the rear of the truck, intentionally not looking in Shiloh's direction. Then, in one swift motion, he pulled his .38 from its holster, aimed the powerful flashlight at Shiloh, and rushed toward him.

Shiloh fought the urge to run.

The man was on him in an instant. "Police! Flat on the ground. Now!"

Shiloh dropped to his knees. "I said, flat on the ground."

Shiloh lay face down on the ground.

"Hands behind your back. If you give me any shit, I'll put a bullet in your ear. Got me?"

"Calm down. I'm not going to do anything. You a cop?"

The man didn't answer.

"Put your hands behind your back!"

Shiloh complied. The man handcuffed him, then took a bandanna from his pocket and, with the weight of his knee on Shiloh's back, tied it tightly around Shiloh's eyes. "What are you doing here, kid?"

"Nothing. I couldn't sleep and saw your lights."

The man put the .38 to Shiloh's temple. "Who else is with you?" He looked around warily to see if he spied anyone else.

Shiloh felt the cold of the revolver. "No, just me."

Satisfied he was alone, the man asked, "You're from Yiqua Pueblo?"

"Yes."

"I thought so. Do you have a weapon on you?"

"No."

"What about your cell phone?"

"I left it at home."

The man patted Shiloh down. "Okay, get up. Let's go." He held Shiloh by his manacled wrists and pushed him toward the pickup.

"Where are you taking me?"

"Just keep walking." At the truck, the man shoved Shiloh hard to the ground, his back against the rear tire. "Now, sit there and keep quiet. I'm going to ask you again. What are you doing out here in the middle of the night?"

"I told you, I saw your lights. And let me ask you, what are *you* doing out here?"

"I'm looking for gold, wise ass," the man rasped.

"Why are you wearing a ski mask?"

"None of your concern, now, is it? What's your name?"

"Shiloh."

"Shiloh what?"

"Youngblood."

"Youngblood? No shit. Well, Shiloh Youngblood, have you been following me?"

"No. I told you I saw your lights from the pueblo and came to see who was out here."

"Okay, pal, don't give me any crap. Got it?"

"How could I? You've got the gun."

"You're no fool."

"So what are you really doing in the desert in the middle of the night?"

"I told you, I'm looking for gold."

How could this be happening? I've been to hell and back, and I come home to this psycho.

The man holstered his gun and started to dig. Using his pick and shovel, he dug in the dry hardpan of the New Mexico desert. After ten minutes, he leaned on his shovel to take a

13

break, then walked to his truck for his bottle of water. "You know, digging in this freaking desert is like trying to break through concrete with a spoon."

Shiloh agreed with the man's comment. "The desert is harder than people think."

"I'm not talking to you."

"Sorry. I thought you were."

The man returned to the hole he had started, grabbed the pick, and swung it hard into the ground. He struck a large rock a few inches below the surface. The shock of the pick's steel hitting rock reverberated up his arm. He threw down the pick. "That's it. I'm through."

The man returned to the truck.

Shiloh wasn't sure if he was talking to himself or if there was someone in the truck he was talking to. He cocked his head to listen for a response, but couldn't tell.

"Good idea. That's what I'll do," the man said, loud enough for Shiloh to hear.

CHAPTER 3

"Okay, pal, you're doing the digging. Here's the deal. I'm going to take off your cuffs and I'm going to watch you dig. You're strong. You should get the hole done in half an hour. Better you than me." The man dug in his pockets for the key to the handcuffs. "Stand up."

The man shoved Shiloh against the truck. "And in case you didn't know, my gun is at your back. You try to fight me and I'll blow you away. Got it?"

"Yes."

"Your blindfold stays on until I tell you to take if off. Now, spread your feet—wide." Shiloh did as he was told.

"Wider!" Shiloh spread his feet wider, and the man removed the handcuffs. "Do not turn around until I say."

"Okay." Shiloh had no choice but to accede.

"If you think you're going to rush me, think again. You'll be dead in a heartbeat. Got me?"

"Don't worry, I know better than to do anything stupid."

"Good." The man stepped back three yards from the truck. "Okay, take your blindfold off. You can turn now."

Shiloh got his first good look at his captor, a lean six-footer wearing a black ski mask, plaid shirt, dark jeans, cowboy boots, and a baseball hat pulled down low, nearly covering his eyes. Two other details caught Shiloh's attention—the badge pinned on the man's shirt and the word *Police* stitched on the front of his cap.

"You're wearing a badge, but you're not a cop, are you?"

The man didn't answer.

Shiloh tried a sympathy approach. "Look, I don't know what your game is. All I want is to get back to my pueblo. I just returned from Afghanistan yesterday."

"So, what do you want—a medal and a chest to pin it on?" The man looked beyond where Shiloh was standing and laughed. "I guess he wants a medal."

Shiloh turned to see who the man was talking to, but saw no one. *Maybe someone's in the truck.* He couldn't tell. He turned back to the man. "Listen, I thought maybe you served in the Gulf yourself, and if you did, you'd understand."

"You're barking up the wrong tree."

"Look, I just want to get back to my mother. She lives in the pueblo and I haven't seen her for nine months. How about you let me go so I can get some sleep. That's the reason I'm out here. I couldn't sleep, so I decided to take a walk to relax and settle my brain."

"In the desert, in the middle of the night? Bullshit. Start digging."

"You know, people from the pueblo are going to come looking for me."

"I don't think so. This is the last time I'm going to say it. Dig!"

"How deep?"

"I'll tell you when it's deep enough."

"Who are you planning to bury?"

"You, if you keep giving me shit."

"So you want me to dig a grave for myself?"

"Nah, I'll let you go as soon as you finish digging," he said. Shiloh didn't believe him. "But Shiloh Youngblood, think about it. We're on your land. It's sacred Indian land. Right? Nothing better for your Indian spirit than to be buried on your own sacred ground, right? So if you give me any more lip, I'll do your soul a favor. Now, just shut the hell up and dig. I'm going to count to three and if you don't start digging, I'm—"

He didn't need to finish his sentence. Shiloh swung the pick down into the hard, rocky earth, but paused after a couple of half-hearted, but futile, efforts. *This bastard is crazy. I need to stall as long as I can to figure out a way to get away from him. I'm not going to dig my own grave.*

The man raised his gun, pointed it at Shiloh's head then dropped it to fire a warning shot just wide of Shiloh's right foot. The sound was muffled. The man was using a silencer. The bullet sparked off a rock and ricocheted into the desert.

Shiloh swore, "What the hell did you do that for?"

"Stop asking questions. The next shot will be at your kneecap," he said with a viciousness that Shiloh did not misunderstand.

After fifteen minutes of hard digging, Shiloh leaned on the shovel. "I need to rest for a minute."

"You know, for a soldier you're pitifully out of shape."

Yeah? Well, I was wounded. I'm still recovering," Shiloh shot back. "It doesn't look like you're in the best shape either."

"No, but that's why you're digging and I'm watching."

"So if I do as I'm told, will you let me go?"

The man waved his .38 in the air, motioning for Shiloh to continue digging.

A half an hour later, the man was satisfied. "That's enough." He pulled a ski mask from his back pocket and tossed it at Shiloh. "Put the shovel down and put that on."

"Why the hell do you want me to put on a ski mask?"

"Because that's what you have to do. Just do it."

Shiloh didn't know what to think, but he pulled the mask over his head.

"Good. Now get the blanket from the back of the truck and put it in the hole you just dug."

Shiloh walked around to the back of the truck. All the while he was gauging how many steps he would have to take to reach the man and wrestle him to the ground. *I need to get closer so he won't use the gun.*

He saw something big wrapped in the blanket. "What's in the blanket, a body?"

"None of your business."

He reached into the bed of the truck to pull the blanket toward him. He sensed movement as he reached to lift it.

"Are you kidding me? There's something in there."

"A dog."

"Bullshit. That's no dog. It's too big to be a dog."

"Pick up the blanket and do what I say."

Shiloh heard a muffled whimper. He unrolled the blanket at one end and discovered a woman who was also wearing a ski mask. He slipped it off her head, freeing a mass of long blonde hair. The woman was about his age, and seemed to be semiconscious.

"What the hell are you doing?" the man shouted.

"She'll suffocate in there. What did you do to her?"

The man fired another warning shot into the ground. "Move away from her."

Shiloh backed away from the truck.

"You know, Mr. Shiloh Youngblood, I'm really tired of your bullshit. You're going to carry her to that hole you just dug."

The woman let out a shrill, piercing scream, startling the man.

Shiloh acted instinctively. He took two quick steps toward the kidnapper, but the man fired his revolver, hitting Shiloh on his left side, stopping him cold. Shiloh threw his hand to his wound then ducked away. The man fired again, but this time the bullet whizzed by Shiloh's head.

Shiloh raced around the side of the truck, yanked the ski mask off, and darted into the desert, running low to the ground and using the pickup as a shield.

The man fired again.

Shiloh zigged-zagged and within seconds was out of the range of fire. As long as the cloud cover hid the moon, darkness was his ally. A moment later, he heard the clank of the pick and shovel being thrown into the bed of the pickup, the tailgate being slammed shut, and the engine start up. He glanced over his shoulder and saw headlights bumping across the desert. The truck was headed right at him. The man shone his flashlight out the window with his left hand and drove with his right.

Shiloh had hoped to reach the safety of the pueblo, but realized he couldn't outrun the pickup. He changed direction and ran toward the Route 14 roadway. He knew the land leading up to the road sat on higher ground and was bordered by piñon trees, junipers, and rocky crevices. The truck would not be able to follow him there.

He was right. The man had no choice but to stop the chase. A quarter mile from the road, Shiloh crouched behind a juniper to catch his breath and examine his wound. He was lucky—the bullet had only grazed his side and his bleeding was minimal.

The man swung the truck around to head back across the desert. Shiloh thought he was safe, for now. He stepped out from his hiding place and watched the truck drive back to the gravesite and stop.

What the hell is he doing?

Ten minutes later, the pickup drove off.

What happened to the girl?

Under the darkness of the cloud cover, Shiloh walked quickly but warily, his acute combat senses primed for danger. With the truck headlights in the distance, he thought it was safe to check the gravesite. Maybe the girl was there. When he reached the grave he saw it was partially filled and a section of the blanket protruded from the ground. He dropped to his knees and frantically scooped out the dirt with his hands. He soon felt the girl's body. He tugged on the blanket to pull it from the grave and unwrapped it from her face. Uncertain if she was alive, he felt for a pulse. He felt a faint beat, then heard her groan. She was alive, but barely.

My God, he buried her alive.

"I'm not going to let you die." He shouted, "Do you understand?"

Shiloh heard the sound of the truck in the distance. He looked up and saw headlights closing in fast. He should have realized the man was going to use the girl as bait to get him to return to the gravesite.

CHAPTER 4

Shiloh picked Angela up and carried her over his shoulder. He hoped to reach his pueblo, but the truck was gaining on him.

Unable to outrun the pickup, Shiloh changed direction and headed back toward the obstacle-laden area along Route 14. He reached the safety of the boulders and high ground with just seconds to spare. They had penetrated fifty yards inside the impassable stretch of desert when the man stopped the truck, got out, and steadied the aim of his gun on the hood of the tuck.

Ping.

A shot hit a boulder to the side of the fleeing pair.

Click. *Click*. The man's gun was empty. He tried feverishly to reload and yelled out in frustration, "I'll find you, Shiloh Youngblood, you son of a bitch. You hear me? You're a dead man!"

Shiloh watched as the man got back in his truck, turned around, and drove south looking for an unobstructed pathway back to Route 14. Shiloh knew they were safe for now. He also knew the man would not give up trying to catch them.

Out of breath, he lowered Angela to the ground. Her hair, face, and body were matted with sand dust. She opened her eyes for the first time, and looked up at Shiloh without recognition. Her eyes reflected panic and she moaned, "Don't! Don't!"

"I'm just trying to help you," Shiloh said.

"Don't! Don't!"

"No, listen to me. I'm not the one who abducted you. I'm trying to help you," he repeated.

Angela slipped back to unconsciousness—her breathing shallow, her eyes rolled to white. She was in shock.

Shiloh saw the lights of a vehicle on the roadway heading north in their direction and ran to the road to flag it down. He climbed the embankment to the road, and from the dirt shoulder, waved his arms frantically for the car to stop. The driver did not slow down and sped out of sight in seconds.

I wouldn't stop either. Shiloh looked up to see the moon still covered by clouds. *It's pitch dark. No one's going to stop. I need to carry her to the pueblo and get help for her there.* He climbed down from the road and returned to Angela.

He brushed the hair off her face. Even with dirt and sand caked to her skin, he observed how pretty she was. "We're going to make it. I promise you," he said, and picked her up again, this time cradling her in his arms.

Another vehicle drove slowly toward them, northbound on 14. There was no other traffic on the road. Shiloh saw the driver shine a high-powered flashlight back and forth on the desert floor. *It's him.* He laid Angela down behind one of the large boulders several yards from the roadway and crouched next to her. The man stopped his pickup on the wide shoulder just above them and continued to shine his light down into the desert, going from bush to bush, boulder to boulder, searching, searching.

Angela groaned and opened her eyes for a moment. Thinking she might scream, Shiloh held his hand over her mouth. She tried to shake it off, but soon fell silent.

"Shh. You need to be quiet. We're hiding from that man. I'm trying to help you." He dropped to his elbows alongside her, and whispered in her ear, "We're running from that man who tried to kill you."

She looked at Shiloh, her eyes rolling aimlessly, unable to focus on him. Her lips were dry. In slow motion, she tried to moisten them with her tongue, but she had no saliva in her parched mouth to draw from.

"My name is Shiloh. Some man is trying to kill you. We're in the desert off Route 14 on the Yiqua reservation. He's on the road above us, shining a flashlight to try to find us. You've got to be very quiet."

"Co-old," she mumbled with violent shivers.

He pulled Angela up and leaned her against the boulder, then took off his jacket and coaxed it over her bare shoulders. To generate some heat, he rubbed her hand between his own.

Her eyes widened. He held his finger to his mouth. "You've got to be quiet. He's up there looking for us. Shh."

The man left the truck engine running and climbed over the guardrail and down the embankment, shining his light on the front of their boulder. The light bounced away, searching other places, but returned to where they were hiding. The beam from the flashlight got smaller as the man got closer. He listened for any sound that would give their hiding place away.

Shiloh looked around and saw a rock the size of his hand. He silently wrenched it out of the ground to use as a weapon, then twisted his body around in a crouch, ready to spring out.

The light from the flashlight continued to get closer. Shiloh tensed. The man was only a few yards away when Shiloh saw the lights from another vehicle on 14. The man saw it, too. He doused his flashlight and waited for the car to pass, but it slowed, then stopped on the shoulder behind the pickup.

Maybe it's a cop.

The man pulled his ski mask off, tucked his revolver into his pocket, and walked back to his truck.

"You okay?" the stranger shouted.

"Yeah. Had to go." It was not a cop. The stranger drove off.

The man got inside his truck and sat for another minute, looking out toward the boulder where Shiloh and Angela were hiding. He pulled away slowly, occasionally shining his flashlight into the desert as he drove off.

"He's gone for now," Shiloh whispered to Angela. "I was hoping that other car that stopped was a cop car, but it wasn't. At least it scared him away."

Angela looked up at him but did not comprehend.

"What's your name?" he asked.

She stared at his mouth but didn't answer. Her eyelids flickered closed.

Gently, Shiloh shook her shoulder. "Can you tell me your name?" he asked again. "My name is Shiloh. What's yours?"

She struggled to focus her eyes. "Ang…"

"Angie?"

"…e… la."

"Angela. Is it Angela?"

Her nod in response was barely perceptible.

"Good. Listen, Angela, do you remember what happened to you? What did he do to you?"

Her eyes closed again, and a tear rolled down her cheek. "Bur…y," she mouthed. "Bur…y."

"He tried to bury you, didn't he? Do you know who he is?"

She gasped, "I… I…"

He couldn't tell if she did. "Where do you hurt?"

She slowly moved her hand and pointed to the back of her arm. Shiloh looked, but in the darkness was unable to see the bruise where the man had injected her with a hypodermic needle.

CHAPTER 5

Detective Clay Bryce of the Santa Fe Police Criminal Investigation Division wove his way through the typical chaos at police headquarters. It was mid-afternoon and the room was filled with cops and detectives pecking on computer keyboards and filing reports, distraught victims giving statements, and handcuffed suspects being warned of their rights. Clay knocked on Captain Matthew Ellsworth's office door, then cracked it open. "Can I see you a minute?"

"Come in. What's up?"

Clay got right to the point. "Captain, it's just a hunch right now, but I think we may have a serial."

"Don't tell me that." Ellsworth ran his fingers through his graying hair and looked at Clay over his wire-rimmed glasses. The fifty-nine-year-old was well liked and well respected by all his detectives. He regarded forty-year-old Bryce as one of his best detectives, one whose intuition usually proved credible.

Ellsworth sat behind a beat-up steel desk that held an in-box stacked three inches high with paper. More files and paperwork surrounded the PC on the credenza behind him. Of course, no crime was a good crime, but he knew a case involving a serial killer would consume the resources of his detectives. It was the worst of all crimes. It made for long days, bad publicity for Santa Fe, and pressure from the chief and the mayor, as well as from the press which would hound him for details and then more details.

Clay explained his suspicions. "Captain, here's what I have." He pulled a notepad from his pocket. In his huge hands, the pad resembled a post-it. Standing well over six feet tall, square-jawed, and broad-shouldered, Clay was an intimidating presence. He had a full head of dark brown hair and equally

25

dark eyes—good looks that were marred only by the slight bend to his nose that had been broken while playing football at New Mexico State. "I got a call today at oh-eight-hundred from Chief Jacoby Johnstone of the Yiqua Tribal Police. He told me a guy from the Pueblo, a Shiloh Youngblood, rescued a Jane Doe on their reservation this morning."

"I know Johnstone. Jacoby's a good guy."

"Well, he tells me Youngblood reported seeing lights in the desert at about oh-two-hundred and went to check them out"

"What was he doing in the desert at two o'clock in the morning?"

"Apparently, he couldn't sleep, saw the lights, and was curious who was out there in the middle of the night. So he went out and spotted a guy digging a grave to put the Jane Doe in. The guy spied Youngblood, seized him, and put him in handcuffs, but the kid was able to escape. When he thought it was safe to go back to see what happened to the girl, he found the guy had buried her alive. He pulled her out before she suffocated and carried her to the pueblo."

"Where is she now?"

"They rushed her to St. Vincent's. I haven't been in to see her yet. Doctors say she's in critical condition, that she may have been drugged, and that it's remarkable she survived given what she went through. They'll let me know when I can talk to her, but it doesn't sound like it'll be any time soon."

"Okay, Clay, and how does an abduction turn into a serial?"

"I think the Jane Doe is twenty-five-year-old Angela Foster from Santa Fe. A state patrolman tagged her abandoned car on Route 14 at oh-three-hundred. I checked her out and learned she's a waitress at Indian Bend. That's when it hit me. I remembered there was another waitress from the Bend who went missing a while back." Clay flipped his pad. "June thirteenth, two years ago. Her car was abandoned on Route 14 just like Foster's."

"And what happened to her?"

"Carrie Kirkland. She went missing and has never been found. I haven't been able to find out a whole lot about her. Still checking her out."

"Come on, Clay, what's your point?" The captain was losing patience. "Two missing persons doesn't make a serial."

"Captain, I understand that, but I checked the state's Missing Persons Clearinghouse and found another waitress from the Bend who disappeared even earlier—three years ago. Emily Coburn. Same pattern. Her car was on 14. She's missing and hasn't been found either. Looks like the same m.o. to me."

Ellsworth leaned back in his chair, folded his hands behind his head, and looked up at the ceiling. After giving Clay's words some thought, he leaned back in, shook his head, and took a deep breath. "Dammit, Clay. I hope you're wrong about this."

"I hope so too, Captain, but I don't think so."

"You think we have a guy who's prowling the highway for women."

Clay wasn't sure if that was a question or a statement. "Maybe."

"What about the guy from the pueblo who rescued Foster? What's his story?"

Clay flipped more pages on his notepad. "Sergeant Shiloh Youngblood, twenty-five years old, on leave from the Army— just back from Afghanistan. He was wounded there and awarded the Silver Star. Chief Johnstone told me the folks from the pueblo threw him a homecoming parade just yesterday—

he's a major hero to the Yiquas. I'm meeting with Chief Johnstone in a bit and I'll talk with the sergeant too."

"All right, Clay, you know you've got to coordinate any investigation on Yiqua land with Jacoby. The tribal police have jurisdiction over any investigation on their reservation, but Jacoby will work with you. Just don't try to usurp his authority. And keep me informed. We have enough on our plate as it is. Let's nip this in the bud quick. We don't need the press on our asses about a serial murderer on the loose. Anything else you have that ties the cases together?"

"That's all I know right now. Three women. All three waitresses. All three worked the swing shift at the Bend. And all three of their cars were found abandoned on Route 14."

CHAPTER 6

Clay Bryce called Chief Johnstone. "I think we know who your Jane Doe is. The State Police found a late model Ford Focus on Route 14, about four miles north of the Indian Bend. Belongs to an Angela Foster. Can you meet me at the car?"

"I'll head out now."

The two men arrived at the crime scene at the same time and exchanged a strong handshake. Chief Johnstone had closely cropped jet-black hair and stood four inches shorter than Clay. His biceps bulged under the short sleeves of his tan uniform shirt and his demeanor was stern, but he gave a half smile when Clay passed along regards from Captain Ellsworth.

"He speaks highly of you, Chief."

"I'd say the same about the captain. Haven't seen him in a while. Tell him I said hello."

"Will do. He did remind me to make sure I don't step over bounds on your reservation. I'm aware you have jurisdiction, but hope we can work together on this case."

"I don't see any problem with that, Detective."

Bryce and Johnstone chatted amiably until crime scene examiner Dan Carton and his two assistants arrived minutes later in a white SUV marked Santa Fe Forensics.

The crime scene examiners established a wide perimeter around the car while Clay explained what State Patrolman Eldridge had reported about the vehicle. "He said there was nothing unusual. He parked behind the vehicle and walked to the driver's side, shined a light in, and saw no one was inside. The car was unlocked, so he popped the trunk, and found it was empty. He checked the plates against his ANPR database. But the car didn't show up as a problem, so he red-tagged it and left. Eldridge assumed the car had mechanical problems or ran out of gas. There was no indication of foul play."

Clay explained his concern that Foster's abduction was part of a series of abductions, possibly leading to the murders of the victims. "It's possible that at least two other missing women were murdered and buried somewhere—maybe even on your reservation—but there's no way to know right now."

"Detective Bryce, if there's anyone buried on our seventeen thousand acres of desert, it will be a heck of a challenge to find them."

"Let's see how this plays out with forensics."

Bryce and Johnstone watched as the examiners worked inward to Foster's car, looking for arcane details and placing numbered yellow tent markers in the dry desert sand. They pointed out two sets of tire treads that were different from those belonging to the Foster car—one belonged to Patrolman Eldridge's car, the other was unidentified. They also ascertained the patrolman and Angela's footprints, and another set of prints they concluded belonged to the driver of the unidentified vehicle.

Carton pointed to the footprints and explained, "These came from the direction of the other vehicle. They lead to the driver's side of the victim's car. Those same footprints, and presumably the victim's, lead from the driver's side of the car around the back of the vehicle to this spot at the passenger side. If you notice, the victim's footprints face the car and are wider than normal."

"Wide, like someone who's being searched?" Jacoby asked.

"Could be. Her footprints stop here. But look at this." Carton signaled an area alongside Foster's footprints where it appeared something had been spread on the ground. "This mark could have been made from a tarp or blanket of some kind. We'll examine the ground closely for fibers. Now see these deeper footprints that lead back to where the driver parked his vehicle? We don't see the woman's footprints. This suggests the driver may have carried the victim to his car in that tarp or blanket."

"Any indication of a struggle?" Bryce asked.

"We can't really tell. But we'll examine the victim's car more closely after we get it back to the garage. We'll also check it for fingerprints and any sign of blood. We've taken photographs for visual documentation, and before we leave we'll take some plaster casts of the tire tracks and footprints. Give me until tomorrow. By then we'll be able to spell it all out for you."

Bryce spoke to Carton. "Chief Johnstone and I are heading out to the Yiqua Pueblo to talk with a witness. After you finish here, and if it's okay with the Chief, I'd like you to examine the scene where Foster was found."

Jacoby nodded his okay.

* * *

Clay followed Chief Johnstone's SUV to the pueblo. They turned down a dusty, unpaved road that led to the Youngblood's small adobe home, one of dozens of similar-looking sandstone homes on the arid pueblo land. Shiloh's mother, a slight, pretty woman with long braided hair and a sparkling smile, was in the front yard. She was watering yellow and gold gladiolas set in large pots at either side of the front door.

"Hello, Mae."

"Hi, Jacoby. Looking for Shiloh?"

"Yes. Is he around? We'd like to talk with him about that girl he rescued last night. This is Detective Clay Bryce of the Santa Fe police."

"Pleasure to meet you, Detective. I hope you can find the man who hurt that poor, sweet girl. When Shiloh carried her into the house, I thought she was dead. Who would do such a thing?"

"That's what we're going to try to find out, Mrs. Youngblood," Clay answered.

"Well, come on in. Shiloh's sleeping, but I'll wake him. He's had a long couple of days, but he told me to wake him if you wanted to talk with him."

Mae escorted the two men into her small but comfortable living room. A gallery of family photos—the most prominent of which were Shiloh in his army uniform— highlighted all four walls.

Moments later Shiloh appeared, his face etched with creases of sleep. "Hey, Chief."

Johnstone explained, "Shiloh, sorry to wake you. This is Detective Clay Bryce of the Santa Fe police. He'd like to ask you about what happened to that girl on the reservation last night."

Shiloh extended his hand to Clay. "Nice to meet you, Detective. What can I tell you?"

"I understand you saved her life."

Shiloh shrugged. "Did you find out who she is?"

"Her name is Angela Foster. She's a waitress at the Bend."

"I figured as much. She near froze to death in that outfit she was wearing. I was able to get her first name from her, but that's about it. How's she doing? I wasn't sure she was going to make it."

"She's at St. Vincent's. The doctors say she's in critical condition and may have been drugged. Time will tell how well she recovers."

"It's pretty unbelievable what that guy did to her. You wouldn't treat an animal like that."

"More like he's the animal, Shiloh. I also understand the guy shot you. Are you okay?"

"Yes. When I tried to rush him, he fired and hit me in my side, but it's no big deal. Just a flesh wound. Mom bandaged it up for me. I'm fine."

"I know you've already spoken to Chief Johnstone, but can you start from the beginning and describe for me what happened? How did you end up in the desert and how were you able to save Angela?"

Shiloh explained the events leading up to his discovery of Angela wrapped in a blanket in the bed of the man's pickup truck, how he escaped, went back and dug her out of the grave, and carried her to the pueblo.

"What can you tell me about the man?"

"I never saw his face. He was wearing a ski mask and a baseball hat with the word *Police* stitched on the front and, let me think, he had on jeans, cowboy boots, and a plaid shirt with a badge on the left side underneath his pocket."

"Can you describe his badge?" Clay showed Shiloh his Santa Fe Police badge. "Did it look anything like this?"

"No, sir."

Chief Johnstone pointed to his own badge. "Was it like mine?"

"No. Neither. It looked like a kid's—like the kind you get in a Cracker Jack box. I really don't think he was a cop."

"What else?"

"He wore gloves."

Johnstone asked, "What kind of gloves, like work gloves?"

"No, the kind doctors and nurses wear. You know, latex or vinyl, I guess. I think they were blue."

"What kind of vehicle was he driving?"

"It was a black Ford F150, but I never caught the license. I do remember it had a bull bar on the front. You know, a front-end protector. It looked like it was made out of welded steel."

Clay nodded. "Anything else you remember about the guy?"

"Detective, the guy was weird. At first, when he had me blindfolded, I swore he was talking to a second person. But when he took my blindfold off, I looked around to see who the other person was, and there was no one. Either the person stayed hidden in the cab of the pickup or the guy was talking to an imaginary person. To tell you the truth, he creeped me out. I thought he was a psycho."

"Did he call the other person by name or identify him in any way?"

"No, sir. Not that I can remember. As I said, I'm not even sure there was another person. He could have been talking to himself."

"Anything else? How big was he? Could you tell if he was white or black? Hispanic? Native American?"

"He was about six feet tall, I'd say. Thin. I couldn't really tell for sure what he was, but I think he was white. Like I said, he was covered up pretty good."

"Do you think you'd be able to identify him in a lineup?" Johnstone asked.

"I don't think so. I mean, I never saw his face. I don't know. Maybe I could identify him by his mannerisms. He walked with a strange gait—like one shoulder was lower than the other."

"When we get a suspect it would be worth it for you to have a look-see."

"How old would you guess he was?"

"That's a good question. Hard to tell. You know, he moved around like he was fit, but honestly, he could have been a hundred years old for all I could tell. I mean, obviously he wasn't a hundred, but, I don't know."

"What about his voice? Did you recognize it? Do you think it could be someone from the pueblo?"

"I guess anything's possible, but I didn't recognize it. I'm sorry."

"Shiloh, you've been a big help. You risked your own life to save Angela's. There's nothing you should be sorry about."

"I suppose."

"Do you think the guy knows who you are or where you live?"

"Yes, sir, he does. He asked me my name and if I was from the pueblo. I was stupid enough to tell him. So, yes, sir, he could probably find me if he wanted to. But I wouldn't be able to identify him, so I don't think he would try to find me."

"He doesn't know you can't identify him, so he might come after you anyway," Johnstone stated.

Clay asked, "How much longer before you head out to your duty station?"

"I'm on leave for another four weeks, then I head back to Fort Hood."

"Chief, I've got a cop at the hospital guarding Foster in case the guy wants to finish what he started with her. What do you think about placing a guard here, too, for the same reason?"

"That's a good idea."

Shiloh shook his head. "No, sir, that's not necessary. I've got weapons here at the house to defend myself. There's really no need to worry about me, Chief. Really, I'll be fine."

Clay didn't agree but he let it drop. "Think about it, though. If you change your mind, just let the Chief know."

"I will."

"Shiloh, we have forensic examiners coming out to look at the crime scene. I know you're tired, but would you mind taking us out there when they show up?"

*   *   *

Clay and Shiloh piled into Chief Johnstone's SUV to drive to the desert gravesite. Crime-scene examiner Carton and his assistants followed. As they had done at Angela Foster's car, they established a perimeter, working inward to the grave Shiloh had dug, recording their findings as they examined shoeprints and tire tracks in the sand.

"Can you tell if the tire tracks are the same as the ones at Foster's car?"

"I can't right now," Carton answered. "We'll cast these too and check them at the lab."

Shiloh showed them where he had been standing when the man blindfolded him and when he was shot, as well as the route he had taken to flee. "The guy followed me in his truck, but then I ran toward 14 to an area where I knew his truck couldn't go. He had to turn around, so when I thought the coast was clear, I went back to see what happened to the girl—Angela. I found her rolled up in a blanket in that grave, covered in sand and dirt. When I pulled her out, I saw she was still alive. That's when I realized he had set me up. He used her as bait to get me to come back. I picked her up, carried her over my shoulder, and ran as fast as I could."

"Did you take her in the blanket?"

"No."

"We don't have the blanket."

"He must have taken it when he came back."

Carton interjected, "Shiloh's story confirms my theory that the suspect rolled her up in a blanket at her car and carried her to his vehicle."

Shiloh remembered something. "Oh, yeah. I forgot to tell you that the guy put a ski mask on me. And he had one on Angela, too."

"Where are they? Do you have them?"

"I pulled hers off when she was lying in his pickup. That's when I first realized it was a girl in the blanket. And mine—I pulled it off when I ducked behind the truck and ran into the desert. The guy probably found it."

"We'll look for it just in case."

Johnstone looked out at the sun setting on the horizon. "We may have to do it tomorrow. It's going to be dark in an hour."

Clay checked his watch and addressed Carton. "Dan, do what you can while you still have light and let me know what you come up with. Chief, can you have the scene guarded until tomorrow if Forensics doesn't finish tonight?"

"No problem."

"I'm going to the Indian Bend to see what I can find out about Foster."

Clay, Chief Johnstone, and Shiloh returned to the Yiqua Pueblo. "Shiloh, thanks for helping us out. Here's my card. If you think of anything else—anything at all—call Chief Johnstone or me any time, day or night."

"I'll do that."

Clay extended his hand to the Chief. "Jacoby, I'll let you know what the examiners come up with."

CHAPTER 7

Built on the Yiqua reservation off heavily trafficked Route 25, the Indian Bend Hotel and Casino was a five-story white stucco building with 108,000 square feet of gaming tables and slots, three restaurants, and 110 hotel rooms. It was surrounded by guest parking lots on three sides and an employee parking lot in the rear. In the center of the entrance turnabout, a fountain highlighted by alternating violet and blue floodlights shot water twenty feet in the air.

It was early evening and the lots were already full when Clay pulled under the porte cochère. He parked his car along the curb, flashed his badge to the valet, and entered the crowded grand lobby. An impressive bronze statue of a life-size Indian Brave astride a rearing mustang appeared to be guarding the entrance. Hotel guests stood in line to check in for the night while gamblers headed straight through the lobby to the casino.

Clay approached a uniformed security guard who was posted beside the executive elevator. He showed the guard his badge and explained he was there to see the person in charge of Security.

"About what, Detective?"

"About a missing person's case I'm investigating."

"That's John Grainger. He's the Operations VP. I'll call his office to let them know you need to talk with him." The guard turned and spoke into a house phone. Within minutes, the elevator doors opened to a thin man with delicate features and prematurely graying hair. He was nattily dressed in a navy pin-stripe suit, white dress shirt, and conservative yellow tie.

"Simon Learner, administrative aide to the vice president. Can I see some ID?"

Clay showed his badge and introduced himself. "Detective Bryce, Santa Fe PD."

"I understand you want to speak to Mr. Grainger about a missing person. Come with me, please."

Clay stepped into the mirrored elevator and the two men rode to the fifth floor in silence. Clay sized Learner up as an ambitious, MBA-educated, twenty-something whose colorless complexion was a sign he worked too many late, sun-starved hours.

Arriving at the executive level, Learner pressed a fingerprint recognition device to open the elevator door. The men stepped into a carpeted corridor, the walls of which were lined with southwestern artwork. Clay followed Learner past a row of mahogany-furnished executive offices to Grainger's corner office suite. Learner knocked on the door. A voice from the office called out, "Come."

"Mr. Grainger, this is Detective Clay Bryce of the Santa Fe Police Department. He would like to talk with you about a case he's investigating."

Clay extended his hand in introduction, but received an awkward no-look fist bump in return. Grainger was movie-star handsome, with a head of dark hair, chiseled cheekbones, and square jaw. Seated at an oversized desk, he stared intently at a closed circuit monitor for another ten seconds before looking up at Clay. "Have a seat." He nodded to Simon to also sit.

After handing Grainger his card, Clay sat in one of two leather armchairs opposite Grainger's desk. Simon sat in the other.

"Great view you have here," Clay said, attempting to break the ice with this man he immediately perceived to be pompous and self-important.

Grainger stood and turned to look out the window over the New Mexico desert landscape. The setting sun cast brilliant shades of orange across the Sangre de Cristo Mountains to the northeast. He, too, wore a blue pin-stripe suit, but unlike Simon Learner's, Grainger's was custom made. His fitted shirt and silk tie were not lost on Clay. *The shirt alone probably cost more than my off-the-rack suit.*

"Yep. The view is beautiful, isn't it?" With his back still to Clay, he asked, "What can I do for you, Detective?"

"I realize it's after hours, so I appreciate you taking the time to talk with me."

Grainger turned to face Clay and offered his well-worn cliché. "We put in whatever hours are necessary to keep our ship moving smoothly in the right direction. Of course, sometimes we have to navigate through rough waters. But that's life, isn't it, Detective."

Clay nodded. "I was told downstairs that you're in charge of security."

"Yes, I am," he said.

Simon added, "Mr. Grainger has responsibility over much more than security."

Grainger smiled and nodded at his aide's sycophantic observation. "In our opinion, we have the best casino security in the country. It's state of the art—not only for the casino but for all of our property."

"That's good to know. It should help me in my investigation."

"What, exactly, are you investigating?"

"I'm looking into an abduction of one of your female employees, and the disappearance of two others. I'm concerned that the three may have been abducted over the past few years. This morning, just after midnight, your employee Angela Foster was abducted from her car on Route 14. Luckily, she was rescued, thanks to a Sergeant Shiloh Youngblood of the Yiqua Pueblo. But we now have reason to believe the other two women who went missing may have been killed—they've never been found. From what we know, all three were waitresses who worked on the swing shift."

Grainger looked first at Simon then at Clay. "Detective, I'm sure you'll explain your theory, but understand one thing, it is imperative that you keep this matter confidential. If word of your investigation leaks out to the public, it could impact our business in a significant manner. You understand, of course, don't you?"

What a condescending SOB. He's more concerned about the Bend's reputation than he is about these women. Clay responded with obvious irritation. "Of course I understand, *Mr. Grainger*, and I'll do my best, but I cannot guarantee that the media won't latch onto the news. They have a way of doing that, you know."

Grainger glared at Clay. He was not used to being challenged. "Again I ask you, what can I do for you?"

"For starters, I'd like to see the closed circuit video you have of the restaurant where Angela Foster worked last night. I want to see if we can spot anyone stalking her or if anything unusual occurred before she ended her shift."

"We can show you that."

"I'd also like to know what other security you have here—anything that can help me examine Foster's actions last night."

"You did hear me say I have the state-of-the-art security in place, didn't you? Follow me. We'll show you." The three men exited the office. They walked to the end of the hallway where Simon pressed another fingerprint recognition device, and the door opened to a surveillance room thirty feet long by thirty feet wide. The room housed men who were scrutinizing dozens of closed circuit television monitors that focused on every gaming table and row of slots in the casino as well as on every area in and around the hotel.

Bryce was impressed. "Hell of an operation you have here. Looks like Houston's space administration center."

"We call this our 'eye in the sky.' All these cameras allow us to view every part of the property. In the casino, we're always on the lookout for cheating by players—as well as cheating by employees. Both happen."

Simon whispered something to Grainger and nodded to a screen at one of the monitoring stations. "Simon tells me we have a couple of guys trying to pull one over on us as we speak. Let's take a look." The three men approached a monitor that was focused on a blackjack table, and Grainger instructed the man who was observing the monitor to roll back the tape. "Detective, see the blackjack table on this screen? Now look at this player." He pointed to a man wearing a black shirt. "Watch him. You'll see how he acts loud enough to draw attention to himself, but not bad enough to be thrown out of the casino."

"Okay. I see."

"Now watch. He distracts the dealer and the other players by telling a joke or saying something stupid. Now watch the man at the other end of the table. Did you see what he did?"

"I missed it."

"Replay it. Watch carefully. See him slip a card from his sleeve?"

"Oh, I see. Yeah."

"The two men are partners. That's actually a pretty crude effort. We've seen it all dozens of times before."

"What will you do with them?"

"They will be escorted from the casino and asked to leave the property. Simon will arrange for it." He added with a wry smile, "Politely, of course."

"Very interesting. I assume, then, we'll be able to follow Angela Foster during her shift last night as closely as we observed those two guys."

"Not a problem."

"I'd also like to inspect the tapes of the employee entrance and the employee parking lot, if you have them."

"Simon will make everything available to you, but I emphasize again that it must be kept confidential. Just as the commercial says, 'What happens in Vegas, stays in Vegas.' I'm sure you know what I mean."

Clay eyed Grainger and shot back, "As I said before, I'll do my best to keep this quiet."

Grainger ignored Clay's prickly tone and said, "Earlier you said there were three waitresses. One was Angela Foster. Who were the other two?"

Finally. It's about time he show some concern. "Two years ago, a woman by the name of Carrie Kirkland went missing, and the year before that, an Emily Coburn disappeared. Both vanished without a trace, and both disappeared in the same way. Their vehicles were found abandoned on Route 14. Do you recall either of them?" Grainger's rapid blink at the mention of the name Carrie Kirkland was not lost on Clay.

"Sorry, I do not. Simon, do you?"

Simon maintained a frozen expression but did not hesitate to respond. "No, Mr. Grainger, I do not."

Clay felt the two men were not being honest with him, and suspected they both knew the women. He elected not to challenge them at that moment. "I'm not surprised, really, that you don't recall. That's probably because there was no sign that either woman was a victim of a criminal act. You wouldn't have paid any attention to them going missing."

Grainger added, "Of course, sometimes people just vanish. This has happened with dozens of employees at the Bend since it opened fifteen years ago. Some just leave without giving any notice. That certainly doesn't mean they were all abducted by some alien force. We may be in the desert, but we're not Roswell, you know." He looked at Simon and smirked. Simon laughed on cue. "Are you sure you're not trying to make a case about a serial stalker when it's nothing more than coincidence that two women went missing?"

"Actually, we believe all three women may have been abducted. Angela Foster was able to escape but, interestingly, all three worked the swing shift, and all three seem to have been abducted in the same manner. You would agree that's a heck of a coincidence, wouldn't you, Mr. Grainger?"

"Let me repeat myself. If word gets out to the media that someone out there has been targeting women from Indian Bend, we stand to suffer a great economic loss. I'm sure you can appreciate that."

Clay let out a heavy sigh at Grainger's condescension, but said nothing.

"Did you see our parking lots as you drove in? Filled to capacity. That's the way we like it. If any word of this gets out, gamblers will bypass us and go to other casinos, which is *not* the way we like it."

Clay seethed over Grainger's repeated admonitions. "Mr. Grainger, that's the third time you've reminded me of possible consequences to the Bend. And I've told you I will do my utmost to keep a lid on this. But you know how things work. This could leak out a lot of different ways. We both know the media has a way of zeroing in on these kinds of intrigues."

Grainger needed to have the last word on the subject. "Speaking for Bend ownership, I would hope you will be more diligent than normal."

What an asshole.

"So, Detective Bryce, what else do you want from us?"

"Copies of the personnel files of the three women I've mentioned, and I'd like to talk to Angela Foster's manager. Did the same person manage all three women?"

Simon answered, "If those women worked the swing shift, then, yes. The manager's name is Hope Archer. She's been managing both the front and back of the house—the hospitality and restaurant employees on the swing shift—for some time now."

Grainger added, "It'll be no problem to get you copies of the personnel files. Simon will see to it that you have them first thing tomorrow." He spoke to Simon. "Buzz Ms. Archer and tell her the detective would like to speak with her after he reviews the security tapes."

"Yes, sir." Simon stepped out to call Hope Archer.

"And, as far as looking at tapes from our CCTV goes, what do you hope to find?"

"We might be able to see if someone followed Angela out of the parking lot."

"What was your name again?" Grainger pulled Clay's business card from his pocket and read it. "Detective Clay Bryce, right? Simon will take you to our video room so you can examine whatever tapes you care to study." He admonished one final time. "But put this investigation to bed *asap*."

Clay extended his hand to say goodbye, but Grainger again offered only knuckles in return before turning to leave the surveillance room. Clay watched as Grainger removed a small bottle of hand sanitizer from his pocket, poured a few drops into his palm, and wrung his hands dry.

CHAPTER 8

Clay Bryce and Simon Learner examined the surveillance tapes together, following Angela Foster's moves throughout her shift. They observed nothing unusual. Well-endowed like many of the Bend's female employees, she was gawked at and flirted with by a number of male diners, but none appeared to act in a way that gave her a difficult time. Clay and Simon also examined the tapes of the employee entrance and parking lot to determine if anyone followed her when she left the casino at the end of her shift. Again, they found nothing unusual.

When Clay was convinced there was nothing more to see on the security video, Simon escorted him back to the lobby and then to a secure door at the far end of the lobby entrance under a sign that read Administration - Human Resources, By Appointment Only. The guard at the door punched in the access code to allow the pair to enter. Inside, they walked down a carpeted corridor to the office of the swing shift manager.

Simon introduced Hope Archer to Clay. "Hello, Detective." She gave him a warm smile.

Clay was immediately taken by Hope's striking good looks. She was model tall and thin, and had high cheek bones and long brown hair that skimmed her shoulders. Her bright, hazel eyes were framed by long lashes and, in spite of the glitz and glamour that surrounded her, she wore little makeup. He guessed her to be in her late thirties, although she could have passed for twenty-five were it not for the tiny laugh lines at the outer corners of her eyes.

"Hope, as I mentioned on the phone, the detective wants to ask you a few questions about Angela Foster. He'll explain. Please help him out any way you can."

"I will, Simon. Thank you," she said.

Simon turned to leave as Clay handed his card to Hope.

"Have a seat, Detective Bryce. What is it you need to know about Angela?"

"Ms. Archer, before we start, would you mind describing your position here?"

"Sure. I'm one of three administrative managers reporting to John Grainger, with a dotted line to Simon Learner. I manage the swing shift—four to midnight—and am responsible for all the activities you see when you first enter the Bend—the desk clerks, customer service, porters, bell hops, the concierges. And I'm also responsible for the operation of our three restaurants, including managing the food and beverage personnel, the waitresses, bartenders, chefs, etcetera. There's other stuff, but I think you get the idea."

Clay was impressed. "That's a lot on your plate."

"Yes, but I love it. Not too many people can say that about their jobs, but I love mine. Frankly, I don't know what I'd do if I didn't have it. I grew up in this job and I'm not sure I could do anything else."

"Let me explain why I'm here."

"Please."

"I understand Angela Foster is an employee of yours."

"Yes, she is."

"Well, she was kidnapped this morning, sometime after midnight. We assume she was on her way home from work."

Hope's eyes reflected her shock. "You're kidding me. Is she okay? Where is she?"

"Well, no, she's not okay. The guy who abducted her tried to kill her, and we don't know why. She's in intensive care at St. Vincent's."

"Oh, my God. Can I see her?"

"I'm afraid not at this time. The doctors say she's in no condition to talk."

"Do you know who kidnapped her?"

"Not yet, but we're working on it. I'm hoping you can help me out."

"I'll certainly try."

"Has she ever talked to you about anyone creating a problem of any kind? Stalking her, for example?"

"No, never." Hope shook her head for several long seconds. "I thought something had to be wrong. I was surprised when she didn't come to work this afternoon, or call in. So, what happened?"

Clay noticed she absentmindedly ran her fingers through her hair, weaving strands into place. He also noticed she was not wearing a wedding band. "I'm sorry. I can't go into that detail. But can you tell me what kind of employee she was?"

"She's been a good employee—rarely missed a day's work or even punched in late. She's been here less than a year— maybe nine or ten months. Other than that, I can't really tell you a whole lot."

"I'd also like to ask you about two past employees, but I must have your assurance that you won't disclose what I'm about to tell you to anyone else. After I tell you, you'll understand why you have to keep this confidential. I don't want to alarm employees or guests about what I'm investigating."

"Of course, Detective. I'm very good at keeping secrets, so ask away."

Clay wasn't sure if she was good to her word, but he had to find out what she knew about the other missing women. "I believe two other waitresses may have been abducted the same way as Angela." He took out his pad and read from his notes. "A woman by the name of Emily Coburn three years ago, and Carrie Kirkland two years ago."

"What do you mean, the same way? Did someone try to kill them, too?"

"At this point, we don't know for sure."

"Detective, please. Call me Hope," she said.

Clay hesitated. He knew he had to remain professional, but he found her captivating. "Okay, I will, *Hope.* So what can you tell me about the two women? Let's start with Carrie Kirkland."

"I remember she was a pretty girl—a little immature, perhaps, but a good employee."

"What did you think when she didn't show up for work? Did she give you notice?"

"No, she just up and quit. Never gave me notice or any reason why she was leaving. She just never showed up for work."

"And Emily Coburn?"

Hope pursed her lips and shook her head. "I vaguely remember Emily, but I can't put a face to her. A lot of women have worked for me over the years. I really can't remember them all. I'm sorry."

"How much turnover do you have?"

"A fair amount—certainly more than I like. It depends on the job, though. The front of the hotel, not so much. But servers and other workers in the restaurants, there's quite a bit. It's the nature of the restaurant business. Yeah, they make pretty good money, but most girls are here to make as much as they can for college, or they're in between jobs, or they're divorced with kids, or whatever. Then they leave. Few expect to waitress as a career goal, if you know what I mean. They usually get burned out pretty quickly."

"Do you have rules about your employees consorting with guests?"

"Yes, we do—very strict rules. We want to make sure people don't get the wrong idea. These women are not hookers. They're waitresses. But some guys who are hanging out with their buddies or away from their wives for a night end up having too much to drink. They think they're at a strip joint and try to put tips in places reserved for strippers. The women do know, that if someone gets out of hand, security is always nearby."

"Has Angela Foster ever told you she had a problem like that—with any customer?"

"No, not that I can remember."

"What about Carrie and Emily?"

She shook her head. "Again, sorry, but I just don't remember them that well."

"But if they did have a problem?"

"If they had any kind of problem, they would have had to notify Security, who then would have had to file what we call an incident report. And the employee would have to sign off on it too. But, as I said, I don't remember that Angela had a problem with anyone."

"I'd like to review those incident reports involving your employees, if I may."

"I don't have them. The reports go straight to Security. You'll have to ask John—Mr. Grainger—or Simon for the reports. John's office is the only one that can release them."

"Okay. I understand."

Hope turned thoughtful. "Detective?"

"Yes?"

"Can you tell me what happened to the other two women?"

"Sorry, I really don't know all the details. All I can tell you is that all three women were abducted from their cars in the same way. Angela appears to be the only one lucky enough to escape."

"Oh. How awful for them all."

"I have one last question for you."

"What's that?"

"Does the casino allow employees to date other employees?"

"Yes, it's allowed, as long as it doesn't cause conflict in the workplace, if you know what I mean. Or if the two people involved aren't in a direct reporting relationship. If you're asking if Angela and those others were dating fellow employees, I wouldn't know, and frankly I don't care. It's none of my business."

"Is it okay with you if I talk to your waitresses on shift tonight to learn what they can tell me about Angela? I promise I won't keep them long."

"I can arrange that, sure."

"Just the servers. I'll only need you to take them off shift for a few minutes at a time."

* * *

Hope set Clay up in the large conference room adjacent to her office. One at a time, she brought in the waitresses from each of the three hotel restaurants for a brief interview. The women were scantily clad in skimpy gold and black waitress outfits that accentuated their chests. Clay had a tough time keeping his gaze from wandering, but he managed to remain professional. He explained to each that someone had abducted Angela Foster while she was driving home along Route 14, and asked if they knew who might have had reason to harm her.

Only one waitress, Holly Paine, was able to shed light on Angela's personal life. Hope had described Holly to Clay as a short, cute, effervescent blonde—a description Clay found more than accurate. Holly's constant smile showed off pearl-white teeth and her single blonde braid swayed across her back with each springy step she took.

"Ooh, poor Angela."

"Do you know her well?"

"Not really, but she told me she shared an apartment with some guy. They weren't romantically involved or anything—he was just someone to share apartment expenses with. She said his name was Denver something or other."

"Did she tell you anything about him?"

"Nothing really. But I do remember one time she came to work and I noticed there were bruises on her shoulder and arm. She had tried to cover them up with makeup. I asked her what happened and she came up with a cockamamie story about how clumsy she was and that she tripped over a rug and fell. I believed her because I'm a klutz, too, you know?"

Clay wasn't sure if Holly was done talking. "Okay. Go on."

"Yeah, well, a couple weeks later there were more bruises. I asked her if she had fallen again, and she just shook her head. That's when I said to her, 'Be honest with me. Did your boyfriend do that to you?' She gave me this nasty glare and said he wasn't her boyfriend and that she didn't want to talk about it, so I just dropped it. None of my business, you know."

"Are you saying you think her roommate is abusive?"

"I can't say for certain, but it sure looks that way to me. If it wasn't him, someone else was beating up on her."

"That's all very helpful, Holly. Thank you for your time."

As Clay did with the other girls, he gave Holly his card and asked her to call him if she remembered anything else.

"And you need to be extra vigilant after your shift. Do not stop along the road—especially on Route 14—or give a lift to any strangers."

Clay gave one final warning. "If a cop tries to stop you, unless you are one hundred percent certain he or she is a cop, do not stop. Keep driving to the nearest police station or public place like a gas station, to make sure it really is a cop."

* * *

It was ten o'clock when Hope informed Clay he had spoken to the last of the waitresses. "Did you learn anything?" she asked.

"Not a whole lot. One of the girls told me Angela has a male roommate, and that he might have abused her. But no one else had any information. I'm going to check out her roommate."

"Did you put in a request for their personnel files?"

"Yes, I'll get them from Simon tomorrow morning. Right now I'm tired and hungry and ready to call it a day. Which of your restaurants is the best for a sandwich and a beer?"

"If you want, I can show you."

Clay did not object. "Great. Can you join me, Hope, or is that against house rules?"

"Technically, you're not a patron. So, yes, I'd love to join you—on one condition."

"What's that?"

"That I can stop calling you Detective and call you by your name."

"You got it. Clay it is."

Clay followed Hope down the corridor, past the HR office, back into the lobby, then through a double door that took them directly into the casino. Clay checked her out from behind and liked what he saw. She wore platform heels and a skirt that accentuated her shapely figure. She sensed he was studying her, but didn't mind, and smiled to herself. "Where are you taking me, Hope?"

"The Hungry Palate. It's exactly what it sounds like. No offense, Clay, but I don't take you for a fine-dining kind of guy."

"You have me pegged right. How about you?"

"I'm just as comfortable at a hamburger joint as I am at a four-star restaurant. I like to cook, but since it's just me at home, I don't spend too much time in the kitchen."

Clay knew he was pushing the envelope, but he said it anyway. "You can cook for me anytime."

Hope stopped in the middle of a maze of clanking slot machines. With bells dinging and people shouting all around them, she looked at Clay and surprised him with her answer, "I just might take you up on that."

They proceeded through the casino and entered the relative quiet of a glassed-in restaurant. Clay looked out at the goings-on in the casino and asked, "Doesn't all this noise and smoke bother you?"

"No. I'm never in the casino very long—usually just to get to a restaurant."

"You said earlier that you grew into your job. How long, exactly, have you been working here?" Clay asked.

"Since just after it opened—going on fifteen years."

"I don't know how you do it—working these hours night after night, and looking the way you do. Aren't you tired?"

"No. I've gotten used to it over the years. I have a lot of free time, so I actually like my schedule. I'm a morning person."

"You're also very pretty," he blurted, totally out of context and, again, in an uncharacteristically forward way.

Hope was taken aback. "Are you normally this brazen with women, Detective Bryce?"

Clay was embarrassed and squirmed in his chair. "Sorry. I'm being pretty blatant, aren't I? I don't know where that came from. I apologize if I've offended you. I'm not usually this bold."

"No, please don't apologize. I think you're good looking yourself, Clay, and I'm not forward that way with guys, either."

They ordered from the light menu and waited for their food. Clay spotted John Grainger and Simon Learner on the casino floor. They made their way toward the café and approached the table where Hope and Clay were seated.

Grainger nodded hello to Hope, then addressed Clay, "Detective, I understand the CCTV tapes you reviewed with Simon weren't of much help."

Clay noticed that Hope looked away from Grainger, and sensed tension between the two. "Unfortunately, the tapes didn't show anything."

"And how did your interviews with Ms. Archer's employees go?"

How did he know I interviewed the waitresses? I didn't tell him I was going to do that. Maybe Hope did.

Clay said nothing about Holly Paine's suspicion regarding Angela's roommate. "They went well. No one had any information about Angela Foster other than to say she works hard and keeps to herself. And no one thought she was being stalked. By the way, Ms. Archer told me about incident reports you keep on file. If you don't mind, I'd like to see any that have been written up involving her staff. Will you arrange that for me?"

Grainger hesitated and glanced at Hope, but she continued to avoid eye contact with him. "They are for internal use only and for review by the State Gaming Control Board. But given the circumstances of what happened to Angela Foster, yes, of course you can review them. They're filed electronically, so we can email those involving Hope's staff to your work email address at your headquarters. I must reiterate, they've got to be kept confidential."

"Confidential! I got it," Clay said. "Trust me, I got it."

Grainger overlooked Clay's obvious irritation. "Simon, take care of that."

Simon nodded his okay, and asked Clay, "How far back do you want to go? And do you want only the waitstaff or everyone in her department?"

"For now, just the waitstaff going back three years."

"I'll arrange to have them sent over to you, but know there are quite a few."

"I understand, and I appreciate your help." The Bend employees all referred to Simon Learner—with more than a little derision—as Grainger's "Mini-Me." He dressed in the same manner as his boss. He slicked back his hair as Grainger did. And, although he couldn't afford the same expensive clothes and shoes as Grainger, Simon dressed with the same tailored look.

Grainger added, "Let me know if you find anything significant in those reports."

"I will. Would you like to join us?"

Grainger shifted his look to Hope once more, and once more she looked away. "No, thanks. We've got to run. I just happened to notice you here as we were passing by."

Yeah, right, just passing by.

"In the future, Detective Bryce, let me know if there are any other employees you want to interview."

Clay looked at Grainger and gave an insincere nod. "Yeah, of course I'll do that, Mr. Grainger." He extended his hand, and again Grainger offered him a fist bump in return. Grainger looked one last time at Hope, then left the restaurant.

"Is he a germophobe?" Clay asked.

"You picked up on that, huh?"

"Hope, did you tell him I was interviewing your employees?"

"No. Why?"

"I just wondered how he knew, that's all. Are you aware if he knew Angela socially?"

Hope looked away when she answered. "I don't know. Maybe."

The two made small talk as they dined until Hope looked at her watch and realized they had been chatting for well over an hour. "My God, I can't believe the time. I've got to get back to work."

Clay stood and said to her, "I'm looking forward to seeing you sometime on *unofficial* business."

"I'm counting on it, Clay," she said, then surprised him with a kiss on his cheek.

CHAPTER 9

Abduction Foiled by Hero Soldier

Sergeant Shiloh Youngblood of the Yiqua Pueblo, a recipient of the Silver Star for Heroism in Afghanistan, foiled the kidnapping and attempted murder of Angela Foster, 25, of Santa Fe, an employee of the Indian Bend Hotel and Casino. Foster was abducted Sunday shortly after midnight on her way home from work. Police found her abandoned vehicle on Route 14. Although the circumstances are not fully known, Sergeant Youngblood, on leave from active duty, was able to wrest Ms. Foster from the kidnapper. Foster remains in critical condition in Christus St. Vincent Regional Medical Center while police pursue leads in their attempt to apprehend the kidnapper. Anyone with information is asked to call 505-222-9999. - Steven Brown

John Grainger picked up the phone and dialed Clay's number. He ranted, "Detective Bryce, you said you wouldn't discuss Angela Foster's abduction with the media. The *Times Journal* and TV news are reporting on her this morning. Is this what you mean about putting a lid on your investigation?"

"Mr. Grainger, good Tuesday morning to you, too. Look, I promised I would try to keep my investigation of Coburn and Kirkland from leaking out, but news about Foster—"

"You said you were going to—"

"Listen to me. I did not give that reporter anything. What he wrote about in his column is publicly available information. It has not been sealed."

"Why not? If anything leaks out about those other women, I'll..."

"You'll what?"

Grainger hung up on Clay.

You have a nice day, too, asshole. Clay logged onto his computer and saw an email had come in from Simon Learner at the Bend. He first opened the attachments containing the three personnel files he had requested. He was surprised to read that Angela's roommate, Denver Stennet, was listed on Carrie Kirkland's New Employee Data Form as her emergency contact. *That's more than just a coincidence.*

Clay next reviewed the incident reports involving Hope Archer's staff. For the most part, they involved tourists who had had too much to drink and became a little too frisky with various waitresses. None of the reports involved Angela.

* * *

That afternoon, Dan Carton briefed Clay on what he found at the two crime scenes. "The tread marks we found near Foster's car were consistent with tires used on a light truck or SUV, and identical to the treads at the crime scene in the desert. We also found something interesting—several woven polyester threads alongside the car, and then again at the gravesite. They probably came from a blanket moving companies use to protect furniture."

"Good job, Dan. I'll see if my suspect has any ties to a moving company."

Carton continued, "Our cast of the guy's partial shoeprint shows he was wearing what appear to be cowboy boots, size ten. And, Clay, here's something else. At the gravesite, the prints show the kidnapper lost the heel off his right boot at some point in time."

"Do you have the heel?"

"No. We searched for it, but the guy was smart enough to take it with him."

"There can't be that many shoe repair shops in Santa Fe. We'll get an alert out to them to let us know if anyone brings in a size-ten boot for repair."

"Anything else?"

"We found four .38-caliber bullet casings. We checked them for fingerprints, but they were clean. We found glove prints in two places on Foster's car—on the driver's-side door handle and at the top of the passenger side door. The prints appear to be from latex gloves, the kind Youngblood said the kidnapper was wearing. But glove prints are no different than fingerprints—they don't help us unless we can match them against prints already in a database."

"So no match?"

"No. We would have to find the gloves in order to match the prints."

* * *

Clay met with Captain Ellsworth to review what he had learned about Foster's abduction. "Captain, if a couple of things fall into place, I could have an open-and-shut case on the guy who kidnapped Foster—her roommate—a guy by the name of Denver Stennet. Here's what I've got. Besides being Foster's roommate, Stennet was also shown as the emergency contact on Carrie Kirkland's employment form at the Bend. She was one of the other two girls that went missing. I don't know what their relationship was, but he may have been her roommate at some point, too."

"Any relationship to the third girl?"

"Emily Coburn. No. Not yet anyway."

"What about people at the Bend? Did they know anything about her relationship with Stennet?"

"Another waitress did. Foster told her that she and Stennet were not romantically involved, that they were sharing an apartment as a matter of convenience to help pay the rent. This girl said she observed some bruises on Foster that she suspected were from abuse, but Angela didn't want to talk about it.

"I also met with the Operations VP at the Bend, a guy by the name of John Grainger. The pompous bastard was more concerned about bad publicity for the Bend than about the missing women. He called me this morning, pissed because he thought I fed news about Foster to the *Journal*. I'm not sure how much cooperation I'm going to get from him. One thing, though. He's got an impressive security system—cameras everywhere, inside and out. It's all state of the art, with a surveillance room full of security personnel doing the monitoring. I thought I might be able to find out if someone was stalking Foster, so I watched the tapes from Sunday night, and followed her inside the casino from when she first punched in to the time she left. I didn't see anything unusual. I was even able to track her when she left the Bend and when she unlocked and got into her car, but I didn't see that anyone followed her when she left."

"You been able to talk with Foster yet?"

"No. The doctors say she's still in no condition to talk."

"Did you find out exactly what happened to her?"

"She was injected with a massive dose of a fast-acting date-rape drug, ketamine, combined with oxycodone. She probably knew what was happening but couldn't do anything to stop it.

She would have been too incapacitated to defend herself. At this point, she most likely won't remember what happened to her."

"Was she raped?"

"No. There was no sign of sexual assault."

"Anything else?"

"Chief Johnstone and I talked with Shiloh Youngblood—the guy who saved Foster. From what he told us, we have a good idea what happened. Our alleged abductor posed as a cop out on the Yiqua reservation. My theory is that he flashed her down on 14 and injected her with the drugs. When Shiloh showed up, he forced him to dig the grave, and then left her in it. And she was alive when the son of a bitch buried her!"

"Did Dan Carton come up with anything?"

"He did. He confirmed the tread marks he found were from a pickup truck. Shiloh Youngblood said the truck the suspect used was a Ford F150, and Carton said that was compatible with his findings. They found four empty .38 shells and fibers from a blanket the guy must've used to wrap Foster in. They think it's the kind of blanket a moving company would use. I'm going to check to see if Stennet worked for any moving company in the area or if he or Foster rented a U-Haul."

"Have you questioned Stennet?"

"Not yet. I'm bringing him in now."

Ellsworth suggested, "With what you know so far, I think you have grounds to hold him while you get a warrant to check his place."

"I plan to do that right after I interview him. Oh, yeah, forensics also told me the kidnapper lost a heel from his boot. Now I just need to find out if Stennet owns a boot that's missing a heel. And if he does, I should be able to wrap this up pretty quick."

"What about Youngblood? Would he be able to identify him?"

"I doubt it, Captain. He said the guy wore a mask and it was pitch-dark, so probably not. But I'm bringing him in anyway, in case he can spot something about the guy."

"Clay, if it was Stennet, why didn't he just kill Foster? Why bury her when she's still alive?"

"I don't know, sir. Jealousy, rage, control, revenge—it could be anything. It's like he wanted to hurt her bad—you know, see her suffer before she died."

CHAPTER 10

"Shiloh, I want you to take a look at someone. Just watch him for a few minutes and tell me if you think he could be the one who tried to kill Angela. I know you didn't see his face, but maybe you can tell by the way he moves or by any of his mannerisms—anything that rings a bell, okay?"

Stennet was seated at a table inside a stark ten-by-fifteen interview room. He was nearly six feet tall, with protruding cheekbones and frizzy hair pulled back in a ponytail. His close-set eyes made him appear cross-eyed.

Shiloh and Clay viewed Stennet from behind a two-way mirror and observed he was clearly agitated. He squirmed in his chair, stood, and sat back down. His eyes darted repeatedly to the two-way mirror and away again. He drummed his fingers on the table, stood again, went to the mirror to try to see who was on the other side, then sat down again, nervously tenting his fingertips.

"The guy sure is one nervous dude," Shiloh observed. "There's no way I can tell if he's the same guy, Detective. He's about the same build I guess, but I can't say for sure it's him. Sorry."

"No problem, Shiloh. It was worth a look-see."

Since Shiloh was unable to identify Stennet, the coincidence of Stennet possibly living with two of the three alleged victims was all Clay had to go on. Clay needed a confession or an incriminating piece of evidence that Stennet was the kidnapper—the heelless cowboy boot, blanket, gun, or fake badge that was used in the Foster abduction.

Clay entered the interview room and Stennet immediately snapped at him. "Why am I here?"

Clay didn't answer. Without looking at Stennet, he sat down across the table from him. Although he had already learned everything he could from the Foster and Kirkland files, he leafed through both files again—slowly. He intentionally delayed starting the interview to put Stennet in a further state of anxiety.

"I said, why am I here? Are you going to answer me?"

Clay looked at Stennet briefly but did not respond. He went back to studying the files.

A silent minute later, Stennet said, "This is ridiculous. I have the right to know why I'm here. Is this because Angela is missing?"

Still no response from Clay.

Stennet pushed his chair back hard and stood up. "I don't have to put up with this bullshit. You're costing me a day's pay. I'm outta here."

Clay slapped the table. "Sit down! You get up when I tell you to."

Stennet sat.

"What are you so nervous about? You on something?"

"No, I'm not on anything." He scowled and asked, "What the hell do you want from me? I have the right to know why I'm here."

"My name is Detective Clay Bryce. I know you're Angela Foster's roommate. I want to ask you a few questions about her. That's all. I'm advising you that this interview is being video-recorded. I'm going to ask you some basic questions. Got it?"

"Yeah, fine, whatever."

Clay read him his Miranda rights. "Do you care to be represented by a lawyer?"

"I don't need any freaking lawyer—not until I find out why you brought me in."

"State your name, age, home address, and occupation."

"Denver Stennet, thirty-one years old. I live at 2134 Via Historica, Apartment 214, in Santa Fe."

"What do you do for a living?"

"I'm an electrician." He pointed to the name *Desert Breeze Electric* embroidered above the left pocket on his yellow buttoned-down shirt. "I work for this outfit—Desert Breeze."

"I see you have paint under your fingernails. Why's that?"

"I'm an artist, too."

"You're an artist?"

"Yeah, I'm an artist. I paint. Why is that so hard to believe? I sell my paintings in the plaza on weekends, mostly to tourists."

"Is that how you find women?"

"What the hell does that mean?"

Clay didn't respond. "Do you live with Angela Foster?"

"Yes."

"How did you end up rooming with her?"

"I put a note on the Twelfth Street Coffee Shop bulletin board looking for a roommate. She called me and we ended up being roomies."

Clay noticed the right side of Stennet's mouth twitch, as though he was about to snarl.

"Do you have an anger issue?"

"No, I don't."

"You look like you do."

"Well, I don't," he snapped back.

Are you romantically involved with Angela?"

"No. We live together is all."

"Are you aware someone attempted to murder her Sunday night?"

"Yes. I read about it in the paper this morning. What happened to her? I reported her missing yesterday. She didn't come home from her shift her usual time yesterday morning so I called the police. They said they couldn't do anything. I asked why the hell not, and they said they wouldn't be able to do anything until she was missing for twenty-four hours. So this morning after I read the newspaper I called them again. They said they knew about her kidnapping and would get back to me. And the next thing I know I got your goon cops hauling me away from my job and putting me in the back seat of a squad car to come here."

Clay stared at Stennet. "*Goon cops,* huh?"

Stennet averted his eyes.

"Did you call her work or any of her friends?"

"No. I figured I might as well just go right to the police."

"She's in critical condition after you tried to kill her."

"What the hell are you talking about? I didn't try to kill her. Why would I do that? We had a good relationship."

"What do you mean *had*?"

"I mean we *have* a good relationship. We've been living together for almost a year, and we're good. We have our own separate lives. If you don't believe me, ask Angela."

"I will when she's able to talk."

"Who would want to kill her?"

"You."

"Bullshit. No way! I did not try to kill her. Why would I?"

"Because of your rage. Because you come across like you have a short fuse. Am I right? That's okay, you can tell me."

69

"That's bullshit! The newspaper says she's in St. Vincent's. Can I see her?"

"No."

"Why?"

"Because I'm afraid you'll try to kill her again."

He raised his voice. "That's ridiculous."

"What size shoe do you wear?"

"What do you need to know that for?"

"I asked you a question. What size shoe do you wear?"

"Size nineteen. Why do you give a shit?"

"Don't be ridiculous. Take off your shoes."

"Okay, I wear a ten."

"Why did you lie just now?"

"To piss you off."

Bryce sat back in his chair, looking directly at Stennet and slowly nodding. "'Just to piss me off,' is that right? You're doing it, pal. Not too smart, is it, to piss off the guy who could put you in prison for the rest of your life?"

"Yeah, well, it's just that—"

"Just what?"

"I didn't do anything to Angela."

"Like I said before, you seem to have some real anger issues, Denver."

"Sure, I get pissed some times. I'm not gonna argue that. Everybody gets mad. But I didn't do a thing to hurt Angela."

"Let's talk about just how angry you get. How often have you hit Angela since you've been living together?"

"Hit her? Never."

"Never? A friend of hers told me she had some bruises because of you."

"That's a lie."

"You mean you never pushed her, or slapped her, or shoved her against the wall?"

Stennet looked away and scratched the side of his neck. He looked back directly at Clay, squinting and willing himself not to blink. He didn't answer.

"Yes or no? You know, when Angela is well enough to talk, we'll find out the truth. And, pal, it ain't gonna be good for you if it turns out you've been lying to me."

"Yeah, okay, here's the truth. There were a couple of times when we got into arguments about stupid stuff, but nothing ever got really bad. Pushing and shoving that's all—kind of wrestling, you know what I mean."

"Kind of wrestling? Is that what you call it?"

"It was—"

"I call it *domestic battery.*" Clay's anger was apparent.

"No—"

"What were the arguments about?"

"I don't remember."

"You don't remember? I'm sure Angela will."

Stennet hesitated for just a second before answering. "Okay, listen. It was always about money. She makes a helluva lot more than me, and I didn't think she was putting up her fair share for groceries and stuff. So we argued a couple of times and she got mad at me and pushed me, and I pushed her back."

"So a little pushing and shoving gave her major bruises on her arms?"

"She didn't get them from me. But you know what? I remember a couple of times that she had black and blue on her arm and I asked her what happened. She said she hit the wall or something. You know what I think? I think someone did it to her. But it wasn't me."

Clay suspected Stennet was lying.

"I'll ask you again. Are you romantically involved with her?"

"No. She doesn't have any interest in me. That's the truth. No sex. No nothing."

"Tell me about your roommate before Angela—Carrie Kirkland?"

Stennet was surprised that Clay knew about Carrie. "How do you know about her?"

"What happened to her? No one has seen her in two years. Did you kill her?"

"No. What are you talking about? I didn't even know she was dead. Is she dead?"

"She's missing and presumed dead."

"If she's dead, I didn't have anything to do with it. And you know what? I don't give a shit if she is dead."

"You're not the sympathetic type, are you, Denver?"

"No. So what? She took advantage of me, just like Angela's been doing."

"Tell me about your relationship with Carrie."

"I met her at a street art fair in the plaza about three years ago. She was by herself, looking at my paintings. She was pretty, but I thought she looked like she was homeless or something. I told her to pick out the painting she liked the best and I would give it to her. And if she wanted, she could sell it and pocket the money for herself. I didn't care. She was so excited, like I offered her a million bucks. We talked a little and she told me she was from Minnesota or someplace like that. Then one thing led to another and, anyway, I said she could stay with me in my apartment for a while until she found a job or something. I got her cleaned up and got clothes for her. I wasn't asking for anything in return. But then, after a while, we were...we started having sex. I mean, she was hot—that girl. When she got cleaned up and dressed up, man, she looked like a million bucks."

Clay had trouble believing Stennet's story. A hook nose and skinny physique were not exactly the qualities women found attractive.

"So what happened?"

"About three or four months after she moved in, she interviewed at the Indian Bend for a waitress job on the swing shift, and she got the job. Said it was a chance for her to make some really good money so she could help me pay for the rent and things, and she could get a car, and you know, buy whatever she wanted without asking me for money all the time."

"And, so?"

"I told her to go for it. Well, it turned out she made some pretty good bucks, with tips and everything, but instead of it being a good thing, it made things rocky for us."

"How so?"

"She used me. Here I'd taken her off the streets and given her a roof over her head. But then when she didn't need me anymore, she couldn't have cared less about me. At first I would drive her to work in the afternoon, and she'd hitch a ride back from people there. But then she was making enough money to buy herself a used car. She'd never driven a car before so I taught her how to drive."

"When she first started working at the Bend, she would get back to the apartment a little after midnight, but after six, seven months, she wouldn't come home until two or three in the morning—sometimes later. I'd ask her why she was so late and she'd always tell me she had to cover for someone. Then she would sleep until ten or eleven, and then get ready and go back to work for the start of her shift at four. We went from having a good thing to having nothing. And just like what's happened with Angela, we started arguing."

"About what?"

"It didn't make any difference. She was, like, picking fights with me for no reason. And it always ended with her yelling that I tried to control her and that she didn't need me anymore. But I was pretty sure she was cheating on me. After all I did for her, the bitch was cheating on me." He snarled. "I know it was someone from the Bend. It had to be."

"Who?"

"I have no freaking idea who. I said to her, 'Okay, you got what you wanted. I got you off the streets, and now you want me out of your life. You got your wish. You can move your ass out anytime you want.'"

"What did she do?"

"She acted like she didn't care. She didn't argue with me, but she didn't move out, either."

"I bet that pissed you off."

"You're damn right it did. I took her off the streets and she pulls that shit on me."

"Is that why you decided to get even with her?"

"What do you mean, get even? You think I killed her because of that? That's bullshit."

"So, you're admitting you killed her?"

"No! I didn't kill her. But one day I'd had it with her."

"Oh, yeah? How so?"

"I told her to pack her stuff and get the hell out—like, *now*. I told her she should go ahead and live with the guy she was screwing. She had to go to work that afternoon, and said she would pack her things when she got back. But when I got up the next morning, she wasn't there. I mean, she never came home. I didn't think anything of it. I figured she was spending the night with her boyfriend, and was just waiting for me to go to work so she could come back and pack up when I wasn't there. But then I had second thoughts. I thought maybe we could work things out. So I waited for her to come back later that day, and when she didn't, I went to the Bend looking for her."

"Did you talk with her there?"

"No. I couldn't find her. And no one knew where she was. That was it. I went back to the apartment and she never came back. I never saw her again. That's the whole story."

"Denver, I don't believe a thing you just told me. You've lived with two women. One went missing two years ago, and I figure she's dead. The other is barely alive. I find that strange as hell."

"Yeah, that's what it is. It's strange. But that's all it is, as far as I'm concerned. Let me say it again, loud and clear I... do... not... know... anything about what happened to either of them."

"Do you own a pickup?"

"Why?"

"Let me explain to you how this works. Try to keep up. I ask the questions. You answer the questions. You don't ask me. I ask you. Got it?"

Stennet looked away and didn't answer.

"I said, do you get it?"

"Yeah, I get it."

"Let's try this again. Do you own a pickup?"

Another hesitation. "No. I used to own one. I don't now."

"What kind of pickup do you own?"

"I just told you I don't own a pickup. What part of *don't* don't you understand? I don't own a car or truck. Period."

Bryce gave Stennet a withering stare. "Man, you've got an attitude that just goes on and on, don't you, Mr. Denver Stennet?"

"Maybe with you I do. You keep pissing me off. You think I'm lying about everything I say. Well, I'm not."

"You say you don't have a pickup anymore, so how do you get to work every day?"

"My company lets me use one of their vans. It's got their name all over the freaking thing, and the company thinks it's good advertising, so they let me drive it."

"What kind of gun do you own?"

"What? I don't own a gun."

"You sure about that? You mean, if I check it out, I won't find any gun registered to you?"

"That's what I mean."

"What happened to Emily Coburn?"

Denver squinted again. "Emily who?"

"Emily Coburn. What did you do with her body?"

"Never heard of her."

"She disappeared three years ago—waitress at the Bend— just like Kirkland. Did you kidnap her, too, like you did Angela?"

"You don't seem to get it. I don't know a thing about Emily Cowborn or whatever the hell her name is, and I don't know a thing about what happened to Carrie, and, guess what, I don't know a thing about what happened to Angela."

"So, you're saying you're innocent of any crime against all three women?"

"That's what I'm saying."

"Since you have nothing to hide, then, you won't mind if we search your apartment."

His answer was immediate. "Hell no, not without a warrant. I don't trust you. So, if you want to search my apartment, get a search warrant. And as of right now, I'm not answering any more questions without a lawyer."

Clay opened the door of the interview room and asked a cop to come in. "Cuff him and book him on suspicion of the kidnapping of Angela Foster. He just lawyered up, so let him have his phone call." Then he whispered to the cop. "But stall him until I can get a warrant."

* * *

That evening, Clay's search of the apartment Denver Stennet shared with Angela Foster did not uncover any evidence that would implicate Stennet in her kidnapping. Bryce was looking for at least one of a number of items—a fake badge, a .38-caliber revolver, a ski mask, a baseball cap with the word *Police* embroidered on it, a mover's blanket, or a size-ten cowboy boot that was missing a heel.

Okay, so I found nothing. But, as God is my witness, I know that son of a bitch is guilty.

CHAPTER 11

Clay decided to return to the Bend. He wanted to talk with Hope Archer again to see if she could help him gain more information about the case.

The truth is, I can't get her off my mind. Maybe that kiss on the cheek last night was nothing—just her normal goodbye. Men shake hands, women offer a kiss on the cheek. I think it was more than that, though—maybe an invitation. She has to know I'm interested. Does she want to get to know me better? What the hell, it's worth a visit to find out.

But he suspected John Grainger had hidden cameras trained on him during his visit the previous night to the Bend—when he interviewed Hope's employees and again when he was having dinner with Hope. Because of that, he didn't want to announce himself to Grainger, and instead went directly to her office.

Clay showed his badge to the guard standing outside the door to the administrative offices and asked him to notify Hope Archer that he wanted to speak with her. The guard recognized Clay from the night before and used the house phone on the wall behind him. "Okay. You're a go." He opened the secure door to the offices and let Clay enter. "Second door on the left." He closed the door behind him.

Hope was seated at her desk and rose to greet him. "What a nice surprise seeing you again." She leaned in to give him a kiss—this one a brief moment longer than her casual kiss of the night before. He was hoping to find out if that was just her way or if she was sending a deeper message.

Clay looked at his watch. "Twelve on the button. I was hoping I'd catch you before you left for the night."

She smiled warmly. "I'm glad you did."

"Do you have a minute to chat?"

"I sure do."

He swiveled his head ever so slightly to glance at the tile ceiling, uncertain if Grainger also had hidden cameras in Hope's office. He didn't see any, but he knew there were many ways to hide a camera and he didn't want to be too obvious looking for one. He said to Hope, "How about we do it over a drink."

"Sounds good to me. Give me five minutes to wrap things up."

"No problem."

"You can sit in here if you like."

Clay watched her put papers away in her file cabinet, check for email messages one last time, and lock her desk and file drawers. She smiled at him when she realized he was watching her every move. "Okay, Mr. Detective, let's get that drink you promised me."

Hope led Clay to the lobby then through one of the double doors leading into the casino. Once again he was appreciative of the view of her tight behind.

Phew! He shook his head.

The casino was jammed with people, and the two struggled to get through the crowd to the lounge without being separated. At one point, Hope reached back for Clay's hand to lead him through a congested aisle of slots and did not let go until they reached the Bender Lounge, where they were finally away from the smoke and noise of the casino. The server was one of Hope's employees. "The usual? Brandy?"

"Yes, please. Clay, how about you? It's on the house."

He ordered a Guinness draft.

They clicked glasses. "It's great seeing you again," she said.

"Same," he said, smiling, but then changed his demeanor. "I'm going to tell you what's going on with the Angela Foster case. I think you can help me. But, Hope, you've got to keep this to yourself."

"Of course. You have my word."

Referring to Dan Carton's analysis of the two crime scenes, Clay first explained to Hope his theory on how Angela was abducted, and then how she was rescued by Shiloh Youngblood. "We have a person of interest, but we don't have proof yet that he's the guy. We think he may have abducted Carrie Kirkland, too, and perhaps even Emily Coburn."

"Who's the suspect?" She squirmed a bit in her chair. "Oh, Lord, I hope it's not someone from here. Do I know him?"

"No, he doesn't work here. The guy's name is Denver Stennet, Angela's roommate. It turns out he was also Carrie Kirkland's roommate and listed as the emergency contact in each girl's personnel file."

Hope bit her lower lip softly and shook her head trying to recall if she knew him. "I don't know anything about him, but I'm glad it's not anyone from here."

"Holly Paine said she thought he might have been abusing Angela. Do you recall ever seeing her bruised up?

"I do, yes, but not anything that would make me think she was being abused."

"Are you sure?"

"Well, now that I think about it, I suppose that's what the bruising on her shoulders could have been from. I guess I should have been more observant."

"Do you know of anyone else here who might have shown an unusual interest in Angela? Anyone from the admin staff, a bartender, janitor, anyone?"

"No."

"Did she ever say she felt she was being stalked?"

Hope shook her head. "No. Sorry, Clay. As I mentioned last night, I don't remember Security ever telling me they filed an incident report that involved her." She exhaled deeply. "So, can we talk about something else now?"

"Okay." Clay smiled. "What do you want to talk about?"

"You, for example."

"Me?"

"Yes. Tell me about yourself."

"Like what?"

"Are you from New Mexico?"

"Yes, right here in Santa Fe. I graduated from New Mexico State. I went there on a football scholarship—my serious love at the time. That explains the bend in my nose, in case you were wondering. Broken playing ball."

"It makes you look ruggedly handsome."

"Yeah, right," he said, and shook his head, although he smiled at the compliment.

Hope smiled and took a sip of her drink, waiting for Clay to continue.

"Anyway, at State I studied criminal justice and decided to join the police force after graduating. My folks weren't happy with my decision, but I always wanted to be a cop. And, yes, I really like my job. Sometimes maybe too much."

"Why do you say that? It's great that you enjoy your job."

"I know, but it cost me a marriage."

"Oh. I'm sorry. What happened, if you don't mind my asking?"

"No, I don't. Nothing really. We went together the last two years in college. I thought she was the one for me and married her a year after we graduated. I was twenty-three and not very mature, I guess. She took offense because I put a lot of time into being a cop. It was my passion—and still is—but she didn't like that. Said I wasn't really married to her, that I was married to my job. The long and the short of it is we just fell out of love and divorced after not quite five years. And that was twelve years ago."

"Are you seeing someone now?"

"No, I'm not. I haven't had a whole lot of luck finding the right girl. You know, someone I can be committed to and who would commit to me. Frankly, any woman I've had feelings toward has had an issue with me being a cop. Seems no one wants to be married to a cop. I guess they don't want to have to compete with my job. More than one has even tried to talk me into finding another line of work. So, I've just accepted the fact that I'm not going to find anyone—and I'm okay with that. I'm tired of the dating game anyway."

"That's too bad. Like the song says, maybe you've been looking for love in all the wrong places."

"Could be. Have any idea where the right places are?"

She smiled knowingly, "Maybe."

"What about you, Hope? I don't see a ring on your finger. Are you divorced?"

"No. I never married. I went with someone for quite a few years, but we finally broke it off."

"Where are you from?"

"I was raised on a farm in Illinois. I attended the University of Illinois, but quit after my sophomore year. I was going with a guy in college. He was a couple of years older than me, and when he graduated, he talked me into following him out here. He always had big ideas and said he was going to make a fortune. I was never sure how he was going do that, but I was naïve enough to believe him. Anyway, I quit school and followed him. That was fifteen years ago. We got jobs when the Bend first opened. He started out as a dealer in the casino, and I got a job as a waitress right here at the Hungry Palate, as a matter of fact. My parents weren't too happy with me, but both my boyfriend and I were making pretty good money, mostly in tips, you know, and eventually we both worked our way up to management. I love my job and I love New Mexico—the desert, the way the desert flowers erupt after a rain, the mountains, the culture, everything. I would never want to live anywhere else. I liked Illinois, too, but I have no desire to go back. I'm a Santa Fean through and through now."

"What happened to the guy you followed here?"

Hope dropped her head and took a deep breath. When she looked back up at Clay, her eyes were questioning. She was uncertain what he was all about, but wanted to trust him. "Like you and your ex-wife, we just fell out of love and went our separate ways five years ago."

Clay saw hurt in her eyes. *That guy left a deep scar.* He reached across the table and rested his hand on top of hers. Just then, from the corner of his eye he sensed a presence at their table. He turned and saw John Grainger.

"Hello, Detective Bryce. What brings you here again this late at night?" Grainger asked.

Clay quickly removed his hand from Hope's.

"I stopped by to ask Hope a few more questions about Angela Foster. I see you're putting in long hours too."

Grainger glanced at Hope, but she looked straight ahead.

"Are you still pursuing this phantom notion of a serial killer?"

"Yeah. Yeah, I am."

"I wasn't happy about the article that appeared in the *Times Journal*."

"I understand, but as I explained to you this morning, there was nothing I could have done to stop it."

"So you said. Anything I can help you with tonight, Detective?

"No, I'm good."

"I was walking by and noticed the two of you, so stopped in to say hello. You take care. Let me know if you need anything." Grainger's manner was unusually pleasant.

Clay watched him walk out of the lounge. "He's full of himself, don't you think?"

"Yeah, I guess."

"You don't believe he just *happened* to be walking by, do you?"

"Probably not." She shrugged.

"Hope, I'm a cop. I notice things that most other people do not. Like I notice how you and Grainger react to each other. Let me ask you something."

"Yes?"

"Is he the guy from Illinois you came out here with fifteen years ago?"

She looked away briefly then turned back to look directly at Clay. She nodded. "Yes."

"He still has a thing for you, doesn't he?"

"He has a thing for every woman. It's just the way he is."

"What about you? Do you still have feelings for him?"

He overlooked her hesitation. "No, Clay, I don't. I really don't. It might sound silly to you, but he's a part of my past, not my future." She reached for his hand. "I think I like the future."

CHAPTER 12

Shiloh Youngblood didn't realize he would face such widespread attention during his leave. Six days had passed since his homecoming and he was tired of it all. His orders were to return to Fort Hood when his thirty-day leave was over. All he wanted was to get some solid sleep, eat his mother's cooking, and hang out with his friends. It was embarrassing enough that people were hero-worshipping him for his bravery in Afghanistan, but the incident with Angela Foster had brought on even more attention.

"Hey, Mom, I'm heading over to Bret's to hang out for a while. I'll be back by five. Need anything?"

"No, I'm good. Thanks, sweetheart."

They heard a knock on the door.

"Son, please see who that is before you go. It's probably for you."

"I hope not." Shiloh opened the door to a well-dressed man. "Yes, sir. What can I do for you?"

"Hello. My name is Steven Brown. I'm a reporter with the *New Mexican Times Journal*. I was hoping to interview a Sergeant Shiloh Youngblood for an article about how he saved a young lady's life. Are you Sergeant Youngblood?"

Mae overheard the man speaking from the front door step. "Shiloh, mind your manners. Ask the gentleman in."

"Please come in, Mr. Brown. Honestly, there really isn't a whole lot I can tell you that I haven't already told the police, and all of that's been made public. I'm not used to all this attention, so I'd rather not talk about it anymore. I did what anyone in my shoes would have done."

"I understand you were awarded a Silver Star for valor, so my guess is you actually acted above and beyond in saving Ms.

Foster. That's what I'd like to write about. I'd like to tie these two acts together. No one likes the idea of war, but everyone likes to hear about bravery and heroism, especially as it relates to saving the lives of your fellow soldiers and then a helpless young lady. Would you let me interview you? I won't be long."

Mae jumped in before Shiloh could say no. She was adamant. "Yes, he will, Mr. Brown. He's always so humble. But from the earliest age, he's been the boy who—"

"Mom, come on now," he chided. "I'll talk to the reporter, but let's not overdo it. Mr. Brown, I'll give you a half hour, but I've got to make a phone call before we start."

"That's great. In the meantime, do you mind if I ask your mother a few questions about the kind of kid you were growing up—you know, human interest stuff?"

Shiloh looked at his mother. He knew she would love nothing more than the opportunity to brag about her son. "Help yourself. But, Mom, please don't lay it on too thick."

"Do you care for some coffee, Mr. Brown?" Mae asked.

"That would be nice, thanks. I'll help you, ma'am."

Mae went into the kitchen and the reporter followed her.

Shiloh finished his phone call and joined the two in the kitchen.

"You look familiar. Do I know you?" Shiloh asked.

"I don't think so."

CHAPTER 13

Clay was relaxed in his recliner watching a Saturday afternoon doubleheader when he got a call from Chief Johnstone.

"Clay, there's been a shooting at Shiloh Youngblood's house."

"What happened?"

Johnstone's voice cracked. "Shiloh was shot and is en route to St. Vincent's. Not sure he's gonna make it. We don't know who did it. Whoever shot him, shot Mae—his mother—too. She's dead."

"What?"

Bryce ran out of his house, turned on the LED lights that flashed from the inside of his unmarked car, and sped to the Youngblood's house. On the way, he called Captain Ellsworth. "Someone just shot Shiloh Youngblood and his mother. Youngblood's on his way to the hospital, but his mother was killed. Could have been the same guy who abducted Angela Foster. I'm on my way there now. I'll fill you in when I get a chance."

* * *

Yellow barricade tape was stretched around the perimeter of the Youngblood home to protect the integrity of the crime scene and keep unauthorized people out. Neighbors had gathered to see what all the sirens and police activity were about. Pueblo women, were crying, some very loudly, while the men fought back tears and stood with their arms crossed stoically. They parted to allow Bryce to duck under the tape and enter the home. Chief Johnstone greeted him at the front door. They walked into the small kitchen thick with the smell of blood and burnt coffee. Blood was everywhere—puddled alongside Mae's body, splattered against the white kitchen cabinets—even on the ceiling. The coffee pot was on and two empty cups and spoons sat in the sink. After studying the scene, the two men walked back into the living room.

"Jacoby, my crime scene guys will be here shortly. Can you tell me what happened? Any witnesses?"

"No, not that we've found. Shiloh was supposed to be hanging out at a friend's house this afternoon. When he didn't show up and didn't answer his phone, the friend drove here and found Shiloh and Mae on the kitchen floor."

Bryce pointed to a man about Shiloh's age talking to one of Johnstone's cops. "Is that his friend?"

"Yes, that's him."

"I'd like to talk to him."

"His name is Bret Colby."

Clay dismissed the officer and introduced himself. "Bret. I'm Detective Clay Bryce from the Santa Fe Police. I'm working with Chief Johnstone investigating the shootings. I'm sorry you had to witness what happened to your friend and his mother, but I need to know what you found when you got here. Are you okay to talk for a few minutes?"

Bret took a deep breath. "Yeah, I'm okay."

Clay observed that Bret could have been mistaken for Shiloh's brother. He had the same round face and broad shoulders, and was as tall as Shiloh. His eyes were red and puffy from crying.

"Can you tell me what time you got here?"

"About two o'clock."

"What happened?"

"Shiloh was going to come over to my house at about twelve thirty but he called to tell me he would be late because there was a reporter from the *Times Journal* at the house who wanted to interview him. He said his mom insisted he talk to the guy, but that he wouldn't be longer than a half an hour."

"He didn't show up when he said he would?"

"No, he didn't. An hour went by and I waited a while longer. It was after one thirty when I got another call from him. But there was no one on the other end, so I called him back."

"And?"

"My call went right to voicemail. That's when I decided to drive over here. Shiloh was always on time—even when we were growing up he would never be late for anything. You know what I mean? He was always good to his word, so I had a feeling something was up. I just didn't know what."

"Tell me exactly what happened when you got here."

"Like I told Chief Johnstone, I parked along the side of the house. Then I knocked on the front door. No one answered, so I opened the door and shouted out for Shiloh. He didn't answer, so I yelled again. Then I called for Mrs. Youngblood, but she didn't answer either. I really didn't think anything of it. I figured they were in the backyard or somehow I missed him when he was on his way to see me. I walked in and started to go through to the kitchen to see if his mother's car was out back, and that's when I saw something on the floor."

"Where, Bret?"

"Over there, outside the kitchen." He pointed to what looked like a partial bloody shoeprint. Johnstone had placed a tented yellow card on the floor near the stain. "It looked like blood, but I wasn't sure what it was. I don't even remember what went through my head, but that's when I opened the

89

kitchen door, and...ah..." He was trying hard to control his emotions.

"Take your time."

Bret took a deep breath to compose himself and continued. "That's when I saw Shiloh face down on the floor. Mrs. Youngblood was next to him, and his arm was wrapped around her waist, like he was hugging her. Her eyes were wide open, but they weren't moving, and there was blood everywhere. I couldn't tell if they were shot or stabbed or what—" Bret was unable to control himself any longer. He lowered his head and put his hand to his brow, embarrassed to be crying in front of Clay and Chief Johnstone.

Clay was not comfortable around anyone who cried, especially a man, but he was trained to study the person, to observe if the tears were legitimate or an act.

Jacoby put his arm around Bret's shoulder. "Hey, pardner, it's okay."

Clay let Bret cry until he was able to compose himself. "I can't tell you how sorry I am you had to witness this. I can't begin to imagine how you feel."

"I just can't get that picture out of my head."

"We can continue later if you like."

"No, no. I'll be okay."

"What did you do when you saw them like that?"

"I panicked. I didn't know what to do. I didn't know what happened or who did it. I thought about what Shiloh said about having to talk to a reporter, and that maybe the reporter did this to them. And if he did, he might still be in the house. So I ran out the front door and screamed for help. Then I called 9-1-1 and ran back into the house to see if they were still alive. I didn't know what else to do," he repeated. "That's when I saw

Shiloh was still breathing, so I turned him over on his back and saw he was bleeding from his stomach. I got a kitchen towel and pressed it hard against his stomach to try to stop the bleeding. There was so much blood I couldn't tell if he'd been shot or what. He was bleeding from his shoulder, too. Oh, Jesus, God, he was bleeding all over. It was awful. I didn't know what else to do."

"You did fine," Jacoby said. "You did all the right things."

"At the time, Bret, did you realize Shiloh's mother was dead?" Clay asked.

"No, I didn't know. I couldn't tell for sure. But, like I said, her eyes were open and they weren't moving, so I think I knew she was dead. She was bleeding really bad too, but I couldn't see if she was breathing. It was horrible to see her like that."

"That's when Chief Johnstone got here?"

"Yeah. He checked on Mrs. Youngblood right away. I asked him if she was going to be okay, and I remember he just shook his head. Do you remember, Chief?"

"I do."

"Then you pulled out your gun and searched the house to make sure no one was still in the house."

Jacoby explained, "That's right, Detective Bryce. I checked the house out and there was no one here. But I can tell you one thing for sure, that if it wasn't for Bret, Shiloh would be dead too. He applied pressure to Shiloh's belly wound to keep him from bleeding out before I got here."

"Bret, did Shiloh say anything?"

"Yes. I could hardly understand him, so I put my ear close to his mouth. You know what he said? He said, 'Hey, buddy, sorry I'm late.' Can you imagine that?" Colby choked back more tears. "That's what he said. And then his eyes started to close. I yelled at him to open his eyes. I told him he couldn't die. I yelled at him to stay awake."

The chief nodded to Clay.

"So you didn't see the reporter who interviewed Shiloh?"

"No. I didn't see anyone."

"Did Shiloh mention the reporter's name when he called you?"

"No. All he said was that he was from the *Times Journal*."

"Clay, it had to have been our kidnapper posing as a reporter," Jacoby speculated. "Remember Shiloh saying the guy knew where he lived? It would have been easy for him to track Shiloh here."

Clay agreed. "I'll check with the *Times Journal* to see if they assigned anyone to interview Shiloh. The question is, was the guy a real reporter or someone posing as a reporter to gain access to Shiloh? Or was it someone else who waited until the reporter left?" He took out his pad. "Bret, let me see your cell phone. I want to see exactly when Shiloh called you so we can establish timelines." Clay figured that if Colby's recollection of time was correct, the killer had a very small window of opportunity to enter and shoot the Youngbloods. He had to wait until the reporter left, shoot Shiloh and Mae, and leave before Bret showed up. The timing would point to the reporter as the killer.

Bret handed Clay his phone. Clay scrolled through the call logs and noted the times calls came in from Shiloh's phone as 12:25 and 1:35. He also noted Bret's outgoing call to Shiloh at 1:36. "Did Shiloh say anything or did you hear anything in the background when he called you the second time?"

"No, nothing. It just went dead."

"And what about when you called him back?"

"Nothing. As I said, my call went right to his voice mail."

"The killer must've turned off the phone."

"Jacoby, let's check Shiloh's phone for fingerprints."

"We can't find his phone. It wasn't on Shiloh and it's not anywhere in the house. I called his number but it went right to voicemail, so the killer probably took it with him."

"Anything else you can think of, Bret?"

"Well, I don't know if this means anything, but when I drove here from my house, I saw an SUV driving in the opposite direction toward the main exit. I didn't recognize it as belonging to anyone in the pueblo. The only reason I remember the car was because, when it passed me, the driver pulled down the sun visor and looked away. Do you suppose that could have been him not wanting to be recognized?"

"Could be. Do you remember anything about the SUV? Color? Make?"

"I glanced at it in my rear-view mirror. It was white. I think it was a Ford. Maybe an Explorer."

"If the reporter is legit, it could have been his car. I'll confirm all this when I get back to Santa Fe. One last thing, Bret. Can you think of anyone who might have had it out for Shiloh?"

"No, Detective Bryce. Shiloh is a hero to everyone in the pueblo. And his mom, my God, everyone loved her, too." Bret teared again. "She was the kindest lady in the world."

Jacoby's voice quivered. "I've known Mae all my life." He shook his head. "I can't imagine anyone who would want to kill her."

Clay noticed Bret's blue jeans were blood-stained at the knees. "Bret, do you remember how you got blood on your jeans?"

"Probably when I was kneeling next to Shiloh."

"Do you remember making that bloody footprint outside the kitchen door?" Clay knew the footprint could not have been Bret's if, as he said, he had noticed the blood stain before going into the kitchen, but he tested Bret to make sure he was telling the truth.

Bret looked at his shoes. He raised first one foot then the other to see if there was blood on the soles. There was. "There's blood on the bottom of both. But, wait a second. I couldn't have made that print. I remember seeing it before I went into the kitchen."

"Would you mind letting us have your shoes so our forensics examiner can look at them?"

"Sure." Bret removed his shoes and handed them to Clay. "Don't you believe me?"

"Of course I do. Standard operating procedure. You said you saw the print before you went into the kitchen, so it can't be from your shoes, right? That means it probably belongs to the killer. We'll get them back to you as soon as we can. You okay with that?"

"I understand. No problem."

"Good. Listen, we'll want you to come into police headquarters at some point to give us a statement."

Bret nodded his understanding and headed for the door.

Jacoby took Clay aside. "If it's the killer's footprint, why only one print? And why outside the crime scene—outside the kitchen?"

Clay suggested, "Maybe that single print was made when Bret showed up. The killer took one step out of the kitchen to see who it was, then took off through the back of the house."

"You're probably right. We know there are footprints leading out the back door."

"Forensics will see if there's a match between the prints out back and this one. By the way, is there a chance this could be a case of domestic violence? Is there a Mr. Youngblood?"

"No. Mae's husband Jack died in an auto accident a couple of years ago."

"Do you know when, exactly?"

"I'm not sure of the date, but if it's important I'll check and let you know. It was a one-car accident—early morning, about one or two o'clock. He ran off the road on his way back from the Bend. That's where he worked as a security guard."

"If it was early in the morning, that means he probably worked the swing shift, right? I'm just curious to see what that accident report tells us."

* * *

Forensics later confirmed Bret's shoes were size twelve. They did not match the bloody shoe print on the floor outside the Youngblood kitchen. The print was from a size-ten boot.

CHAPTER 14

Clay left the Youngblood crime scene and sped to the *New Mexican* Times Journal Building in Santa Fe to learn if a reporter had been assigned to interview Shiloh Youngblood. It was nearly five o'clock—it was going to be a long Saturday. On the way, he called St. Vincent's to check on Shiloh's condition and was told Shiloh was in surgery. "Would you have Doctor Moran call me after surgery?"

Clay parked on the street directly in front of the building and went straight to the security desk inside where he showed his identification. "I need to speak with the editor in chief immediately."

Within minutes, a *Times Journal* receptionist arrived and escorted Clay to the fourth floor where a number of reporters and editors were working.

Editor in Chief Luis Garcia looked up from a large round table in a glass-enclosed conference room where he and his section editors were finalizing the details of the Sunday edition. He lifted his index finger and mouthed "one minute" to Clay, who nodded back that he understood. The receptionist escorted Clay into Garcia's office.

Observing the organized chaos of the city room, Clay saw reporters and editors working on computers while others conferred about their articles or talked on their cell or office phones. It was a frenzied environment not unlike that of police headquarters.

A minute later Garcia entered his office. "It's always a push to get an edition finished in time, especially the Sunday edition. But you caught me at the right time. What can I do for you?"

"I'm Detective Clay Bryce of the Santa Fe PD." He handed Garcia his card.

"Nice to meet you, Detective. Luis Garcia, editor in chief of the *Journal*." They shook hands. Garcia looked exhausted from the challenge of getting the Sunday news out in time. He exhaled deeply and plopped down in his chair. He pointed to a side chair for Clay to sit.

"Do you know who Sergeant Shiloh Youngblood is?"

"Yes. We learned he was shot and his mother murdered a short while ago."

"You got that news fast."

"We did. In today's digital world it's critical for us to learn news in real time."

"I'm here because of those shootings—straight from the pueblo, in fact. I was told Sergeant Youngblood was interviewed by someone who identified himself as a reporter of yours, but we think the guy may have been using that as a cover to get in to see him. If you really did send a reporter out, I'd like to talk to him."

"It was our reporter. Steven Brown interviewed Sergeant Youngblood. He had to edit his report to include information about the shootings, but his column will be in tomorrow's paper."

"Is he here now, Mr. Garcia? He may have been the last guy to see Shiloh and Mae Youngblood before they were shot."

Garcia leaned to one side and looked around Clay through the glass office partition to see if his reporter was at his desk. "He's in the city room right now. I'll call him in." Garcia stood and leaned out his office. "Steven, a minute."

Steven Brown walked into Garcia's office, clearly irritated at the interruption. He was dressed in a navy blue blazer, gray slacks, and white shirt with a yellow bowtie—and an outlandish pair of Keds high-top fluorescent-green sneakers.

"Steven, Detective Bryce is with the Santa Fe Police Department. He's investigating the shootings of Shiloh and Mae Youngblood and wants to ask you a few questions."

Brown peered at Bryce over the reading glasses perched on the tip of his large nose. His comb-over gray hair was held securely in place with heavy-duty amounts of hair spray. Between his looks and high-pitched squeaky voice, he had the air of a cartoon character. "What do you want to know?" His tone was prickly, matching the sour look rooted on his face.

"Did you interview Shiloh Youngblood this afternoon?"

"Yep. A few hours ago. I don't remember the exact time."

"When did you learn that he and his mother were shot?"

"After I got back here. We picked it up from the police scanner. It must have happened right after I left their house."

"What can you tell me about your visit to the pueblo?"

Brown exhaled loudly, impatient with Bryce's questions. "Is this necessary? You can read about it in tomorrow's edition."

"Steven, just answer his questions so we can all get out of here," Garcia said.

"What do you want me to say? The sergeant was a humble kid and said he was being overwhelmed with all the attention he was getting—you know, about his hero status with the Silver Star and then that girl's abduction. He said he had plans with a friend and didn't want to keep him waiting, so he gave me a half hour. He and his mother answered my questions and apologized for cutting the interview short. That was it. I thanked them and left. That's all I can tell you."

"What kind of vehicle were you driving?"

Brown looked into space before answering, more aggravated with each question Clay posed. "Why do you ask?"

"Shiloh's friend said he saw a car he didn't recognize at the pueblo. I'm wondering if it was yours."

"A Ford Explorer. White."

"When you left did you see any other vehicle parked in front, back, or anywhere near the house? A black pickup, for example?"

"Not in front, and I didn't have any reason to look in the back."

"Because the times of your visit and the shootings were so close, it's possible the guy who shot Shiloh and his mother was in the house the entire time and waited until you left, or he could have been lurking in the back. You were lucky to leave when you did."

"I suppose."

"Can you tell me anything else about your interview?"

"It was innocuous, a human interest story. Mae offered a few comments about Shiloh growing up. That kind of thing. That's it. As I said, you'll be able to read my column in tomorrow's paper."

"Mr. Brown, we may need you to come to police headquarters to give a statement."

Upon hearing that, Brown became even pricklier. "What the hell for?"

"I'm sorry, what did you just say to me?"

"I said, what the hell for?"

Clay looked quizzically first at Garcia then back to Brown. In his most patient tone, he explained, "We're trying to determine the timeline of events leading to the shootings of two innocent people, and how the killer was able to get in and out of their house unseen."

"Fine. Whatever."

"I can't help but notice your outfit—green Keds with a nice blazer. Is that what's in nowadays? If it is, I'm way out of touch, as you can see." He laughed as he pointed to his own scuffed up brown dress shoes.

Brown responded sharply. "No. Of course it's not a *style* thing. I have problems with my feet—bunions. These sneakers are the most comfortable shoes I can wear, so I keep them in my car and change into them when my feet hurt."

"Just curious, were you wearing those sneakers when you interviewed Shiloh?"

"No, I changed into them when I got back into my car. Why?"

"Just curious, that's all. Would you let me see the shoes you wore to the interview?"

Brown shook his head and spat out a no.

"No, you won't let me look at your shoes?"

"That's what I said. What do you need to see them for?"

"Curious."

"You think I had something to do with the Youngblood shootings, don't you? That's a hell of an insult. I had nothing to do with it, and if you knew anything about the Fourth Amendment to our Constitution, you would know I don't have to show you a thing without a warrant."

Clay continued to show patience. He shook his head, perplexed at Brown's attitude. "Mr. Brown, what's the big deal? I'm sorry if I insulted you and, no, I don't think you had anything to do with the shooting, but it's my job to examine all the elements of the case."

"Detective, my guess is, because you're a cop, you don't know bupkis about the Bill of Rights and the prohibition of unreasonable searches. If you're that curious about my shoes, bone up on the Constitution and, as I said, get a warrant." He turned to Garcia and said, "Boss, I'm out of here." Without waiting for an okay from Garcia he turned and walked out of the office and back to his desk.

Clay looked for a show of support from Garcia. "What's that all about? He's got an issue with cops?"

Garcia shrugged. "Sorry. I can't help you. He is what he is, but he's a damned good reporter."

CHAPTER 15

Clay left the Times Journal building and called Captain Ellsworth from his car. He briefed him on the details of the Youngblood shootings and his conversations with Shiloh's friend Bret Colby and reporter Steven Brown.

"How did it go with Brown? I know him. A real pain in the ass, isn't he? I've had run-ins with him a dozen times," Ellsworth said.

"Yeah, well, then you know what he's all about. He copped a major attitude toward me. I'm in his boss's office, and he comes in dressed to the nines, you know, blazer, slacks, but then I see he's wearing these crazy-ass lime-green sneakers. I asked him what was up with them. He said he has foot problems and wears them when his feet hurt. But I'm thinking about the killer who left a bloody footprint at the scene. Was it Brown's footprint and that's why he changed his shoes? I asked to see the shoes he was wearing when he interviewed Youngblood. I didn't accuse him of anything. I just wanted to make sure there was no blood on the shoes, and eliminate him as a potential suspect. You'd think he'd know that."

"Listen, Clay, I know Brown. He acts like a one-man ACLU. He threw out the Bill of Rights to you, didn't he?"

"Yeah. But it's enough to make me wonder what he's all about. He ends up giving me a lecture about the Fourth Amendment and unreasonable searches, and said if I wanted to check his shoes, I had to get a warrant."

"You know, if there was blood on his shoes, they would have been tossed by now."

"I'm sure you're right, Captain, but I think I'll stick around and wait for him to leave the building. I want to ask him nice one more time."

* * *

Clay waited in his car. It was nearly six when Brown exited his building. He was still wearing his green sneakers and drew stares from passers-by. Clay honked his horn and called out to him, "Hey, Brown, wonder if I can talk with you for a second?"

At first, Steven Brown wasn't sure who was calling him. When he stooped down and saw Clay inside the car, he said, "Oh, it's you. What do you want now?"

Clay got out of his car. "You know, I'm suspicious by nature. It's my job to be suspicious. No offense, but your choice of footwear bothers me."

Brown looked at his sneakers, then back at Clay. "Have you studied up on the Constitution?"

"Yeah, I have a copy in my car. I've been reading it while I was sitting here waiting for you. I think I have it down pat." His sarcasm was not lost on Brown.

"Did you get a warrant?"

"No, not yet—"

Before Bryce could finish his sentence, Brown rolled his eyes and said, "So, you *do* think I shot Mae and Shiloh Youngblood, don't you?"

"Here's what I think. We found a bloody footprint in Shiloh's house, and I'm wondering if it could be from your shoe. I'm not saying it is. I'm just saying I wonder about the coincidence of you saying you had to change your shoes after you left his house. You see what I mean about being suspicious by nature? I want to make sure it's only coincidence and not something more."

"So you want to examine my shoes for blood?"

"Yes. Can we agree to that much?"

"No, we can't. I told you before. You want to look at my shoes, get a warrant." Brown walked away but made a U-turn after just a few steps. "You know what, Detective? It pisses me off that you think I had anything to do with that shooting. Until you have a warrant, you can go pound sand."

CHAPTER 16

HERO SOLDIER SHOT, MOTHER MURDERED
AT YIQUA PUEBLO

On Saturday afternoon, an unknown assailant invaded the Yiqua Pueblo home of Mae Youngblood, 52, killing her and critically wounding her son, Sergeant Shiloh Youngblood, 25. Only one week ago, the sergeant was in the news for rescuing Angela Foster, who had been abducted after ending her shift at the Indian Bend Hotel and Casino. Detective Clay Bryce of the Santa Fe Criminal Investigation Division and Chief Jacoby Johnstone of the Yiqua Tribal police report that mother and son were discovered early Saturday afternoon by a close friend of Sergeant Youngblood. The sergeant is on leave from the U.S. Army after having served his second nine-month tour in Afghanistan, during which time he was awarded the Silver Star for extraordinary heroism. Youngblood remains hospitalized in critical condition. The police ask anyone with information about this crime to call 505-222-9999. All calls will be held in confidence. The interview this reporter had with Sergeant Youngblood shortly before he was shot appears on page A6. - Steven Brown

On Monday afternoon, one week after Angela Foster was kidnapped, Clay called a very irritated Steven Brown in for questioning. Captain Ellsworth witnessed the interview in the adjacent observation room.

"Steven, I need your help with my investigation of the Youngblood shootings. I just want to ask you a few questions."

Brown leaned back in his chair, folded his arms across his chest, and sniggered. "All this because I wouldn't let you examine my shoes? Ha! You couldn't get a warrant, could you? Imagine that."

"I didn't even try. What would have been the point? If you did have blood on your shoes, you would have tossed them by now anyway. But if you didn't get rid of them, I thought you would just do your civic duty, show me the shoes, and then answer my questions to help me find out who shot Shiloh Youngblood. I'm not sure what the big deal is. I had a simple request, but you've made it a constitutional issue. What's up with that?"

"This is what a judge would call *harassment*. You cops are good with that tactic, aren't you? Instead of doing your jobs in the proper manner, you strong-arm, abuse, and harass law-abiding citizens. I, for one, will not put up with your police-state misconduct."

"Good Lord, Steven. What the hell are you talking about? The Santa Fe police force has one of the best reputations of any in the country."

"Not as far as I'm concerned."

Clay let the comment slide. "So there's no way I'm going to change your mind about cooperating with me?"

"Not a chance."

It was Clay's turn to smirk. "Okay, listen. At your suggestion, I've gone so far as to study the Supreme Court's 1966 Miranda ruling. With that said, Steven, I'm going to read you your Miranda rights."

"You've got to be kidding me."

"No, no I'm not."

"This is pure and simple provocation," Brown barked.

"Mr. Steven Brown, this interview is being recorded." Clay smiled and read Brown his rights. "Your choices will be to get a lawyer to represent you, cooperate with me and answer my questions, or, if you do not cooperate, I may publicly announce that you are a person of interest in this case—which of course you are."

"This is laughable—exactly what I mean about police harassment. I ought to take you to court for this."

"It's your choice, Steven."

Brown said nothing.

Clay continued, "Fine. We'll start with the identifying questions. Please state your name and age."

Again Brown did not answer.

"We can sit here until the cows come home, if that's what you want. I've got all day. No problem from my end."

Brown relented. "My name is Steven Robert Brown. I'm fifty years old."

"Married?"

"No."

"Ever been married?"

"No. Like that's an important question to ask."

"What size shoe do you wear?"

"I'm not answering that. You're back to asking about my shoes."

"And you deem that question to be harassment? Are you saying you're not going to tell me your shoe size?"

"Ten."

"Thank you. What do you do for a living?"

"I'm a reporter for the *New Mexican Times Journal*."

"How long have you been a reporter for the *Times Journal*?"

"Going on four years."

"Where did you work before that?"

"The Louisville Kentucky Bulletin."

"Why did you leave that position?"

Brown squirmed. "I'd rather not say."

"I'll say it for you, then. You were forced to resign because you and your paper were sued for libel by two police officers in Louisville. True?" Clay did not wait for him to respond. "Is it not true that you accused them of exactly what you're accusing me of—harassment? With that history in mind, Steven, I would welcome the opportunity to have a judge determine in a court of law if your defamatory remarks of a few minutes ago are slanderous. I think they are. What do you think?"

Brown shook his head repeatedly and pursed his lips, but said nothing.

"What were you doing this past Saturday afternoon between the hours of noon and two o'clock?"

"I was at the Yiqua Pueblo interviewing Shiloh Youngblood for my column in the *Times Journal*."

"Now that wasn't too hard, was it?"

Brown glared at Bryce.

"You know, I think it's kind of peculiar you won't honor my simple request. We have a dead woman and a decorated Army sergeant lying in the hospital in critical condition, and all I'm asking is for you to cooperate with my investigation so we can get what may be a serial murderer off the streets."

"You already so much as told me a minute ago that you didn't think I was guilty, so why are you making such a big deal out of this?"

"You're a smart man. Why do you think? Why don't you just show me the shoes? Then all would be good and we can be friends."

"I don't care if we *can all be friends*. I don't want to be your friend, your confidante, your buddy. Let me ask you, Detective,

108

what the hell do you think my motive would be to kill Shiloh Youngblood?"

"Maybe you're the guy who abducted Angela Foster and you thought Shiloh could identify you. I'll say it again. You're the one making a thing out of this, and I don't understand why. What do you think the court of public opinion would say about the fact that you wouldn't cooperate with me when a war hero was shot within minutes of you interviewing him? And on top of that, you've got a thing against cops?" Clay answered for Brown. "I'll tell you what people would think. They'd think you have a thing against authority figures, and they'd start to wonder what you're all about."

"You're full of shit, *Detective* Bryce." Brown practically spat the words out of his mouth. "It's the principal that matters here. You cops think you can get away with all kinds of shit, but not with me. Get a search warrant and you can see my shoes. The Fourth Amendment prevents unreasonable searches—"

"Give me a break already. Don't lecture me on Fourth Amendment rights."

Brown glared at him. "Charge me with something or I'm walking out of here."

Clay realized his attempt to get Brown to cooperate was fruitless. "You're free to go." Frustrated at Brown's attitude he added, "And, Mr. Greenshoes, you can rest assured that I will be keeping a close eye on you."

Brown got up to leave. On his way out the door, he grinned at Clay and said, "See you in the funny papers."

Ellsworth left the observation room and met Clay in the hallway. "As I said, he's a pain in the ass. But you know what, Clay? There's nothing you can do except keep him on your radar."

CHAPTER 17

Ten days had passed since Clay started his investigation into the abduction and attempted murder of Angela Foster, and he had made scant progress. He had a lot more questions than answers. While still suspicious of Steven Brown's story about why he changed into sneakers after leaving the Youngblood residence, Clay's prime suspect was Angela's roommate, Denver Stennet. His search of Stennet's apartment, however, had not yielded anything incriminating, certainly not the smoking-gun evidence he had hoped to uncover. He had found no records that Stennet or Foster had rented a U-Haul or other vehicle in the two years prior. Nor was he successful at locating a shoe repair shop that had recently repaired the heel of a size-ten cowboy boot.

Shiloh Youngblood remained in intensive care after successful surgery to repair the damage done by two gunshot wounds. On Wednesday, Doctor Moran, phoned Clay to tell him Shiloh was well enough to be questioned about the shooting. "The Sergeant was in phenomenal shape. He lost a lot of blood, but he's awake and lucid. He'll be in here for a while, but he should be fine when all is said and done."

"That's good news, Doctor. He's one lucky man."

"He is. The bullet that did the most damage, the one to his abdomen, missed every organ by centimeters and lodged in his rib cage. So, yes, he's a lucky man. He'll be moved to a private room shortly. You can talk to him, but don't overdo it."

"There will be two of us, and we won't overdo it."

"I'm sure you won't, Detective."

"One other thing, Doctor."

"What's that?"

"We need to guard against him being a target again. When you move him out of ICU, I'd like him moved to a private room adjacent to last week's abduction victim, Angela Foster. I'll be putting a cop on guard for both of them twenty-four seven."

*   *   *

Chief Johnstone met Clay in the main lobby at the hospital. They rode the elevator to the third floor and walked to the end of the corridor where Shiloh and Angela were in rooms across from each other. A cop who was in a chair against the far wall stood when he saw the two men approach.

Clay asked, "How's it going?"

"No problem, Detective."

"Good. Which room is Youngblood in?"

The cop pointed to the room on his left. Clay and the Chief entered and found Shiloh propped up in bed with oxygen and IV connections. A nurse was checking the morphine drip and taking his temperature. She cautioned, "He's not allowed out of bed yet. Doctor Moran left strict instructions limiting the time you spend with him."

Both men acknowledged her orders. Clay stood at the foot of the bed while Jacoby pulled up a chair and sat alongside Shiloh. "How're you doing, pardner?"

With strained voice, Shiloh answered, "I hurt a bit, but I'll be okay. Tell me, is Mom okay?"

Jacoby and Clay exchanged glances. The chief knew he would have to be the one to tell Shiloh his mother had been killed—best to hear the news from him instead of from someone on the medical staff or a TV newscast. "Listen, pardner, I've got some really bad news." He rested his hand on

111

Shiloh's arm. "Shiloh, Mae is dead. Whoever shot you, shot her too."

Shiloh stared at Jacoby for a few seconds then slowly turned away. He closed his eyes and tried to keep from crying, but tears escaped and rolled down his cheeks.

"I'm sorry, Shiloh," Clay said. "We're going to find the son of a bitch who did this. I promise."

Shiloh opened his eyes and looked up at the ceiling in silent prayer to the mother he adored.

"We've notified your commanding officer at Fort Hood about what happened. He wants you to be totally recovered before you go back on duty, so he's extended your leave to ninety days."

Shiloh stared blankly at the Jacoby. "How I can help you find him?"

"Do you remember anything that happened right before you were shot?" Clay asked.

Shiloh blinked and again looked up at the ceiling. "I remember a guy—I forget his name—he said he was a reporter and wanted to talk to me about how I saved that girl. Brown—that was his name. Mom insisted I talk with him, so I called my friend Bret to tell him I was going to be late. But then afterward... Bret... I remember Bret was there. Jesus, is Bret okay?"

"Yes, he's fine," Jacoby assured him. "He's chafing at the bit to visit you."

Clay said, "The reporter was Steven Brown, Shiloh."

"Right. Steven Brown."

"Are you saying Bret was there when Brown was interviewing you?"

"Yes... No... No." Shiloh shook his head. "I don't remember."

"That's okay. It'll come back to you in time. Do you remember if Brown left as soon as he was done interviewing you?"

"I think he did... Yeah, I think he left. Why are you asking? You don't think he's the guy who shot us, do you?"

"We're not sure," Clay answered. "Right now we're looking at every possibility. Can you remember anything else?"

Shiloh opened, then closed, his eyes, trying to recall the sequence of events. "After he left, I went to my bedroom to get... I think I went to get the keys to Mom's car. I was using her car... Then I think I dialed Bret, but I never talked to him. And, oh yeah. Oh my God, I remember. I heard Mom scream from the kitchen. I remember thinking she had fallen, so I ran back to see if she was okay... and... and there was a guy..."

"Can you describe him?"

"I think it was the same guy from the desert... He had on a ski mask... I saw Mom on the floor... She was bleeding... and... That's all I remember. Then I woke up here."

"Do you remember if you heard a gunshot before running to the kitchen?" Jacoby asked.

"No. I don't think so."

"He probably used a silencer," the Chief said to Clay.

"You're pretty sure, Shiloh, it was the same guy who tried to kill Angela Foster?"

"Yes, I think it was."

"Do you think the reporter could have been the shooter?"

"I don't know. He could have been. I remember seeing him leave—I think. No, I don't know for sure. I'm sorry. I'll have to think about all this some more." His voice trailed off.

Bryce recognized that Shiloh was tiring. "We're going to leave you alone for now. I know Bret and a lot of folks from the pueblo want to visit you, but Doctor Moran thinks it's best to wait a few more days before you have company. Under the circumstances, I've assigned a cop to be on guard outside your room to make sure no one tries to come after you again. That girl you saved, Angela Foster, is recovering across the hall. The cop I've got stationed in the hallway will be guarding both of you. When you're up to it, we'll have you and Angela reconnect. She's still in a pretty bad state. Maybe hearing your voice will get through to her."

Shiloh nodded, closed his eyes, and instantly fell asleep.

On their way out, Chief Johnstone told Clay he had been able to get a copy of Jack Youngblood's accident report. "I'll send it over to you, but basically it said the state police who investigated the accident scene on Route 14 found skid marks from his pickup in the dirt shoulder fifty yards before it sideswiped a telephone pole, and then another fifty yards later it went off the road and crashed into a ravine. It happened about one o'clock in the morning."

"Had he been drinking?"

"No. He had a zero blood alcohol level, and there were no drugs in his system. The police labeled his death 'driver inattention.' They think he either fell asleep at the wheel or maybe swerved to avoid an animal, but they really don't know."

"Was there any suspicion another car was involved?"

"The report says nothing about another vehicle. They just labeled it a one-car accident."

"Any idea where his truck is now?"

"I figured you were going to ask me that, so I looked into that, too. It was hauled to a junkyard outside of La Cienega, but it was totaled. The owner of the junkyard checked his records

114

and told me the truck had been stripped for parts and the rest sold for scrap metal."

"What was the date of that accident?"

"June fourteenth, two years ago."

Clay stopped in his tracks and nearly shouted at Chief Johnstone, "You're kidding me! That's the day after Carrie Kirkland disappeared!"

CHAPTER 18

Five days after the shootings, Shiloh Youngblood was not well enough to attend his mother's funeral. Mae Youngblood was to be interred in a cemetery at the northern end of the Yiqua Pueblo—the final resting place of many in her long family line. Clay obtained permission from Shiloh and from the Pueblo governor to attend the ceremony and pay his respects to Mae. He would be the only non-Yiqua present to witness the traditional funeral ceremony.

Under the brilliant New Mexico afternoon sun, several pallbearers, including Jacoby Johnstone and Bret Colby, transported Mae's body on a wooden crib to a gravesite located between two piñon trees. As tradition dictated, her body had been wrapped in a colorful blanket.

The governor gave the eulogy, lauding her pride in her son Shiloh, her humility, her humanity, and her love of the Pueblo heritage. After the eulogy, several women gave all those present a handful of cornmeal to spread over Mae's blanketed body as an offering of food that would serve to nurture Mae as she made her way to eternal life.

In a natural burial, the pallbearers lowered Mae's body into the grave on the crib that was to be her bed for all eternity, and people dropped flowers and branches of evergreen into the grave. After that, everyone in attendance, including Clay, assisted in shoveling dirt into the grave until it was completely filled.

* * *

Clay returned to police headquarters after the funeral to do paperwork. At seven o'clock he called Hope.

"Hello?"

"Hope, hi. It's Clay."

"Oh, what a nice surprise."

"Say, I know it's late, but I've got to head back out to the Bend to talk to John Grainger. Can I stop by afterwards to say hello and maybe buy you some dinner?" Clay was tentative in his request. Without a doubt he was attracted to her, but he didn't know her feelings toward him. And while he had seen other women since his divorce, he hadn't had much success at the dating game. But then he had never met anyone like Hope. She took his breath away. She was different—smart, beautiful, and self-assured.

Without hesitation, she responded, "I look forward to it, Mr. Detective-man."

* * *

John Grainger was blunt. "It seems you're becoming a regular around here, Detective Bryce. Are you sure you don't have ulterior motives?"

"What do you mean by that?"

Simon Learner was standing next to Grainger's desk. Granger glanced at him. "We've noticed that you and Hope Archer seem to be getting along rather well."

Clay felt himself turn red but ignored Grainger's insinuation. "Yes. She's been helpful in my investigation."

Grainger smiled knowingly. "I'm sure she has."

Once again Clay disregarded the innuendo. "I assume you've heard about the shootings that took place Saturday at the Yiqua Pueblo."

"I have."

"Shiloh Youngblood's the one who rescued Angela Foster from her desert grave. It's possible that whoever kidnapped Angela found out where Shiloh lived and tried to eliminate him as a witness. He survived the shooting, but his mother was killed."

"What did his mother have to do with all this?"

"Probably nothing. My guess is she just happened to be in the wrong place at the wrong time."

"I've told you this before, but I think you're exaggerating the whole serial killer thing. Now you're suggesting the Youngblood shootings are related to Angela Foster's kidnapping?"

"Yeah, I am."

"In that case, I'll ask, *again*, what do you want from us?"

"I learned you employed Shiloh's father, Jack Youngblood, as a guard."

"Yes, I remember the name. I think he died in an automobile accident a few months back."

Uncharacteristically, Simon corrected his boss. "Actually, it was two years ago, Mr. Grainger. He died in a one-car accident on his way home from the Bend."

Grainger did not appreciate that his assistant corrected him. He gave Simon a blistering stare before turning his attention back to Clay. "Detective, why does Jack Youngblood interest you? He died in an auto accident—*two years ago*—according to Simon." Grainger glared at his assistant again but Simon looked away.

"Because I'm looking into the possibility that his accident was not an accident at all. That, in fact, someone may have run him off the road."

"Right," Grainger said, half-smiling. He shook his head and asked in a derisive tone, "And why would someone do that?"

"I'm not sure yet. Maybe Mr. Youngblood witnessed what happened to the other waitress, Carrie Kirkland, and her kidnapper decided to eliminate him by ramming him into a ravine. It's only a theory on my part, but his death occurred on the day after Kirkland disappeared. That's a hell of a coincidence, don't you think?"

"Interesting but far-fetched." Grainger turned to his assistant. "Simon, do you remember anything about Jack Youngblood?"

This was Simon's opportunity to get back in Grainger's good graces. "Yes, sir, I do. He was from the Yiqua Pueblo, and was stationed outside the Administrative Offices on the afternoon-to-midnight shift. We sent flowers to his wife Mae when he died."

Grainger shook his head, feigning disbelief. "Simon is like a walking computer. He has an incredibly retentive mind—I think even a photographic memory. But he says no, don't you, Simon?"

Simon smiled and stood straighter and taller at the compliment. "Thank you, Mr. Grainger, but that's not quite true, sir."

"But it is. It's amazing, Detective. He can remember the most minute detail about anything that has gone on at the Bend. He's been my loyal aide for five years."

"That so?" It was more of a statement than a question.

"We're expecting big things from Simon. I see him running this place down the road."

"Then what else can you tell me about Mr. Youngblood, Simon?"

Simon glanced at Grainger for permission to answer. Clay looked in Grainger's direction too and saw him give an approving nod. "Mr. Youngblood was always very protective of the women who work for Hope Archer. Every night, as the women clocked out, he took it upon himself to escort them safely to their cars."

"Now here's something curious about him. Were you aware he never filed an incident report? I went through all the reports you sent me—as you know, there were quite a few—but there was not a single one completed by Jack Youngblood. Given that he was an employee in your security department, I found that pretty unusual."

Again Simon looked at Grainger then at Clay. "Detective, maybe you missed them. I think there have to have been reports submitted by Mr. Youngblood in what I sent you."

"You think? You don't know for sure?" Grainger asked.

Simon's face turned red at another rebuke from his boss. He stammered, "I... I'm sorry, but I'm not absolutely sure."

"Double check on that, and make sure you sent everything the detective requested."

"Yes, sir, I will. My apologies, Detective Bryce, if I failed to send you all of the reports."

Clay wondered if Simon had intentionally failed to send him Jack Youngblood's reports. For now, he masked his suspicions. "No problem. There were a lot of reports, so maybe some slipped through the cracks. These things happen."

"Is there anything else you need?" Grainger asked.

"Not right now. But, Simon, please send me Youngblood's reports as soon as possible."

"I will."

"And, now, I would appreciate it if you could take me down to Hope Archer's office. I have a few more questions for her."

Learner looked again at his boss who nodded his okay.

Grainger fished again about Clay's relationship with Hope. "She's been helpful to you in your investigation?"

"Yes, she has." Clay abruptly ended the conversation, avoiding further discussion that would indicate his interest in her. He followed Simon out of the office without extending his hand to Grainger or giving a word of thanks.

* * *

Hope closed her office door after Simon left. She turned to Clay and surprised him with a sweet kiss on the lips. He didn't know how to react. Was she just teasing? He wanted to reach out to her, to pull her close, but thought twice of it and stepped back, confused.

He stammered, "Good Lord, Hope."

She let out a nervous giggle. "I'm sorry, Clay. I shouldn't have done that. Honest, I'm not usually like this. I don't know what has gotten into me. Really, I'm sorry."

Clay put his hands around her waist and stepped in close. "Hope, don't. I mean, listen. Don't *apologize*. I feel like a high school kid with you, too, and I've only seen you, what, three times and—"

"Shh," she leaned in and kissed him again.

Clay took in the fragrance of her hair and her subtle perfume. He felt her breasts against his chest and tried to control his breathing. Looking over her shoulder, he nodded toward the door.

"What?"

"Someone could walk in on us. We'd better not. Let's get something to eat."

"Then what?"

Clay exhaled audibly. "You're making this very hard for me, Hope."

She smiled mischievously. "Good."

* * *

Clay led Hope to an empty table at the Hungry Palate. After they sat down, Hope leaned in toward Clay and whispered, "I guess you can tell I am attracted to you. I have been since we first met."

"Damn if I know why, Hope, but one thing I do know for sure—the feeling is mutual."

She picked up a menu and fanned herself with the charm of a Southern belle.

Clay smiled at her playfulness and felt himself falling deeper for this woman. "You know, you are not only beautiful, you're a hell of a tease."

"A tease? No I am not."

"Yes, you are."

"Well, I think you're a very handsome man, and I think you're the one who's the tease."

They laughed. "We're acting like a couple of school kids." Clay looked around and whispered, "Okay, let's forget about eating and get a room."

"One of these days I might take you up on that, but it won't be here. Too many eyes—if you know what I mean. Besides, I'd like to get to know you better. And I am not a tease," she insisted. "You'll see."

Clay suddenly had an uneasy feeling they were once again being watched. He stretched his neck pretending to relieve stress, but as he did, he scoured the dining area for cameras. The camera positioned near the servers' station moved slowly to fixate on him and Hope. He softly shushed her. "Careful what you say. We're being watched."

Hope slowly nodded that she understood. "Well, I know what I want, Clay. Are you ready?"

"Yes." He motioned to the server to come and take their order.

Five minutes later, Grainger walked in with Simon at his side. "I figured I'd find you here."

Hope said nothing, but Clay gave an insincere laugh. "Are you spying on us with your eyes in the sky? That's what you called it, right? Your eyes in the sky?"

Grainger didn't flinch. "I suppose you can say we spy on everyone." He gave Clay his own insincere smile in return.

"Isn't that an invasion of privacy?"

"No. We're permitted to have cameras directed to every part of the premises as long as we don't go where we're not supposed to."

Obviously irritated, Clay asked, "And, eavesdropping? Is that allowed too?"

Grainger did not like his accusation. "No, Detective, it is not. And we are not eavesdropping on you." He turned to his aide. "Are we, Simon?"

Simon shook his head. "No, sir, we are not."

"Frankly, I'm offended you would make such a suggestion. But let me ask you something. Isn't seeing Ms. Archer on a social basis a conflict of interest? After all, you are the lead investigator for this sham case you're working on."

"I'm asking her some questions regarding Jack Youngblood. What makes you think this is a social get-together?"

Grainger avoided answering directly. "I'm sure she knows the rules regarding casino employees patronizing with guests."

For the first time, Clay noticed Hope react visibly to Grainger's words. She looked at him and shook her head in disgust. She was about to respond to his comment, but Clay preempted her. "Mr. Grainger, I'm here on official business. I am not a *guest.* If I were, I'd be checked in at the hotel or in your casino playing the slots or blackjack. I have invited Hope to have dinner with me so we can discuss the case involving Angela Foster, if that's okay with you."

"Oh, my God, of course." Grainger's voice dripped with sarcasm. "Do what you think you must. Simon and I are going to get a bite to eat, too. I hope our presence doesn't bother you. Simon, let's let these two alone so Detective Bryce can continue his interview of Miss Archer."

Simon squinted at the camera above the servers' station. Within an instant, the camera slowly shifted direction. After Grainger and Simon walked away, Clay said, "I think he and I have officially become adversaries."

"That happens with a lot of the people he deals with, Clay."

"No surprise there. You know, from what I could see, I think Grainger's bugged your office."

"Yeah. He probably has."

A sudden thought crossed his mind. *Were those kisses in her office for my benefit or for Grainger's?*

"Listen, I have to ask you something, but I don't want to dwell on it. And if you don't want to answer that's okay."

Hope wasn't sure what was coming.

"What happened between you and him?"

She sat silent for several seconds, fidgeting with a strand of hair. Before speaking, she tucked the hair behind her ear. Her earlier smile had long disappeared. "A lot. He's not the man I moved out here with. If you can believe it, I was totally in love with the guy at one time." She looked toward the far end of the restaurant where Grainger and Simon were sitting.

Returning her gaze to Clay, she said, "He's a changed man. He doesn't care whose toes he steps on. He gets what he wants, no matter the price to anyone else. That's how he became vice president here by the time he was thirty-five."

"So he's got ambition. What's wrong with that?"

"Because... because after a while I could see he wasn't the same guy. Look at him. It's obvious. He started with nothing, and now wears thousand-dollar suits and thinks the world revolves around him. I know for a fact that he makes a ton of money. And with that kind of money comes power. He's on the make with any pretty girl he wants. And there are a lot of pretty, young women here. When I first learned he was being unfaithful to me, screwing around like he was, I thought it was a one-time thing, so I forgave him. But then it happened again, and again. I told him I couldn't take it anymore, and that's when he told me to leave, that we weren't—to quote him—compatible any more, that I was too controlling, and he needed more space. Can you believe that? He needed more space? So, that's what happened with us."

Hope was sincere when she added, "You know, you're the first man in a long time I feel I can trust, and I don't even know you."

He studied her face, not knowing how to respond.

"I shouldn't have said that—the last part, that is. But as you can see, Clay, I don't hold back on my emotions."

"I'm glad you don't hold back. That's just one of the things I like about you."

"Thank you. I appreciate that—more than you know. By the way, why did you need to see John again?"

"I'm sure by now you've seen the news about what happened to Shiloh Youngblood and his mother."

She nodded.

"Well, I learned that Shiloh's father Jack worked here at the Bend as a guard. He died in a car accident the day after Carrie Kirkland disappeared."

"Jack Youngblood? Of course I knew him. Funny, but I never put two and two together that he and Shiloh Youngblood were related. I can tell you Jack was a very nice man. He was so sweet and protective toward my girls—like a father to them."

"I was hoping John Grainger or Simon might be able to shed some light on him."

"Were they any help?"

"Not at all. Simon remembered Jack but couldn't tell me much more than that he worked on the swing shift and saw to the safety of your female employees."

"When we're done here, would you arrange for me to talk to Holly Paine again? She's the only one who seemed to know anything about the guy who rooms with Angela."

"You mean Denver Stennet?"

"Yes. Good memory. That's the guy."

"Do you really think Holly can help you? She's pretty flakey. And watch out for her. In case you hadn't noticed, she's a big flirt."

"I'll make sure she doesn't put her tentacles in me."

"Good. I reserve the right to be the only person allowed to insert my tentacles in you."

CHAPTER 19

"Have a seat in the conference room, Clay. I'll call Holly right in."

Within a minute Holly Paine bounded in, her long ponytail swinging behind her head. "Hi, Detective Bryce. You wanted to talk with me?" She was effusive in her greeting. "It's great to see you again."

Clay stood to greet her and, without warning, the flirtatious little blonde gave him a hug and kneaded his biceps in a not-so-innocent way. She noticed Hope watching from the hallway and quickly pulled back. Clay, too, saw Hope frown at Holly's show of affection. He shrugged his innocence to her and left the door to the conference room open so there would be no accusations of impropriety.

"Holly, have a seat. Thanks for talking with me again."

"*Any*time," she said. "I mean *any*time."

Clay dismissed her flirts and continued. "When we spoke last week, we talked only about Angela Foster."

"Right. I told you everything I know."

"I understand, but now I'd like to ask you about a waitress who worked here a couple of years ago—a girl by the name of Carrie Kirkland."

"Okay."

"Now, before going any further, understand that what we discuss here is confidential. You can't discuss it with anyone. If word got out, the publicity would hurt both my investigation and the Bend."

"I understand. I won't say anything. I'm good at keeping secrets."

Clay had no choice but to believe her vow. "Tell me what you know about Carrie."

"She was very sweet. She actually helped me learn the ropes when I was first hired, but she left after I was here only a couple of months."

Clay explained his concern. "I think she may have been the victim of a crime. I don't have any evidence to support that yet, but I believe she was abducted and may even have been murdered."

Holly put her hand to her chest. "Oh my God. You mean, abducted, like what happened to Angela?"

"Yes, perhaps. Did you ever talk to her about her personal life? Her love life? Her boyfriends?"

"Not really. I mean, we weren't that close. I was pretty new to the Bend, and she was always very helpful, but we never really talked about our personal lives."

"Let me ask you about another employee—a security guard. His name was Jack Youngblood. Did you know him?"

"Oh, yes. He always walked us girls out to our cars at the end of our shift."

"Well, it turns out that Mr. Youngblood died in an automobile accident the day after Carrie went missing. Do you know if they had any kind of relationship?"

"Mr. Youngblood and Carrie? Oh, no. Mr. Youngblood was a sweet man. A romantic relationship with Carrie? No way. He was a lot older than she was, and besides, he treated us all like we were his daughters. Very respectful. I mean, he really was concerned about us. A real gentleman, if you know what I mean."

"I understand. Do you know if Carrie had any problems with anyone stalking her, anything like that?"

"I don't know about that, but I do remember one night something happened after our shift ended."

"What was that?"

"Mr. Youngblood was walking me out to my car when we heard a loud argument in the far corner of the parking lot. Jack told me to stay where I was, and he went over to where the people were arguing. He came back a few minutes later and I asked him what was going on. He said it was Carrie and that she was in an argument with someone. The person ended up driving off."

"Any idea who it was?"

"No."

"Man or woman?"

"I don't know. I asked Jack, and he went like this." She put her finger to her mouth. "He said shh. Don't say anything about this to anyone. He didn't want me to know who the person was."

"So, there was no incident report written up about what happened in the parking lot? Why do you think that would be?"

"Oh, no, I think Mr. Youngblood did write a report. I mean, they drill that into us all the time. They tell us that any problem we have *has* to be written up. No exceptions. If we don't comply, the casino regulators would come down hard on the Bend—like, they'd be fined like a zillion dollars. Carrie told me that she didn't want to get fired, and she didn't want Jack to get in trouble, either, so she agreed to sign the report."

CHAPTER 20

Clay's cell phone rang Friday mid-morning. "Detective Bryce, this is Simon Learner. I've checked and double-checked all the incident reports on file and did not find any written by Jack Youngblood. Either he never wrote any—which, I agree is unusual—or they were somehow purged from the system."

"Who has access to the report database other than you and Mr. Grainger?"

"No one else."

"Your boss says you have a photographic memory. Do you recall seeing any kind of report involving an incident that occurred in the parking lot between Carrie Kirkland and an unknown person?"

"Contrary to what Mr. Grainger said, I don't have a photographic memory. And, no, I don't remember any such incident."

"I'll be back to talk with Mr. Grainger and you about that report this afternoon."

* * *

Simon met Clay in the lobby to escort him to John Grainger's office. Clay knew his comment about Grainger spying on him and Hope hadn't sat well. "Simon, look, I apologize for insinuating last night that you were eavesdropping on Hope and me."

After a pause, Simon extended his hand. "Apology accepted."

"I'll apologize directly to Mr. Grainger too."

"Might be a good idea."

Grainger was poring over documents when Bryce and Simon entered his office. Not hiding his disdain, he said, "Yes? What is it now?"

Clay extended his hand. "I want to apologize."

"For what?"

"I made some unfair insinuations last night about you spying on Hope and me. That was wrong. I've already apologized to Simon."

Grainger said nothing, but after a few seconds, swiped his hand across Clay's palm. "I accept your apology."

"I know you probably consider me a nuisance, but—"

"Detective, you *are* a nuisance. I'm very busy. Now what do you need?"

"Well, you see, here's an interesting thing. When we spoke last night, I told you I didn't see any incident reports written by Jack Youngblood. Simon called me this morning to confirm that he could not find a single report ever written by Jack Youngblood."

"What's your point?"

"My point is, I learned from one of Hope's employees— Holly Paine—that Mr. Youngblood did, in fact, write up at least one report."

"Is that so?"

"Yes. It turns out that one night, when Mr. Youngblood was escorting Holly to her car, there was an incident in the parking lot involving Carrie Kirkland and someone else. You may recall that I mentioned Carrie earlier as one of your employees who'd gone missing."

"I see. And, who was the *someone else*?"

"I don't know. Holly never found out who it was. She didn't know if it was male or female."

Grainger looked to his assistant for an answer. "What do you suppose happened to that report, Simon?"

Simon disputed the claim. "Mr. Grainger, I've been thinking about this since I talked with Detective Bryce."

"And?"

"Well, since neither of us ever saw this report, my guess is that it was probably never written."

Clay pushed back. "I disagree. I believe Holly Paine when she says Jack Youngblood wrote up a report."

"What else did she say about it?" Simon asked.

"Not much, since she didn't know what the disturbance was about and Carrie wouldn't talk about what had happened. She did, however, say that Carrie didn't want the report filed, but Mr. Youngblood said they had to comply with Bend's policy. Holly also said Carrie signed the report to protect Jack Youngblood from getting in trouble."

"Simon, Youngblood's manager was James Donovan, wasn't it?" Grainger asked.

"Yes, sir."

"Well, then, Jim would have had to sign off on the report, right?"

"Correct. I guess it's possible he never passed the report on to us."

Clay was curious about the chain of command. "Assuming Jack did his job right and gave the report to Jim Donovan, what would Mr. Donovan have done with it?"

Simon looked at Grainger before he answered. "He would have given it to me."

"And what do you do with the reports you receive from Mr. Donovan?"

"I review them, determine if any action is required, and if so, I fix the problem. If it's noteworthy, I discuss it with Mr. Grainger."

"Again, I want to make sure I've got this straight. Neither one of you saw the report in question?"

Grainger answered for both. "Not that we can remember. It appears, in this case, that, *if* there was a report at all, and *if* it was given to Jim Donovan, he must have failed to pass the report along. Those are two big *ifs* to get past."

"Would you arrange for me to speak with Mr. Donovan?"

Simon answered, "He's no longer employed here. He left a couple of years ago. He stopped coming to work after Mr. Youngblood was killed."

"That seems to happen a lot around here. People just stop showing up for work," Clay observed.

Grainger glowered. "You're off base on that, Detective. Sure it happens, but it's unusual for people to leave without giving any kind of notice. Isn't that correct, Simon?"

Simon hesitated enough for Clay to notice. "Yes, I think that's an accurate assessment."

Clay's curiosity about James Donovan had been piqued. "I'd still like to see Mr. Donovan's file—and Youngblood's, too. Okay with you, Mr. Grainger?"

He nodded his okay. "Simon will arrange to get them to you. You'll have them first thing Monday morning."

"Thank you, both. Oh, and Mr. Grainger, as I said earlier, I'm sorry for my insinuations about you spying. I was way out of line."

Grainger nodded and returned to the paperwork on his desk. A conciliatory handshake was out of the question.

CHAPTER 21

As promised, Simon Learner transmitted the personnel files of James Donovan and Jack Youngblood early Monday morning. Clay discerned no unusual information from either file. He decided to drive to the address shown on Donovan's W-9 taxpayer identification form, an apartment at 1600 Calle del Rio in Santa Fe.

The front door to the three-story pueblo-style building was locked, requiring an access card to gain entry. Clay buzzed Donovan's apartment, but received no response. He buzzed a second time for good measure and, when no one answered, he buzzed the building manager's apartment.

"Who is it?"

Clay spoke into the intercom and held his badge up to the security camera. "Detective Clay Bryce of the Santa Fe Police Department. I'm here to see a Mr. James Donovan."

Building manager William Pelling came to the front door and studied Clay's badge through the glass before allowing him in. Pelling was in his mid-sixties with sparse gray hair and pale skin that was equally ashen in color. Reading glasses hung from a chain around his neck. "Mr. Donovan is no longer a tenant here, Detective. He left a couple of years ago."

"I'm investigating a case and would like to talk to him. Do you know where he might be?"

"I have no idea. He left without notice and didn't leave a forwarding address."

"What about other information on him, like his rental application?"

"Of course, yes. I'll show you what I have. It's not much, though."

Clay followed Pelling into his two-room apartment—a combination living-room-office-kitchenette with a separate bedroom. The shelves along one wall were filled with orderly rows of books and neatly piled magazines. The smell of freshly brewed coffee wafted through the apartment. Clay accepted Pelling's invitation to have a cup.

Two small CCTV monitors hung above Pelling's desk. "I see you have cameras at the front and rear entrance. So you see all the comings and goings of your tenants, huh?"

"Well, not all, but a lot. I'm not always in my office. But I'm responsible for keeping the tenants as safe as possible, and the cameras help me keep an eye on things."

"You said that James Donovan doesn't live here any longer. My last known address for him was apartment 333."

"As I said, I have no idea where he moved to. One morning I found a note he'd left under my door that said his mother was sick and he had to leave to take care of her. He apologized and told me to keep his security deposit because he had to break the lease. I've got that note still. Obviously, he left in a hurry because he left all his furniture and clothes behind. He said he would come back for them but never did. Let me get his paperwork. Give me a second." Pelling retrieved Donovan's folder from a two-drawer metal file cabinet and handed it to Clay.

"Everything I have relevant to him is in there—his application form, credit references, the termination notice, and the inventory of what he left behind."

Clay pulled the termination note from the folder. He observed it was computer generated, not handwritten. Holding the note carefully by one corner, he read. *"Sorry, I have to break the lease. My mother is very sick and I have to go to Albuquerque to take care of her. Please keep the security deposit with my apologies. I'll be back for my belongings. James Donovan."*

"It's not signed and doesn't have a forwarding address. I'd like to take it with me to examine back at the police lab. Is that okay with you?"

"Sure. You know, when he didn't come back for his belongings I tried to get hold of him but I could never reach him. I checked for Donovans in Albuquerque and called every one of them, but none of them had ever heard of him. After a month and a half, I rented his apartment, so I had all his things put in the basement storage."

"This note was printed from a computer. Did he leave his computer and printer behind? I'd like to have my lab look at them, too."

"To my knowledge, he didn't have a computer. If he did, he must have taken it with him."

Clay scanned the list of furniture and belongings. "You're right—no computer or printer on your list. Could you have missed these items when you took inventory?"

Pelling was miffed that Clay questioned the accuracy of his list. "Absolutely not, Detective. My list contains every item he left behind. Whatever it shows is what was in his apartment after he left. I can take you to the storage room so you can see for yourself. It's all still there. Actually, I was about ready to donate it to Purple Heart."

"I'd like to take a look. What about his mail? Did he tell you where to forward it?"

"No. He never notified the post office. His box was overflowing. I had to tell the postman to stop delivering."

"What date did he break the lease?"

"It should be on the inside back of the file."

Clay turned to the back cover. "June fourteenth two years ago? Is that right?"

"If that's what it says."

"That's the same day Jack Youngblood was killed."

"Who's Jack Youngblood?"

"Someone involved in the case I'm investigating."

"And it involves James Donovan too?"

"Yes, it does, but I'm not at liberty to discuss it. Can you take me to the storage room now?"

"Follow me." Pelling took Clay down a flight of stairs to a large but orderly basement storage room crammed with items left behind by tenants. Labels identifying former tenants by name hung from the low ceiling above their respective belongings. Pelling pointed out James Donovan's belongings, and said, "Help yourself. Stop back to my office on your way out."

Clay put on gloves and did a cursory examination, but there was too much to go through—furniture, four large boxes of miscellaneous items, and two garbage bags overflowing with clothes. He decided to bring in Dan Carton and his forensics team, and have them take a closer look for potential evidence.

Back at the manager's apartment, Clay said, "Mr. Pelling, I'm going to get a search warrant to have our forensics people inspect all of Donovan's furniture and belongings more closely."

"Do what you have to. The sooner the better. I'd like to get rid of it all."

"I may need you to stop by police headquarters to see if you can identify a suspect. I'll call you if I do."

"Be happy to help."

"And, if it's okay with you, I'm going to hang onto his file for now. Can you think of anything else?"

"Just that he was a quiet tenant, never any trouble. It surprised me when he left so suddenly."

"One last thing." Clay pulled three photos from his inside coat pocket. "Did you ever see any of these women?"

Pelling shuffled the photos from front to back and back again, studying each one. "Her," he said.

Carrie Kirkland.

CHAPTER 22

On his way in to Police Headquarters the next morning, Clay stopped by the hospital to check in on Shiloh. Officer Gary Hausen, the cop on guard duty, pointed to Angela Foster's room when Clay approached. "Youngblood's in there. I figured it was okay for him to visit her."

"Sure."

"By the way, a friend of his has been in trying to see him, a guy by the name of Bret Colby. I told him no visitors were allowed."

"Good. No one gets through." Clay gave the cop a thumbs up then entered Angela's room. Shiloh was seated next to Angela's bed, holding her hand, his IV drip pole perched alongside hers. Occasionally she emitted a soft whimper causing Shiloh to gently rub her cheek.

"Hey, Shiloh, good to see you up. You doing okay?"

"Yes, sir. Every day some progress. The doctor said I could be discharged soon. I can't believe I've already been here over a week." He continued to hold Angela's hand. "I check in on Angela and just sit here and talk to her. The doctor said it was okay."

"She respond to you?"

"A little. She's pretty heavily sedated. Every once in a while she tries to open her eyes. I keep telling her she's gonna be fine. I'm not gonna let her die. Right, Angela?"

Upon hearing her name, Angela opened her eyes briefly, then closed and opened them again. They rolled toward Shiloh. He looked quickly at Clay then directed his full attention on Angela. "Hi, Angela. I'm Shiloh. Do you remember me?"

A solitary tear fell down her cheek. Shiloh gently wiped it away. "It's okay. You're gonna be okay."

She tried to nod.

Shiloh looked at Clay and said, "Sometimes she mumbles things I don't understand. The doctor says that's normal. He even thinks my being here might be helping her come to."

In a faltering voice, she said, "Shi... loh."

"Hi, Angela. I'm happy you remember my name. Do you see this other man here? That's Detective Bryce. He's in charge of investigating what happened to you."

Angela lifted a finger toward Shiloh's IV drip pole. "Happened... you?" she mumbled.

"Someone tried to hurt me. The doctors thought it was a good idea if I stayed in the hospital for a while. And you know what? It's given me a chance to get to know you. Okay if I hold your hand?"

"O... kay."

Clay was anxious to find out if she knew who had harmed her, but would have to return when the doctors gave him permission to question her. "Angela, we're going to find out who did this to you. But the most important thing right now is that you work on getting better."

"I'll take care of you, Angela," Shiloh said, and smiled at her. "I won't let anything happen to you. I promise."

Angela's eyes flickered as she tried to stay awake.

Clay placed his hand on Shiloh's shoulder to indicate he was leaving. "I'll be back to talk to her when she's better. You take care of yourself too, Shiloh."

"Will do."

In the hallway, Clay reminded Officer Hausen to stay alert. Just before stepping on the elevator, he heard Shiloh call for him.

"Detective Bryce, hold on a minute." Clay turned and saw Shiloh walking as quickly as the drip pole would allow. Hausen followed close behind, his hand on his revolver, ready for anything.

"What's up, Shiloh?" Clay asked.

"Listen, Detective, I know I'm hardheaded. Maybe if I wasn't, my mom would still be alive. You suggested we have a guard at the house and I turned it down. Remember I said I could defend myself?"

"Yes."

"Well, I was wrong. I didn't really think the guy would come after me. But now I know he'd do it again if he has half a chance."

"Yeah, that's possible." Clay wasn't sure where Shiloh was heading.

"So, hear me out. Since I have a permit to carry a concealed weapon, I'd like to have my piece with me here, just in case."

Clay started to object. "I don't think so—"

"Look, Detective, we know the guy's not going to stop at anything to get at me. At least my weapon will give me a fighting chance to defend myself. I can tell you where to find it and bring it to me."

The prospect of Shiloh having a gun inside St. Vincent's was not one Clay wanted to consider. He pointed to Hausen and said, "That's why we have a guard outside your door."

"I know and I appreciate it, but all I'm saying is I would feel better if I was armed."

"I'll think about it."

"Come on. You know there's no downside. I can handle myself, and I'm not going to go around shooting people just for the heck of it."

After a moment's hesitation, Clay relented. "Okay, but you're not to use it unless there's a real emergency. My badge is on the line if you screw up. You think twice before drawing the gun on anyone. Got it?"

"Yes, sir. I promise."

"Tell me where to find it, and I'll get it to you in the next couple of days."

* * *

At police headquarters Clay met with Captain Ellsworth to update him on what he had uncovered since their last briefing. He explained who Jack Youngblood and Holly Paine were, and that they had witnessed an incident in the Bend parking lot involving Carrie Kirkland and an unknown person. He went on to detail the mysterious disappearance of the incident report Youngblood had given to his manager, James Donovan. "We don't know if Donovan passed it along to his boss—which is normal procedure—or what happened to it. The people at the Bend tell me they never saw that report."

Ellsworth asked, "Have you spoken with Donovan?"

"No. He's gone. No one knows where he is. When I went to his last known address, the apartment manager there, a William Pelling, told me Donovan left two years ago. He just upped and left. Slipped a note under Pelling's door to tell him he was breaking the lease. He left his clothes and furniture behind, and said he'd be back for them. But he never returned, and didn't leave a forwarding address. The most interesting thing of all is the date he broke his lease—June fourteenth— the same day Jack Youngblood was killed in an automobile accident and the day after Carrie Kirkland went missing. As I've been saying all along, all this is too much of a coincidence."

"Have you looked into Donovan's finances? Any chance he could have been on the take at the Bend?"

"I thought that too. I checked his bank account with the Second National Bank, but there was nothing unusual about it—no large deposits or withdrawals—and it's been inactive for two years."

"And what about the Albuquerque police?"

Clay nodded. "I checked with them too. There are three James Donovans living in Albuquerque, but none match our guy. If he's in Albuquerque, he's there under an alias."

Ellsworth sensed Clay was frustrated at his lack of progress in the case. "You're thinking the parking lot incident is what ties everyone together?"

"Yes, sir."

"Let me see if I've got this right." Ellsworth outlined the facts of the case, then pointed out the obvious. "First off, you don't know for sure that anyone other than Shiloh's mother has been killed. All you know is that Angela Foster was abducted and Shiloh was shot, and you have suspicions about the two other missing women."

"Right."

"And you don't actually know that Jack Youngblood wrote a report about an incident in the Bend parking lot. But if he did, you don't know if he turned it in to Donovan."

"True."

"So you're taking Holly Paine's word on all this."

"Yes."

"Isn't it possible she's mistaken about the report or just plain lying about it for some reason?"

"Anything's possible, but I believe her. I see no reason for her to come up with a story like that if it wasn't true."

Ellsworth leaned back in his chair, deep in thought.

"Captain, two weeks ago I told you I thought we had a serial. I'm convinced now more than ever that's exactly what we have."

There was a knock on Ellsworth's door. Dan Carton stuck his head in and asked, "Are you ready for me?"

Clay had been successful at getting a search warrant to have Forensics inspect James Donovan's belongings, specifically to look for evidence that might tie Donovan to the killings. His instructions were for Carton's team to check for fingerprints on the lease termination note and to check all Donovan's belongings for anything that might point to him as the killer.

Carton reported, "The only prints we found on the note Donovan left for Pelling were Pelling's."

"So we can't confirm if Donovan typed the note?"

"No, we can't. But, it's doubtful he did. Whoever typed that note made sure their prints wouldn't be on it."

Ellsworth asked, "What about Donovan's computer? Did you find anything on that?"

"Unfortunately, the computer was not in with Donovan's stuff," Clay said. "I don't know if he took it with him or if the person who wrote the note did."

"The computer is obviously valuable to whoever took it," Ellsworth commented.

"You're right. It's probably got incriminating information in it," Clay remarked. "Did you find anything else, Dan?"

"We looked through all of Donovan's clothing and found something of interest in the pocket of one of his jeans."

"What?"

"Latex gloves."

Clay blurted out, "Yes! Angela Foster's kidnapper was wearing latex gloves. Were you able to come up with a match?"

"No. We checked them against the glove prints found on Foster's car and also against the prints we found on the back door of Youngblood's house. They didn't match, but that doesn't mean anything. The kidnapper probably tossed each pair of gloves he used since they're cheap and disposable. But, Clay, here's one more thing. We found two ski masks in one of the bags of clothing."

"Ski masks? Black, I bet. Dammit, that cinches it!"

Ellsworth tempered Clay's euphoria. "Hold on. That doesn't make Donovan the killer."

"No, it doesn't. But it *does* mean he could be. Or someone is setting him up to take the fall. Denver Stennet is still my prime suspect, but this takes me in a whole different direction now. When I questioned Stennet, he told me he thought Carrie Kirkland was involved with someone from the casino. It's possible she was having a fling with Donovan, then Stennet finds out, and kills them both."

"All right, bring in Pelling to see if he can identify Stennet."

"Will do, Captain. He's already recognized a photo of Carrie Kirkland as a woman he's seen at Donovan's apartment, so it's possible Stennet was there too."

CHAPTER 23

Denver Stennet walked into the brightly lit police lineup room with five other men of similar height and build. Each stopped in place where a mark on the floor corresponded to a number on the wall behind them. Over a speaker they heard, "Everyone face forward, toward the mirror."

Pelling and Clay watched the men from the adjacent observation room. "Mr. Pelling, I want you to look at these six men and tell me if you recognize anyone. Take your time. And, understand, it's possible you've never seen any of them before."

Pelling didn't hesitate. "Number five. I've seen him before."

Clay wasn't surprised, but he wanted Pelling to be certain. "Number five. Are you sure? Take another look."

"I'm absolutely certain!"

Denver Stennet.

"Can you tell me where you've seen him before?"

"At the apartment. He came to the apartment complex the night before Mr. Donovan vacated his apartment. I'll tell you how I remember. I don't know if this guy was drunk or what, but he buzzed me nonstop from outside the main entrance. I was dozing, and he woke me up. I went to the front door and asked him who he was and what he wanted. He said his name was Denver something or other. I don't remember his last name. And he demanded to be let in to see Mr. Donovan. He said all he wanted to do was to talk to him. I told him Mr. Donovan obviously was not in his apartment, and if he wanted to wait for him he could wait in his car because I wasn't going to let him in. He cursed me a blue streak, called me a liar, and accused me of covering for Mr. Donovan. Crazy talk. I remember he looked real angry. I told him I didn't know what
146

he meant when he said I was covering for him, and if he didn't leave, I was going to call the police. He kicked the door—you know, like a kid throwing a temper tantrum—cursed me out again, and finally left."

"Did you happen to see the kind of car he was driving?"

"You bet I did. I watched him all the way out to the parking lot to make sure he was going to leave. He was driving a black or dark-colored pickup—I couldn't really tell because it was dark out. I couldn't tell you the make or model either. But he sat in the parking lot for quite a while. I assumed he was waiting for Mr. Donovan, but then he finally took off."

* * *

"Denver, I'll remind you of your Miranda rights and that this interview is being recorded. Do you understand you have the right to an attorney and anything you say may be used against you in a court of law?"

"Yeah, yeah, yeah. I'm not gonna get a lawyer until I need one. The last one cost me for no reason at all. What do you want from me now? Is all this more bullshit about Angela?"

"It's about Angela, yes. Don't you want to know how she's doing?"

Stennet squirmed. "Yeah, ah, how's she doing?"

"Not good."

"I'm real sorry to hear that, but I had nothing to do with her kidnapping—nothing."

"You want to know something, Denver? I don't believe anything you tell me. You lied when I talked with you the last time, and you'll probably lie to me now, too. But if you lie to me one more time, I will charge you with obstruction. Got it?"

Stennet raised his voice. "I didn't lie about anything. I told you the truth. Period. Everything. I don't give a shit if you believe me or not."

"You know, pal, I suggest you start hoping I believe you. Let's talk about pickup trucks. You told me you didn't own a pickup?"

"I don't."

"Let me refresh your memory." Bryce read from the transcript of their earlier interview. "I just told you I don't own a pickup. I don't own a pickup. What part of *don't* do you not understand? I don't own any car or truck." He looked at Stennet and asked, "Remember saying that?"

"Yeah, that's what I told you. So?"

"Well, here's what I now know. I've learned that when Carrie didn't come back to your apartment two years ago, you went looking for her at James Donovan's apartment on Calle del Rio and you were driving a black pickup."

Stennet looked away from Clay and didn't respond.

"So you want me to believe you when you lied to me about your truck the first time we spoke?"

"I didn't lie to you. I don't have a pickup. I used to have one, but it was totaled the same night Carrie went missing. I don't have any vehicle now. Ask Angela."

"Angela is in no condition to talk to me. You know that."

"What does my pickup have to do with anything?"

Clay did not answer. "What did you expect to find out by visiting James Donovan at his apartment?"

"I don't know what you're talking about."

"Let me refresh your memory a second time." Clay paraphrased from the transcript. "You said you thought maybe you could patch things up with Carrie, so you waited for her to come back. And when she didn't, you went to the Bend looking for her, but no one knew where she was. You said you went back to your apartment and she never came back, and you never saw her again. But, Denver, that's a lie isn't it? You went looking for her at James Donovan's. Another one of your lies. Something you forgot to tell me?"

"It wasn't a lie. I didn't think it was important."

"Why did you go looking for him?"

"I thought he knew where Carrie was. That's all."

"Why didn't you tell me that?"

"I just said I didn't think it was important."

"Are you kidding me? You suspected she was having an affair with Donovan and didn't think it was important to tell me that? So you just lied about it?" Clay pounded the table, startling Stennet. "Didn't you?"

"Okay, so I thought she was having an affair. I told you before I thought she was cheating on me."

"And did Donovan know where Carrie was?"

"I could never find out. I told you the last time I was here. When she didn't come home, I went to the Bend thinking someone had to know where she was. I asked the other waitresses, and no one knew anything. One girl told me I should go talk to this guy Donovan. He was the security manager or something, and she thought he would be able to help me."

"So you went looking for him?"

"Yeah, but when I asked to see him, I was told he wasn't at work either. That's when I put two and two together. She's missing. He's missing. So she had to be with him. I found his address and drove to his apartment. But when I got there, the jerkoff building superintendent wouldn't let me in. I asked him if he'd seen Carrie, and he said he didn't have any idea who I was talking about. So I left. That was it."

"So you didn't think all that was important enough to tell me?"

"No, I didn't."

"Tell me about your pickup. You said you totaled it."

Denver shook his head several times and took a deep breath. "Okay, this is the truth. I was pissed at Carrie and that asshole she was screwing. I sat in my truck waiting for them to show up, and I popped a few beers. I waited for an hour at least. Finally, I said, screw it. She ain't worth it, and I left. Next thing I know I'm heading back to Santa Fe and a truck comes flying up behind me. It was a pickup with flashing lights on top of the cab. I thought that apartment manager called the cops on me, so now I think I'm toast because I'd been drinking. I'm thinking he's going to nail me for driving under the influence."

Stennet hesitated, shaking his head as he recalled what happened that night.

Clay wasn't sure if he was telling the truth, but wanted to hear him out. "Go on. Finish your story."

"Yeah, well, now I'm pissed at myself, but what could I do? I slowed down and pulled over. I stopped, and as soon as I did, the son of a bitch rammed me from behind. Hit me hard enough to snap my head back. I thought he accidentally hit me, you know, like, he slid in the dirt shoulder. But when I tried to get out of the car to go talk to him, he backed up and hit me again."

"What did you do then?"

"I yelled at the asshole, but couldn't do anything. He had me stuck in the truck. I couldn't get out and I couldn't get away from him. He kept pushing my car. I jammed on the brakes as hard as I could and yanked the emergency brake, but he was pushing me all over. I tried to steer back to the road, but he kept pushing me to the side of the road where there was, like, a gully. Scared the shit out of me when I realized what he was trying to do. I tried again to jump out but couldn't. The last thing I remember was my truck doing cartwheels down the embankment. I woke up in the ambulance on the way to the hospital. That's the truth. I missed a month of work because of that son of a bitch. I was lucky I wasn't killed."

"What kind of pickup was the guy driving?"

"I think it was black pickup—a Ford, an F-150. I'm almost positive of that. I can't tell you anything else about it except it had one of those front end guards—a bull bar."

"Did you see the driver?"

"Nah, but I did notice one thing."

"What?"

"You probably won't believe me about this either. I didn't tell the cops this, but I swear the driver was wearing a ski mask."

* * *

Clay checked State Police records from two years earlier. Two major accidents had occurred five miles apart on Route 14, one the evening of June thirteenth and one on June fourteenth. The reports confirmed that Stennet was the driver in the first one and had been taken to St. Vincent's by ambulance after suffering non-life-threatening injuries, and Jack Youngblood was killed in the second. The report also indicated that Stennet had suffered multiple contusions, a concussion, and two broken ribs. His pickup was totaled and removed to a salvage yard outside La Cienega, which was the same salvage yard where Jack Youngblood's truck was hauled the following night. The police report did not, however, confirm Stennet's story about being run off the road, although it included his unverified account of the accident and indicated there were no witnesses. The accident report read in part:

"A 911 was called in by an unidentified motorist at 0200 hours for an overturned vehicle in a ravine alongside Route 14. Two state patrol cars and an ambulance were dispatched to the scene. The vehicle's owner and sole occupant, Mr. Denver Stennet, was unconscious at the time he was extracted from the vehicle. He was taken by ambulance to Christus St. Vincent Regional Medical Center in Santa Fe. Upon regaining consciousness, Mr. Stennet offered the following information. He reported a vehicle he initially believed to be a police car ran him off the road at approximately twenty hundred hours the night of June 13. He described the vehicle as a black Ford F-150 outfitted with a bull bar. Analysis of the victim's blood sample found a blood alcohol level of .07. There was no evidence of drugs. The victim did not recognize the driver of the other vehicle. There was no indication at the crash site that his vehicle was struck by another."

Clay realized that, on the face of it, Stennet indeed appeared to have been a victim and was fortunate to have survived. He drummed his fingers absentmindedly on his desk. No, he was not ready to eliminate Stennet as a suspect just yet. But he now had a new person of interest in James Donovan.

CHAPTER 24

Clay had been putting in sixteen-hour days trying to develop a case to support his theory that there was a serial killer—or at least a serial abductor. Although exhausted and frustrated, thoughts of Hope Archer buoyed his spirits. Like a love-struck schoolboy, he could not get her out of his mind. They called each other nearly every day. At first the phone calls were small talk about getting-to-know-you subjects. More recently, their tone was flirtatious, suggestive, even sexual.

* * *

Hope had the weekend off. She invited Clay to go on a picnic with her on Sunday, an invitation he accepted with high expectations. He knocked on the door of her Camino de las Brisas condo, located in the northeastern suburbs of Santa Fe. Hope opened the door and greeted him with a hug and a warm kiss. "I am so pleased you're here, Clay. Come on in. I was just putting a bottle of wine and some beers in a cooler for us."

Clay followed her into the small but tidy kitchen, wondering how she was able to pour herself into the skin-tight jeans she had on. He shook his head at her incredible figure.

"Nice place, Hope. How long have you been here?"

"About three years. After I split with John, I looked at a lot of different places until I found this one. I love it. I have some of the most beautiful views of Sangre de Cristo. And when the sun sets, I see a radiant glow that sometimes flashes green—for just an instant. It's breathtaking."

"You sound like a poet."

"Well, I'm hardly that. Come on. Let me show you around. This little kitchen is my pride and joy. It may not look like it, but it's got everything I need to cook you a gourmet dinner tonight."

"I'm looking forward to it."

She took him by the hand and showed him around the rest of her brightly decorated apartment. Hung throughout were vibrant paintings of the southwest—canyons along the Rio Grande, the plaza in Santa Fe, sunsets over the desert, and the red-hued Sangre de Cristo Mountains.

"I like paintings like these that bleed on the sides. They give it a 3-D effect," Clay said. He looked more closely at a painting of a Native American woman to see who the artist was. *H. Archer.* "You painted this?"

Hope smiled but didn't answer.

"It is you, isn't it?" He went to several other canvasses. "These are yours too. Wow. Sexy, gorgeous, and talented artist in one beautiful package. You continue to amaze me."

"Thanks, Clay. Painting is my way to relax." She walked him into her bedroom where she featured a painting of a brilliant yellow-gold sky above pastel hues of the Sangre de Cristo range.

"My God, Hope, that's beautiful."

"Thanks. The view overlooks the Pecos River. That's where I'm taking you today."

"Looking forward to it."

"Me too. It's one of my favorite places. I've spent hours and hours painting there. It's such a beautiful spot—and so peaceful. My stress all seems to disappear when I'm there. You'll love it. I promise."

Clay noticed a photo of an older couple on her dresser. "Are these your folks?"

"Yes. My adoptive parents, Loraleigh and Christian Archer, the sweetest people in the world. My mom suffered from dementia. When she died, she didn't even know who I was. And then my dad died a year later—probably from a broken heart—unable to cope with my mom's death."

Clay put his arm around Hope's shoulder. "I'm sorry to hear that."

She looked at him with doleful eyes. "Thanks. I miss them terribly."

"Did you know your birth parents?"

"Well, from what I remember about my mother, I don't think she was exactly the most stable woman in the world. She would leave me overnight by myself some times when she went drinking with her men friends. I was just a little girl. I was so scared something would happen to me when I was alone. I remember sleeping under the bed so bad people wouldn't get me. I was terrified every night."

"What about your real father?"

"If you can call him that. I don't think he ever cared what happened to me. I remember the day he told me he was going to put me in foster care. I was five years old. I didn't know what that meant. I remember asking him if that meant I wouldn't see him or Mama anymore. He never answered my question, and just told me I should behave in the foster homes. Then he gave me a teddy bear, told me it would be my best friend, and that I should treat teddy the same way—like I was his best friend. I don't know what happened to my father afterward, because I never saw him again. I have never been able to forgive him for what he did to me."

"Hope, I'm sorry you had such a rough time growing up. Do you know if your parents are still alive?"

"I don't know and I don't care. I don't ever want to see them again anyway."

Clay was surprised to hear the bristling anger in her voice.

"Do you know, Clay, I spent five years going from one foster home to another, crying myself to sleep every night, wondering what family I was going to be shuffled to the next morning? I lived in ten foster homes in five years. Ten! Maybe that's not unusual, but you know what, it was really hard on me. I guess I wasn't able to cope like most kids."

"Jesus, that's gotta be tough on any kid."

"But I wasn't *any* kid. I was me. And it was unfair that I didn't have a childhood like most other kids." She teared up.

"Let's not talk about this anymore. You don't have to explain to me."

"I know I don't, but I don't mind telling you. It's part of who I am today."

Clay realized Hope wanted to unburden herself, but he thought he would try to change the subject to distract her. He noticed a dozen teddy bears lined up on her bed with the largest in the center.

"They're very cute," he said, pointing to the bears, "all those stuffed animals, lined up like that."

"Thanks. They're part of my teddy bear collection."

"Is one of them the one your father gave you?"

She sat on the edge of the bed and cradled the largest one in her arms.

"No, but I guess you can say my father's the reason why I collect them."

"Why's that?"

"Because when I was going from one foster home to the next, I slept every night with the bear my father gave me. Since he said I should make it my best friend, that's what I did. After a while, teddy ended up getting pretty raggedy, but he was the only friend I had in my entire life. I carried him everywhere with me. Then, one night, these mean foster parents I was living with pulled the covers off me and took teddy away. They said I was too big to be sleeping with a stuffed animal."

"You're kidding me."

"No, I'm not. I remember screaming to them to give it back to me. I said he was my best friend. I wanted my friend back. I cried and cried. But they never gave it back. They said they threw it away. They just threw it away—like it was trash."

"That's unbelievable that they would do that to a child."

"It was awful. Finally, when I was ten years old, out of the clear blue, I got adopted by the Archers. They didn't have any children of their own. They owned a small farm, and they just loved me to death." Her mouth quivered and she could barely get the words out. "They were so nice, but then they died and left me too."

"But they didn't leave you—they died."

She shook her head. "No, they left me."

"You know what, Hope? From what I can see, you turned out pretty damned good, in spite of everything you went through."

"You think so?"

"Absolutely." He looked at the bears lying across the bed. "So, all these are because of the one those foster parents took away from you?"

"Yes. This one I'm holding is the one the Archers gave me when I first went home with them. And then I started to collect them. We lived on a farm and there weren't a lot of kids my age around, so the teddy bears became my friends. All of them. I know it may sound silly, but I love them. I have a lot more of them in my closet."

Clay laughed. "You have more? Well, Hope, if you love them all, then I'll love them too."

Hope gave the teddy she was holding a quick kiss and put it back in its place on her bed. She then stood and gave Clay a peck on the lips. "You're like my new teddy," she laughed.

"You can hug and squeeze me anytime."

Suddenly, Hope's demeanor changed. Her eyes fixed on Clay, she said, "I hope I'm not wrong, but I'm looking forward to the future." She turned and walked out of the room.

Clay followed her back to the kitchen, wondering exactly what she meant.

Apparently recovered from their discussion about the turmoil of her youth, Hope finished packing a basket and cooler for their picnic. Clay watched, turned on by the way she moved, the way she carried herself, and how she smiled at him. He reached for her hand. He couldn't help himself. She looked up at him and didn't say a word as he leaned toward her and gave her a tender kiss. She put her arms around his neck and they kissed again. He slid his hand down her back, stopping at the small of her back. She purred. His breathing quickened. As did hers. They kissed again until she pulled away. "You've got lipstick all over your face now." She used a tissue to gently rub his lips clean.

"My God, you turn me on," he said, trying to catch his breath.

"You do the same to me, too. Come on. We'd better get out of here." She reached for the picnic basket. "I'll let you carry this." Clay saw her eyes well, but didn't understand why.

* * *

They parked off a remote trail and hiked a quarter of a mile through a strand of ponderosa pines to a bluff overlooking the Pecos. The river nurtured lush green vegetation as it meandered through the pastel and gold desert. Hope turned to Clay. "This is the spot. Isn't it beautiful?" Together they unfolded a blanket and spread it under a tree with a full view of the river. "Come on. Sit." She pulled out a bottle of beer and handed it to him.

"You're right, Hope. This is beautiful."

"This is what I meant. You'll see after a few minutes. Whatever troubles you think you have will disappear. I promise you."

"And if they don't?"

"You know, you're a devil."

He smiled at her.

"Well, if they don't, I think I know something else that will take care of your stress."

They talked and enjoyed their picnic lunch. Hope had prepared assorted tea sandwiches along with cheeses and bread, fruit, deviled eggs, and almond Bundt cake. Clay thought about the contrast of being with Hope in this quiet, sylvan setting after the ostentations of the Indian Bend.

She stretched out on the blanket and looked up at him. He was cradling a Corona. "Do you know something, Hope?"

"What's that?"

"I honest to God think you are one of the most beautiful women in all of Santa Fe."

She smiled. "You are sweet, but I don't think so. There are a lot of pretty women in Santa Fe."

"No, I'm serious. You are beautiful." He meant it.

"I feel like I've known you for a long time, Clay. You make me feel so good when I'm with you."

He set his Corona on the blanket, stretched out next to her, and leaned on his elbow inches from her face. Neither said a word. She smiled self-consciously and lifted her head to kiss him. He kissed her gently, savoring her soft lips, his tongue reaching for hers. He stroked her arms. She allowed his hands to slide onto her breasts and didn't resist when he arched his body on top of hers and unbuttoned the top button of her blouse. Just then they heard voices approaching in their direction. Clay quickly rolled off and they both sat up. Hope straightened her blouse and combed her hair with her fingers. In his haste, Clay knocked over his beer. They looked at each other and giggled like school kids.

"I thought this was your private place," he said.

A young couple walked to the edge of the rise with the same thing Hope and Clay had in mind. They waved knowingly and moved out of sight.

Clay let out a low whistle. "My troubles were about ready to disappear, but now they're worse."

"You're funny. I think I can make them go away. Let's go home."

* * *

The drive back to Hope's condo was a blur for Clay. At first, Hope held his free hand, but then let go and teasingly rubbed his thigh.

He looked at her. "You are killing me again."

She smiled. "Okay, I'll stop," she suggested.

"No, that's okay. You don't have to."

She giggled.

Back at the condo, they barely made it inside when their passion exploded. They rushed into each other's arms and kissed hard with open mouths, searching, exploring with their lips and tongues, neither satisfied, both wanting more, harder and harder. He lifted her up to carry her into the bedroom in his powerful arms, and gently lowered her onto the bed among her teddy bears.

"Oh, my God," she moaned.

*   *   *

The next morning, Clay woke before Hope did. He turned to look at her breathing softly at his side. She was as beautiful a woman as he had ever been with. Her emerald-green eyes, her soft skin, her toned body. Everything about her took his breath away. Without a sound, he got out of bed, collected the clothes strewn on the floor, and went into the bathroom to shower. Afterwards, he was in the kitchen writing a note for Hope when she shuffled in, carrying one of her teddy bears.

"What are you doing?"

Clay wasn't certain, but he thought she sounded angry. "Hi," he smiled. "Did I wake you?"

"Yes. I thought you had left."

"I was writing a note to tell you I had to get to headquarters and would call you later today."

Hope picked up the note and read it. *I loved our day (and night) together. I've got to get to work but I hope we can see more of each other. By the way, my stress seems to have disappeared. I hope you have a great day. I know I will!!!!*

She smiled and sat on Clay's lap, running her fingers through his hair. "Are you sure you have to go?"

"I've got to."

"No. You can stay a little longer, can't you?" She persisted and kissed him softly.

He fought the urge to take her into the bedroom. "Hope, I can't. It's eight o'clock already. I've got to get going."

"What about breakfast?"

"I'll grab a donut on the way."

She stood and insisted. "No, sir, you're not going until you sit right down and have a decent breakfast, Mr. Detective-man."

"I can't. Really, I can't."

"If you leave now, I'll believe last night didn't mean anything."

"Why would you say that, Hope? That's not true, and you know it."

"Then stay and have breakfast with me."

"I can't," he insisted, but her pretend angry look convinced him to relent. "Okay, *Mom*, I will," he teased. "But I'm good with cereal or a bagel. I don't want you to go to any trouble."

She would not compromise. They sat and chatted over a breakfast of crepes, bacon, fruit, and juice.

"Hope, with that figure of yours, you can't possibly eat a breakfast like this every morning."

"No, but this morning I'm trying to impress you. I really don't want you to go. Are you sure you have to?"

"I have to go. Honest. Angela's case is still weighing on me. In fact, I'm beginning to think there've been other victims."

"You mean besides Emily Coburn and Carrie Kirkland? Who else?"

"Jack Youngblood, for one. There's a strong possibility he didn't die from a car accident and that he may actually have been murdered. I'm still looking into that. Someone might have driven him off the road and into the ravine. And I'm not sure about James Donovan, either. He may have been murdered, too. By the way, do you know anything about him?"

"Not a whole lot. I remember he left the Bend a couple of years ago. No notice or anything. But he seemed nice enough. I'd run into him at the Hungry Palate every once in a while and we'd have a bite to eat. He was always by himself. But honestly? I think he was on something."

"You mean drugs?"

"Yes, his eyes were always glassy, with black circles under them, like raccoon eyes."

"Do you know what happened to him?"

"No, I don't. But I wouldn't be surprised to learn he died of an overdose somewhere. He left the Bend about the same time Carrie Kirkland left."

"My point exactly."

"That's interesting, isn't it—first Carrie left, then Jack died in that car accident, and then Jim left—all in a couple of days. I never looked at them being tied together."

"Hope, I shouldn't be talking to you about any of this. Please keep it to yourself, okay? I don't want the newspapers to get wind of anything. And I especially don't want John Grainger to jump down my throat again."

She crossed her chest. "Cross my heart and hope to die."

CHAPTER 25

Clay's cell phone rang as he was leaving Hope's condo. "Hey, Jacoby. What's up?"

"Morning, Clay. Remember Shiloh's friend Bret Colby? He called to tell me he was out on the reservation riding his bike in the desert this morning, and found what he thought were human bones. I drove out there and he's right. There's no question they're human remains. I'm still at the site."

"Where did he find them?"

"Not even a hundred yards from where that guy tried to bury the Foster girl. Coyotes must have dug up the bones."

"Can you tell if they're recent?"

"They're not ancient tribal, if that's what you're asking."

"Be there in half an hour. I'll have Forensics and our medical examiner with me."

* * *

The normal procedure when remains are discovered requires the Santa Fe Medical Examiner, Doctor Aaron Safford, to take control of the crime scene. Trained in the anthropological examinations of skeletal and mummified remains, Safford methodically coordinated his excavation of the gravesite with Dan Carton and the forensic team, and found additional bones, remnants of clothing, three pieces of costume jewelry, and bits of black woolen cloth attached to a skull.

"The desert's dry environment has contributed to the partial mummification of the body, which makes identification a bit easier," the ME told Clay. "I can tell you with certainty the remains belong to a female. We'll take them back with us and work to develop the cause of death. They could be from one of your missing persons. For full identification, I'll need to check DNA from what you've found against that of a living relative, assuming there are any."

Clay said, "I'll get you samples. Once I do, how long before you'll have results?"

The ME responded, "At least a few days."

Dan added, "In the meantime, we'll find out if the other items in the grave tell us anything."

Clay turned to Chief Johnstone. "Chief, I'm going to contact State to have them bring in a cadaver dog ASAP to check for other graves in this same area—with your permission, of course."

"That's a good idea. Let's go for it."

Clay looked beyond the chief to Bret Colby, who was sitting on the front bumper of the chief's SUV. Colby gave a half-hearted wave back at Bryce. He was nervous, and wondered if they were talking about him.

"Chief, what can you tell me about Colby?"

"As far as I know, Clay, he's a good kid. He lives with his wife Janine and their two boys in a small house at the western end of the pueblo."

"What's he do for a living?"

"He works at the Bend."

"I should've guessed that."

"Yeah, a lot of folks from the pueblo work there. Bret's a blackjack dealer. He's been there four or five years."

"He ever been in trouble?"

"Not that I know of."

"So, what was he doing out here?"

"I asked him that. He said he's been having a tough time getting over finding Shiloh and Mae, so he rode his bike out here to clear his head. You can draw your own conclusions after you talk with him. You don't think he's involved, do you, Clay?"

"I don't know. I don't think so, but let's find out for sure. Let's have him come downtown to talk. But I'd like you to join me if you would."

"Of course. He's been through a lot. It might be a good idea to have him see a friendly face."

Clay went to where Bret was waiting. "Hey, Bret. How're you doing?"

"Hi, Detective Bryce. I'm okay." His tone suggested otherwise.

"It doesn't sound like you're okay."

"First Shiloh and Mae, and now this."

Clay empathized. "I know, man. More than you needed to see. You're still having a tough time getting over that scene in Shiloh's kitchen, I bet."

"Yeah, I can't get it out of my head. I sure would like to talk to Shiloh but the guard outside his room won't let me see him."

"The guard's there on my orders. I'll tell you what. I'll make sure you get to see him. How about coming to police headquarters to give me a statement about what you found here, and afterward we can go over to St. Vincent's and check on Shiloh together?"

Bret nodded.

"By the way, what brought you out here this morning?"

"I like to ride my bike through some of these trails every once in a while to get some exercise and zone out, you know? I work at the Bend as a blackjack dealer on the swing shift, and I don't get a whole lot of exercise dealing out cards all night. It may sound strange to you, but when I'm out here I get a sense of my heritage, like how my forefathers survived all those years ago. I know people look at the desert as just sand and dirt, but it has special meaning to me. It helps me put things in perspective."

"I understand what you're saying. You must be proud of your birthright. I know I would be if I were in your shoes."

Bret teared up. "I am proud. Shiloh and I used to talk about our heritage and what it must have been like to live here in the desert generations ago."

"Speaking of Shiloh, tell me about the two of you— you guys were best of friends, weren't you?"

"Still are. We've been friends, like, forever. We grew up together, went to school together, hung out together, played football and baseball together." Bret gestured to the desert and said, "Detective, Shiloh isn't just my friend—he's a brother to me. We've always stuck up for each other. He was the best man at my wedding. We're all so proud of him, his service—" He got emotional again.

"Tell me how you found the bones."

"I was riding the trail past Shiloh's house. It goes right into the desert. I rode for about ten minutes, and out of the corner of my eye, I saw a bone a couple of feet off the trail. It just kinda caught my eye. I'm not even sure why. Anyway, I've seen a lot of skeletons—you know, mule deer, cows, coyotes—so I figured it was from an animal. But then it hit me that it looked different from the bones I'd seen before, so I picked it up, and even then I didn't know for sure that it was from a human. But I saw part of another bone a little farther off the trail, and a skull sticking out of the ground alongside a sage bush. That's when I got spooked, and I called Chief Johnstone. He told me to stay where I was and that he'd come out. That's it. I showed him what I'd found when he got here. He agreed he thought it was bones from a human, and that's when he called you."

"You did the right thing."

"Are they going be able to find out who that was?"

"We're sure going to try. The Medical Examiners say it's probably a woman. We've been investigating a case where two women went missing a few years back, so it could be one of them. In fact, they worked at the Bend. Maybe you knew them."

"Who were they?"

"Do you remember a waitress by the name of Emily Coburn? She went missing about three years ago."

Bret tried to put name and face together. He shook his head. "No, that name's not familiar."

"What about a Carrie Kirkland?"

"Carrie? Yeah, I knew Carrie. You've got to be kidding me. Are you saying that could be her?"

"Could be, Bret. She's been missing for a couple of years. How well did you know her?"

"Not very. She worked as a waitress only for a little while. I remember she was pretty—sexy-looking with long blonde hair. You couldn't help but notice her, if you know what I mean," he said, and used his hands to draw a silhouette in the air of a buxom woman. "I remember asking people what happened to her because all of a sudden I didn't see her anymore. No one knew anything. She just didn't come to work one day."

"Can you tell me anything else about her?"

"Like what?"

"Like, was she seeing a guy there by the name of James Donovan?"

"Jim Donovan? I remember Jim. He was really a quiet guy— shy. I just can't picture him with someone like Carrie."

"She was too much for him, huh?"

"Yeah, but now that you mention Jim, whatever happened to him? He just disappeared into thin air, too. Some people said he had a drug problem."

"No one seems to know. What about a guy by the name of Denver Stennet? Do you recognize that name? He was Carrie's live-in boyfriend back then."

"No. That name doesn't ring a bell. But if you're looking for names of guys who were all over Carrie, there was one guy who hung around her a lot—but he hangs around all the women."

"Who was that?"

"The Operations VP. If you've been at the Bend, you probably know who I'm talking about. He's always dressed like he stepped out of a magazine or something—we call him the *Chief Suit.*"

"John Grainger?"

"Yeah, that's the guy. Carrie would brag about going to bed with a vice president. She had a mouth, that girl. It was probably him."

"Okay, Bret, thanks. That's helpful."

"No problem."

"I need to ask you to keep our conversation to yourself, okay?

"Okay."

"I'll let you know when you should come in to give us your statement, and then we'll visit Shiloh."

CHAPTER 26

Tuesday morning the New Mexico State Police brought in a Human Remains Detection dog—a cadaver dog—to check a wide area around the grave Bret Colby had discovered. The dog, a golden retriever with a history of success in finding human remains buried as long as thirty years, had the uncanny knack of discerning the difference between human and animal bones.

Conditions were ideal. A slight breeze enhanced the dog's senses. With skillful control by his handler, the golden found two additional shallow graves with skeletons substantially intact—both relatively close to the first series of bones found by Colby.

The ME informed Clay of the findings.

"Shit, that makes three. I was worried about that. There could be a hell of a lot more bodies out there. It's a damn big desert, and bodies could be buried anyplace. It would take months to cover all seventeen thousand acres."

"Detective, I'll let you know the results of all three sets as soon as our DNA results come in."

* * *

Two days later, Clay received the news he feared most. He shared the update with Captain Ellsworth. "The ME tells me the DNA shows that two of the three sets of skeletal remains found on the Yiqua reservation belong to the missing girls, Carrie Kirkland and Emily Coburn, but the third set is unidentifiable. Doctor Safford hasn't been able to find a match to anyone in our database."

"What about Carton? Has he been able to come up with anything?"

"Yes. He identified the bits of black cloth attached to the skulls in each of the three graves as coming from ski masks, which seem to be a signature in all the killings."

"Can you track where the masks came from?"

"The labels were cut out, so we don't know who made them or where they could have been bought. They can't be traced."

"All right, stay on it. Let's kick this thing into high gear. Do you need support?"

"I'm good for now. I'll let you know."

Clay called Grainger as soon as he left Ellsworth's office. "I'll be there in half an hour. I need to see you. Alone."

"What now?"

"I'll explain when I get there."

* * *

Clay was escorted to Grainger's office and got straight to the point. "We've located human remains in three graves on the Yiqua reservation, close to where Angela Foster was buried. Two have been identified as Emily Coburn and Carrie Kirkland."

Grainger flinched and looked away briefly. "Are you sure it's them?"

"Yes. DNA tests prove it. We don't yet know who the third person is, but it could be another Bend employee. It's looking to me like someone is targeting your female employees. I need your help in identifying the third set of remains."

"My help? How could I possibly help? And why do you insist there's a serial killer stalking casino employees?"

Clay was incredulous. "What the hell are you saying? You mean, even with what I just told you, you still don't believe there's a serial killer out there? What is wrong with you, man? Are you that dead set against reality?"

Grainger eyed Bryce sharply. The last thing he needed was more negative publicity for the Bend. "If word of a serial killer gets out, the Bend could be out of business. There would be no way to survive this kind of news, knowing the killer is still on the loose."

"Look, Grainger, right now I don't give a shit about the Bend. I care about who's been killed and who else might be killed if we don't get the sick dude who's out there targeting innocent women."

Grainger just shook his head, and fell silent.

Clay was out of patience. He snapped, "Listen to me, Grainger. I'm convinced now more than ever that we have a serial killer on our hands. At first I thought these two women were the only two victims, but I was wrong. You know what else I think?"

Grainger was afraid to ask. "What?"

"I think the killer is associated with the Bend. He works here, he's a former employee, a gambler in your casino, or he has dealings with the Bend—like a vendor or a salesman. He's someone who blends in. It's what a serial killer does. I need for you to help me find out who was buried in that third grave. I need a list of all the women who've left the Bend without notice over the past four years—not just waitresses, but every female employee."

Grainger realized he had no choice and agreed to Clay's demands. "Okay, fine. Whatever. Simon will get you the information."

"No, not Simon. No one else is to know about this. Can you get this information on your own for me by tomorrow—Friday?"

Grainger nodded.

* * *

The next morning, under the guise of wanting to study employee turnover at the Bend, Grainger had Human Resources gather the files of former employees who had left their jobs without notice. Their terminations were documented as *RWN*, Resignation without Notice.

In addition to Emily Coburn and Carrie Kirkland, three other women fit the profile. Grainger presented the files to Clay. "Detective, I knew one of these women. Gwen Willington. We had begun to date at the time she left. I know you think I have little concern for people, but I do care. Gwen was different. She was... sweet. I really liked her."

"What kind of a relationship did you have with her?"

"If you're asking did I have sex with her, no. Our relationship never reached that point. Not that I didn't want to—it's just that she—she wasn't like that."

"Like what?"

"She was old fashioned, wanted to take things slow. I thought the world of her, so I respected her wishes. But then one day she just disappeared. I haven't seen her since. It was as though she fell off the face of the earth. The first I knew she was resigning was when I got a note from her saying she was leaving—something about trying to find herself. As I recall, it was on Bend stationery and I received it through the interoffice mail."

"You still have the note?"

"No. I had no reason to keep it."

"Did the note say anything else? Anything that might suggest what she was planning to do?"

"No. It didn't go into any detail. I remember it was typed, and she didn't even sign it. I was surprised she decided to tell me through a *Dear John* letter." In a rare show of self-deprecation, Grainger alluded to his reputation as a womanizer. "I mean, I know I'm no saint, but I thought it was a pretty cold way to end a relationship."

* * *

Using the police department's database, Clay was able to track the status of two of the three women whose names Grainger had given him. One was a married mother of two living in Minneapolis. Another was a school teacher in Los Angeles. The whereabouts of the third woman, Gwen Willington, were unknown. According to her file, she had been the administrative secretary to the Bend's director of Human Resources, Jason Alvarez. Her RWN file was dated three years prior and contained a color photograph of an attractive woman with shoulder-length brown hair, blue eyes, and a bright smile. Clay couldn't help but wonder if her pretty face had once been hidden under a ski mask.

Her file also contained an unsigned letter of resignation to Jason Alvarez saying that she had enjoyed working for him, but felt it was time for the next chapter in her life and that she was relocating to New York.

CHAPTER 27

In the five days since their picnic, Hope thought of little more than Clay and the night they had spent together.

She could not get him out of her mind.

I don't think I've ever fallen this hard for anyone. I know I can't get too carried away, but I really think this could be the beginning of what I've been searching for my entire life.

"Hi, Clay. It's Hope."

"Hey, Hope, I was just thinking about you."

"Well, great minds, you know," she laughed.

"So, what are you doing?"

"I just got to work, but my heart's not in it today. Thought I'd call and see if we could get together tonight. I can't wait to see you again. How about meeting me for dinner? I can probably check out of here early."

"I'd love to, but I'm heading to Albuquerque right now. I've got to interview someone about the Angela Foster case and not sure when I'll be back."

"Is that a no?"

"It's a yes, but let's make it a takeout and a movie?"

"You're on. My place okay?"

"See you there as soon as I can get free."

"Just let me know when you start back. I'll have a surprise ready for you."

"I love surprises."

They both laughed.

* * *

Even though Clay was unable to track down Gwen Willington, he did locate Gwen's mother, Marian Willington from the information Grainger had provided him. He arranged an appointment with her to discuss Gwen and to obtain a DNA swab to check against the DNA of the remains from the desert. He knocked on the door of her adobe-style house, and was greeted by a tall, striking woman he guessed was in her fifties.

"Mrs. Willington?" He flashed his ID badge.

She was expecting him. "Yes, please come in, Detective Bryce."

"Thank you."

"I've been on pins and needles since you called. You've found Gwen, haven't you?" Her eyes welled.

"No, Ma'am, we haven't."

Her disappointment was apparent. "Then, what is it?"

"Actually, I'm here to ask if you know where she is."

She led him to her living room. "Have a seat. May I get you something to drink?"

"No, thank you."

Marian sat across from Clay, anxiety written on her face. "Why are you asking about Gwen now? Why, after three years, do the police show an interest in her?"

Clay avoided mentioning the discovery of human remains in the desert. "I'm investigating a case involving the disappearance of two other women from the Indian Bend and was hoping Gwen might be able to shed some light."

"You're being very kind, Detective. But I know you're not telling me the truth. You're looking into Gwen's disappearance, aren't you? You think something bad has happened to her. I understand. I've been scared out of my mind for the past three years that someone would knock on my door to tell me she was dead."

Clay looked at her intently. Marian clearly needed to hear the truth. "I won't beat around the bush. The fact is, I *am* concerned about your daughter."

Marian's shoulders slumped.

"I'm trying to learn if Gwen's disappearance is somehow connected to that of the other women from the Bend."

"I see."

"What can you tell me about Gwen's disappearance?"

"We were very close, Detective. I didn't ask her to, but she called me every day. She was like that. She always worried about me. I guess because I live alone. Then one day she didn't call."

"I have a photo of her from her personnel file at the Bend. She looks a lot like you."

"That's kind of you to say. I have other photos if you need them." She nodded toward a series of framed photos that filled a drop-leaf table at the end of the sofa. "She is a wonderful daughter, a beautiful girl."

"After she stopped calling, what happened?"

"Well, after two days, I got concerned. I called her to find out if she was okay. But I couldn't reach her. My calls to her cell phone went right to her voicemail. Then I really got worried that she was sick or hurt, since she lived alone. So I drove to Santa Fe and used the spare key she gave me to get into her condo. I couldn't tell when she had been there last. But her car was still in its parking spot, so I figured she went out with someone and, you know, stayed overnight. I actually was a little embarrassed that she would come home and find me in her apartment checking up on her."

"It's only natural that you'd be concerned."

"I didn't know what to do next, so I knocked on a neighbor's door. An older woman who lived there said she hadn't seen her in a couple of days but thought she might have been on vacation. That's when I went to the hotel where she worked to talk to her manager. She worked for the head of Human Resources there."

"Jason Alvarez."

"Yes. Jason was a very nice man and he tried to help. He told me that at first he'd been concerned about her, but then he found a note she'd written to him saying she was quitting her job and relocating to New York. He said he was disappointed in the way she left, but had no hard feelings toward her. He even asked me to tell her he wished her well. He thought they had a good relationship and had held her to high standards. I told him that quitting without notice was not something Gwen would do. She was too nice and considerate to just up and leave. He said he had spoken with her fellow employees, and no one had any inkling she was thinking of quitting. He suggested that if I didn't locate her, I should consider going to the police and report her as missing."

"Did you?"

"Yes, but they wouldn't do anything. They had checked with Mr. Alvarez and found out she'd written that letter of resignation from the Bend. As far as they were concerned, they didn't consider her a missing person, let alone think any kind of crime might have been committed. They believed she went to New York and said I should look for her there."

"And did you?"

"Well, I thought about it, but there was no sign she ever left Santa Fe. I mean, she wouldn't have left her car and her clothes and just leave without telling me. The police said they would continue to look for her, but I don't think they ever did."

Marian pulled a tissue from the box on the table near her and dabbed her eyes. "I'm sorry, Detective Bryce. I'm not faulting the police. I know they have a lot of people calling them about someone gone missing and then that person shows up after a day or a week or whatever. I think they never took me seriously and put Gwen in that same category. I just know I'll never see her again."

Clay spoke to Marian with all sincerity. "Mrs. Willington, I am so sorry to upset you. I know this has to be a nightmare for you."

"They just didn't know her. She would always let me know what she was going to do. Always! I've been frightened every minute of every day for three years thinking that something terrible has happened to her. If you have children of your own, you must understand how hard it is."

"I don't have children, so I can't begin to imagine what you're going through. But I do hope to find closure for you."

Her tears turned to sobs. "My husband passed away when Gwen was four years old. She was my only child."

"I'm so sorry." He waited until she composed herself. "Mrs. Willington, can you tell me anything else about her? Do you know if she was seeing any one before she disappeared?"

"I don't know. I mean, as close as we were, she never told me about her love life. I'd ask her from time to time if she was dating anyone, and her answer was always the same—there was no one serious."

"Does the name John Grainger ring a bell? He's a vice president at the Bend."

She shook her head. "I'm sorry, no."

Marian Willington didn't question Clay's request for a DNA sample. She knew why he was asking, and was resigned to the reality of his request. She had suffered so much anxiety and needed resolution one way or another.

* * *

On Monday, Clay received the DNA results that proved the skeletal remains discovered in the desert were Gwen's. He called Grainger.

"The Medical Examiner has concluded the third set of human remains found on the Yiqua reservation belonged to Gwen Willington."

Grainger was suddenly unsteady. He reached for his chair and plopped down in it. There was a long silence.

"Hello, Mr. Grainger, are you still there?"

Several more seconds passed. "Yes, I'm here. I can't believe you found her."

CHAPTER 28

Serial Murders at Indian Bend

Over the past three years, an apparent serial killer has been targeting employees of the Indian Bend Hotel and Casino in a perverse tale of death in the desert. The killer first abducts and then buries his victims in the vast high desert of northern New Mexico on the Yiqua Indian Reservation. That's the conclusion of Detective Clay Bryce of the Santa Fe Criminal Investigation Unit and Chief Jacoby Johnstone of the Yiqua Pueblo Tribal Police.

Three women—Gwen Willington, Carrie Kirkland, and Emily Coburn, all of Santa Fe—went missing at various times over the past three years. All three were employees of the Indian Bend at the time of their disappearance. Their remains were discovered Monday by an unidentified resident of the Yiqua Pueblo, and DNA testing confirmed the women's identities. The police are not disclosing the identity of the person who found the remains for his own protection.

Adding to the mystery, another Bend employee, Angela Foster, was kidnapped and found in the desert one month ago. Ms. Foster was abducted from her vehicle on Route 14, north of the Indian Bend. She remains hospitalized, recovering from injuries suffered at the hands of her abductor.

Army Sergeant Shiloh Youngblood of the Yiqua Pueblo, a Silver Star hero of the Afghanistan conflict and on leave from the Army, saved Foster's life. Within days, in what the police believe was an act of retaliation, Youngblood was shot and critically wounded, and his mother, Mae Youngblood, was murdered. The sergeant is recovering from his wounds at Christus St. Vincent Regional Medical Center.

Police believe Kirkland and Coburn were abducted in the same manner as Foster. They have not yet determined Willington's manner of death.

Detective Bryce and Chief Johnstone have expanded their investigation to include reopening the case of the death of Jack Youngblood, Shiloh Youngblood's father. The elder Youngblood, also an employee of the Indian Bend, died two years ago in what is now deemed to be a suspicious one-car accident. The authorities believe all the deaths, abductions, and shootings are connected.

Are these crimes the work of one person? The police believe they are. Police are not providing details of suspects or persons of interest, but it has been reported that one of two unnamed suspects may be a past employee of the Indian Bend, and the second suspect may have been involved with at least two of the victims. Anyone with information about any of these crimes is asked to call the Santa Fe Police at 505-222-9999. - Steven Brown

Tuesday morning, Captain Ellsworth called Clay into his office. He was not happy. He tossed the *Times Journal* across his desk for Clay to see. The banner headline was about the serial killings. "This is not what I had in mind when I told you to keep a lid on this investigation. Are you giving Brown the information for his columns?"

"No. I don't know how he's getting his stuff, Captain. I asked Chief Johnstone, and he swears he hasn't talked to Brown either. But the Chief said he talked to Bret Colby, the guy who found the remains in the desert. Colby's coming in later this morning to give a statement, so I'll try to find out then if he's the one who's been feeding Brown."

Ellsworth was not satisfied. "Listen, I've got a dozen reporters setting up camp outside headquarters hounding me about what's going on. Find out who Brown's source is and shut the guy down. Pronto!"

* * *

Bret Colby was nervous. He fidgeted in his seat and repeatedly turned his head to the door in anticipation of Clay entering the interview room. After ten minutes, Chief Johnstone walked in, shook Bret's hand, and sat at the table next to him. "Hey, Bret, how're you doing?"

"I'm okay, Chief. I didn't know you were going to be here."

Clay had asked Jacoby to sit in on the interview to help put Bret at ease. The chief spoke in a comforting tone. "Detective Bryce thought I should be here since I know you from the pueblo."

"He doesn't think I was involved with the murders of those three girls, does he? I don't know why, but I'm nervous about what he thinks of me."

"Don't be nervous. We just want to get to the bottom of these murders."

"What do you think I should tell him?"

"Just tell the truth, pardner. He's a good guy. Tell him the truth so you can help us nail who's killing all those women."

Clay was scowling when he entered the room. He sat down at the table across from Bret and slid a copy of the *Times Journal* in front of him. He pointed to the article by Steven Brown and said, "Do you see that, Bret? Do you know what that is?" Without waiting for a response, he added, "I need to first read you your Miranda rights."

"What? Why? I thought you just wanted me to give a statement. You don't think I had something to do with those girls, do you?"

Clay looked at Chief Johnstone then at Bret without answering his question. He read him the Miranda warning.

Bret shifted in his seat again, unsure what to expect.

Clay said, "I'm a little concerned about you. To be the first person to come across not one, but two, crime scenes is strange, don't you think? First you discover Shiloh and his mother shot in their home and then you find the remains of those girls in the desert. Do you see why I'm curious about that?"

"Well, yeah, it's weird, but I didn't have anything to do with any of that."

"Let's talk about Shiloh and his mother."

"I swear I didn't have anything to do with shooting them. Shiloh's my best friend. I wouldn't do that."

"Is he your best friend, really, Bret? Didn't you guys have some kind of conflict—maybe over a girl—your wife, maybe?" Bryce was fishing, trying to fluster Colby with innuendos about his wife and Shiloh to see if he would say anything incriminating.

"That's not true. Nothing like that ever happened. He dated Janine a couple of times in high school, but they weren't close. What are you saying?"

"Bret, the detective is not accusing you of killing anyone," the chief said. "We're trying to learn more about the goings-on at the Bend. He thought you might be able to tell us more about the three murdered women because you worked with them."

Bad-cop Clay interrupted. "No. Wait a second, Chief. I think we're on to something here. Tell me about your wife and Shiloh, Bret."

"Nothing to tell you. Honest to God. Nothing." He looked at the Chief, incredulous at Clay's accusation. "I don't know what he's trying to say, but as God is my witness, I did not shoot Shiloh and I did not kill Mae."

Jacoby asked, "When Shiloh came back from Afghanistan, and the Pueblo threw him that big welcome home celebration, how'd that make you feel?"

"I was proud of him—very proud. You know that. We all were."

"What about Janine?"

"Huh? What about her?"

Clay smirked. "Come on now, Bret. Weren't you a little jealous of Shiloh? I mean all your life it was Shiloh this, and Shiloh that, and—"

Bret turned to Chief Johnstone. "You've got to believe me. Janine and I are good. I don't know what he's trying to say. I love Shiloh like a brother. I would never hurt him."

Jacoby patted Bret on the back. "Okay, okay."

"You do believe me, don't you, Chief?"

"Yeah, I do." Jacoby gave Clay a slight nod.

Clay took Jacoby's cue and lightened up. "You know what, Bret? I do too. Let's chalk it all up to a helluva coincidence that you were the first at two of our crime scenes. Okay?"

Bret nodded.

"So, help us out then."

"Whatever you want."

"Obviously, we don't know who the killer is. We think it may be someone from the Bend. We have our suspicions, but we just don't know for sure. Now, what about you? You know anyone at the Bend capable of killing these women? I mean, you and your buddies probably talk about the murders, right? You ever think maybe it's a guard in the casino, or one of the kitchen help, maybe the bartender, or a janitor—you know, anybody like that who acts weird sometimes? You know what I mean?"

Colby took a deep breath. He was relieved to know he was no longer considered a suspect. He nodded and swiped a tear from the corner of his eye.

"Yeah, we talk about it. That's true. And everybody knows about me finding Shiloh and Mae in their house. But we've never thought it was someone we know. I'm just a blackjack dealer. What the heck would I know?"

"You probably know more than you think. Like, tell us what you know about Gwen Willington."

"Not a whole lot. She was nice, I mean sweet—you know what I mean."

"Do you remember if she was going with anyone?"

"I can't say anyone in particular. Actually, I was surprised there weren't more guys all over her. She was pretty good looking."

"What about John Grainger? Remember you told me he was all over Carrie Kirkland? What about Gwen? Was he all over her too?"

Bret looked thoughtful. "Yeah, now that you mention it. I remember he was with her a lot. But it looked to me like they were always talking business." He shrugged. "I don't know. Mr. Grainger makes a move on every good-looking woman who sets foot in the Bend. Remember I told you Carrie used to brag about doing it with a VP? It was probably him."

Clay said, "I do remember. What else can you tell me about Grainger?"

Bret felt more at ease and opened up to Clay. "If it wasn't Carrie Kirkland, he was with someone else. At first, he was with Hope Archer for the longest time. She's another pretty lady. The word was they came to Santa Fe together from someplace in the Midwest when the Bend first opened, but then she caught him screwing around, cheating on her, and she ended up leaving him. Don't know if it's true or not, but that's what people think. Actually, I wonder what any woman sees in him. It's like one girl after another. I don't understand why, but I guess women think he's hot shit. Maybe it's the power thing, you know what I mean?"

"Did you ever see him with Angela Foster?"

"Angela? Yeah. How's she doing, anyway? Do you think she'll make it okay?"

"I think so, Bret. She's getting better."

"Well, to answer your question, I've seen Grainger with Angela from time to time. Of course, he would be. She's a knockout too. He's smooth, that guy. There's probably not a girl around that he hasn't tried to screw. I don't think he got to first base with Angela, but I'm sure he tried."

"What about Jason Alvarez, the HR guy? Did you ever see Gwen with him? You know, socializing, not just work related."

"No, it always seemed like business between them. But he was funny."

"Funny? Ha ha funny?"

"No, but the way he acted with Gwen was laughable. Even though we never saw anything between him and Gwen, we used to laugh about how he was all jealous-like when Grainger and Gwen were together. I mean, from my table you can see people coming into the casino from the lobby. Sometimes I'd see Grainger come in with Gwen to have lunch at the Hungry Palate. Then, like clockwork, Alvarez would come into the casino a few minutes later, looking around nonchalant like, but I knew he was trying to see where they were."

"Tell me about your friend Steven Brown. How well do you know him?"

"What do you mean?"

"You know, the reporter for the *Times Journal*."

"He's not my friend."

"But you must know him. I'm not sure how else he would get information about Gwen Willington other than from you." Clay turned to Jacoby and said, "Chief, didn't you say Bret was the only person you told about Gwen?"

"Yes. I thought he had the right to know who the remains belonged to, since he found them."

"So, Bret, how do you know Steven Brown?"

"He interviewed me after Shiloh's mother was killed. I told him what I knew—which wasn't a whole lot—and that was it."

"Have you been feeding him information about our investigation?"

Bret's jaw tightened and his eyes darted around the room. Clay noticed. He asked for a glass of water.

"We'll get you water, but answer my question first. Have you been feeding Steven Brown information about the case?"

Bret looked at Chief Johnstone, who gave him a shrug in return. "Just tell him the truth, pardner. I've believed everything you've told us so far, so don't lie to us now."

"Okay," Bret blurted out. "I gave him some stuff."

Clay was annoyed. "*Stuff.* You mean like after Chief Johnstone told you about Gwen and Carrie and Emily, you told

188

Brown about them and about our suspicions too. Is that what you mean by *stuff*?"

Bret exhaled deeply. "Yes."

"Why, Bret?" Jacoby asked. "I told you to keep that information under your hat."

"I didn't think it was such a big deal. Everyone's been talking about the murders, and Mr. Brown told me I'd be doing them a favor."

"How so?"

"He said people should know there was a serial killer out there so they could be on guard against the guy."

"Did he pay you for the information?"

Again Bret hesitated.

"Yes or no."

"Okay, yes."

"How much?"

"He would give me a hundred bucks if the information was good enough to use in his column."

Clay was now clearly angry. He leaned forward in his chair and narrowed his eyes. "You listen to me. I'm going to say this loud and clear so you totally understand. This interview is confidential. Get it?"

Bret nodded nervously. "Yes, sir."

"You are not to say anything more to Steven Brown or any other reporter. If I learn you have, I will charge you with obstruction. Do you understand?"

"Yes."

CHAPTER 29

Clay headed to the Times Journal building as soon as his interview with Bret concluded. He intercepted Steven Brown before he entered the lobby. "Hey, Brown, I want to talk to you."

"Yeah? About what? Did you get a warrant?"

"I can haul you back to the station right now or you can stop and talk to me out here. Your choice."

Brown stopped and faced the detective. "I know what you want."

"What's that?"

"You want to look at these, don't you?" He pointed to his cordovan wing-tip shoes. "The shoes I wore when I interviewed Shiloh Youngblood."

Clay shrugged. "Nope, I'm over that."

"Really now!" Brown shot Clay another one of his smirks. "That has to mean you haven't been able to get a warrant. Ha! This is as close as you'll get to them."

"You think this is funny, huh? You know why I want to talk with you? Among other things, my captain is pissed because of your column in today's paper. And the management at the Bend is pissed at me, too. In fact, I'm not sure who *isn't* pissed at me because of you."

"Tough shit, Detective. You don't get it, do you? You and your crony cops don't know the Bill of Rights from your big toes."

"Look, I promised my captain that I would keep a lid on these murders until I had a suspect. Right now this case is blowing up on us. Thanks to your columns, the media from across the country are honing in on this story and they're

190

trying to make it the crime of the century. You've done nothing but put Santa Fe, and especially the Indian Bend, in a bad light."

Brown gave Clay a self-satisfied smile. "Good. I'm happy about that. Does this mean you're confirming my story?"

"No. This conversation is off the record."

"I can't agree to that."

"What the hell is wrong with you? I'm trying to find a killer and you're playing games."

A stiff westerly wind threatened to lift Brown's comb-over hair. He turned away from the wind. "What, exactly, have I written that harms your investigation? Understand this—the Bill of Rights is the basis of our democratic society, and I'm not going to let you or your insidious police department abrogate those principles."

"I ought to haul your ass off in cuffs and see what a judge has to say about it. We've got a serial killer who's killed three women from the Bend, Mae Youngblood as collateral, maybe more, and is most likely planning to kill others."

"First Amendment. It's called freedom of expression."

"Give me a break. What the hell do you think you're accomplishing by leaking information to the public?"

"That's what we reporters do. We inform our readers of what's happening in the world, and alert them about bad guys. So what if people stop going to the Bend? Maybe we save lives by writing about these murders. I'm not sure why *you* don't get it."

Clay waited for Brown to finish his mock lecture. "You know, Steven, your holier-than-thou attitude is laughable."

"What's your point?"

"Ethics. And scruples. You appear to lack them both."

"I have no idea what the hell you're talking about."

"Do you know Bret Colby from the Yiqua Pueblo?" Brown looked about nervously. He suddenly found himself on the defensive.

"You know I do."

"What is your relationship with him?"

"I don't have a relationship with him."

"Is that right? Funny, I talked to him this morning, and he told me otherwise."

Brown shot back, "Yeah? So what did he say, that he provided me with information about the murders? Big deal."

"How much did you pay him for that information?"

"What do you mean *pay* him? I haven't paid him a penny. I don't pay anyone to report information to me."

"Don't lie to me. You're lucky I don't talk to your boss about how you get your information, about how you single-handedly—what's the word—*abrogate* your paper's standard of integrity. If I told him what you've been doing, that would do wonders for the reputation of the *Times Journal*, wouldn't it?"

"Are you threatening me?"

"Yeah, I guess I am. You should know that Bret told me you've been paying him for information about the murder investigation. Where are your ethics on this now? What are you, a reporter for some two-bit tabloid rag?"

Brown said nothing.

"Bret's your confidential source—the source you wouldn't divulge to me. You know I can't do anything about what you've already written, but I will tell you that you've sensationalized my investigation, and—"

"And *what*?

"Write what you want. But understand this, if you write anything else that *impedes* my investigation, not only will

Garcia know about your methods, but your publisher will, too. And you can look forward to a date in court."

"You think your threat is going to change the way I do my job? Ain't gonna happen. Besides, Garcia won't give a rat's ass how I get the information for my column. It's the story that counts. And you know what, Detective Bryce? Maybe that's what you need—people who can feed you information, because you sure as hell aren't solving these crimes. You want me to admit that I paid Bret Colby for information? If that makes you happy, then, yeah, I admit it. Okay. I did. But *you* understand something." Brown spoke as slowly as possible, just to annoy Bryce. "He's just one of my sources—but he's not even the confidential one. And, pal, don't hold your breath waiting for me to tell you who it is."

CHAPTER 30

After three weeks of recovery, Shiloh was anxious to be discharged and return to the pueblo. First and foremost, he wanted to pay his respects to his mother at her gravesite. He also knew he needed at least another month of rehab before being deemed fit to return to active duty.

In the four weeks since Angela was kidnapped and buried alive, Shiloh's initial care and concern had grown into a sweet affection for her. Angela, too, developed a fondness for Shiloh and looked forward to his daily visits to her room. Although unspoken, a longer-term relationship seemed destined for their future. Angela recovered steadily, and was comforted when Shiloh was near. Her physicians and psychologist felt that, with time and continued therapy, she would be able to confront the root cause of her trauma. In addition to the medical and psychotherapeutic care Angela received, her personal relationship with Shiloh was clearly beneficial therapy for her.

Clay made good on his promise to Bret that he would be allowed to visit Shiloh. Clay met him in the lobby of St. Vincent's and they rode the elevator to the third floor where they were surprised to see Shiloh and Angela walking hand in hand down the corridor with Officer Hausen following close behind.

Upon seeing his friend, Bret shouted, "Shiloh!" and hurried toward him with arms outstretched. "What a sight for sore eyes."

Shiloh gave him a heartfelt, emotional embrace. "Bret, honest to God, it's great to see you."

"Don't get me going. I'll end up slobbering all over you. I can't tell you how much it means to see you up and about."

Shiloh slapped Bret on the back and said, "Hey, let me introduce you to Angela." Facing Angela, he said, "This ugly dude is Bret Colby. Hate to say it, but he's my best friend."

Bret laughed. "That's the thanks I get. I've heard all about you, Angela. I'm pleased to meet you."

She smiled and looked back and forth between the two friends. "He looks like he could be your brother, Shiloh. You're both very handsome."

"And I guess I should mention Bret's the guy who happened to save my life."

"Just like you saved me."

Bret joked, "But, Angela, you were worth saving. I'm not so sure he was."

Shiloh hugged Bret again. "I love you, man. Chief Johnstone told me that if it wasn't for you, I would have been a goner. He told me how you saved me from bleeding out."

"No different than what you would have done for me. But you scared the hell out of me, you know? I just wish I could have done something to save your mom."

Shiloh momentarily lost his smile. "You couldn't do anything about it. I know you would have."

Clay had been standing to the side to let the friends reunite. He stepped in toward Angela and introduced himself. "Angela, I'm Detective Bryce. We met once before, but I don't know if you remember me. I'm investigating your case."

"I'm sorry, Detective, I don't remember you, but I'm very pleased to meet you—again," she said, and smiled warmly.

"I mean this when I say I'm happy to see how well you're doing. The last time I saw you, you were just waking up. What a turnaround. You're a resilient woman." Although tempted to question her about the kidnapping, her psychologist had cautioned Clay not to broach the subject for fear that undue pressure on her fragile psyche would drive her back into her traumatic, near catatonic shell.

Angela surprised Clay, however, by volunteering some information. "Well, I'm sure you're eager to know what I remember about the night I was taken from my car. The one thing I can tell you is that a man dressed as a cop and driving a pickup truck stopped me when I left the Bend. I don't think he was really a cop. I've tried to remember more, but that's all that I can think of now."

"Let's not talk about it now, Angela. I'll have time to interview you later. Maybe by then you'll remember more."

"When are you getting out of here?" Bret asked Shiloh.

"Today. I'm waiting for them to discharge me now."

"So you've been slumming for over three weeks. Man you're going soft," Bret laughed.

"Yeah, I think you're right. But it's given me a chance to get to know Angela. Actually, I was supposed to be discharged last week but the doctors said they wouldn't let me go until my temperature was normal for seventy-two hours straight. It had spiked for some reason or another."

"Well, just to let you know, I've got a fridge full of cold beer waiting for us."

"Jesus, that sounds good. How's Janine?"

"She's good. She says hi, and she'll see you when you get home."

"Come on, guys, let's get out of the corridor," Clay urged. "You can talk in your room." Shiloh and Angela turned around and headed back down the hallway, with Bret following. Clay stayed behind with Officer Hausen and asked, "What are they doing out here unprotected in the middle of the hallway?"

"I thought it would be okay as long as I was with them," Hausen responded.

Shiloh overheard Clay's scold. Before going into his room, he stood up for the cop. "Detective Bryce, it was my fault. I just wanted to take one last walk with Angela before I left. I talked Officer Hausen into letting us walk out here, but he insisted on staying right with us."

"How about we stop tempting fate. You can't take chances like this," Clay warned. "The shooter is still out there and, I promise you, he's still waiting for the right time and place to take both of you down."

"You're right. You made your point."

Back in Shiloh's room, a nurse entered with discharge paperwork. She looked at Clay and Bret over her glasses. "Okay, Sergeant Youngblood, you're almost ready to go. I need to go over some information with you first, so I'm going to ask your friends to leave."

"We were headed out now anyway. I'll be in touch, Shiloh, and remember what I said. Please be careful."

"I will, Detective. Thanks for visiting. Hey, Bret, you think you can give me a lift home?"

"Of course. I'll wait for you out front."

"I'll be down as soon as I'm done here." He turned to the nurse. "Half hour or so?"

She nodded.

"Can Angela come in here until you're through?"

"Sure."

On his way out, Clay spoke to Officer Hausen one last time. "Keep an even closer eye on the girl after Shiloh leaves."

* * *

Shiloh put his personal items, including his revolver, in a white plastic hospital bag.

"You have a gun at the hospital?" Angela asked.

"Detective Bryce let me have it. Self-protection only—and to protect you, too, if I had to." He took Angela's hand and together they stepped into the hallway. "You can't walk me to the elevators. I promised the detective. But I'll be back tomorrow to see you, okay?"

Angela beamed and reached up for their first kiss. "That's called sealing your promise with a kiss."

Shiloh looked in her eyes and smiled. "That cinches it—I'm going to be making a lot more promises."

A doctor dressed in scrubs, his face covered with a surgical mask, walked down the corridor toward the couple. Other than Officer Hausen, no one else was in the hallway. Angela saw him approach and pulled hard on Shiloh's hand. She screamed. "It's him!"

Shiloh was startled, "Who?"

"It's *him*. It's that guy."

Hausen leaped out of his chair and drew his revolver. By the time he could take aim, the doctor had pulled a .38 from his pocket and fired twice. The first bullet caught the officer in the shoulder, the force spinning him around and throwing him to the floor. The second bullet whizzed between Angela and Shiloh and thudded into a wall.

Shiloh yanked Angela into her room and slammed the heavy door shut. He dumped the contents of his bag to retrieve his revolver, and told Angela to call 911. "Stay here," he ordered. With his gun drawn, he cracked the door and peeked into the corridor. The shooter had escaped down the exit stairwell. Shiloh suspected as much and raced after the man with his gun drawn. He came across a pile of green scrubs on a landing and knew the man was now in his everyday clothes. By the time Shiloh reached the ground floor, the shooter had disappeared.

Shiloh returned to a shaken Angela. "Who was it?"

"It was him."

Shiloh called Clay. "Some guy just tried to kill Angela and me in the hospital. We're okay but your cop was shot in the shoulder. They just rushed him down to emergency."

"Where are you now?"

"Angela and I are in her hospital room. Security is with us now. We're okay."

"Stay in the room. I'll be right there."

Clay made a U-turn, sped back to the hospital, and pulled up to the curb behind Bret Colby, who was outside standing by his car. He raced through the lobby, taking the steps two at a time up to the third floor, and hurried to Angela's room. Shiloh was doing his best to comfort Angela, who was crying convulsively.

Clay immediately tried to ease her fears. "Angela, everything will be okay."

"Why is he trying to kill me?"

"We don't know that, but I promise, you *will* be safe," he vowed. "We're going to make sure this doesn't happen again. Shiloh, tell me what happened."

"I was walking Angela across the hallway from my room to hers when I saw this guy walking toward us. He was dressed like a doctor. I didn't think twice about him, but then all of sudden Angela screamed, 'It's him.' Before I knew what was happening the guy started shooting. He missed us, but hit your cop. If it wasn't for Angela, we'd all be dead. When she recognized him, he was a good twenty, thirty yards away. Any closer, he wouldn't have missed us. We got into her room here and slammed the door shut. I pulled out my revolver, but by the time I was able to chase him down, he had ditched his doctor outfit and escaped down the exit stairs. I took the steps down to the ground floor, but he was gone."

"Angela, tell me, how did you recognize it was the man who kidnapped you? Was it Denver Stennet, your roommate?"

"No."

"How then?"

"I don't know exactly. There was something about the way he walked with one shoulder lower than the other. I really don't know. But he was wearing a surgical mask, which I don't think a doctor does outside the operating room."

"Okay, Shiloh, stay here with Security. I'm going to check on my cop to see how he's doing. I'll be right back."

* * *

In the emergency room, Clay learned that Officer Hausen was in surgery and that his injury was not life threatening. He called Captain Ellsworth. "We've had a shooting at the hospital."

"I'll be right there."

* * *

With sirens blaring, Captain Ellsworth arrived at St. Vincent's in a matter of minutes. After checking on the condition of his wounded officer, he hastened to Angela's room.

Clay made introductions all around. Although calmer than she had been ten minutes earlier, Angela appeared to still be in a state of shock.

Ellsworth did his best to assure her, promising to find the shooter and do what was needed to keep her safe. He and Clay stepped into the hallway and spoke in private. "Listen, Clay, we need to move them out of here. It's obvious the guy knows Angela can identify him. He'll just redouble his efforts to get her—and Shiloh too. Too many people know she's in St. Vincent's. Let's get them to a safe house until we find this son of a bitch."

CHAPTER 31

SHOOTING AT ST. VINCENT'S HOSPITAL

On Tuesday, Angela Foster and Sergeant Shiloh Youngblood, key witnesses to the ongoing series of abductions and murders of current and former employees of the Indian Bend Hotel and Casino were the intended targets of a shooter at Christus St. Vincent Regional Medical Center. Thanks to the quick actions of Sergeant Youngblood and Santa Fe Police Officer Gary Hausen, 52, the two were unharmed.

Officer Hausen, on guard duty to protect the two witnesses, was shot and wounded by the unidentified gunman. He is expected to make a full recovery. The suspected shooter masqueraded as a surgeon and managed to fire multiple shots before escaping. Police are reviewing hospital security tapes for clues to his identity. Anyone with information about this incident is asked to call the Santa Fe Police at 505-222-9999. - Steven Brown

Wednesday morning, escorted by a cop in an unmarked car, Clay drove Shiloh and Angela to a house off Route 588, three miles northwest of St. Vincent's. The cars kicked up dirt, dust, and gravel as they followed a long road past four other homes to the end where the safe house was located.

Overlooking the vast uninhabited desert, the only access to the house was up the narrow dead-end road. It was the ideal safe house—remote, isolated, and secure. Cars could not approach without being seen from the house.

Clay set expectations for Shiloh and Angela. "Okay, folks, this is where you'll be staying until we can solve this case. You have both agreed to be here and to abide by what I say. The most important requirement is you are to stay inside the house at all times and not divulge your location to anyone. That means no walks or sunning yourself or going to the nearest convenience market. You must stay away from windows, pull the shades at night, and otherwise make yourselves invisible to anyone outside these walls. You get the picture?" Clay didn't wait for them to answer. "Three plainclothes cops will rotate guard duty and be in the house on eight-hour shifts. Make yourselves comfortable for the long haul. You have two bedrooms. Take your pick who sleeps where. The kitchen will be replenished periodically. We will provide you with whatever you wish. Any questions?"

Shiloh and Angela shook their heads. "Okay, good. Use this time to get to know each other. Watch TV, read—you see the shelves of books—do anything you want. Angela, your psychologist, Doctor Albright, will visit three times a week to continue with your therapy. Other than the doctor, the cops, and me, no one else—I repeat, no one—will be allowed to visit. Got it?"

They both nodded their understanding. Clay reached into his jacket to extract a cell phone. "I don't want anyone to track you here, so the only phone you can use is this secure cell phone. Its sole purpose is to contact me and me alone, or for me to contact you. No one else will have access to the phone number, not even the doctor or any of the cops. In other words, you can't use it to order a pizza or do any on-line shopping. Got it?" he joked.

Shiloh smiled and was pleased to note that Angela smiled too. He asked, "Detective, how long do you suppose we'll be here? I've got about a month left on my leave from Fort Hood."

"We've been in contact with your commanding officer. He's aware of the situation. Let's hope we can nail these bad guys before then. I think we're close."

Angela hugged Clay. "I can't tell you how much I appreciate what you have done for us—for me and for Shiloh. Thank you from the bottom of my heart."

* * *

On his drive back to town, Clay received a call from John Grainger.

"I want to see you about Steven Brown's column in yesterday's *Journal*."

Clay suspected Grainger wanted to tear into him again. At the Bend, Grainger wasted no time. "What have you got against the Bend? Or is it me you have something against? It's got to be something, because it sure as hell looks like you're doing your best to close us down. What are you telling that reporter? First it was Angela Foster. Now it's Gwen Willington and the others. In four weeks you've managed to scare people to death. Who the hell wants to stay here or gamble if they think we've got a serial killer lurking around the corner?"

Grainger's rant put Clay in a foul humor. "Listen, *Mr.* Grainger, the sooner you stop hiding your head in the sand and accept that there *is* a serial killer lurking around the corner, the sooner you can help me solve this case and get your business back to normal."

"Oh, I accept that there's a killer. What I don't accept is your inability to keep a lid on this and how you're scaring the shit out of people."

"You know, only a handful of people knew about Gwen Willington's death—you being one of them."

"Yeah? What are you insinuating?"

"Nothing. I'm just saying you know the details of the case. So let me ask *you*. Who did *you* talk to about it?"

"You told me to keep the details of Gwen's death confidential and I have."

"You haven't told anyone?"

"Only Simon."

Clay raised his voice. "You've got to be shitting me. I told you to keep it confidential. Why did you tell him?"

"He's my aide. He wouldn't disclose anything I told him in confidence."

"Where is he right now?"

"Either in his office or down in the casino."

"Well, bring him in so we can find out if he's been talking to anyone else about Willington."

*   *   *

Simon noticed Grainger's jaw muscles tense and slacken repeatedly. He knew his boss was upset.

"Sit down, Simon."

"What's the problem, Mr. Grainger? Have I done something wrong?"

Grainger gave him a sour look. "We'll soon find out. Detective Bryce wants to ask you some questions about that reporter from the *Times Journal*."

Simon was intimidated by Clay's imposing presence.

"Did you see the *Journal's* article that mentioned we found Gwen Willington's remains?" Clay asked.

"Yes. It also mentioned two other women."

"Do you know the reporter who wrote the article—Steven Brown?"

"I may have met him. If I have, I don't remember."

"I understand Mr. Grainger told you about Gwen Willington." Simon shot a glance at his boss. "Did you tell anyone else about what happened to her?"

Simon did not allow himself to blink. His face was frozen. Clay recognized Simon's demeanor to be that of a liar.

"No, sir, absolutely not," Simon protested. "I never talk to anyone about any subject that's discussed in this office. I discuss confidential matters with no one. Mr. Grainger has instilled that in me. I did not talk with the reporter, or anyone else for that matter. No one!" He finally allowed himself to blink and took a breath. "Mr. Grainger knows I honor my vow of confidentiality. Isn't that right, Mr. Grainger?" He nervously scratched the back of his neck, waiting for his boss to respond.

Grainger hesitated before nodding his concurrence. "That's very true, Detective. I trust Simon implicitly."

"Simon, how well did you know Gwen Willington?"

Simon rolled his neck. "Do you think I had something to do with her death?"

"Did you?"

"No, I did *not*. I knew who she was, and I knew she worked in HR, but that's it. I had very few dealings with her."

Clay elected not to challenge Simon further in front of Grainger. "Okay. You can go."

Simon looked at Grainger for direction.

"That's fine. You can go."

Clay waited for Simon to walk out of the office and close the door behind him. "Do you believe him?"

"Yes. I believe he's telling the truth. He's been loyal to me for some time now. No reason for me to believe that he lied about Gwen."

"What more can you tell me about your relationship with her?"

Grainger bit his lip and inhaled deeply before answering. "You know, Detective, I have never met such a sweet person. She was beautiful—inside and out. I actually felt she was someone I could settle down with."

"How long were you dating her?"

"Three or four months. I tried to keep it quiet. But you can imagine how hard that is to do here with so many prying eyes."

"You mean like your eyes in the sky?"

"I'm going to let that comment go unanswered."

"Do you know if she talked to her mother about you?"

"I don't have a clue, but probably not. I don't think she was sure about my...intentions." Grainger made air quotes when he said the word *intentions.* "My reputation is not the best when it comes to women, so I doubt Gwen told anyone about us. Look, I've had relationships with a lot of woman, and I confess I'm not proud of everything I've done. I know I've made mistakes, including with your *girlfriend,* Hope."

"Tell me about Gwen's boss."

Grainger tilted his head. "Jason Alvarez? What about him?"

"Would he have had any reason to harm her? I mean, did Gwen ever talk about him?"

"No. I think they got along fine. She never said anything bad about Jason, but then she never said anything bad about anyone."

"And you heard nothing from her after you read her note saying she was leaving the Bend?"

"Nothing. For three years I've been thinking how strange it was for her to leave the way she did, but I never thought for a second that she would have been murdered. Honestly, I'd always hoped she'd just show up one day so we could continue where we left off."

"You said you received her note through your interoffice mail. Do you remember if it came from Human Resources?"

"I don't remember. Those envelopes get reused and go back and forth between departments."

"I want to ask you about Emily Coburn and Carrie Kirkland."

Grainger laughed. "Do I need a lawyer?"

"Do you think you need one?" Clay asked.

"I was kidding."

"All I want to know is if you had a relationship with either Coburn or Kirkland."

"I didn't know either one of them."

"That's strange that you say that. I have information that you had been seeing both girls when they worked here."

"Who told you that?"

"It doesn't matter."

"No offense intended, but if they were waitresses, they wouldn't have been my type."

"Who's your type?"

"Gwen Willington was."

"Why?"

"She was beautiful. She had brains. And, there's no other way to say it, she was sweet. She had it all. She was a hell of a woman."

"Do you know if Gwen ever dated James Donovan?"

"From the little I remember about him, I doubt it. I don't think he was her type."

"Do you think he was capable of killing her?"

"I can't tell you yes or no."

"Are you not yet convinced that someone associated with the Bend could be our serial killer?"

"No, I'm not. Show me proof."

Clay shook his head. "You'll be the first to know when I have it. Now, do me a favor and let Jason Alvarez know I'd like to talk with him. I assume he reports to you, right?"

"He does."

Grainger buzzed Simon and instructed him to notify Jason Alvarez of Clay's intention to interview him.

"Detective, I hope you're getting closer to putting an end to all this. It gets more and more painful with each passing day."

He got a curt nod from Clay. "I'm sure you'll let me know if you think of anything else. By the way, let me ask you a personal question off the record—about Hope."

Grainger arched his eyebrows. "Ask away. But I'm not promising I'll answer."

"What happened between the two of you? She told me she followed you here fifteen years ago."

"*That* I can answer, although I don't really know how to explain it. She was a babe in the woods when we first came out here from Illinois. She was different—a farm girl—and she had some baggage because she was adopted and all that. She always said her real parents abandoned her, and I guess they did. I'm sure she's told you about her early childhood. I heard about that, and about her teddy bears, a hundred times. Lord help me if I wasn't careful with those stuffed animals. I think they meant more to her than I did. She was young, pretty, naïve, and I molded her to be the Hope you know today—smart and confident."

"You molded her? Aren't you being a little full of yourself?"

"Yeah, I guess. But it's true. You may find it hard to believe, but she was like a little girl lost. She didn't know what to say, what to do, how to talk to people, how to dress. Honestly? I built her up and told her she was as good as or better than anyone else, and I meant it. But then she started questioning everything I did. I couldn't leave the house without her wanting to know where I would be every hour."

"She said you ran around on her, and after a while, she couldn't forgive you anymore."

"I did. She's right about that, but only after she became such a control freak and so damned jealous. I mean, sometimes she went crazy at me, off the walls, if you know what I mean. After a while I felt like I was in prison. I didn't need that. I was busy trying to build a career. So, yeah, I started to screw around. And I admit I was responsible for our breakup because I couldn't keep my hands out of the cookie jar, so to speak."

"So what finally happened?"

"I can't tell you if I initiated it, or if she did, but we both knew it was time to go our separate ways. I know she hates me. But in some ways, I still love her. Listen, she's a wonderful lady, and for sure, a better person than I am."

Clay wondered if he was witnessing another side of Grainger—a self-deprecating good guy. *This is probably what he was like before success went to his head.*

As Clay walked out of the office, Grainger reached for his hand sanitizer.

CHAPTER 32

Clay didn't know how to interpret John Grainger's description of Hope. *Jealous and controlling.* He hadn't seen much of that. But, then, he hadn't known her all that long. He was surprised at how quickly they had become intimate, but he rationalized that the world had changed in the years since his divorce. Nevertheless, their mutual attraction excited him. He was definitely enjoying the company of this beautiful woman, but regretted asking Grainger about her. He would make his own determination in time.

Simon accompanied Clay down to the Administrative offices, and directed him to Human Resources, adjacent to Hope's office. Jason Alvarez had been expecting Clay, and greeted him with a firm handshake. "Simon Learner told me you wanted to talk with me. Probably about Gwen Willington, right?"

"You're right, Mr. Alvarez. Thank you for meeting with me on such short notice."

"Call me Jason. Have a seat, please." Alvarez was a balding, middle-aged man with a thick waist and a sallow complexion. Clay glanced around the office. There wasn't a paper out of place. A yellow-lined pad, a pencil, and an open laptop were the only items on Jason's desk. His wall hangings were benign photos of the Bend. *He's either very efficient or very anal—or both.* Nevertheless, Jason's wide smile, expressive eyes, and friendly demeanor were in complete contrast to how Grainger comported himself.

"So, yes, I'm looking into the disappearance of Ms. Willington. I understand she worked for you as an administrative assistant. Can I assume you've read in the *Times*

Journal that her remains were discovered in the desert a few days ago?"

"Yes. I was shocked and sad to read that. Everyone who knew her really liked her. Have you found out who killed her?"

"Not yet, but I think we're getting close. What can you tell me about her?"

"Oh, she was a beautiful woman, and very smart. Very pleasant. I mean, just an all-around ten in my book. She didn't have a mean bone in her body." Alvarez rose from his desk to close his office door, then lowered his voice. "She was easily the best assistant I ever had. I thought she had a bright future, including taking over my job at some point. I was planning to promote her to manage some of the elements of HR, like recruitment, but then she disappeared. One day, she just didn't show up for work—and that shocked the heck out of me. Of course, I never learned the truth why she left so suddenly."

"Did she have any enemies that you can think of?"

"Enemies is a strong word. But no. No one that I'm aware of. She could deal with people at all levels and, like I just said, she was really well liked and respected. She enjoyed the freedom I gave her to do her job. What else can I say? She liked being challenged with different projects that I would give her." He shook his head as he reminisced about her lost future. "Too bad, huh?"

"What did you think when she suddenly didn't show up for work?"

"I was surprised, to say the least. And I was concerned, too. I asked people here if anyone had heard from her. I called her cell after a few hours to see if she was okay, but she didn't answer. I was about to go to Security to have them check on her whereabouts when I noticed an interoffice envelope addressed to me on her desk. I opened it and found out it was her letter of resignation. She said she had enjoyed working for me, but that it was time for her to move on to the next chapter in her life. She didn't say what that was, except to say she would be moving to New York City. The truth is, at first that made me angry. It wasn't like her. She had been so loyal. I thought we had a great relationship."

"Did you ever suspect she may have had an abuse problem and that's why she left so suddenly?"

"You mean like drugs or alcohol? No. Never. Not Gwen. She was straight-laced and very conservative in everything."

Clay pushed the envelope. "Were you romantically involved with her?"

The question caught Jason by surprise. His head snapped back involuntarily. "Absolutely not. I was twice her age. I thought she was terrific looking. As I said, a ten in my book, and so sweet, but—" He paused.

"But what?"

"Frankly, Detective, I'm offended by your question." His eyes expressed anger. "I'm happily married and would never do anything to jeopardize my position here. What's more, I don't condone sexual harassment in the workplace."

"I'm sorry, Jason. Didn't mean to offend you. I had to ask. It wouldn't be the first time a boss had an affair with an employee."

"I'm not that way. And that kind of innuendo can destroy my reputation and my credibility." Then, just as suddenly as Alvarez had shown anger, he reversed his expression and his wide smile returned. "Mind you, I don't think I'm out of line by telling you that I *did* admire her looks. She really was drop-dead gorgeous."

Clay wasn't convinced that Jason was being honest about his relationship with Gwen, but decided to move on. "What about a romantic relationship she might have had with anyone else? Did she ever mention if she was seeing anyone?"

"No. She rarely spoke about her personal life. I would ask her on Monday if she had a good weekend, and she would usually say 'Yes, thank you,' and only once in a blue moon would she elaborate, maybe talk about seeing her mother. It was clear she wanted to keep her personal life to herself. She was a private person."

"I can't help but think that if she was a ten, as you put it, guys had to be swarming all over her."

"She was friendly with everyone. I suppose it's possible that led some to mistake her intentions."

"That's certainly possible. By the way, did you ever see her with your boss?"

"John Grainger?" Jason's demeanor changed slightly and he sat a bit more upright. "Yes, I think I did. Ah, I mean, I saw them together sometimes, but... Well, frankly, I wondered about their relationship, but I never asked her."

"She never talked about him?"

"No. As I said, Gwen didn't talk about her personal life."

"You're giving me the impression that Grainger and Gwen were involved."

Clay struck a chord—something irritated Jason. He raised his voice a notch. "No. I didn't mean to imply that. I said she just never talked about anything in her personal life. If she was involved with John, she didn't disclose that fact to me—and it was none of my business."

"Did you ever notice any kind of problem between them?

"No, I did not. Detective, you keep bringing up John Grainger and her relationship with him, and I keep telling you I don't know if they had a relationship."

"I understand Gwen's mother visited you after Gwen went missing."

"Yes, she was distraught. She said she hadn't heard from Gwen in several days and was concerned for her. She had been to her apartment but didn't find her there. I suggested she go to the police and report Gwen as missing. She called me later and told me the police weren't able to help. We kept in touch for a while. Mostly she would call to ask me if I'd heard anything. But after a time, the calls just ended."

"I'm also investigating the abduction case of Angela Foster and now the murders of Emily Coburn and Carrie Kirkland. They were all employed here."

Alvarez became defensive. "I don't know anything about any of them either. I'm the Director of HR, but that doesn't mean I know everyone's personal lives. I do know Emily and Carrie left abruptly, and were labeled as having resigned without notice. As you can imagine because of what's being reported, some of our employees are now terrified to come to work. I wouldn't be surprised if we start to see more sudden resignations."

"Those newspaper reports are pretty much scaring everyone. And they're not helping my investigation any. But, you know, perhaps it makes people more aware of their surroundings."

"I suppose you're right about that. May I ask you a question, Detective?" Bryce nodded. "You said earlier you were close to apprehending the killer?"

"Yes, but not close enough. My investigation has taken me to a few people. One, in particular, is a fellow by the name of Denver Stennet. Do you know the name?

"No."

"Maybe he's someone you've seen in the casino. I'm going to need you to come to police headquarters to see if you recognize him in a lineup. A quick trip into headquarters won't break your schedule, will it?"

"No problem. Let me know when you want me there."

"Another person of special interest is someone else who used to work here—James Donovan. Are you familiar with that name?"

"Yes. Jim was a shift manager in Security. He's another RWN. But I'm confused. I find it hard to believe Jim had anything to do with Angela Foster's abduction or the murders of those other girls."

"Why do you say that?"

"Well, he left a couple of years ago, and I don't know if anyone's ever seen him since."

"Any idea why he left?"

"No. Jim was different, I'd say, but well thought of. I do know there was talk of drugs, but it was just a rumor."

CHAPTER 33

After leaving Jason's office, Clay stopped in to see Hope. It was a little before five. "Hi, beautiful. Thought I'd stop by and say hello. I've been talking with Grainger and Jason Alvarez."

Hope closed the door, turned to face Clay, and stood in place. She folded her arms across her chest and tapped her right foot repeatedly.

By her glare and jutted chin, Clay knew she was mad, but he didn't know why. "Uh oh."

"Have you ever heard of this new invention? It's called a telephone?"

Clay laughed. "What are you mad about?"

"Mad? Why would I be mad? It has nothing to do with the fact that I haven't seen or heard from you since last Friday night."

He thought she was kidding and tried to make light of his inattention to her. "Today's Wednesday? By my calculations, that's about a week?"

Hope's glower worsened.

Clay realized his humor wasn't cutting it, and tried a different tact. "Actually, Hope, it seems like a month. I've missed you. Just so you know, you've been on my mind—constantly."

She wasn't about to let up on him. "First you called every day, which got me to thinking how great it was to find someone who cares enough to keep in touch all the time. And then—nothing! You couldn't have called? Clay, you know what I think? I think maybe our days together don't mean anything to you. Just a few one night stands? Is that all I've become?"

Clay saw she was serious—angry and unrelenting—and she was right. He'd been occupied with the investigations and getting Shiloh and Angela to their safe house, and hadn't called her in days. "Good Lord, Hope. I hardly look at you as a one-night stand."

"Then are you seeing someone else?"

"No. I told you already. I have no interest in anyone but you. Now stop it about me seeing someone else." He moved to hug Hope but she kept her arms tightly crossed. "I'm sorry I haven't called, but let me size up my week for you." Clay ticked off the list on his fingers. "Yesterday, someone tried to kill Angela and Shiloh, my boss has been on my ass to solve this case, John Grainger is more pissed at me than ever, and now you're pissed at me too. And you know what? I'm no closer to solving these crimes than finding cheese on the moon."

Hope softened her expression. "What do you mean someone tried to kill Angela and Shiloh?"

"Just that. Someone tried to kill them at St. Vincent's."

"You're kidding me."

"I wish I was."

"Are they okay?"

"Yeah, but we've had to move them both out of the hospital so they can be better protected."

"Was it the same guy who tried to kill Angela before?"

"We don't know yet, but she said it was. In all the hubbub she was able to identify him as being the same guy."

"Where's Angela now? Is she okay?"

Clay had to avoid divulging anything further regarding Angela. "All I can tell you is that she's getting the care she needs on a regular basis from one of the hospital psychologists, and that she and Shiloh are safe."

"Oh, thank God."

"I know you're worried about Angela, but we've got them both under round-the-clock protection."

"Clay, I'm sorry you've had such a bad time of it—and I'm sorry I got mad at you, but can't you promise you'll stay in touch from now on? It doesn't have to be every day, but more than once a week. Even if you just text me once in a while, ask me how my day is going—just a note so I know you're thinking of me. It would mean a lot."

"It's been a tough few days, for sure. But that's no excuse. You're right, I should have called. I will do better in the future. I promise."

Hope uncrossed her arms and took a step toward Clay. Tears slid down her cheek. "I really missed you," she said.

He held her close and gently brushed away her tears with his thumbs. "Yeah, I missed you too. I really did."

"I read in the paper that you found the remains of all those girls. I was totally shocked. That had to be tough on you."

"It was. But the worst was having to tell Gwen's mother that we found her daughter."

"I'm so sorry I was mad. I'll make it up to you. It's not fair of me after what you've been through."

"No, listen. You had a right to be mad. It's a lesson learned."

"Let's not talk about it anymore." She looked at Clay with a mischievous smile. "Maybe we can go on another picnic soon, like, in one of the hotel suites?"

"I thought you said there were too many eyes here."

"Yeah, well, I changed my mind. It's not like John hasn't done it himself a hundred times."

CHAPTER 34

Hope returned from the front desk. "Here's the room key. There will be a six pack of Guinness in the fridge and room service will be up in half an hour with a steak dinner and a wedge of chocolate cake. Anything else you want, call me."

"What about you?"

"I'll be up after I get a few things done."

* * *

In the hotel room, Clay called to check in with Shiloh and Angela on the secure cell phone he had given them. They reported all was well and that a shift of cops had occurred earlier.

It had been a long day, and Clay was grateful to sit down to the dinner Hope had ordered for him. After his second beer, he got in the shower and let the hot water stream down his back and neck. His thoughts turned to the pleasures that lay ahead.

As if on cue, Hope entered the large marble bathroom and peeked in on Clay. She saw his outline through the opaque shower door and asked, "You doing okay?"

"Now that you're here, yes," he said from the shower.

He opened the door. "Hi, beautiful."

She was unashamedly naked. Tall, slender, achingly beautiful.

"And what, exactly, are you doing, Mr. Detective-man?"

"Thinking of you. Want to join me?"

"I thought you'd never ask."

Clay stepped aside and let Hope enter the shower. She smiled. "I think they call this makeup sex."

He laughed and reached for the bar of soap. With the shower streaming onto their faces, Hope swept her hair behind her ears, looked at Clay, and kissed him with an open mouth, hard and long. He turned her around, holding her tight against his body, and gently lathered her breasts as he kissed her neck. She cooed contentedly and reached down knowingly.

They were both ready. She turned back to face him, and rubbed her breasts side to side against his chest, until he lifted her and, with deep surges of passion, they climaxed together.

"I don't want you to ever leave me," Hope said.

Clay thought she was crying, but the shower camouflaged her tears. "Are you still mad at me?"

"A little."

He kissed her neck and shoulder. "Still?"

"Maybe not." She breathed hard with fresh desire and reached for him again.

* * *

Clay woke early, and couldn't help but feel good about Hope. Lying on his back, he looked up at the ceiling, his mind replaying their long night of sex. She had said she didn't want him to ever leave her. Why would he? He felt the same way about her.

She woke a few minutes later, saw Clay was awake, and nuzzled his neck. She whispered, "How did you sleep?"

"Very, very well. You know I did. And you?"

"Me too." She gently stroked his bare chest.

Clay wrapped her in his arms and pulled her tight against him, enjoying her soft skin against his.

"I really like you, Clay. Really."

He kissed her gently. "I really like you too."

"What are you thinking right now?"

"A lot of things. You and me. Wonderful sex. How beautiful you are."

"I bet you're thinking about your case too."

"It's crossed my mind."

"How about I try to uncross it? I think I know just how to do that." Hope reached for Clay and he didn't fight her, allowing her to do whatever she wished.

* * *

"Do you still have your work on your mind?"

Out of breath, Clay rolled over onto his back. "Not nearly as much."

They laughed.

Hope ordered room service breakfast. Clay had wanted only coffee but, not surprisingly, she ordered a full breakfast for them.

"Did you know, Hope, that John Grainger had been seeing Gwen Willington before she disappeared?"

With obvious bitterness, she sneered, "No, but that doesn't surprise me—not one little bit. It's not like he hasn't had affairs with a dozen different women."

"Do you think he was capable of killing her?"

She momentarily looked away from Clay before answering. "I guess anything is possible, but I don't think so."

"Why did you hesitate? When you were with him, was he ever abusive to you?"

Again she looked away. "No, not really."

"Hope?"

"Verbally, maybe. I mean, he made me feel awful sometimes, like I could never please him. He used to criticize me a lot, and he'd do it in front of people. If I had a drink, he'd say things like 'Looks like I'll have to pour you into bed tonight.' Or if he didn't like what I was wearing, he'd say 'Where did you find that dress—in a dumpster?'"

"And you put up with that?"

"Yes, I did, at first. You have to remember. I was a naïve farm girl from the Midwest who'd never been any place in the world outside of Illinois. I looked up to John. He was two years older and like a god in my eyes. Whatever he said, I thought was gospel."

"Why didn't you leave him when you found out what he was doing?"

She teared up. "I kept forgiving him. I didn't want him to leave me. I was such a fool. But it finally got to the point where I didn't believe a word he said about anything. I was just so miserable."

"Come on. Let's not talk about him anymore. I can see why it upsets you."

Hope turned thoughtful. "Clay?"

"Yes?"

"Who do you think is killing all these people?"

"I wish I knew. At first I was certain it was Angela's roommate, Denver Stennet, but I can't find the evidence to link that sorry bastard to the crimes."

"What about the fact that he roomed with both Carrie and Angela—isn't that enough to arrest him?"

"No, it doesn't prove anything. And it certainly doesn't point to the reason why he would have killed Gwen. I still think it could be Stennet, but we found evidence that also incriminates James Donovan. Our problem now is that Donovan's been missing for so long, we don't know if he's a suspect or a victim."

"And with someone trying to kill Angela and Shiloh again, this is really getting out of hand, isn't it?"

"The case has taken a bad turn. At first it appeared the killer was targeting only waitresses. But after Gwen was killed, it clearly involves others at the Bend besides waitresses. Honestly, I'm concerned about you too."

Hope reached across the table and rubbed Clay's arm. "You're sweet to worry about me, but I can handle myself. I've got a .45 that I carry with me in my purse. All legal. I've got a permit to carry it concealed, and I know how to use it."

"I've heard that line before. That's what Shiloh said before he was shot. Just be careful, okay?"

"I will, Clay. I promise. How about talking to my girls again and telling them what's going on and how they should protect themselves, what they should be on the lookout for, etcetera."

"Okay by me."

"I'll arrange it for this this afternoon, before the next shift. I'm being selfish you know."

"Why do you say that?"

"Because I'll get to see you again."

CHAPTER 35

Hope arranged for all the women on her shift, including restaurant employees and the lobby hospitality personnel, to report to work fifteen minutes early to attend a briefing on what the media was now calling the Desert Serial Killer.

Clay and Hope entered the conference room together. "Hello, ladies. Thank you for coming in a few minutes early. Miss Archer thought it would be a good idea to update you on my investigation regarding Angela Foster. Have you been keeping up with the newspaper accounts of what's been happening?"

The women all nodded.

"All right. Then you know there is a serial killer on the loose, but I'm here to tell you there's no reason to panic as long as you use common sense. I want to review a few things about our suspect that will help keep you safe."

For the next ten minutes Clay divulged what he could about the killer. He explained that, although the suspect didn't focus entirely on waitresses from the Bend, three waitresses had, in fact, been abducted, and it was particularly important for them to be wary and to always be on guard. "Remain vigilant and, when leaving the casino, travel in pairs or request an escort. Make sure someone else knows the times you'll be traveling to and from the casino. Keep your car doors locked at all times, and don't stop for any pickup truck, even if it has flashers and appears to be the tribal police. Drive to a public place and then stop. That's when you want to find out for sure who it is. Ask them to show you their ID." The women indicated their understanding of his reminders. Clay asked again if they knew of anyone who had been stalking Angela or the other women who were killed, but no one offered any more information. Hope dismissed her crew to start their shift.

An uncharacteristically subdued Holly Paine remained seated after the other women left. "Detective Bryce, I have something to tell you about Gwen Willington. It's been on my mind since I read that the police found her. I don't know if it's important, but I thought I ought to tell you and let you decide."

Hope asked, "Is it okay for me to stay?"

Holly and Clay both nodded.

Clay asked Holly how well she knew Gwen.

"Not very well. We'd talk every once in a while when we'd run into each other. I mean, just about different stuff... nothing important. She was very sweet. She treated everyone nice. You know, she had it all—looks, smarts."

"So what is it you wanted to tell me?"

"You know Mr. Grainger, don't you?"

"Yes, I know who he is."

"Well, I could tell he had a thing for her. He was, you know... I mean, he was like a puppy dog with her. He was, like, head over heels about her. A man had to have a lot of confidence to even talk to her because she was so beautiful. Mr. Grainger has that kind of confidence. You probably do, too, because you're a good-looking man like he is."

Clay glanced at Hope and felt himself turn red. Holly had a way with words that made him blush.

"Go on, Holly."

"Well, I thought you should know that once when I was coming to see Hope about something, I caught Gwen and Mr. Grainger in the corridor outside of the HR office having an argument. Gwen's back was to me, so, for a second, she didn't know I was there."

"Do you know what they were arguing about?"

"No, I couldn't hear. And anyway, as soon as he saw me, he shushed her. She turned around, and when she saw me, she didn't say anything else. It was obvious she was really mad about something. I'll be honest with you. I don't like Mr. Grainger. I was really surprised that a girl like Gwen would want to be with someone like him. But it takes all kinds, doesn't it?" Holly suddenly recalled Hope's history with Grainger. "Oops," she said, and gave Hope a sheepish look. If Hope was embarrassed by what Holly had just said, she didn't show it.

Clay had been suspicious of Grainger since first learning of his involvement with Gwen Willington, so he hoped Holly could help him narrow down her date of disappearance. "Do you know how long it was after that incident that Gwen went missing? Understand, Holly, I'm not trying to imply anything about Mr. Grainger, but just develop a timeline for her disappearance."

She shrugged. "I don't remember exactly when Gwen disappeared, but I'll think about it and let you know." She stood to leave and added, "I don't know if what I saw was important. I just thought you should know."

"Thanks, Holly." Clay handed her another of his cards. "Please let me know if you remember anything related to that timeline. Call me anytime."

Holly examined the card, tilted her head, and, reverting to her flirtatious way, asked, "Anytime?"

Clay turned red again. "Call me if you think of anything else that might be helpful to my investigation."

"You know, Detective, you better watch yourself around here. All the girls think you're pretty hot."

"Really? I don't know why but that's nice of you to say."

Hope cleared her throat.

Holly turned to her. "I guess I'd better get to work or my boss will fire me."

"I'll talk to your boss. You'll be okay." Clay smiled at Hope, but saw only anger in return.

After Holly left, Hope offered a wry smile. "I'm not happy about her hitting on you. She's not too obvious, is she?"

"She's harmless. She's probably like that with every guy." Clay attempted sarcasm in response. "That's the only reason I agreed to talk to everyone again—so I could see Holly."

Hope twisted her face to show disgust. "I hope you're not serious."

Clay shook his head. "No, of course not."

"It's too late anyway. You're mine now."

He smiled and was about to hug her when he caught a glance of a small camera in the ceiling above the entrance to the conference room.

Dammit. That's a new one. It wasn't there before. He's got them everywhere.

CHAPTER 36

Captain Ellsworth, under pressure from the Chief of Police, asked the FBI's Investigative Support Unit at the Academy in Quantico, Virginia, to lend assistance in the serial killing case. The Captain called a special meeting that Friday in one of the conference rooms at police headquarters. FBI Special Agent Mark Stephenson studied reports on the serial killings and spoke to the captain as they waited for everyone to arrive.

Clay and Jacoby entered the conference room together.

"Special Agent Stephenson, meet Detective Clay Bryce and Chief Jacoby Johnstone. Clay is our lead investigator in this case. As I mentioned earlier, he's the one who first recognized we had a serial on our hands. And Chief Johnstone is the chief of police of the Yiqua Native American Pueblo, south of Santa Fe. He's been working closely with Detective Bryce. As you know, any investigative work on the Yiqua reservation requires the approval of the tribal police. The Chief has been accommodating, and has worked hand in hand with Clay to help us resolve this case. He has given his authorization to have the Santa Fe PD and the FBI involved."

"It's nice to meet both of you."

The conference room door swung open and Assistant District Attorney Hank Kincaid joined the meeting.

"Special Agent Stephenson, I'm sure you remember ADA Kincaid. I asked the DA to assign Hank to this case."

"I remember. Good to see you again, Hank."

"Same here. It's been a while." They shook hands.

Captain Ellsworth filled Clay and Jacoby in on the two men's history. "Special Agent Stephenson and ADA Kincaid were part of the team that worked closely to solve the Breeze Canyon serial killings a few years back. Since they worked so well together, I asked the FBI if we could have Special Agent Stephenson assist us again."

Hank shook his head. "An interesting case, wasn't it, Mark?"

"Yeah, it was. That's for sure."

Ellsworth explained, "I have designated this group the Desert Killer Task Force. What's discussed in these meetings is to remain confidential, with disclosure only on a need-to-know basis. As he did with the Breeze Canyon murders, Special Agent Stephenson is going to help us better understand this killer's character and motives."

Clay was not happy that Ellsworth had asked the FBI for assistance, but with the growing clamor from the media, the chief of police, the mayor, and even the governor about the effect the case was having on Santa Fe tourism, he had little say in the matter.

Stephenson was aware that local police departments sometimes considered the FBI intrusive. He understood the sentiment and worked hard to not be looked upon as an interloper. "To reiterate what the captain said, my role is purely advisory. I'm here to help you any way I can."

Stephenson was a tall, lanky man with narrow shoulders, closely cropped brown hair, and angular facial features. He provided his insights in an articulate, professorial manner, as though reading notes from behind a podium. "Captain Ellsworth has filled me in on the details of the case, and I've read your reports, Detective Bryce. I understand you were the first to see commonalities with all these murders."

"It was a hunch at first," Clay said. "Other than Angela Foster's attempted murder, this was initially just a missing persons case, but when we discovered the remains of the other women, it morphed into a case of serial killings."

"Let's get started, gentlemen. We'll begin by focusing on the common elements to develop a profile that hopefully leads us to the person responsible for these murders. First, though, some information on my background. I've been with the Bureau for fifteen years. For the past four, I've been in the FBI Investigative Support Unit at the Academy in Quantico. Thanks to the popularity of all the police shows on television, we're commonly referred to as FBI profilers. Some years ago, the Bureau recognized that serial murders are a strain on the resources of local police departments. As a result, they put together the Investigative Support Unit to assist in areas such as psychological profiling and advanced forensics techniques. As I said a minute ago, my sole objective here is to provide advice, specifically as it relates to the killer's tendencies. In other words, I'll be involved in the psychological or human behavioral aspects of the case. Unless you have any questions about my background, let's get started."

When no one had a question, Stephenson stood and went to the whiteboard on a side wall of the conference room on which he had drawn a series of vertical lines. In each column he had clipped the names and photos of the victims in the case. Pointing to the photos in the first column, he said, "From what I've read in the files, these are the individuals we know for certain were murdered."

Emily Coburn, Carrie Kirkland, Gwen Willington, Mae Youngblood.

"In this column we have Jack Youngblood, who, as I understand may have been murdered."

Clay added, "Yes, it's our belief that he was murdered, but we do not have the evidence to support that supposition."

Jack Youngblood.

"Okay. And one person has been missing for two years and is either a victim or a suspect."

James Donovan.

"Finally I understand two persons were targeted by the killer but survived."

Angela Foster, Shiloh Youngblood.

Stephenson pointed to the photos of Angela Foster and Shiloh Youngblood. "Let's focus first on these two. Foster was abducted from her car on a minimally traveled road—Route 14. The circumstances surrounding her abduction give us the clearest picture of what might have happened to the three women whose remains you found in the desert. By the way, how is Foster doing after the shooting at the hospital on Wednesday?"

"As you no doubt know, we've moved her and Youngblood to a safe house," Clay said. "She's recovering nicely, but she's not quite to the point where we can question her in depth about her abduction."

"And how's Youngblood doing?"

"He's doing remarkably well and was actually in the process of being discharged from the hospital the day of the shooting."

"Would you summarize his role in Foster's kidnapping?"

"Youngblood rescued her from the desert the night she was abducted. Because of that, he's been targeted twice—the first time in his own home, and the second time this week at the hospital. We think the guy believed Youngblood would be able to identify him. Unfortunately, during the first attempt, his mother, Mae, was killed."

"Mae was most likely an innocent bystander," Jacoby added.

232

Stephenson put an *X* through Mae's name. "She was a collateral victim. By doing away with Mae, the killer is letting us know he'll do away with anyone who wanders into what is his sometimes schizophrenic world."

Jacoby asked, "Is a serial killer always mentally ill—a schizophrenic?"

"No, Chief. Contrary to popular belief, that's not always the case. If it were, serial killers would be judged legally insane and never brought to trial. No, most often these people suffer from antisocial behavior and know what they are doing is wrong. On that basis, they are rarely deemed as mentally incompetent, and almost always stand trial for their crimes."

"Like a Ted Bundy or John Wayne Gacy?"

"Yes. Exactly."

Clay said, "I have another question for you about collateral targets. Going on the assumption Foster's kidnapper thought Youngblood would be able to identify him, Youngblood should also be considered a collateral target, shouldn't he?"

"Yes. From what we know, he was not a primary target. But let's talk about the individuals who were primary." Stephenson underlined the names *Foster*, *Willington*, *Kirkland*, and *Coburn*. "What are the common elements among these four people?"

Clay began, "We connected the first three victims by their job and work schedule—they were all waitresses who worked the four-to-midnight shift at the Bend. Learning that Gwen Willington was also a victim threw those two common elements out the window. She wasn't a waitress. She worked a nine-to-five schedule in the Bend's HR department."

Hank said, "Isn't it true that the day shift and swing shift overlap by an hour? Willington worked until five, and the others started at four."

"That's a good point. Let's consider swing shift common to all victims." Stephenson headed a new column, *commonalities*, under which he wrote *Indian Bend* and *swing shift*. What else do the victims have in common?"

"Obviously, they were all women. Young women," Jacoby said. "And from what we know, all attractive women."

"That's good." Stephenson wrote *women, young, attractive.*

"They all lived in Santa Fe. Is that important?" Ellsworth asked.

"We don't know yet, so we'll put that down."

Santa Fe

Hank asked, "Did they live near each other, Clay? For example, in the same apartment complex?"

"We looked at that and found no pattern in their addresses. They all lived in different parts of town."

"Their mode of travel?" Stephenson asked.

"Cars, but Willington's was not involved in her killing. While the other three women appear to have been abducted while driving along Route 14, Willington's car was located in the parking lot of her apartment complex."

Stephenson included *Route 14* as a commonality of three of the four victims.

Jacoby added, "We have to include the fact that all the victims were buried on our reservation."

"Okay, good. They could have been buried anywhere in the desert, but the killer chose the Yiqua reservation. Why? What's the relevance?"

Clay shook his head. "I don't think there is any. I think it was convenient to the killer. He buried them off the beaten path and not visible from the roadway."

"Let's put it on the list for now, although I agree it may not be relevant. Do we know if they were sexually assaulted?"

Clay answered, "We know Angela Foster was not. If the other abductions were similar, it's not likely the women suffered any sexual abuse."

"That's a good assumption. Okay, anything else about the women?"

Stephenson looked at the four men seated at the table one by one. In turn, each man shook his head no.

"Let's look next at the abductions. What was common to the manner in which the victims were abducted?"

Jacoby spoke, "We believe the killer wore a ski mask, and also had each victim wear one."

"How do you know that?" Stephenson asked.

"Youngblood told us he and Foster were forced to wear ski masks, and also that the abductor was wearing one."

Clay added, "And Forensics found traces of fiber from ski masks in the desert graves."

Stephenson added *ski masks* to the list, then ticked off each commonality.

Swing shift
Indian Bend
Women, young, pretty
Santa Fe
Route 14
Buried on Yiqua reservation
Ski mask

"Let's talk about ski masks. Why would the killer put masks on his victims? What does that tell us about him?"

235

No one replied.

"Okay, let's see if I can lead you to an answer. What are the usual reasons people wear a ski mask?"

"To guard against the wind and the cold, like for skiing."

"Right. What else?"

"A burglar or a mugger would wear one to hide his identity," Jacoby said.

Stephenson nodded. "That could explain why the killer wore a mask. What about the victims? Why put a mask on them?"

Again no response from the men seated around the table.

"What if it's to hide the identity of the victim? To hide the face of the victim from the killer himself?"

"What does that mean?" Clay asked.

"Here's a theory. It allows the killer to rationalize what he's about to do—first, kill without being seen, and then, not see who he's killing. To use a cliché, it's like hiding your head in the sand."

Clay shook his head, "But that doesn't make any sense. He knows who he's killing."

"You lost me too," Ellsworth said.

"Let me explain it another way. Maybe the killer has a grudge against the person he's going to kill. But he also doesn't want to regret his actions. There's that other side of him that doesn't want to act on that grudge, so what does he do? He covers the face of the person he's got the grudge against, and when he kills her, he easily erases that memory from his mind. He can say to himself, 'I didn't kill her. I don't even know what she looked like.'"

Captain Ellsworth nodded. "Okay, I get it."

Clay agreed, "Yes, I get it too, and it seems to me that if we knew what the grudge was, it would go a long way toward learning who the killer is."

"Let's ask the question," Stephenson said. "What's a possible motive?"

Ellsworth said, "Here's my theory."

"Good. Let's hear it."

"We've all heard about men who fixate on religious revenge. They believe God mandates that they kill certain types of women for their sins. In this case, would the fact that the women were young and pretty and wore sexy outfits motivate the killer to believe they were prostitutes?"

Clay argued, "But, Captain, the women were not prostitutes, and Gwen Willington didn't wear sexy outfits. I still think it has to do with the swing shift. Hank's earlier point is well taken. Even though Gwen didn't work the swing shift, her hours overlapped with the swing shift employees."

Jacoby had been following the conversation closely. He nodded in concurrence. "I agree it's the swing shift that seems to hold the clue to motive, but why that shift?"

"That's the sixty-four-thousand-dollar question—one we don't have an answer for," said Stephenson.

Ellsworth asked, "Just to digress for a second. What are other common reasons a person becomes a serial killer?"

"There's no one cause. But keep in mind, studies have shown that some serial killers have been the object of some type of abuse themselves—physical, sexual, psychological, even neglect abuse. The impact of any one of these types of abuse can create dysfunction in the way the abused person deals with others. A man might transfer his abuse rage to a certain type of woman who reminds him of his abuser. In light of that, what was it about these women that set off the killer?" Stephenson tapped the white board with his marker. "Does anything else on this list of commonalities hint to a motive?"

Jacoby shook his head and was frustrated at the psychological analysis. "I understand everything you're saying about abuse and religious fanaticism and other things that influence early childhood, but can't there be a simpler explanation? Isn't it just as possible this guy is killing women *not* because of abuse rage, as you call it, but because he's got a grudge against each woman he kills? Maybe they rejected his advances and the guy can't handle rejection."

"I agree with Chief Johnstone," Hank said. "Let's go back to the way Angela Foster was abducted. We know she was injected with drugs to prevent her from fighting back. We know her car was left on 14 and she was taken into the desert where the suspect tried to bury her alive. But there's one point I think is key to determining motive—she was not sexually abused. Nor do we think the other women were sexually assaulted."

"A very good point," Stephenson said.

Jacoby asked, "What person would go to those lengths to kidnap someone and not do it for ransom or to sexually assault the victim? It sounds to me like a grudge or revenge motive."

Stephenson agreed. "Good points. And to add to the Chief's comments, it's possible the suspect never had a relationship with the women he abducted, and didn't want anyone else to have one either. His grudge could exist only in his fantasy obsession, not in actuality."

Ellsworth said, "Can you help us understand how that scenario might have played out?"

"Sure, Captain. Let's say you have a romantic interest—real or fantasy—in Jane Doe. Along comes Detective Bryce who takes Jane away from you. What are your options? You can eliminate Detective Bryce, or, in your twisted way of thinking, kill Jane for being with him. It's your way of getting even with Jane for rejecting you. At the same time, you've gotten even with the detective because he can no longer have Jane. The guy who is going with the woman stokes the killer's anger, yes. But ironically, it's the woman the killer obsesses about, not the guy who's got him enraged."

Clay offered a thought, "We don't know if anyone other than Angela was buried alive, but let's make the logical assumption the others were alive when they were buried. What does that signify?"

"That's a virtual certainty. When someone does something as extreme or cruel as bury another person alive, it demonstrates that person's height of anger and their compulsive desire to hurt that person to a degree beyond the realm of normal anger. In plain language, because he feels tortured, he wants to torture others in turn."

Captain Ellsworth let out a low, soft whistle. "Man, that's deep." He looked at the others. "Does everyone get this?"

"Makes sense," Jacoby said. "Bottom line, what are we looking for? Do we narrow the suspect down to a guy who had either a real or fantasy relationship with all the women?"

Stephenson nodded. "I think that's the direction in which we should proceed. Given what we know, it's probably someone from the Indian Bend who's in the company of the women who work late afternoon. An employee, a guest, a vendor—someone associated with the Bend in some manner."

Clay said, "That's a lot of people."

Stephenson continued with his profile. "That's true, but let's see if my profile helps narrow it down. Keeping everything we've discussed in mind, here's the person we're looking for. He's an ordinary guy. He might be married. If he is, he's unhappy with his wife, his marriage, and probably his life. He may be looking for the perfect woman to be with, and when he thinks he's found her, he becomes obsessed with her. She may not even know he's interested. Chances are, he's someone who goes about his daily life in a manner that seems normal to anyone. He follows a routine. Work, play, sleep, work, play, sleep. And he controls his routine religiously. If someone interferes with the object of his fantasy objection, he feels the need to act, but it tortures him to do so. Once he does, however, he goes back to his routine."

"Is the guy a control freak?" Jacoby asked.

"Probably. It's important for him to have control of everything he's involved in. And he has intense anger issues. Outwardly, he controls his temper, but inside he seethes and plots his revenge until he acts on the object of his anger. In effect, he controls his own emotions by not showing his anger."

Clay remarked, "So we should be looking for someone who swings from mild mannered and pleasant to raging lunatic if things don't go his way—but who doesn't show his rage."

"That's correct."

"Not to be flip, but if the guy doesn't show his emotions outwardly, how will we know he's masking his anger? It seems to me we'd have to get every suspect on a psychiatrist's couch to learn what they're like."

"You're right, Detective. It's probably not going to be readily apparent. But, who, among all the people you and Chief

Johnstone have met in this case, do you think could have the hidden characteristics we've profiled?"

Clay looked at Jacoby, who nodded for Clay to respond first. "At the top of my list is Denver Stennet."

"Who's that?" Stephenson asked.

"Well, his only association with the Bend is that he was Kirkland and Foster's roommate. I haven't been able to pin anything on him, but the coincidence of him living with two of our victims has bugged me from the beginning."

Stephenson wrote in the last column on the whiteboard. *Denver Stennet.*

"John Grainger, the Operations VP at the Bend."

"Tell us about him."

"Talk about controlling," Clay said. "This guy controls everything that goes on at the casino. He's got closed circuit cameras everywhere. Every time I'm at the Bend I feel he's got cameras focused on me. And he's one who put Gwen Willington on a pedestal. She's been gone for three years and he still gushes over her—the lost love of his life, that kind of thing."

John Grainger

"Who else?"

"Jason Alvarez. He's the Bend's HR director. From my conversation with him, it's pretty clear he was taken by Gwen Willington too. Described her as a ten. I think he lied to me about his level of involvement with her—or at least about his infatuation with her. He was mild mannered until I asked if he had a romantic relationship with her."

"What did he say?"

"It's not what he said so much as what he *did*. He showed his prickly side—no visible anger, but I sensed it was just beneath the surface. When I asked, he said he was happily married, but I'd bet he's not. To him, Gwen could do no wrong. I'd even say he was obsessed with her."

Stephenson said, "He fits the profile," and wrote *Jason Alvarez* on the whiteboard.

Clay continued, "Then there's Steven Brown—Mr. Green Sneakers—the reporter for the *Times Journal*. I know he doesn't work at the Bend, but I just don't trust him." Clay explained that Brown had gone to Shiloh's house to interview him at about the same time as the home invasion that killed Mae Youngblood occurred, and afterwards changed out of his shoes and into lime-green sneakers. "He's refused to let me see the shoes without a warrant. I'd put that pain in the ass on the list too."

Steven Brown

Jacoby offered another name. "I hate to say it, but Bret Colby from my pueblo—and close friend of Shiloh's. He was the first person to show up at two different crime scenes. And he works at the Bend. My gut tells me he's not involved, but the fact that he discovered not one, but two, crime scenes is a coincidence we shouldn't ignore."

Bret Colby

Clay offered one additional suspect. "There's one other guy—mystery man, James Donovan. He was the swing shift security manager at the Bend. He disappeared two years ago—the day after Carrie Kirkland disappeared. The same day that Jack Youngblood was killed in an auto accident. No one knows what happened to Donovan. We don't know if he's a victim or a bad guy. Heck, we don't even know if he's alive or dead. Circumstantial evidence points to him as the possible killer, but nothing conclusive."

James Donovan

"Speaking of Jack Youngblood, Detective, what do you know about his death?"

"The State Police reported that he died in a one-car accident believed to have been caused by driver inattention. To me, his death is suspicious."

"Why do you say that?"

"Because it was Youngblood who wrote up a report about an incident that occurred in the Bend parking lot involving Kirkland and an unknown person. Youngblood turned the report in to his boss, Jim Donovan, but it mysteriously disappeared. Youngblood, Kirkland, and Donovan are all tied into this, but I don't know how yet. It's conceivable that unknown person in the parking lot incident is our serial killer."

"Okay, it's fair to say that the unknown person in the parking lot could be our killer. He could be one of the men we've discussed or it could be someone else yet to be identified. I'll show him as Mr. X."

Mr. X - Unknown person.

Captain Ellsworth summarized, "Gentlemen, Special Agent Stephenson has given us a preliminary profile of the type of person we should be looking for. Let's find out which one fits the profile the best."

"I'll start with Alvarez on Monday," Clay announced.

CHAPTER 37

Clay arranged to have an informal meeting with Jason Alvarez, Human Resources Director at the Indian Bend, at police headquarters first thing Monday morning. Before their meeting, Clay did a thorough check into Alvarez's background. He had been married for twenty-five years to Rebecca Harris, a high school teacher who retained her maiden name. They had no children and lived in the bedroom community of Sage Mesa, twenty miles south of the Bend toward Albuquerque. Work was the centerpiece of his life. He was at the Bend early and typically did not leave until seven or eight each night. Although he was well liked by his employees, they thought him a workaholic and anal retentive. He ran a tight ship, micro-managing all aspects of the Human Resources department.

Clay had told Alvarez he would be looking at mug shots to help in the Angela Foster abduction case. But his real reason was to see if he could uncover any further details about Alvarez's infatuation with Gwen Willington. He also wanted to learn what else he could about Grainger and Willington's relationship.

"Jason, thanks for coming in. I know you're busy, but I thought you might help me identify a suspect in the Angela Foster abduction case. I'd like to show you photos of several men and would like to know if you have ever seen any of them at the Bend."

"Sure, anything I can do to help."

Clay opened his folder and extracted six photos. "Take a look at these. Do you recognize anyone? Could you have seen any of them in the casino, or talking to Angela, or even to Gwen Willington?"

Jason shuffled through the photos, shaking his head to each. "No, I can't say I've ever seen any of these men before. I'm pretty good with facial recognition, Detective, and I don't recall ever seeing any of them."

"Take your time. Look at them again, please. Are you sure?"

He shuffled through the photos again. "No, sorry. No one looks familiar."

Clay wanted to put Jason at ease. He leaned back in his chair and went into a casual conversation. "Man, this is a tough case to figure out. You've been at the Bend a while, haven't you? Ever see anything like this before?"

"No, never. It's terrifying now for the women employees because of all the murders."

"How long have you been there?"

"Actually, I started working at the Bend a year before it opened."

Clay was aware of this already, but acted surprised. "A year? Why would they hire you a year before it opened?"

"The owners wanted to have all the employees in place for the casino, the restaurants, and the hotel. And they wanted me to help develop systems and procedures before they opened."

"I see. Does that mean you personally hired everyone?"

"Yep."

"Man. *That* was a hell of an accomplishment. Congrats."

"Thanks. We thought we did a pretty good job. It was a challenge."

"You were telling me about Gwen Willington when I was over at your office. Did she help in the hiring?"

"Oh, no, not at the beginning. She didn't come to work at the Bend until about four or five years ago."

"Speaking of Gwen, what do you think could have happened to her? I mean, who could have done such a terrible thing? Anyone at the Bend you've known over the years who could have done something like that?"

"You mean kill her? I can't imagine anyone who would do such a thing. She really was a sweet and remarkable woman."

"You know what I found out?"

"What?"

"Remember when we talked last time I asked you about John Grainger and Gwen?"

"Yes, and I told you I didn't know anything about them."

"Well, guess what? I found out they were dating before she went missing."

Jason rolled his neck. "Is that right?"

"Oh. You really didn't know that?"

"Uh, no. No, I didn't. As I told you, Gwen was a very private person."

"Do you think Grainger could do such a thing to her? Say, hurt her in a fit of anger, even if unintentionally?"

Jason clenched his jaw and narrowed his eyes. "Detective, I don't know where this is leading, but if you think I know what happened to Gwen, I don't, other than what you've told me and what I've been reading in the papers lately."

"No, I didn't mean to imply that I wanted you to snitch on a fellow employee. I was just curious. After all, you report to Grainger, don't you?"

"Yes."

"You don't hold him in high regard, do you?" His words were more of a statement than a question.

"Sure. Sure I do," he said.

Clay was unconvinced. "I forget who told me, but I understand you competed with Grainger for the Vice President position he now holds." No one had told Clay that. He threw it out to see how Jason would respond. "How is it that he jumped ahead of you on the corporate ladder when you had such massive responsibilities from the very beginning?"

Jason said nothing.

"I understand Grainger started out at the Bend as a dealer. You probably hired him too, didn't you?"

"I did."

"That has to eat at you. I mean it would eat at me if I was in your shoes." Clay was baiting Jason, hoping to see an explosion of anger.

Jason finally responded. "Well, it's no secret I wanted that job. Even John knows that. But he earned it, and I don't have anything against him. Besides, he's younger than I am."

"You think that's the reason? Because he's younger? I'm no lawyer, but from what I know about age discrimination, isn't it against the law to hire or promote someone solely because he or she is younger than another person? I mean, couldn't you file a suit against the Bend for age discrimination if you believe that was the case?"

Jason realized immediately that Clay had perceived his comment about the age differential as a barb against Grainger. "No. I misspoke. I didn't mean to imply that I was discriminated against. I like my job and wouldn't want to jeopardize my position there. John earned the promotion. Period!"

"You told me you were happily married. Any kids?"

"No, my wife couldn't have children."

"I'm sorry to hear that. By the way, where did you work before coming to the Bend?"

"In Cincinnati."

"Ohio? How did you end up here in the great state of New Mexico?"

"I always wanted to live in the Southwest, so I when I saw the classified ad in the New York Times for this position, I jumped at the chance to come out here."

"What did your wife think about moving to the desert?"

Jason's laugh was forced. "We live in Sage Mesa, a helluva change from Cincinnati. She wasn't too happy at first, you know, moving away from her friends in Cincy. But she's up and down on it now. I mean, she's happy when she reads about all the snow and ice they get in the winter. Other times, when she misses her friends, it's not so good. She goes back to visit a lot."

"What does she do? I mean does she work?"

"Yes, sir. She's a high school teacher, and she's very active in the New Mexico Commission for Women, in our church, in the YWCA, and other organizations too."

"Wow, I'm impressed. I bet that's time consuming for her."

Jason shrugged. "You're right. It is. But we both enjoy being busy—and active. She's always doing something or other—going to a board meeting, grading papers, whatever."

"What about you? You're major busy, too, I bet."

"Yes, I am."

"Long hours, huh? Me too." Clay worked to develop a working-man's bond with Jason. "Sometimes it's like the day never ends. Am I right?"

"Yes." Jason smiled and nodded in agreement.

Clay laughed. "You know, I'm divorced. My wife used to say I was more in love with my job than with her. She was probably right. Does the same thing happen to you? I mean, as hard as you both work, I bet you don't have a lot of time to do things together. You know, travel, go out to dinner, go hiking—that sort of thing. I know my wife—my *ex*-wife—and I never found the time to do anything together."

Jason laughed. "Yeah, the truth be told, we don't have much time to do things together. We do have our common interests, but mostly we're like two ships passing in the night."

"So your wife is in all these organizations. What about you? What's your thing?"

"Work."

"Work, and that's it?"

"Yes, pretty much. That and church."

"Who did you work for in Cincinnati?"

"A company that went belly up."

"What was the name?"

Jason looked quizzically at Clay. "Why do you want to know that?"

Clay shrugged. "Just curious."

Jason bristled at the line of questions from Clay. "Say, listen. I thought you called me in to help you try to identify a suspect, but now you're asking about my married life and where I used to work. What's that all about?"

"Ah, I was just seeing similarities in our backgrounds and our jobs. And I was hoping you could shed some light on John Grainger. You know, tell me any scuttle on what makes him tick, anything you know about his relationship with Gwen."

Jason nodded but didn't respond. He had become leery of Clay's intention to have him visit police headquarters.

"Gwen was pretty, wasn't she? But you said you were never tempted to do anything with her. I mean sexually, you know?"

Jason sat more upright in the chair. He squinted at Clay. "Yes, that's right. Why are you asking me that?"

Clay ignored the question. "Didn't you ever think about asking her out for a drink, or for dinner after work?"

"No, never."

"That's not true, is it?"

Jason was now agitated—worked up and breathing hard. He had had enough of Clay's persistent questions about Gwen. "What is going on here? What are you after?"

"Just wondering if you were telling the truth about her, that's all."

Jason stood. He appeared ready to stomp out of the interview. "Yes, I'm telling you the truth. First off, Gwen would not have been interested in me, and second, I would never do anything to jeopardize my position at the Bend."

Clay continued to bait him. "You say that a lot. 'I don't want to jeopardize my position.'"

"Yeah, well, it's a fact. I'll say it again. I won't do anything to jeopardize my position. I don't get involved sexually with anyone like John does all the—"

"All the time? Is that what you were going to say?"

Jason scanned the ceiling in the conference room, looking for telltale spyware similar to what he knew was omnipresent at the Bend. "Listen, Detective Bryce, I respect John Grainger. I don't know what you expect me to say about him."

"Aw, sit down, Jason. No reason to get mad."

Jason sighed deeply, uncertain what he should do. Reluctantly, he sat back down.

"Are you worried about your job?"

"No, I'm not worried about my job. I know John could let me go at any time if he wanted to, with or without cause. But

I've worked too hard all these years to give him any real reason to fire me. I'm not about to risk getting charged with some complaint from a female employee."

"I'm not sure what you mean. You mean a sexual harassment-type complaint?"

"That's exactly what I mean."

"I can't imagine what you'd have to worry about. As much as Grainger fools around, he wouldn't have any basis to fire you if you had been shacking up with someone like Gwen. Talk about the pot calling the kettle black."

"I'll say it again. I never had any kind of relations with Gwen. As you can imagine, as head of HR, I'm well familiar with the issue of sexual harassment. So, no, John would have no basis to fire me—not because he'd fear retaliation from me, but because there won't ever be a claim levied against me."

Clay shifted his line of questioning, coming at Jason rapid fire. "Do you know if he was having an affair with Angela Foster?"

"I don't know."

"What about Emily Coburn and Carrie Kirkland?"

"That's really not for me to say."

"So you're saying he did?"

Jason stood his ground. "I'm not going to answer that."

"I'll take that as a yes."

"Whatever."

"Has anyone ever filed a sexual harassment suit against Grainger?"

"I'm not at liberty to say."

"I'm taking that as a yes."

"You need to understand—I'm not answering your question one way or the other. Confidentiality concerns."

"Who filed the suit?"

"Did you not hear what I just said?"

"Oh, give me a break. I can find out easy enough. Save me the trouble."

Jason looked away and did not respond. Clay changed tactic—he would wait Jason out. He did not ask again. He simply stared at him, knowing the man would eventually break. A full thirty uncomfortable seconds went by.

Jason caved. "Two suits were going to be filed—one from Emily Coburn, the other from Carrie Kirkland. But both women went missing before the EEOC could act on their claims and before notice of the claims went to the Gaming Commission."

"Are you serious? How did you hear about those claims?"

"Emily came in to talk with me. She told me John continually harassed her to have sex. She wanted to know what to do—should she file a claim, how to go about it..."

"So you helped her?"

"Of course. Sexual harassment is against the law. It's my duty to help her. I advised her confidentially, but then she disappeared days before a scheduled hearing on her claim."

"Did you think at the time that John forced her to leave?"

"Yes. At first I thought she left because of the stress John was putting her through. But then it occurred to me that he probably settled with her."

"You mean paid her off?"

Jason nodded. "I don't know if he did. I just thought that was a possibility."

"And Carrie?"

"I never spoke with her. John came to me. He told me he found out she was underage and that she threatened to sue him He was remorseful and asked my advice."

"You're kidding me. Underage? The great John Grainger resorting to sex with an underage girl?"

"Detective Bryce, in his defense, I don't believe he knew she was underage."

"We'll see."

"So what happened to her?"

"I don't know what happened to her afterward. All I know is she disappeared, just like Emily."

"Didn't you find it strange that both women went missing before they formally filed their claims against him?"

"Yes, but I thought he paid them both off so he wouldn't have to deal with their claims. That's all I know. Happy now?"

"Don't worry. I won't let on to Grainger that you told me all this. But I intend to find out more from him."

"Detective, I'm done answering your questions." Jason stood and headed to the door. "You weren't honest about why you wanted me to come in."

"Yes, I was," Clay lied. "I thought we were having a good conversation. Don't be angry. You got me interested in John and Gwen's relationship. You know I've got a case to solve, and I would like to know more about Grainger from you."

"Then I suggest you talk with him."

"I will do that, but let me ask you—"

"I'm not answering any more questions without my lawyer."

CHAPTER 38

On Wednesday, Holly Paine did not report to work at the start of her four o'clock shift. By six thirty, Hope was frantic and phoned Clay. "I'm so glad I got you. I think something's happened to Holly. I'm really worried."

"Hope, slow down. What are you talking about?"

"Holly Paine. She hasn't shown up for work."

"Are you sure she's not just late?"

"Yes. She's never late. I called her cell phone and it went right to voicemail. I'm afraid something's happened to her. You need to find out where she is."

"Okay, now, relax. I'm sure she's fine." Clay was, in fact, concerned, but he didn't want to admit as much to Hope.

"This can't be happening again. Do you think she's been kidnapped like Angela was?"

"Listen, Hope. Come on, slow down. Talk to me."

She took a deep breath. "Clay, this is not like her."

"Really, I'm sure she's fine. Let me have her phone number. I'll try to reach her."

Hope recited Holly's number.

"I'll let you know what I come up with. In the meantime, if you hear from her, let me know right away, okay? Everything'll be fine. Don't worry. What's her address?"

Hope searched her employee listing. "1600 Calle del Rio in Santa Fe."

Clay stopped writing. "Are you sure that's Holly's address?"

"Yes. Why?"

"That was James Donovan's address."

* * *

Clay called Holly's number but got no answer. He drove to her apartment building and rang for William Pelling.

"Hey, Detective, how are you? Still looking for that fella Donovan?"

"No, I'm not here for him. I'm sorry to bother you, but this time I'm looking for a woman by the name of Holly Paine. I understand she lives here."

"She does. Something wrong?"

"Her boss at the Indian Bend notified me Holly didn't report to work today. You know everyone at the Bend's spooked by the serial murders. I'm just checking to make sure she's okay."

"She's in apartment 103. Come with me."

Clay knocked on Holly's door but she did not answer.

"Do you have the key, Mr. Pelling?"

"Of course." He sorted through the several keys on his key ring and located the master key.

Clay knocked one more time. After a few seconds with no answer, he nodded to Pelling. "Okay, go ahead and open it."

Pelling pushed the door open allowing Clay to enter the apartment. "Holly? This is Detective Bryce. Are you in here? Holly?" No response. They walked into a messy living room—clothes hung from chairs, magazines littered one corner, and a partially filled glass of wine rested on the coffee table.

The TV was on—and loud. Clay turned the volume down then knocked on the closed bedroom door. Again no response. He stood to the side, turned the knob, and pushed the door open. Inside, they saw rumpled bed covers, clothes scattered on the floor, and more magazines piled on the bedside table.

"She's not the neatest tenant, is she?" Pelling observed."

Clay didn't acknowledge his comment.

"You don't really think she could be a victim of that serial killer like those other girls, do you?"

Clay answered truthfully. "Yes, actually. Now I'm very concerned."

He opened the closet and found it surprisingly clean and organized. He was drawn to one end of the clothes rack where he noticed a man's shirt and trousers hanging neatly on wood hangers. "Looks like Holly has a friend who spends some time here. Any idea who he might be?"

"I see her with men on occasion, but no one guy all the time."

Clay pulled the hanger off the rack to examine the clothes more closely. The shirt was custom-made and the initials *JG* were embroidered on the cuffs.

John Grainger

"Mr. Pelling, have you ever noticed Holly coming or going with a well-dressed man? He'd be about forty years old, black hair, slicked back?"

Pelling shook his head. "Nope, can't say I have."

"What about last night? You see her with anyone?"

"Not like anyone you just described, but I did see someone. He had his arm around her waist as they walked down the hallway toward her apartment. Come to think of it, he was carrying a small suitcase."

"Can you describe him?"

"Not really. His back was to me, but I saw he had a beard and was wearing a baseball cap. Oh, and he had a ponytail."

Clay noticed the door to the bathroom was ajar. He was about to push the door open when a clicking noise from inside the bathroom made him hesitate. He put his forefinger to his mouth to quiet Pelling and motioned him to back away. "Holly, is that you in there?"

No answer. Clay drew his service revolver, then threw the door open.

The window was up and a slight breeze caused the cord from the venetian blind to hit against the window sill.

"It's okay. It's just the cord from the blind." Clay re-holstered his revolver, then noticed the shower curtain was completely drawn closed. He pulled it back and saw Holly's fully clothed body submerged in the bathtub.

CHAPTER 39

Bend Waitress Murdered - Another Victim of the Indian Bend Serial Killer?

Santa Fe Police are investigating the death of Holly Paine, 25, of Santa Fe, who was found dead in her apartment on Calle del Rio last evening. Police spokesman Captain Matthew Ellsworth reported drowning as the cause of death. There are no suspects to Paine's murder at this time. Police report Paine was murdered in the early hours of Wednesday morning when she returned to her apartment upon completing her shift at the Indian Bend Hotel and Casino.

What is going on at the Bend? Over a period of five weeks, Detective Clay Bryce of the Santa Fe Police Department and Chief Jacoby Johnstone of the Yiqua Tribal Police have discovered five, now possibly six, homicides of people associated in some manner to the Bend. Bryce and Johnstone continue to lead the investigation into these homicides, but the murders continue. Is our police force equipped to deal with such crimes? To date no suspect or person of interest has been identified. One has to wonder. It may be time to turn this case over to a more experienced task force of police professionals better suited to deal with crimes of this heinous magnitude. Police are not disclosing any further information at this time. They ask anyone with information to contact police at 505-222-9999. - Steven Brown

Dan Carton reviewed his forensics findings with Clay. "The collar tag on the shirt you found in Paine's closet said *Made for John Grainger*, and we found Grainger's business card in the shirt pocket."

"That's awfully tidy, isn't it?" Clay asked.

Carton agreed. "Either he's an idiot of a killer or someone is trying to frame him. It's just too obvious."

"Finger prints?"

"The only prints we found belong to the decedent."

"No others?"

"Nope."

"Not Grainger's?"

"No, we didn't find his anywhere."

"None of this makes any sense. I'm bringing him in. I want to know what the hell his relationship was with Paine."

* * *

Clay summoned Grainger to police headquarters. Finding Grainger's clothes in Holly's apartment, and learning from Jason Alvarez that he had been in a sexual relationship with an underage Carrie Kirkland had Clay eager to pursue these new leads in his investigation.

The other members of the Desert Killer Task Force—Captain Ellsworth, FBI Special Agent Stephenson, Chief Johnstone, and ADA Kincaid—observed the interview from the adjacent room.

Grainger was in a foul mood when he arrived with his attorney, Mark Flores. "I don't appreciate being dragged down here for no reason at all. What the hell is this all about? You have screwed up this investigation from the beginning. First you drag the Bend through the mud and now you're trying to take me down too."

Clay didn't acknowledge Grainger's outburst, but instead read him his Miranda rights and let him know the interview was being video-recorded. "You're familiar with video recordings, aren't you? You know, *eye in the sky* kind of thing."

"Are we back to that again?" Grainger shot back.

"For the record, you are represented by counsel, Mr. Mark Flores. I asked you to come in today to answer questions about the murder of Holly Paine, one of your employees at the Indian Bend. What do you know about her?"

"I read that she was murdered. That's it. You can't think I had something to do with that?"

"We have reason to believe you were in a relationship with her."

Flores asked, "Are you accusing my client of murder?"

Clay avoided a direct answer to his question. "Mr. Flores, we do have a central concern about your client. When we investigated Holly Paine's murder, we discovered articles of clothing in her closet that belong to your client—a shirt and trousers. Since he left his clothes there, he must have had an ongoing relationship with her, one we assume was sexual in nature."

Flores objected to Clay's conclusion. "Detective Bryce, you know we're going to require verification the articles of clothing belong to Mr. Grainger. Unless we receive that assurance, we disavow—"

Clay slid a sheet of paper across the table. "That's a sworn affidavit from Mr. Grainger's tailor attesting he custom-makes much of his clothing for him. He specifically states that he made the shirt and trousers we found in Holly Paine's closet."

Flores scanned the report.

"If you still wish to *disavow* that these clothes belong to your client, I suggest the definitive way to prove any of this is to have him submit to a DNA test to determine if, in fact, he wore the clothing."

Flores hesitated.

"Look, I can get a warrant in half an hour to collect a DNA sample, so why don't we make this easy? Yes or no?"

Flores looked at Grainger and nodded as a sign he agreed to Clay's request.

"You can have whatever the hell DNA you want, but I want to make it perfectly clear to you right here and now—I never set foot in her apartment," Grainger said.

"Apartment?" Clay's voice rose as he pronounced the word. "How did you know she lived in an apartment? Why not a house or a condo? I didn't say we found your clothes in her *apartment*. I simply said the shirt and trousers were in her closet."

Grainger shook his head and looked to Flores for advice.

"Don't answer that, John. Detective, I, too, assumed you were talking about her apartment. Shame on us for thinking *apartment*, but that was a totally innocent misspeak."

"Misspeak, huh? Let me ask you this, Mr. Grainger. How do you suppose your clothing got into Holly's closet—at her apartment?"

"You don't have to answer that, John," Flores advised again.

"No, Mark, that's fine. Listen, Detective, the fact is I have no idea how my clothes got there."

"Were you having, or did you have a sexual relationship with Holly?"

"No. Absolutely not. I did not have sexual relations with that woman." Grainger raised his voice. "Listen to me. I don't have a clue how my clothes got into that woman's closet. I didn't even know her."

"To refresh your patchy memory, Holly Paine was the waitress at the Bend who told me about the *incident report* Jack Youngblood wrote up involving an argument in the employee parking lot at the Bend. Now do you remember?"

"Oh, yeah—the report he *supposedly* wrote."

Grainger's breathing became more rapid. Flores put his hand on Grainger's arm to calm him down. "It's okay, John. Let me answer. Detective, you cannot be thinking of accusing my client of murdering Ms. Paine on the basis of clothing you found in her closet."

"On the contrary, Mr. Flores, that's exactly what I'm thinking."

"Do you have any other evidence to suggest that my client has knowledge of Ms. Paine's death or that he was ever in her apartment? Have you discovered fingerprints in the apartment belonging to Mr. Grainger?"

"No, but the fact his fingerprints haven't been discovered can simply mean he was careful to wipe everything clean. You're missing my point. All I want to know is how Mr. Grainger thinks his clothing got into Holly Paine's closet. They didn't appear there by magic. *Some*one put them there. If it wasn't your client, then who?"

Grainger offered, "Someone must be trying to frame me for her murder, but I have no idea who or why."

"You have no idea why? Let's assume for the moment that someone really is trying to frame you. From what I understand, you've stepped on quite a few toes to get to where you are today. So, of those people you ran over, who would have motive to frame you for murder?"

"I've made enemies, yes, but I can't think of a single person who would kill a girl so they could get even with me. Frame me for murder? How sick do you have to be to do something like that?"

Clay's tone became conciliatory. "Again, assuming your argument about being framed makes sense, will you cooperate with me in determining who had access to your clothing?"

"Of course I'll cooperate."

"Good." Clay looked first at Flores then at Grainger before continuing. "Tell me this—have you ever left your clothes at the homes of the women you've been with? And if you did, I need you to identify those women."

Grainger's breathing picked up again. He was adamant in his response. "I have never left clothing at a woman's home, or at anyone's house for that matter."

"Could someone have taken your clothes when you were at your gym?"

"I don't go to a gym. I don't have time."

"Then who had access to your closet at home?"

"Maybe the women I..." He hesitated.

"Entertained?"

"Yes, those women."

"Will you give me their names?"

Grainger looked to Flores for advice and whispered something in his ear.

"My client will give you that list as long as you retain it in confidence. There are some relationships he feels will... how shall we say it... cause issues."

"I assume that by that you mean it will cause issues with their husbands?"

"Yes."

"No, counselor, sorry. I can't give your client that assurance."

Grainger shoved his chair back and stood. "Then I'm leaving. I'm not giving you any names."

Clay spoke firmly to Flores. "Your client isn't going anywhere until I say he can go. Now, kindly tell him to sit down, or I will charge him with murder and shackle him to this table."

Flores took hold of Grainger's forearm and urged him back into his chair.

"We've got a few other things to discuss still," Clay said.

Grainger glared at Clay. "Like what?"

Thanks to the information garnered from Jason Alvarez, Clay was ready to drop the hammer on Grainger, who now appeared to have had motive to kill both Emily Coburn and Carrie Kirkland.

"We need to talk about Emily Coburn and Carrie Kirkland—your murdered former employees."

"Not again. What am I supposed to tell you about them now?"

"When I first brought up their names as former employees of yours, you said you didn't know them. Do you remember telling me that?"

Grainger stared straight ahead without answering. He knew what was coming. Flores interjected, "Where are you heading with this, Detective?"

Clay kept his eyes trained on Grainger while answering Flores. "Well, counselor, I've learned that, in fact, Emily Coburn and Carrie Kirkland were both going to sue the Bend and your client for sexual harassment, but they both somehow went missing before the complaints were formally filed with the EEOC. As we now know, both women were murdered and buried in the desert. Mr. Grainger, do you still say you didn't know them?"

"I never said I didn't know them."

"Yes, that's exactly what you said."

"You must have misunderstood."

"So is this another case of you *misspeaking*?"

"No, I did not misspeak. You misunderstood."

"Okay. I don't agree with your interpretation, but I'll play it your way for now. What can you tell me about them?"

"I have no idea what happened to either one."

"So, for the record, you acknowledge you knew them."

"Yes, I never denied it. I hadn't thought about either one until the day you walked into my office and told me you thought they might have been abducted and even killed."

"Did you have affairs with them?"

"Why is that important to know?" Flores asked.

Clay was shocked the lawyer would even ask that question. "Really? Are you serious? Maybe because they were both killed and your client knows more than he's letting on."

Flores directed Grainger to answer the question.

"Look, frankly, I was happy they both left."

Clay corrected him. "You mean, *went missing*. They didn't just *leave*."

"*Went missing,* whatever. Listen, I never did have sex with Emily Coburn. Believe me, I tried. She said if I didn't stop asking her, she was going to file a sexual harassment suit against me. I thought she was playing hard to get, and stupidly, I didn't stop."

"Were you served a formal complaint?"

"No. When she disappeared—*went missing*—we didn't have to worry about being sued."

"How convenient. What about Carrie Kirkland? Did you actually have sex with her?

"Yes, I admit I did."

Clay wanted Grainger to repeat his admission for the task force witnesses. "So you admit that you and Carrie Kirkland were in a sexual relationship involving sexual penetration?"

Flores advised him, "Don't answer that, John."

"Why not? That's what it was."

"How did you react when she suddenly went missing?"

"I was okay with that. It meant I didn't have to be the one to break off our relationship and worry about what she was going to do or say about me. She didn't file a sexual harassment suit either, although she threatened one. The whole matter was dropped because she wasn't around to pursue it. Isn't that right, Mark?"

"That's correct. Detective Bryce, we were ready to defend John—in either case—but the whole issue became moot when both women disappeared."

"I certainly didn't want them killed, and I have no clue who killed them," Grainger asserted.

"Was it public knowledge that they were going to sue you?"

Flores said, "No, it never got to that point. In fact, very few people knew about it."

"Who did?"

Grainger answered, "Simon, Jason Alvarez, and Gwen Willington are the three I believe knew about it."

"No kidding. Even Gwen Willington knew about it?" Clay found that odd. "Who told her?"

"I did. I told her in confidence."

"How did she handle that news?"

"Not well."

"Did you argue about it outside the HR office at the Bend?"

"Yes. How did you know that?"

Clay avoided answering his question. Instead, he asked, "Is that why she didn't want to have a relationship with you?"

"Yes, probably. But I told her because I wanted to be honest and aboveboard with her."

"Frankly, we believe Kirkland filed suit against John to blackmail him. If word had gotten out to the Casino Gaming Commission, John would have been fired and the Bend would have had their casino license suspended. As far as Coburn is concerned, she wasn't in it to make money off John. She merely appeared to be a principled woman."

"Principled, but not *un*willing to take my money," Grainger said sarcastically.

"You paid her off."

"Yes."

"Did you pay off Carrie too?"

"I prefer to say we *settled* with her," Flores responded, "to protect John's reputation."

"I wanted to settle with them even though Mark disagreed. I should add, I did not use the Bend's money. The money came out of my own pocket," Grainger said.

"How much did you settle each claim for?"

Flores answered, "Significant amounts. But I'd rather not say how much. That's not important."

Clay was thoughtful for half a minute, drumming his fingers on the edge of the table and looking off at nothing in particular. Finally, he looked back at the two men. "I'm sure you can understand my point of view. The fact that you paid both women off, they go missing, and we find their remains in the desert is more than just a little suspicious."

Flores nodded. "I understand that. But my client knows nothing about their disappearance."

"Fill me in on their complaints. What about Coburn— Emily?"

"There's nothing to tell. I flirted with her, cajoled her, but never threatened she would lose her job or anything like that."

"You never succeeded at getting her into bed?"

"That's correct. As I said before, I didn't know when to take no for an answer. Totally my fault for trying."

"Tell me how your sexual relationship with Carrie came about."

Flores said, "We don't need to get into that. John, you don't have to answer."

"That's okay, Mark. I want to. How else am I going to clear my name?"

Flores sat back, resigned to his client's desire to talk. Clay just stared at Grainger, waiting for him to begin.

"Listen, Carrie was hot. But she came onto me, not the other way around. Did we have sex? Yes, and she played me for a fool—the fool that I was. She said if I didn't agree to pay her, she would claim I raped her and she would go to the cops. Understand, I don't need to rape anyone. Any sex I have with a woman is consensual."

"You're saying Carrie threw herself at you?"

"She did. She wasn't the first woman to do that. Of course, I didn't realize she planned to blackmail me. I should have, but I didn't. I made sure we were discreet. She was not to acknowledge she knew me, and vice versa. We would meet at my house—not do anything at the Bend."

"Apparently she didn't understand the meaning of the word *discreet* because she bragged to her roommate about her relationship with you—that she was having sex with you."

"It doesn't surprise me now."

"I'm going to tell you something you already know."

"What?"

"Carrie Kirkland was only sixteen years old when you were having sex with her."

Flores stiffened in his seat while Grainger gave Clay a sharp look.

"It's true. I verified it. Carrie Kirkland turned seventeen a week before she went missing. That means you were having sex with a sixteen-year-old. You knew that, didn't you?"

Grainger remained motionless in his seat. Clay prepared himself for Grainger's lies.

"No way! She told me she was twenty years old. There's no way she was just sixteen. She didn't have the body of a sixteen-year-old."

Clay gave him a look of whatever-that's-supposed-to-mean.

"And she knew more about sex than most women I've ever been with. As usual, Bryce, you've got your facts screwed up. She could never have gotten a job at the Bend if she was just sixteen."

"John, that's enough. Do not say anything else."

"You knew she was sixteen, so stop the bullshit," Clay said. "Listen to me, Grainger. You've admitted to having sex with an underage girl. Mr. Flores is certainly aware of New Mexico Statute Section 30-9-11, but let me read it to you. *Whoever commits criminal sexual penetration on a child thirteen to sixteen years of age when the perpetrator is at least eighteen years of age and is at least four years older than the child is*

269

guilty of a fourth degree felony. That's enough to put you in prison for a—"

"She wasn't underage. I don't believe it. She didn't look sixteen. She certainly didn't act sixteen. Show me proof."

"I'll do that." Clay pulled a document from his file. "Here's her birth certificate."

Grainger shook his head as he studied the certificate in front of him.

"You still want to argue she wasn't sixteen when you were having sex with her? You know what I think? I think you knew she was underage. I think you knew your career was shot. Done. Over with."

"That's ridiculous."

"What recourse did you have? Her death had nothing to do with her filing a sexual harassment suit. You killed her because she would have nailed you for having sex with her—underage sex—and then you buried her in the desert thinking no one would ever find out."

Flores jumped in. "That's enough. You're hounding my client. John, do not respond to him. He's baiting you."

Grainger brushed his attorney off again. With raised voice, he said, "You know, Bryce, if you really believe I killed her because she was sixteen, you're dumber than I think you are."

"As dumb as you leaving your clothes at a murder victim's apartment?"

"I already told you I don't know how my clothes got there."

"Let me understand what you're saying. First, you were having sex with a sixteen-year-old girl but you claim you didn't know she was that young."

"You got it."

"Then, your clothes were left at the apartment of another one of our murder victims and you claim you don't know how they got there. Get the picture I'm painting?"

Flores interrupted again. "John, don't respond."

Clay directed his attention straight at Flores. "I believe your client is guilty of multiple murders."

"I haven't killed anyone!"

"You told me you were not having an affair with Gwen Willington, but I have reason to believe you were."

"I'm telling you—I did not have sexual relations with Gwen. I swear to that."

"What about Angela Foster? Have you been having sex with her too?"

"No. Absolutely not."

"You think about that. I'll ask you again, because I've got witnesses who'll attest you've been hanging all over her."

"I don't know who's telling you that. Yes, I was interested in her, but I've never had any relations with her. Not saying I didn't want to. It just never happened."

Clay kept the jabs coming. "You're a pretty smart guy, Grainger. I mean, how else would you have gotten to the position of Vice President at the Bend? Help me out here. How should I look at the fact that—let me name them—Emily Coburn, Carrie Kirkland, Gwen Willington—are all dead, and I have witnesses that tell me you had a relationship with all three, or at least *tried* to have a relationship with all three—and then there's Angela Foster and Holly Paine."

Flores argued, "You have nothing more than purely circumstantial suggestions of guilt, with no proof of any of your allegations."

"Counselor, your client claims he never saw the report about the parking lot incident Holly Paine told me about, implying the incident never occurred. Or, if it did, James Donovan, a play-by-the-rules kind of guy, destroyed the report that detailed the incident before he could see it."

"I don't remember you asking me about that report," Grainger lied.

"You're kidding me, right? I didn't ask you about the report? You know, you keep digging yourself in deeper every time you lie to me."

Grainger was on the defensive. "I'm not lying."

Clay was not about to let Grainger get away with another lie. "At the time, you said you didn't know anything about the report. But let me tell you something. I'm convinced it was *you* who was arguing with Carrie Kirkland in the parking lot, and when you got hold of Youngblood's incident report, you made sure to destroy it."

"No way. That's not true!"

"What did she tell you to get you so mad your own security had to go to her rescue? Is that when she told you she was going to file suit against you? Did she tell you she was only sixteen years old? Is that what happened? You knew you'd be toast if word got out, so you killed her."

Flores insisted his client stop answering Clay's questions. Grainger shook his head. "Stop! Everybody stop. I can't go on like this. Mark, I'm sorry. I need to tell him what really happened." Grainger took a deep breath, and confessed. "Listen, Detective, you're right. You know pretty much everything that happened. I'm not a bad guy. Yes, I did have an argument with Carrie."

Flores tried to stop him but Grainger wouldn't listen. In an unburdening of his conscience, he recounted, "No, listen. Here's what happened. I got a note from Carrie telling me to meet her in the parking lot after her shift. I didn't know what she wanted. I thought maybe she wanted to set up another rendezvous. But that's when she told me she was only sixteen. I freaked out. She said she wouldn't tell anyone and would disappear if I gave her money to keep quiet. She said if I didn't, she would tell the cops I raped her. How could I defend myself? It was my word against hers, and she said she had proof we were having sex. I didn't ask her what kind of proof, but I got the idea. I still don't believe she was only sixteen. Honest to God, I can't believe it. I told her she was crazy to try to blackmail me, and if she tried, I would go to the cops myself and tell them what she was doing. She yelled 'Rape, rape.' I said, 'Okay, okay. Stop screaming. I'll give you what you want.' But it was too late. The next thing I knew, Jack Youngblood came running over to find out what was going on. She screamed, 'I'm only sixteen and he wants to have sex with me.' I was beside myself. I had no idea about her age. I got in my car and got the hell out of there. That's when I called Mark and told him what had happened."

Flores commented, "He did. I told him not to say anything to anyone, and that I would see him in the morning."

"Tell me about the incident report. You denied it initially, but I assume you will now admit that Jack Youngblood did, indeed, write one up?"

"Yes. He did exactly what he was supposed to do."

"And who did he give it to?"

"Jim Donovan."

"Was there anything in the report about Carrie's age?"

"Yes. Youngblood mentioned it in the report."

"What happened to the report?"

"I couldn't have anyone else know about it, so I intercepted it the next morning before Donovan could read it. It was on his desk. I took it and shredded it."

"Did Youngblood tell anyone else?"

"I think he talked to Donovan about it the next afternoon."

Clay slapped the table hard, startling both Grainger and Flores, and accused Grainger of killing Jack Youngblood. "And then Youngblood got killed. Is that why you killed him? You ran the guy off the road to his death? You murdered him, didn't you? One less person around who knew the truth."

"Absolutely not! I'm being honest. No more lies. I did not kill Jack Youngblood. What was I to do—kill everyone who knew anything about my relationship with Carrie? I didn't kill him. I didn't kill Carrie. I didn't kill Emily. I didn't kill anyone."

"Do you know Denver Stennet?"

With the tip of his forefinger Grainger flicked away a tear that had pooled in the corner of his eye. He spoke in a soft monotone. "I know who he is, yes."

"How do you know him?"

He inhaled deeply and faced Clay. "I know he was Carrie's roommate and... I don't know, probably her lover too. I do know one thing—he most likely set up the whole blackmail thing. I can't prove it, but it's the only thing that makes sense to me. She wasn't smart enough to do it on her own."

"Is that why you tried to kill Stennet, too, by running him off the road?

Grainger was caught by surprise. "What? No, I didn't do that. I didn't even know that happened. This is the first I've heard of it."

"Who would have had reason to kill him?"

"How the hell would I know? You're the detective. You tell me."

"What about Holly? Was she part of the scheme to blackmail you along with Carrie and Stennet? Is that why you killed her?"

"I *didn't* kill her. I didn't even know who she was."

"What happened to Gwen Willington? Now that you say you're being honest with me about everything else, tell me what really happened to her."

"I was devastated to hear she was murdered. I really did think the world of her. Everything I told you about the two of us is true. I really have no idea what happened to her."

"I'm going to ask you again. Were you having sexual relations with Angela Foster?"

Grainger shook his head before answering. "No. I did not lie to you about that. I never had sex with her. I admit I tried, but I did not."

"Did you abduct her and then try to kill her because she wouldn't have sex with you?"

"I did not!"

"What about James Donovan? Did you kill him? Is he buried in the desert like the others?"

Grainger hit the table with his fist. "You are out of your mind! I think this investigation has gotten to you. I'm going to say it one last time. I didn't kill anyone. No one! Got it? I may be a lot of things, but I'm not a murderer."

"You admit to having sex with a sixteen-year-old. That's true, isn't it? We have it on tape that you admitted to that. I believe you killed Carrie and all the other women for reasons that are so clear to me now. There's only one thing I don't know."

Flores had had enough. "John, I insist you not say another word. Detective, turn off that video recorder. I want to talk to my client privately."

Clay stood and signaled to the technician in the observation room to turn off the equipment. "I'll give you ten minutes." He closed his file, left the room, and joined the others members of the Serial Task Force in the observation room.

"What does everyone think?"

ADA Kincaid was the first to offer his thoughts. "You don't have enough to hold him for murder, but you can hold him on a fourth degree felony for criminal sexual penetration. I think you should continue to build on the motive you've established that he murdered each woman in turn to safeguard his position at the Bend. Further, finding his clothes in Holly Paine's apartment will lend to the circumstantial evidence stream you're developing. Although he denied it, it's conceivable he offered a quid pro quo relationship with each of them for sexual favors. But unless someone can bear witness to that, we don't have enough for a murder rap to stick. You're close, but right now it's all circumstantial."

Clay added another observation. "Well, here's something else to add to all the other circumstantial evidence. A couple of days before she was killed, Holly Paine talked to me about Grainger. She told me she had caught Gwen and Grainger arguing just a few days before she, Gwen, went missing. When Holly and I finished talking, I noticed a camera in the ceiling of the conference room. It had been trained on us. What's the chance Grainger killed Holly to eliminate her as a witness to his argument with Gwen?"

Kincaid answered, "Even if we could prove Grainger eavesdropped on your conversation, it doesn't prove motive that he would kill her for that."

Ellsworth instructed Clay to book Grainger for statutory rape, then asked, "Hank, can we get a warrant to search his house based on what we now know?"

"Yes. I'll talk with the DA about what we've uncovered," Kincaid said. "He wants this thing to end too. Let's get the search done quickly. I'm sure Grainger's attorney will have him out on bail in no time at all."

"I agree," Stephenson said.

Two cops followed Clay back into the interview room, and Clay announced, "The video recording will continue at my signal." He gave the thumbs up to the video technician through the mirror, and then turned to Grainger. "John Grainger, I'm arresting you for the criminal act of sexual penetration as defined under New Mexico Statute 30-9-11 of the then sixteen-year-old Carrie Kirkland."

"I told you I didn't know she was sixteen," Grainger shouted.

"Take him away." One of the cops grasped Grainger's elbow to stand him up and handcuff him.

Grainger's shoulders slumped. He showed none of his normal pretensions. He was scared. "I can't believe this is happening. I'm not what you think. I'm not a rapist. I didn't know she was sixteen. I didn't kill anyone."

* * *

The search of Grainger's house did not turn up any items known to have been worn or used by the killer.

Within twenty-four hours Grainger was booked, arraigned, and released on one-hundred-thousand-dollar bail. A trial date was set and he was ordered to surrender his passport. The Bend put him on a leave of absence until a verdict was rendered in his case, and appointed Simon Learner to fill Grainger's position as the interim Operations Vice President.

CHAPTER 40

INDIAN BEND EXECUTIVE ARRESTED
FOR UNDERAGE SEX

John Grainger, 40, Operations Vice President of the Indian Bend Hotel and Casino, was arrested on charges of criminal sexual abuse of an underage employee of the Bend. Captain Matthew Ellsworth, spokesman for the Santa Fe Police Department, addressed the media and announced Grainger was also a person of interest in the serial murders of four Bend employees. How an underage employee came to be hired by the Bend in the first place is being investigated by the New Mexico Department of Labor and the New Mexico Casino Gaming Commission, with possible significant penalties in store, including monetary penalties and suspension of operation. Grainger professes his innocence in all criminal matters but has been put on leave of absence from the Bend until adjudication of his case is complete. - Steven Brown

Clay made it a point to text or talk to Hope every day. In spite of her over-the-top anger for his not keeping in touch with her, he had fallen hard for her and managed to rendezvous with her at the Bend on other occasions. Their relationship blossomed the more time they spent together. Hope was convinced Clay was her soulmate—the man with whom she wanted to share her future.

She realized he was under intense pressure to solve the serial murders. As an antidote to the stress, she arranged for them to have a quiet dinner on Sunday at Le Chanticleer, a French bistro high up on Canyon Road in Santa Fe—far away from the grind of his investigation. Hope also planned to propose a way to fast forward their relationship, and she felt the restaurant, with its romantic ambiance, was the perfect setting to do so.

Clay and Hope had just ordered drinks when they noticed a hostess leading Simon Learner and his date, a woman Hope recognized as Liza Williams, an employee of the Bend's accounting department. Simon caught Hope's eye as he and Liza approached, and stopped to say hello. Clay observed that Simon was dressed casually in blue jeans and a yellow golf shirt.

"Hey, Hope, fancy meeting you here. You remember my friend, Liza. Detective Bryce, this is Liza Williams."

Clay stood and greeted the two while the hostess stepped aside to wait.

Liza leaned down and gave Hope an air kiss. "Hi, Hope. Good seeing you again." Liza looked all around her and giggled. "There's no pool to fall into is there?"

Hope smiled. "I think you're safe here."

"I'm still so embarrassed."

"You shouldn't be. It wasn't your fault."

"Thanks for saying that. I managed to survive when all was said and done."

"See? No harm, no foul," Hope added. "Enjoy your dinner."

"You too. It was nice to meet you, Detective." Liza turned and followed the hostess to their table, with Simon right behind her.

"They're a cute couple," Hope observed.

Clay agreed. "Actually, I'm stunned to see him looking like a normal human being—not a sycophant in a pinstripe suit. I almost didn't recognize him at first."

"I know." Hope laughed.

"What was that all about, falling into the pool?"

"Oh, my God, the poor girl was mortified. Remember I told you about how I had to go to a party at John Grainger's house last month?"

"I remember, yes. You said it was like a command performance."

"It was. All his direct reports and first-line managers were there. It was almost like he was taking roll and, Lord knows, it wouldn't have gone well for anyone who didn't show up. Of course, I had to be there. Anyway, Simon was there too, and Liza was his date."

"So what about the pool?"

"There were a bunch of us out back near John's pool, just chatting and sipping our drinks. Suddenly, there was a splash and a shriek. Liza apparently tripped over Jason Alvarez's foot and fell into the pool. Luckily she fell in the shallow end. But still, she was immersed up to her waist. Jason said it was an accident, but I don't know. Sometimes Jason is... well, Jason. Surprisingly, he can be a real cut-up."

"Jason? He sure doesn't come across that way."

"I know, but he really has a great sense of humor."

"So tell me about your relationship with John. Do you still see him socially?"

"No, absolutely not. I hope you don't think something is going on between John and me. Are you jealous?" Hope reached for Clay's hand with both of hers. "You are, aren't you?"

"No, I'm not jealous. I'm really not." He paused. "You can do whatever you want and go wherever you want. I mean, it's not like I have chains around you."

"I wouldn't mind that," she smiled, and arched her eyebrows in a sexually inviting way.

"You're a devil, young lady, but hold that thought." Clay directed the conversation back to Grainger. He was curious to know what Hope thought about him now that he was charged with the criminal offense of statutory rape.

"I'm not ashamed to admit that John was a good executive. He knew how to get things done. To a large degree, he was the one who put the Bend on the map and made it the most successful casino in New Mexico. I'm actually sorry to see what happened to him. He should have known that sooner or later his messing around with employees would get him in trouble. And, Holly Paine, I don't know about her, but I can tell you one thing—I think she was trouble."

"What do you mean, trouble?"

"Well, I mean look at the way she came onto you."

"Aw, Hope, come on now. She was harmless."

"I don't think so. She really was quite the flirt. Now it's my turn to be curious. Did you go to bed with her? You did just say we don't have chains around each other."

"Where did that come from? Absolutely not."

Hope stared at Clay for a few seconds. He stared back, waiting for her response. Finally, she appeared to soften. "Okay, I'll have to take your word on that." She picked up her menu and started to read. Clay did the same, but his mind was elsewhere.

"Hope, what's the buzz about Grainger at work?"

"I knew you wouldn't be able to let work go completely. I'll answer your question, and maybe we can move on to just you and me. Deal?"

"Deal."

"Okay, everyone is shocked. John wasn't the most popular guy, but people respected his ability and his authority. Now they're saying ugly things about him, dredging up all kinds of unfair nonsense."

"Like what?"

"Oh, like they always knew he was a bad guy, and he took advantage of his position. Things like that."

"Do you agree, Hope?"

"In some ways, yes. But I really don't believe he knew Carrie was underage. Had you seen her, you would understand how John could have been mistaken. She was really built—I mean, mature beyond her age. You know he could have any woman he wants, so why go after an underage girl? He couldn't have known. It's like he was set up, you know what I mean?"

Clay got pensive and stared through Hope, disquieting her.

"What's the matter?" she asked.

"Tell me about Simon."

"Simon?"

"Yes. How's he doing at the Bend?"

Hope glanced in the direction of Simon and Liza, then focused back on Clay. She wasn't certain where he was going with his questions. "He's doing okay. Nothing has really changed. Simon's a pretty capable guy. He's very intelligent and now he can show his abilities without worrying about what John will say or do. It's on his shoulders to make sure all this bad publicity doesn't end up hurting the Bend."

Clay stared through Hope again.

"Are you okay, Clay?"

"What you said about John being set up with Carrie makes sense. It's pretty obvious that Simon had the most to gain with John out of the picture."

"What are you saying?"

Clay looked toward Simon and Liza, who were seated on the opposite side of the dining room. He spoke in a voice barely above a whisper. "Well, look. If John's out of the picture, Simon takes over. He would no longer be a lackey at John's beck and call—he'd be the one calling all the shots. You're right. Simon's a bright guy. He's ambitious. He wants to get ahead. But he wasn't ever going to get a chance to climb the ladder as long as Grainger was the boss. He wasn't going to retire anytime soon."

"You think Simon killed Holly Paine and framed John just so he could get John's job? That's crazy."

"I know it's a hell of a stretch, but it's certainly plausible. All the evidence against John is just too perfect. Now that I think about it, he may very well have been framed. I think I'll pay Simon a visit on Monday."

"Okay, that's fine. Now, can we please talk about something other than John and Simon? I have something to ask you."

"The answer is yes," he said with a suggestive smirk and a wink.

"No, listen, Clay. I'm serious." She looked around at the nearby diners and made sure they weren't eavesdropping. She leaned in and spoke in a low voice. "I can't believe how much I've fallen for you."

"I feel the same way about you, Hope."

"Do you agree we have a future together?"

Clay was stunned by the serious tone of her question. "Uh, oh. This doesn't sound good. I hope we do. What are you getting at? Should we talk about this later at your place?"

She shrugged. "No, I'd really like to talk about this now. No one can hear us."

"Okay. What are you saying?"

"It's just that, sometimes… I don't know what you want from me."

"You know what I want from you," he said, and mischievously reached for her hand.

She put her other hand on top of his and rubbed it gently. "I know *that*, Mr. Detective-man. You always want *that*. But, be serious for a second. Do you think we can have—" She stopped midsentence.

"Have what?"

"A normal life together?"

Clay slowly withdrew his hand. He sensed she was asking for a commitment of some kind. "A normal life? I don't even know what that means."

"That's exactly what worries me. I sometimes think there something's wrong with our relationship. I'm not sure where it's heading. I'm pushing forty and I want to know I have a future."

"Listen to me, Hope. I think the world of you. You know that. I don't know what's in store for us. I love being with you, but I don't want us to go the route of my first marriage, where my ex and I started off so in love and ended up in total hate. That's the last thing I want to happen to us."

"So something *is* wrong. Is there someone else?"

There's that damned jealousy thing again. Clay was surprised by her insistence that something was wrong. He kept his voice low, almost to a whisper. "No, there's no one else. And I don't know what you mean when you say something's wrong. Nothing's wrong. We both love our jobs, and maybe that works against us—you working until midnight and me working days. That makes it hard, because we can't see each other as much as we would like. I know plenty of people who work different shifts for years and have a good life together, but would we be able to have that too?"

Hope dabbed at her eyes with her napkin. The people at the next table looked their way, suddenly aware something was wrong.

Another long pause, an uncomfortable silence—neither Hope nor Clay knew where the other was headed. They sipped their drinks and looked at each other. Hope tried to gird her emotion, but finally said, "I don't want to lose you."

Clay did not respond. He remembered Grainger's description of Hope as controlling. *Is this what he meant?*

"You know, Clay, when I see you with my girls, I know they think you would be a real catch. And then I think, what am I getting into again? All that time with John, I worked so hard to make it work for us, and he just threw me aside like I meant nothing to him."

"I understand how much John hurt you, Hope, but I'm not John. I'm not like that."

"I want to believe that, Clay, I really do."

"Look, I've had the best time of my life with you," he whispered. "I've had the best sex of my life with the prettiest girl I've ever been with, and she's stolen my heart—my cold, lonely heart—and warmed it deeply. I never thought I would feel this way again. I want nothing more than to be with you. But, honest to God, I don't know what you're asking of me right now."

"I'm asking if we can make it work."

"I don't know what you mean by *if we can make it work*. Of course we can make it work."

"Then let's try?"

"Try what?"

As if the idea had just occurred to her, Hope asked, "What would you think of us moving in together? You could move into my place."

Clay wasn't ready for that commitment. He looked at her, unsure what to say, and visibly squirmed in his chair. Finally, she drew the only conclusion she could from his silence. "Well that speaks volumes. You know, I talked with a friend of mine about you moving in with me, and we guessed you were going to say no."

"What friend?"

"Oh, that's not important."

"Hope, we've known each other for, what, less than two months? Come on. Do you want me to say we should just dive in? And then what happens if it doesn't work out? I've fallen for you like a ton of bricks. I think I've made that clear. All I'm saying is let's give it a little more time. Let's get to know each other better. As much as I'd enjoy it, we can't base the rest of our lives on sex alone. I know you believe that too."

She leaned back in her chair, nodded several times, and smiled—a condescending smile, one that said she had heard it before. *It's not you. It's me.* That's what John had told her. "You're not saying that as an excuse to leave me, are you?"

"No. I don't want to leave you, Hope. Why are you thinking that?"

"Oh, you know, Clay. Everyone else who's meant something important in my life has left me. You don't need an excuse if that's what you want to do."

"And the same goes for you, too, doesn't it?"

Hope took a deep breath and looked wistfully toward Simon and Liza, who were holding hands at their table. "Okay, let's not do anything. I agree we should get to know each other better. Let's keep talking about it."

"Hope, I think time will tell us what we should do."

She nodded. "I've fallen hard, Mr. Detective-man. You can see that can't you?"

CHAPTER 41

On Monday Clay arranged to meet with Simon at the Bend. When he arrived, he found Simon seated in the oversized leather chair at John Grainger's desk, staring at a CCTV monitor. Clay's first thought upon seeing Simon was how much he dressed and acted like Grainger.

"It was good to see you at Le Chanticleer."

"Same here."

"And your girlfriend is lovely—Liza, right?"

"Yes, Liza Williams."

"Looks like you've settled into the job."

"I'm only here on an interim basis until Mr. Grainger is acquitted and returns. I've been asked to hold down the fort."

"Let me ask you a question, Simon. How do you feel about the mess he's in? Do you think he knew Carrie Kirkland was only sixteen?"

"I can't answer that. My guess is he did not. There really wasn't any reason for him to be... to be with, um, an underage girl. I've seen him flash his smile and make women melt. Doesn't make sense he'd knowingly go with a sixteen-year-old."

"What did you think of him as a boss?"

"Mr. Grainger has always been tough but fair—and a genius at marketing. He's worked at it practically twenty-four-seven with an energy and passion that's been hard to match. I've had a tough time keeping up with the hours he's put in."

"Sounds like you're doing a political endorsement for the guy."

Simon shrugged. "I'm a fan. What can I say? He loves this place and deserves the bulk of the credit for making the Bend a success."

"How did you end up here? I understand you have an Ivy League degree. You could have gotten a positon at any company you wanted."

"I graduated from Brown University, but I was born and raised in Santa Fe. I decided to return after I got my MBA. When I first started here, the Bend was struggling to survive. That's when Mr. Grainger was promoted to the Operations VP position. He needed an assistant, so I applied and got the job. Why work here instead of at some Fortune 500 company? Well, the pay's good, it's in my home town, and my family lives in Santa Fe."

"If memory serves me, you've been here about five years."

Simon nodded.

"Did you ever think in your wildest dreams that you'd be the Operations VP while still in your twenties? I mean, Mr. Grainger's only forty. It would have been a long wait for you to take over, if not for his legal troubles."

"To be honest, I recently came to the conclusion that my future here isn't for the long term anyway. Mr. Grainger has always allowed me to take on new responsibilities, but he wasn't going anywhere. What more could I hope to accomplish by staying here?"

"I see what you're saying, Simon. But then this happens. Your boss gets into legal trouble, and all of a sudden, you're the man in charge."

"Yes, true. I didn't expect it but that's how it happened."

"Do you feel guilty sitting in his chair, behind his desk, giving orders to people instead of taking orders from Grainger?"

"No, not at all. I was asked to fill in, and that's what I'm doing."

"Were you aware he was going to be sued twice for sexual harassment?"

"Yes, I was aware of those *potential* suits, but they never materialized. They were never filed because the women left the Bend without notice."

"Did he ever ask you to lie about Emily Coburn and Carrie Kirkland—to claim you weren't aware of his relationship with them?"

Simon hesitated briefly before answering. "I don't remember."

"You don't remember? Let me refresh your memory." Clay pulled his note pad from his jacket pocket and flipped back through pages of notes until he found what he was looking for. "The first time I met you and Mr. Grainger, you both said you didn't know anything about Emily Coburn or Carrie Kirkland. Obviously Mr. Grainger was lying. Why did you lie too? Because he told you to?"

Simon took his time to answer the question. Finally, "I don't remember what I did or didn't tell you all those weeks ago."

"Really? You surprise me, Simon. Your boss once said you have an encyclopedic memory. And you're telling me you don't remember what you said just a few weeks ago? You know what? I know what you said. It's all right here." Clay waved his pad at Simon. "If you gave false statements to cover for Mr. Grainger, you could be looking at charges of obstruction of justice. And if I prove that you assisted him so he could avoid prosecution and then he's found guilty, I will charge you with accessory after the fact."

"I'm telling you—I'm not lying."

"Let me throw out a theory I have about you."

"Go ahead."

"I think you put incriminating evidence in Holly Paine's apartment—evidence that suggested Grainger was involved in her murder. You have a lot to gain by him going to prison—this job, this office, the power, the perks." Clay swept his hand around the office. "This would all be yours, right?"

Simon looked nervously back and forth, but his voice remained calm. "Detective Bryce, first you suggest I lied to cover up for Mr. Grainger and now you say I planted evidence against him. I can tell you unequivocally I would never even conceive of doing something like that. I owe my livelihood to him. Has he been tough on me? Absolutely. But I am beholden to him. I would *never* turn on him. Never!"

Clay was relentless. "Here's something else. Mr. Grainger told you we had discovered Gwen Willington's remains in the desert. And when I asked you if you told anyone else about that, you said you did not. You lied about that too. You are, in fact, Steven Brown's confidential source, aren't you?"

"The reporter?"

"Yes, the reporter." Clay was losing patience. He watched Simon squirm in his chair. "I'll ask you again—"

Simon cut him off. "Okay, yes, I've had discussions with Steven Brown."

"Good Lord. You lied about that too? Why would you disclose confidential information about the investigation to him?"

"Because of my girlfriend."

"Your *girlfriend* asked you to tell Brown what you knew?"

"She didn't ask me. It was my idea."

"Why?"

"Because women are being murdered and it was being kept a secret from the public—I'm concerned for Liza's safety, worried she'll become a victim too. I want it out in the open so Liza and others will know to protect themselves."

"As of right now, I'm prohibiting you from disclosing anything further to Brown. In the future, you will tell me the truth. I don't care what Grainger told you to say or not to say. Do you understand?"

Simon nodded uneasily. "Yes."

Clay leafed through his note pad again until he found what he was looking for. "Speaking of your girlfriend, there's something about a party a while back at your boss's house. I understand Liza fell or was pushed into Grainger's pool. Tell me about that."

"There's nothing to tell. It was an accident. No big deal."

"How did it happen?"

"A group of people were standing near the edge of the pool when Liza tried to get by them. My back was to her, so I didn't see what happened, but all of a sudden I heard a splash and saw her in the pool. She told me she tripped over Jason Alvarez's foot."

"She tripped?"

"She told me later she thought Jason tripped her on purpose."

"No kidding? Now why would Jason do something like that?"

"No idea. Maybe he thought it would be funny. Or he had too much to drink. Anyway, I never saw her fall, so I can't tell you anything else about it."

"What happened afterward?"

"I helped her out of the pool. She was totally embarrassed. Then Jason's wife took her to Mr. Grainger's bedroom to help her get dried off and do whatever to make her look presentable. I guess they ran her dress through the dryer."

"Interesting. One more thing. Do you think your boss will be allowed to come back to work here if he is acquitted?"

"I can't answer that. When the CEO offered me this position, he said it was on an interim basis. He was upfront about it. But he did say he wasn't sure he'd have Mr. Grainger back even if he was acquitted because the charge is so onerous and the publicity has hurt the Bend's reputation. He wants to see how I do before considering making my title permanent. And he'll consider other candidates for the job too."

"Like who? Did he say?"

"They'll look outside, I'm sure. And they're going to interview Jason Alvarez too."

CHAPTER 42

Clay's suspicions about Jason Alvarez grew each time he spoke with him. Jason was a close fit to Stephenson's profile of the type of person who outwardly appears normal but tries to dictate how everything around him is done, and bristles when challenged. Clay's earlier interview with Jason at police headquarters had ended abruptly with Jason stomping out in anger.

Clay decided to conduct a more in-depth interview. The incident at Grainger's party with Jason tripping Liza Williams into the pool drew his suspicions. Had the HR director intended to create a diversion for some reason?

Clay searched for previous employment information on Jason, and discovered that he had worked for J. J. Nephew Company, a trucking carrier in Cincinnati, for fourteen years, the last five as their HR Director. He also uncovered disquieting information about a suit in which Jason was named as a defendant before J. J. Nephew went bankrupt.

* * *

Jason Alvarez and his lawyer, Earl Woods, were seated facing the one-way mirror in the interrogation room at police headquarters. Clay walked in stern-faced, and nodded to Woods. He did not acknowledge Jason until he read him the Miranda warning. He explained the obvious. "Understand, Jason, that although you are represented by Mr. Woods, your answers to my questions may be used against you in a court of law."

Jason was stunned. "Why in the world did you read me the Miranda warning? What are you accusing me of?"

Woods raised his hand, gesturing to Alvarez to calm down. "Detective Bryce, what is this about? Why are you interviewing my client?"

"If you've been keeping up with the newspaper accounts of the serial killings, counselor, you know that the skeletal remains of one of the victims, Gwen Willington—a former employee of Mr. Alvarez—were discovered on the Yiqua reservation. We think your client might be able to provide information about Ms. Willington's disappearance, including how and why she was murdered."

Jason's anger at Clay's response was immediate. "You're accusing me of murdering Gwen? You have *got* to be kidding. I wouldn't do *any* harm to that girl. I told you I thought the world of her."

Woods shushed his client. "Hold on, Jason. The detective didn't say you killed her. He said you might be able to provide information about your employee's murder. Is that not correct, Detective?"

"Jason, why the overreaction to my reading you your rights? It's normal procedure."

"No, it's not. If it was normal procedure you would have read it to me the last time you interviewed me."

"You know, you're right. The truth be told, you've made clear how you felt about Gwen, so here's the reason I brought you in. I did some checking on your background and found that you have a history of sexual harassment suits being brought against you. Isn't that true?"

"You're exaggerating. There is no history. I mean, there was one time. An employee of mine in Cincinnati filed a bogus suit against me, but it was never brought to trial."

Clay knew there was only one suit against Jason, but decided to bait him by exaggerating, "Maybe you didn't hear me. I said *suits*. Like in more than one."

"Sarcasm is not necessary, Detective," said Woods.

"Suits? That's totally not true. *One* claim by *one* woman who worked for me at my former company, and she tried to profit by suing me."

"Can you explain that suit to me?"

Woods interrupted, "Jason, you don't have to answer that. How is this relevant, Detective, to your investigation into the death of Gwen Willington?"

"I just want to know what that complaint in Cincinnati was about, and how it got resolved."

Jason turned to his attorney. "Earl, it's okay. I want to answer."

Clay nodded, "Go ahead."

"Look, I told you it was one complaint, not multiple complaints. And this woman—Tracey Linville—was a total sham. She was my administrative assistant in HR, and it turns out she played me for a fool."

Woods pleaded with his client. "Jason, please. Do not discuss this any further. You may be incriminating yourself."

"No, Earl, I have to clear this up."

Clay said, "Jason, okay, continue."

"The company was having major financial problems and, as head of HR, I was directed by management to come up with a plan to reduce our workforce by twenty per cent. Tracey and I put in some long hours working on that plan. One night, she came on to me. It's the truth. *She* came on to *me*, not me to her. She was a good-looking woman, I admit—single mother, just divorced, with a kid. I think she was scared she'd be laid off too, which might be why she came on to me. I mean, look at me. Do you think attractive women just throw themselves at me? I think she thought I would protect her from being laid off if she had sex with me."

"Did you have sex with her?"

"Yes. Consensual. I'm not proud of that. I felt guilty as hell about what I did. But, yes, we did have sex."

"Just the one night?"

Jason felt sheepish. He shook his head and mumbled, "No, a few times."

"I guess you didn't feel that guilty, huh? So, what happened?"

"We met with every department head and came up with a plan of who to lay off—administrative staffing, drivers, warehouse employees, traffic people—every department. The president asked me to review the plan with the board of directors, which I did. After a lot of discussion, they basically approved the layoffs as a last-ditch effort to reduce payroll and save the company. Except..." He hesitated.

"Except what?"

"Except they wanted me to lay off everyone in my own department—everyone—including Tracey. I was to stay on to deal with the unions, but everyone else was to be laid off. When I told Tracey what they wanted me to do, she went berserk. She screamed that I used her, that I took advantage of her, that I never had any intention of keeping her on board. And then she accused me of sexual harassment, of forcing her to have sex with me. She swore she was going to sue me and tell my wife all about it."

"What happened from there?"

"Just as she said she would, she told my wife and then filed a suit against me and the company. She claimed I demanded quid pro quo—that I promised I wouldn't lay her off if she performed sexual favors for me. And she claimed the company knew about me having sex with her and didn't do anything about it. It was absolutely, totally not true. Her claim was for $300,000." Jason paused and glanced at Woods, not knowing if his lawyer would allow him to go on.

Woods nodded his consent.

"Then the union got involved. First off, Tracey lied to them, saying it was my idea to have such a major layoff. Well, saying the word *layoff* to a union steward was like waving a red flag in front of a bull. They fought the company tooth and nail even though they were biting their nose off to spite their face. They had to know the company was doomed if we didn't lay people off. But it was, as the saying goes, damn the torpedo, full speed ahead, we're all going down with the ship. And, of course, they provided legal support to Tracey against me and against J. J. Nephew."

"How did it end up?"

"The worst way possible for all involved. The country was in a recession. When the owners of the company realized they couldn't fight the union mentality about layoffs, they threw up their hands and filed for bankruptcy."

"Are you saying J. J. Nephew filed bankruptcy because of the sexual harassment suit against you?"

"Not directly. It was all cumulative—a number of things— the economy, competition, the unions fighting the layoffs, the sexual suit against us. There were a lot of reasons why."

"Why would the Bend offer you the HR job if you were facing a charge of sexual harassment?"

Jason leaned in to whisper something to his attorney, who again nodded his assent.

"The Bend didn't know about the claim against me. They still don't."

"You're telling me they didn't reference check you?"

"No. They did. See, Tracey filed her charges against me a couple of months *after* I interviewed with the Bend. *After* I interviewed with them! Initially they told me I was one of two final candidates for the job and, of course, all the reference checks they did on me were good. But I didn't get the job at first. The other guy did."

"And you're saying a couple of months went by before Tracey filed her sexual harassment suit? Two, three?"

"Yeah, something like that. But, then a week after she filed her suit I got a call from the Bend telling me the guy they hired didn't work out and they had to let him go. They wanted to know if I still wanted the job. Of course I said yes. As luck would have it, instead of them starting the hiring process all over again, they offered me the job based on the information they had on me from before the harassment claim was filed. So that's it. That's the whole story. The Bend never knew anything about that claim."

"What happened to Tracey Linville and her claim against you?"

"It never came to pass. There was absolutely no proof that I demanded sexual favors from her. And the claim just lapsed without action for two reasons. Tracey died in a car accident a month after I left, and J. J. Nephew was dissolved. They wouldn't have had any means to pay the amount she was suing for."

"Were you still in Cincinnati when she died?"

"No, why?"

"Curious."

"Oh, I see where you're trying to go with that. But, no, I was here in Santa Fe."

"So, your assistant in Cincinnati dies in an auto accident. And your assistant here dies under suspicious circumstances."

Earl Woods interjected, "The world is full of coincidental occurrences, but that is no reason to implicate Jason as a sex offender or murderer. He's a professional who made a mistake fifteen years ago. His record both before and after that incident has been spotless."

"For the record, Jason, are you saying you did not have a sexual relationship with Gwen Willington?"

"Absolutely true. Never."

"Have you had a sexual relationship with any other Bend employee?"

"No!"

"Do you obsess over women?"

"Don't answer that, Jason."

"Simple question, counselor. I'd like to know if he obsessed over Emily Coburn, Carrie Kirkland, or Angela Foster."

"No, I do not obsess over women."

"Would you have any reason to frame John Grainger for the murder of Holly Paine?"

"What are you talking about?"

"John Grainger has been implicated in the death of Holly Paine, but he believes he's been framed."

"Are you kidding me? No! Why would I try to frame him for anything?"

"To get the job of Operations Vice President."

"Why would you think that?"

"Because a week ago you told me how much you wanted that job. And you felt you should have gotten it instead of Grainger."

"I wanted that job. I still do. I deserved it for all the time I put into that place. It's not Grainger who made the Bend what it is today, but he always gets the credit. I may have wanted his job, but I don't want it so bad that I would kill someone and frame John to get it. That's crazy. Even if he got fired there would be no guarantee they would promote me to that job. As it is, they gave the job to Simon Learner anyway."

"Yes, they did, but on an interim basis. Simon told me they would probably consider you for the job. Did you know that?"

"No, I didn't." Jason appeared genuinely stunned that he was being considered for the Vice Presidency. "No one's told me that."

"Speaking of Simon, that reminds me. There was an incident at a recent employee party at Mr. Grainger's house where Simon's date, Liza Williams, tripped and fell into Grainger's pool."

"I remember that. So?"

"I hear you tripped her—perhaps intentionally?"

"Oh, my God. I tripped *her*? Who told you that? Simon? She's the one who tripped over me. I did nothing intentional to make her fall into the pool. The whole thing was an accident."

Woods asked, "What does this have to do with anything?"

"Just curious about it. I understand, Jason, your wife tended to Liza afterward to help her get dried off."

"That's right."

"Did you trip Liza to create a diversion?"

"A diversion?"

"He's not going to answer that, Detective. The interview's over."

"Jason, I'd like to speak to your wife. Are you okay with that?"

Jason hesitated before answering. "Sure. Why not? I have nothing to hide."

CHAPTER 43

Clay visited the Sage Mesa High School where Jason Alvarez's wife worked. The school principal pulled her from her class, and she met with Clay in an empty office.

Rebecca Harris was a tall woman with a wide bottom. Her wattle neck and stern demeanor contributed to her overall unattractive look. She looked years older than her husband, thanks to her salt-and-pepper gray hair pulled taut in a bun. Speaking gruffly, she said, "This had better be important to pull me out of my class."

Clay explained he was the lead investigator on the serial murders that involved female employees at the Bend. "Of course I've spoken to your husband, as HR Director there, but I've also learned about his previous employment at J. J. Nephew in Cincinnati. He told me what happened there, but I'd like you to confirm some of the elements of his account."

"Like I said, this had better be important."

Clay disregarded her comment. "If you've been keeping up with the news, you probably know that we recently found the remains of one woman who was a former employee of your husband's—Gwen Willington. Did you know her?"

"Yes, I knew Gwen from when she worked for my husband. She was a sweet girl. I did read about her and the other girls who were murdered. What does that have to do with Jason?"

"I questioned him about the nature of any relationship he might have had with Ms. Willington such as he had with his employee at J. J. Nephew, Tracey Linville. He told me you were aware of his affair and the fact that it led to a sexual harassment suit being filed against him."

"Yes, I know about it."

"Did you know the woman in question?"

"Tracey Linville? Yes. I met her several times."

"What can you tell me about her?"

"I remember she wore skirts much too short for an office workplace. And she wore a cheap perfume that smelled like baby powder and trailed her everywhere she went like a room deodorizer."

"Did Jason confess to his affair with her?"

"Not at first. But he didn't have to. I was pretty sure he was seeing someone, and I figured it was her. He's not the best liar in the world."

"What do you mean by that?"

She exhaled with a loud *hmph*. "Just what I said. He's not a good liar. He would be on the phone with her and hang up abruptly when I walked into the room. And when he started working longer hours than normal, he would come home with that baby powder smell all over him. And you know how naïve he is? He didn't realize I knew. When I told him he smelled of her, he said he couldn't help but have that smell on him since he worked closely with her. He flat out lied and expected me to believe it. But I knew. There were so many hints."

"So, Mrs. Alvarez—"

"My name is *Harris*," she said. "Rebecca *Harris*—not Alvarez."

"Oh, of course. I'm sorry. So, Jason said Tracey called you about their affair."

"That's right. I remember I had to hold the phone away from my ear she was so loud and crass. She called Jason every name in the book. Told me they had been having an affair and that he forced her into having sex. She said he promised he was going to leave me and marry her, and that he would protect her from being laid off if they had sex. I listened to her rant and then I hung up on her. She called back but I didn't answer. You know, she never even told me who she was, but I knew. I swear I could smell her perfume through the phone line the whole time she was screaming about Jason."

Clay tried to show empathy. "Not a pleasant call, huh."

"Hardly. I told Jason about it when he came home that night. He denied everything at first, but the truth is, I almost didn't care." Rebecca was matter-of-fact about Jason's denial.

"Why not?"

"Probably more than you care to know, but I don't mind telling you we don't exactly have the best sex life. I used to tell him that if he met someone who could satisfy him, it was okay for him to go for it."

"You gave him the okay to be with other women?"

"In a way. But you know what really ticked me off about that—pardon my French—that *bitch* Linville, was that she sued him. A sexual harassment suit would become public knowledge and I had my reputation to protect. No, I wasn't happy about that."

"What happened?"

"Nothing, really. Jason finally admitted to the affair. He explained what happened and said she came on to him first. I told him to find a way to get himself out of the mess he was in, and that was that."

"So, then, Tracey filed a grievance against him, which is when he got an offer to work for the Indian Bend. Is that true?"

"Yes."

"What happened to her?"

"The company went bankrupt and she lost her job. A month later she died in an auto accident when she was under the influence of some drug or other."

"What happened to her suit against Jason and the company?"

"It was dropped. The union tried to litigate it on her behalf, but it just died a natural death because J. J. Nephew filed bankruptcy."

"I'm curious about one thing."

"What's that?"

"Do you recall where your husband was when Tracy was killed in that accident?"

Rebecca tilted her head and looked at Clay. She was not happy with his implication, and shot back, "He was in Santa Fe, starting his new job—over a thousand miles from Cincinnati."

"And you?"

"Oh, now I'm a suspect too?"

"No. I just want to know where you were when Tracey Linville was killed."

"Maybe I don't want to answer that."

"You don't have to if you think it will be self-incriminating. But I can publicly identify you as a person of interest if that's what you prefer."

Rebecca thought twice about not answering Clay's question. "No need to. I was in Cincinnati when I learned she had died. I was trying to sell our house and clean up things there."

"A minute ago you said you told Jason he could have sex with any woman who would want him. Has he had any affairs since he began working at the Bend? In particular, with Gwen Willington?"

"Gwen Willington! Ha! You've got to be kidding me. She was a beautiful girl. There's no way she would have had an affair with Jason. That would be like the eighth wonder of the world. First off, she would have had no reason at all to have an affair with him—she would have been able to pick and choose anyone—and it certainly wouldn't have been my husband."

"Did Jason have an affair with any other woman that you know of?"

"I don't think so, but I don't know for sure. He still works long hours, so, maybe, yes, I don't know. I guess I don't really care."

"Anyone you can think of in particular?"

"Nope. I wouldn't have a clue."

"Mrs. Harris—"

"It's *Ms.* Harris."

"Sorry, again. Several weeks ago, Ms. Harris, you and Jason were at a party at John Grainger's house."

"Yes. What about it?"

Clay exaggerated the event. "I was told an incident occurred where Jason threw Simon Learner's girlfriend into the pool. You know Simon, don't you?"

"Yes, I know Simon, and Jason did no such thing," she barked. "Who told you he threw her into the pool? The girl fell in after tripping over Jason's foot as she tried to step past him near the edge of the pool. At first we thought she had too much to drink, but she's probably just clumsy."

"What happened after she fell in?"

"Simon helped her out. She was wet from the waist down, so I took her into John Grainger's bedroom and helped her change into some dry clothes. Jason immediately apologized to the girl, to Simon, and to John. But he didn't trip her on purpose. I saw the whole thing. It was all just an accident. Period. We left the party early because Jason was so embarrassed."

"One last question. Has Jason ever mentioned a guy by the name of Denver Stennet?"

"Sounds familiar, but I can't say for sure."

CHAPTER 44

Denver Stennet was stretched out on his couch watching late-night TV. He was well on his way to finishing off his second six-pack of beer when he heard a knock on his door.

"Who is it?"

There was no response.

"What the hell—"

He set his bottle of beer on the coffee table and went to the door. Through the peephole he saw a bearded man in a baseball cap pulled low over his forehead.

"It's one o'clock in the morning. Whaddaya want?"

"I want to talk to you."

"What about?"

"I'd rather not say from out in the hallway. Can I come in for a second?"

"No. I don't know who the hell you are."

"I'm a friend of Carrie Kirkland's. I need to talk with you. She left some money that I'm supposed to give you."

"What are you talking about? What money?"

"You know, the Grainger deal? Do I have to spell it out for you?"

"Grainger? It's been two years. Why now?"

"If you let me in I'll explain."

Stennet's beer-addled brain was piqued about the money. "Just slide the money under the door," he said.

"I'd be here all night to put this much under the door."

"How much do you have?"

"Hey, listen pal, if you don't want the money I'll just hang on to it for myself. Yes, or no? I'm out of here in, like, five seconds if you don't open the door."

Shit, Stennet said to himself, and opened the door.

310

The man walked in carrying a small black case.

"So, who are you?"

"That's not important. The money is."

Stennet eyed the case. "Is it the money Carrie got from Grainger?"

"Yes."

"I wondered whatever happened to it. I wasn't sure she ever got it. Why am I getting it now? And who the hell are you?"

"Whoa, slow down. You ask a lot of questions."

"You know, I don't really give a shit who you are. Give me the money and adiós yourself outta here."

"I'll tell you what. How about you get me a beer and I give you the money and tell you all about what went down? Deal?"

Stennet puffed out his chest. "I told Carrie it would work. I can't believe the asshole couldn't tell she was sixteen. That's because he used his pecker for brains."

"Yeah, well, guess what. She looked older than sixteen. Her plan worked pretty good, didn't it. It's making you a pile of money."

"It was my plan, not hers."

"Whatever. Do you know the police think you're the guy who killed her?"

"Yeah, but I don't give a rat's ass what they think."

CHAPTER 45

Chief Johnstone called Clay. "Denver Stennet committed suicide."

"No! How?"

"He shot himself."

"Where did you find him?"

"Near where we found the remains of those three women on the reservation. He left a note confessing to all the serial murders."

* * *

Clay pulled up to the crime scene followed by Forensics and the Medical Examiner. Yellow crime scene tape cordoned off a van he presumed was Stennet's work van. It was labeled Desert Breeze Electric Company and painted with a gold and blue desert scene on either side. Twenty yards away Bret Colby sat on the bumper of Jacoby's SUV. Bret's mountain bike was propped against the side of the vehicle and his helmet hung from the handle bars.

Clay spoke quietly to Jacoby. "Why is he here?"

"He found the van and called me."

"You have got to be kidding me. Another crime scene and he's the first to discover it?"

"I told him you would want to talk to him."

"You know, Chief, this is the third time he's come across a crime scene. The third damn time. This can't be just coincidence."

"I know. I agree."

"Where's Stennet?"

"In the van."

"Let me check that out before we talk to Colby." Clay opened the driver's door. Stennet was dead in the passenger seat, his mouth open, and his chin resting on his chest. He held a .38-caliber revolver in his left hand. Clay unlocked the passenger door to allow the Medical Examiner to get a closer look at the body.

After a cursory exam, Doctor Safford said, "I'd say he's been dead eight to twelve hours. He appears to have been killed by a self-inflicted gunshot wound, but I'd have to get him on the table to know for sure."

Jacoby stood alongside Clay and provided additional details. "I have a typed suicide note, Clay, admitting to all the serial murders. It's bagged and in my car."

"What else?"

"We found a ski mask, a couple of vinyl gloves, and a fake cop badge in the glove compartment. It could be the same badge worn by the guy who abducted Angela Foster."

"Everything seems cut and dry, huh," Clay remarked.

"It sure seems that way. Evidence in the van and the suicide note point to this guy being responsible for all the killings."

"It does, Jacoby. But I'm thinking this is almost *too* cut and dry. Let's talk to Bret."

The two cops approached Bret.

"I see how you're both looking at me. I know you suspect I had something to do with this. When I found that guy dead in the truck, I thought, man, here we go again. They're never going to believe me. Let me get the hell out of here and let someone else find him. I ain't no cop, so it's none of my business. I started to ride back to the pueblo, but then thought it wasn't right to just leave this guy out here. Who knows how long it'd be till someone found him. So I rode back here to the van, and that's when I called the chief."

Neither Clay nor Jacoby acknowledged Bret's comments. "Tell us how you first discovered him."

"Like I already told Chief Johnstone, I was out for a morning ride when I saw the van in the distance. It got me curious. I've seen four-by-fours and ATVs out here—you know, off-road vehicles—but never a van. When I got close enough my first thought was that someone was screwing off from his job at Desert Breeze."

Clay asked, "Why would you think that? If someone was going to screw off, why would they do it in the middle of the desert?"

"I thought the same thing. I couldn't imagine why the driver would do that and risk getting stuck in the sand. I mean, the sand out here is pretty hard, but there are some soft spots, too. Then I remembered the newspaper reports of the killings and thought maybe it was someone who wanted to see for himself where they happened. You know, like a gawker at a traffic accident. Anyway, I rode my bike in a wide circle around the van and then approached from the front so the guy would see me coming."

"Show us what you mean, Bret."

Bret pointed to the route he took. "There. I don't think you can see my tire tracks, but that's where I came around."

Clay remained suspicious. "Didn't you worry that maybe he was the guy who killed those three girls from the Bend and you could have been in danger yourself?"

"Honestly? No. Call me stupid, but I didn't."

Clay shook his head. "Okay, go ahead. What did you do next?"

"When I rode closer to the van I saw someone in the passenger seat. I thought the guy was taking a siesta, you know? He looked like he was asleep. I yelled out to him, but he didn't answer. So I pulled alongside the van and knocked on his window. I looked in, but really couldn't see much because of the sun reflecting on the glass. But the guy never moved. I asked if he was okay, but he didn't answer. I could see his door was locked so I went around to the driver's side. When I opened the door, I saw he had a revolver in his hand and a bullet wound to the left side of his head. I could tell by his color that he was probably dead."

"Did you touch anything inside the van?"

"No, sir. I don't think I did."

"You didn't pick up the suicide note?"

"No. As soon as I realized he was dead, I closed the door."

"What did you do then?"

"Then I left and started to ride back to the pueblo."

"But didn't you say you came back?"

"Yeah, I didn't want to leave him out here. It wouldn't have been right.

"And that's when you called Chief Johnstone?"

"Yeah."

Clay trained his eyes on Bret to see if he displayed the traits of someone who's lying, but saw none. "Okay, Bret. Wait here. We'll want you to give us another statement and, of course, keep all this to yourself. You understand, right?"

"Yessir. I know exactly what you mean. I'm not gonna talk to that reporter. I promise."

Clay went to Jacoby's SUV to see Stennet's suicide note. *I confess I killed those three girls from the Bend. And Jack Youngblood too. And I shot that Shiloh kid and his mother and then I tried to kill Angela because she was cheating on me with that Grainger guy. This is the only way I can stop killing. Sorry."*

Clay turned the note over to see if anything was typed on the back side. "That's it? That's his suicide note? It doesn't make sense."

"What do you mean, it doesn't make sense?" Jacoby asked.

"Stennet was a cocky, obnoxious son of a bitch. This note doesn't sound like anything he would write. We'll have to see what the ME says, but I think we're looking at a murder, not a suicide."

"You think?"

"Yeah. I mean, look, Stennet says he's *sorry*. That's bullshit! He probably never said the word *sorry* in his whole life. And the note itself? I bet there aren't any fingerprints on it. I think someone else typed this, so we wouldn't be able to check the handwriting. And then they killed Stennet and staged the scene to look like a suicide—the revolver, the badge, the ski mask, the whole nine yards."

"But, Clay, if it was murder, the killer would have had to drive the van out here, then walk back to 14."

Clay thought about Jacoby's observation. "You're right. And if he did, someone would have had to pick him up there. Or another vehicle followed him out here to pick him up and they headed back to 14 together."

"If someone drove here to pick him up, there would be another set of tire tracks. We haven't seen any sign of that."

"Either way, that means there's probably more than one person involved in this."

"I think it's more likely the guy walked back to 14.

"I agree. Let's have your men search for tracks leading back that way."

Jacoby ordered his men to spread out and walk toward the roadway in search of footprints.

In less than five minutes, one of the cops shouted, "I've got something here."

"Whaddaya have?" Jacoby asked.

"A partial. Looks like someone was sweeping his footprints away as he headed toward 14, but he missed this one."

Clay stood looking out across the wide desert. "Jacoby, do you remember Shiloh telling us he thought there might have been a second person in the truck the night he was out here with Angela Foster?"

"I do."

"Well, this just might prove he was right about that. Let's head over to Stennet's apartment to see what we can find there."

CHAPTER 46

The next morning, Captain Ellsworth convened a meeting of the Serial Killer Task Force. Clay Bryce, ADA Hank Kincaid, Chief Johnstone, and Special Agent Mark Stephenson listened first to Dan Carton's forensic report and then to Aaron Safford's autopsy findings.

Carton reported finding Stennet's fingerprints in the Desert Breeze van and on the .38, but not on the suicide note or fake police badge that was found in the glove compartment. "Clay also asked me to check the Stennet suicide note against the note James Donovan left for his apartment manager. I've concluded the two notes came from the same printer."

"Dan, what about the partial footprint we found at the crime scene leading to Route 14?" Jacoby asked.

Carton leafed through his notes. "It was a size-ten print. We couldn't match it against the prints found at Angela Foster's crime scene, but it was the same size shoe or boot so it may have been made by the same guy wearing different shoes."

Clay added, "When we examined the suicide scene, the chief and I concluded that if, in fact, Stennet was murdered, there were probably two people involved. Our conclusion was based on the fact that someone had to pick up the driver of the van after he left Stennet in the desert."

"And the footprint Dan just described supports that theory," Chief Johnstone said.

Kincaid asked, "So now we're looking for two killers, not one?"

"That's our belief," Clay observed.

Stephenson commented on the possibility of two killers. "Usually, one offender acts alone, but it's not uncommon for two or more people to team up in serial killings. Understand,

I'm not referring to terrorist organizations, but individuals who join together for some other motive."

Captain Ellsworth jumped in. "Before we get too engrossed in the psychology of all this, let's hear what Doctor Safford has to say."

The ME explained his conclusions. "Stennet's death initially appeared to be a suicide, but the autopsy turned up traces of ketamine in his blood—a slight amount, but enough to incapacitate him."

"Isn't that the same drug found in Foster's system?"

"Yes. And because of that similarity, I'm calling Stennet's death a probable homicide."

Clay said, "Here's what we've got. I agree with the ME that Stennet's death was not a suicide. A search of Stennet's apartment turned up two six-pack beer carriers but only eleven empty bottles. I don't think this scenario is a stretch. I believe Stennet knew the killer or killers and allowed one or both of them into his apartment. They spiked his beer with ketamine, which incapacitated him. Then they drove him out to the desert where they shot him with the .38, and put the gun in his hand, to stage the scene like a suicide."

"So you think the killers took the bottle that had the ketamine in it—bottle number twelve?"

"Yes. But the search of the van turned up nothing. I have to believe the killer disposed of that bottle so we wouldn't be able to test it for the drug."

Captain Ellsworth said, "So, this charade of a suicide means they're obviously trying to shake us off. They must feel we're getting close to finding out who they are."

"Exactly," Clay concurred.

"So, if we assume Clay's assumption is correct," Ellsworth continued, "let me ask you all a question. What if we take the killers' bait and announce to the press that Stennet confessed in writing to the serial killings and then committed suicide? What would the killers do after that?"

"There is no certainty what they'll do," Agent Stephenson said. "I don't think they're through killing. They may be on pause. That's part of the erratic pattern of serial killers. They could murder again whenever the urge grips them. These people are not spree killers who kill multiple people in a short period of time. This case demonstrates that months or even years can pass between murders. We really have no way of knowing when they will kill again."

Chief Johnstone asked, "Bottom line, what do we do? Do we publicize the fact we know Stennet was murdered and continue our investigation, or do we play along and announce he committed suicide?"

ADA Kincaid voiced his opinion. "From what Special Agent Stephenson is saying, we can expect the serials are going to kill again, but it could be quite a while from now—maybe years before they kill again. If we play along and announce Stennet's death was a suicide, it may keep them from killing again in the short run. They could go undercover, and leave this case unresolved for who knows how long until they strike again. However, if we announce we know Stennet was murdered, it might bring them out in the open now, and just maybe they'll screw up somehow. I get the sense they think they're smarter than we are. The suicide ploy makes them believe they can manipulate us any way they like. Bottom line, to answer your question, Chief, I suggest we announce Stennet was murdered.

Let's bring these bastards out in the open, and hope it's just a matter of time before they screw up."

No one disagreed with Kincaid, although Clay was concerned. "I agree with Hank. But no matter what we do, we've got to nail these bastards sooner versus later. I'd hate to think we announce Stennet's murder and that causes the killers to rage even more."

"I agree there's risk in whatever we do," Ellsworth announced. "But since everyone is in agreement, I'll schedule a news conference to report Stennet's death as a murder."

CHAPTER 47

SUSPECT IN DESERT MURDERS KILLED

There has been yet another murder in a growing series of murders involving the Indian Bend Hotel and Casino. Denver Stennet, 31, of Santa Fe, was killed overnight Tuesday. His body was found Wednesday morning on the Yiqua reservation. Stennet was considered a suspect in a string of murders that have come to light over the last six and a half weeks.

Police found a suicide note in which Stennet allegedly confessed to the murders. Captain Matthew Ellsworth of the Santa Fe Police Department informed the press that, although Stennet's death was staged to look like a suicide, the Santa Fe Medical Examiner declared his death a homicide.

There appears to be no end to the killings, most of which involve employees or former employees of the Bend. Since Stennet went from suspect to victim, we must ask if our police department will ever be able to solve these heinous crimes. Given that the police are so misdirected, unskilled, and ill-equipped to deal with this investigation, perhaps our mayor should appoint a new task force to take the lead in the investigation. - Steven Brown

With Denver Stennet murdered, Clay was left with two suspects—John Grainger, who had the motives to kill the women from the Bend, and was the most likely suspect, and James Donovan, who no one had heard from or seen for two years.

Clay had built a circumstantial case against Grainger, but he didn't feel good about it. Grainger could not have been

322

stupid enough to leave his business card at Holly Paine's apartment. And it was conceivable Grainger had been set up by Denver Stennet to be blackmailed by the sixteen-year-old Carrie Kirkland. The case against Grainger as a prime murder suspect was all too neat and clean.

On Sunday morning Clay drove the short distance from the police department on Lincoln Street to Grainger's luxury home on the outskirts of Santa Fe. He rang the doorbell and stepped back so Grainger's security cameras would capture his image.

Grainger opened the door within seconds. "Yes? What?"

"Can I come in? I'd like to talk to you."

"Not without my lawyer."

"Look, I don't feel good about the way this is going down. I have a gut feeling you could be right about someone trying to frame you."

Grainger stared at Clay trying to discern his motives. "Why do you feel that way now, after you've brutalized me?"

"I know we haven't seen eye to eye on most stuff."

"Like from the beginning."

"I've just been doing my job. All I can tell you now is that something doesn't feel right. I'd like to talk with you to see if we can come up with someone who would want to frame you."

"I don't think so. I don't trust you in the slightest. You've cost me my job, my reputation—my life."

"I get it, Grainger. I get it. I understand you don't trust me. I understand you're pissed. But the way I look at it, you have nothing to lose by talking to me. You're in deep shit now and you know it. If you don't talk to me, I'll just continue to build my case against you for murder."

"And if we do talk?"

"I promise that whatever you say is strictly off the record unless it helps prove your innocence. It's your choice. If you feel I'm stepping out of bounds at any time, call your lawyer or kick me the hell out of your house."

Grainger was not convinced. "What do we talk about— Holly Paine's murder or the Carrie Kirkland rape charge?"

"Both. They may be related."

Grainger was dressed casually and had a day-old beard that showed streaks of gray. He looked older than when he was clean shaven and dressed in his custom-made suits and Italian shoes. Though still reluctant, he finally agreed to let Clay in. "All right. Let's see where this leads."

Clay was impressed by the home's luxuriousness, the high-beamed ceilings and expensive artwork covering every wall throughout. "You have a beautiful house."

"Thanks." Grainger was wary of the compliment, still uncertain of Clay's intent. "We can sit out back. Can I get you something? Consuela—my housekeeper—is off today but I can get you whatever you like."

"No, thanks. I'm good."

Clay followed Grainger through a spacious, open kitchen, and stepped out through the open slider to the backyard, where beautifully maintained gardens surrounded an infinity pool.

"Looks like you've done all right for yourself."

"I can't complain. But I've worked my ass off to get all this."

Clay noticed a copy of the *Times Journal* on the patio table open to Steven Brown's column. "That reporter has been having a field day, hasn't he—with you and me both."

"Yeah. He's made me out to be a sexual predator. But, then, so have you."

"Listen, Grainger, all I'm doing is my job. I let the facts sort themselves out. I believed you when you said you didn't know Carrie was sixteen. But she *was* sixteen and you had sex with her. What do you want me to do? Sugarcoat it?"

Grainger shook his head and didn't respond.

"I'll say this again. Nothing you tell me will be used against you. This is strictly off the record. Let's start with Holly Paine. I'll ask you one more time how you think your shirt and trousers could have gotten into her apartment. Help me out. You said you were never there. I want to believe you. So who could have put your clothes there?"

Grainger stared straight ahead for a moment before answering, "I've been thinking about that since you first told me about finding the clothes. Whoever put them there had to have taken them from my closet. I've never left my clothes at anyone's house."

"I see you have a security system in place here. Do you use it?"

"Yes, religiously."

"Like when?"

"At night when I go to bed, when I leave the house, even for a short trip."

"Not during the day when you're here?"

"Not normally."

"Is it possible someone could come in when you're out back here, steal something, and be gone before you would notice?"

"Yeah, anything is possible. But my doors and windows chime to alert me when they're opened, so I would have heard."

"Could any of your lady friends have taken them and tried to frame you because you pissed them off somehow?"

"I don't think so. My *lady friends*, as you call them, are not going to slink out carrying my clothes with them. A little too obvious, don't you think?"

"What about when you have your buddies over for a beer or when you have people over for a party like the party for your employees last month?"

"What are you saying?"

"Could someone have taken your clothes then?"

Grainger replayed mental images of recent events he'd held in his house and concluded, "Yeah, it's possible."

"Could you name everyone who has been in your house— for any reason whatsoever—over the past two, three months?"

"Yes, I can put together a list. But understand, I told you the other day, I'm not giving you the names of certain women."

"Look, Grainger, you're a suspect in one murder case and a person of interest in at least three others. I understand you want to protect certain people, but you're not doing yourself any favor by withholding information."

Grainger knew Clay was right, but he still wanted Clay's full assurance. "I'll give you a complete list, but with the understanding that, for some of the women named, you will speak only to them and not involve their husbands."

"Okay, I can promise that. But you need to include everyone who's been here, whether for a drink, a poker game, or a party, and anyone else with access to your house, including service people like plumbers, air conditioning people—everyone."

"Give me until tomorrow."

"Okay. I'll be back tomorrow to see what you've come up with."

CHAPTER 48

Consuela greeted Clay at John Grainger's front door the next day. She spoke little English, but comprehended Clay's request to see her boss. "Sí, sí," she said, and beckoned Clay in. She led him through the house to the patio where Grainger was reviewing the list of names he had prepared for Clay.

"Looks like you've worked up more than one list," Clay said.

"Yeah. I have everyone who's been here over the past couple of months, broken down in three different groups." He handed Clay the first list. "This one includes the names and phone numbers of the women who have been here." Clay scanned the list. He did not recognize any of the women named, but he planned to discreetly interview each one.

"And the next list?"

"That includes men and women from the Bend who were at my party last month." Clay recognized a number of the names—Hope Archer, Simon Learner, Liza Williams, Jason Alvarez, and Jason's wife, Rebecca Harris.

"Hope told me she was here," Clay commented.

"Yes, she was. And did she tell you it was a typical employee cocktail party—the kind no one wants to go to—everybody pretending they're having a good time while they're here, but as soon as they get in their cars to head home, they all bitch about having to be here?"

"No, she didn't tell me that," he lied, "but she told me there was a little excitement—something about Simon's date falling into the pool."

"Liza, yes. Poor girl."

"Anything that stands out about that incident?"

"No, not really." Grainger was clearly sympathetic to Liza's embarrassment. "I thought she had had too much to drink, but it turns out she doesn't drink at all and was sipping ginger ale all night. She said she tripped over Jason Alvarez's foot."

"Do you think he tripped her on purpose?"

"I couldn't tell you that. At first, I thought she jumped into the pool. You know, to liven things up and get everyone to jump in with her—clothes and all. You know, sometimes you see that in raucous scenes in the movies. But that's not what happened. When Simon pulled her out of the pool, she was in tears. Rebecca—Jason's wife—took her into my bedroom to tend to her. She ran Liza's dress through the clothes dryer and got her looking presentable."

"Could that have been an opportunity for someone, say, Rebecca, or even Liza, to steal your shirt and pants?"

"You mean that Liza fell into the pool on purpose or was tripped by Jason intentionally as a diversion?"

"Yes, something like that."

"I guess that's possible. But I didn't see anyone wearing my shirt under their cocktail dress or stuffing it into their purse, if you know what I mean. So, no, I don't think her falling into the pool was a diversion of any kind for anyone."

"And the party went on."

"Yes. Jason apologized to Liza profusely. He felt so bad about what happened that he and Rebecca left the party early. But then the next day—it was Sunday—Simon called to ask if he and Liza could come back over."

"Why?"

"Liza wanted to dunk her dress in the pool. Since she was in the water only up to her waist, the bottom half of her dress was bleached from the chlorine. She thought if she put the entire dress in the pool it would bleach evenly."

"You're kidding me. She really thought that was going to work?"

"Yes, she did. I thought she was joking. I told her I would buy her a new outfit instead. But she said that was her favorite dress and she wanted to see if she could save it. So she and Simon came back Sunday."

"Did Simon stay with Liza while she was dunking her dress in the pool?"

"I guess so, but I don't remember."

"Curious, how does Simon get along with Jason?"

"I think okay."

"How about you? How do you and Jason get along?"

"Fine, as far as I can tell."

Clay wanted to better understand the history of their relationship. "I understand five years ago the two of you were vying for the Operations VP job. Is that true?"

"Yes. Frankly, I thought Jason was going to get the job. I think everyone did. Jason actually hired me fifteen years ago, and did a hell of a job getting everyone in place when the Bend first opened. As successful as he was, I think everyone was shocked he was passed over. I mean, *he* hired *me*. I'm sure he was disappointed at the time. Initially things were awkward between us, but as far as I'm concerned today, we get along fine. You'd have to ask him if he feels the same."

"I will."

Grainger's third list included service companies. He listed Consuela, a swimming pool company, a landscaper, and the Desert Breeze Electric Company.

"Why was Desert Breeze here?

"The night of my party, Jason backed over a light bollard in my driveway as he tried to get around a car that was parked in front of his. The cars were packed in pretty tight. He came back into the house to tell me about the bollard and said he would send an electrician over to repair it."

"Jason arranged for it?"

"Yes."

"Do you know the name of the electrician who was here from Desert Breeze?"

"You'd have to ask Consuela."

"I assume she's the only one from your list who has regular access to the inside of your house."

"That's correct. There's no reason why anyone else would need to get in. Consuela has been with me for five years and is like family to me. She has my security access code, and I trust her implicitly. You're welcome to talk with her any time."

"Were you at home when the electrician showed up?"

"I was, but I was out back here, working on my laptop."

"So you wouldn't recognize the guy if I showed you a photo?"

"No, Consuela dealt with him."

"Would you ask her if the electrician came into the house?"

Grainger called for her. "Consuela, cuando vino el electricista el mes pasado, ¿entró él en la casa?"

Consuela nodded. "Sí, señor. Tuvo que apagar la unidad para reemplazar el bolardo."

"Yes, he had to get to the electrical panel to turn off the electricity while he fixed the bollard."

"Where's the panel located?"

"In my bedroom closet. What are you thinking—that he's the guy who stole my shirt and trousers?"

"Could be. Hold on. I'll be right back. I want Consuela to look at the photos."

Clay retrieved the photos from his car and went back to the patio where he spread them on the table. Among them was one of Denver Stennet. "Ask Consuela if she recognizes any of these as the electrician who worked in your house."

"Consuela, ¿fue uno de estos hombres el electricista que vino a la casa?"

She pointed to the photo of Denver Stennet. "Este hombre."

"Are you sure?"

"Sí, señor."

"That's Denver Stennet, one of my murder suspects. I should say, *was* one of my suspects. He's the guy they found dead in the desert a couple of days ago."

"You're kidding. Damn. The same guy? What does that mean?"

"Not sure yet. What date would he have been here to replace the bollard?"

"It was the Monday after my party. The party was last month on Saturday the fifth, so it had to be the seventh."

Clay pulled out his cell phone and looked up the phone number for Desert Breeze Electric Company. He dialed the number and asked for the service department.

"Service. Judy speaking."

"Judy, I'm Detective Clay Bryce of the Santa Fe Police Department calling on official business."

"What can I help you with, Detective Bryce?"

"We think one of your electricians, Denver Stennet, worked at the home of a John Grainger last month—on the seventh. Can you tell me the circumstances as to why he was sent on that job? Did someone ask for him specifically?"

"Detective, Denver is dead."

"I know that. But I need to know if he was assigned to do work at John Grainger's house on the seventh of last month."

"One moment."

Clay listened as she typed into her computer. "Yes, I'm showing he was sent to John Grainger's house that afternoon to repair a driveway bollard light."

"You can definitely confirm it was Denver Stennet?"

"Positive. My records show that a Jason Alvarez called and asked specifically for Denver to be sent to the Grainger residence."

Clay thanked the woman and hung up. He explained the conversation to Grainger, who said, "That's strange, isn't it? Why Stennet specifically?"

"I'll have to ask Jason."

* * *

Clay's next call was to Jason Alvarez. "Jason, I understand you ran over a light bollard in John Grainger's driveway the night of his employee party."

"Yes, I did. I told John about it and asked one of our maintenance guys at the Bend to go over to repair it the following Monday. But John must have handled it, because later that afternoon, the maintenance man called me and said when he went out, the housekeeper told him someone from Desert Breeze had already been there to repair it.

CHAPTER 49

Seven weeks had passed since Angela was kidnapped and left to die in the desert, and three weeks since she and Shiloh were moved to the safe house. Physically, both were recovered from their injuries, but psychologically, Angela remained fragile. The shooting at St. Vincent's had set her recovery back.

Three times a week, Doctor Ariana Albright, a board-certified clinical psychologist, walked out the main entrance of St. Vincent's hospital, got into an unmarked police car, and was driven to the safe house where she continued Angela's counseling and therapy.

Today, the unmarked car had company. A pickup truck followed the car undetected the entire route. When the cop turned off Route 588 onto the unpaved road that led to the safe house, the driver of the tailing pickup sped on by, certain the cop had not spotted him. A half mile down the road, the pickup made a U-turn at a 7-Eleven convenience store and raced back to the remote dead-end road. Slowing at the entrance, the driver watched the unmarked car climb the long, steep road till it stopped, its brake lights illuminating bright red in the driveway of the last of the five houses on the road.

*   *   *

Doctor Albright and Angela sat in the privacy of the study for their therapy session. The gray-haired, middle-aged psychologist had a warm and empathetic manner. She recognized that Shiloh and Angela's affection for each other had been growing with each passing week. And more than that, she believed Shiloh's care and concern was central to Angela's recovery.

It was during this third week that Angela confessed to Albright she had fallen in love with Shiloh, but didn't know if Shiloh felt the same way. "There's only one way to know," the psychologist said. "Ask him."

"But what if he doesn't feel the same?"

"Then you'll know."

Angela was disappointed at the thought.

"At the sake of sounding schmaltzy, Angela, I've seen how the two of you are when you're together. You've been here for three weeks, and before that, he sat by your side at St. Vincent's for the better part of another three weeks—caring for you, supporting you... isn't that right?"

"Yes."

"Do you think your affection toward him is because he rescued you? Or do you feel genuine love for him—for what he is—not just because he saved you?"

"I've thought about that a lot. What I find most appealing about him is how very caring he is. We've talked so much about each other's lives—his growing up a Yiquan Indian, me being from Connecticut, how different our lives have been. But, somehow, our differences have made me feel that much more attracted to him. I don't think there's a thing he doesn't know about me and me about him. We know we're different in some ways and in other ways we're the same. But I don't know if that's good or bad."

Albright spoke in her soothing manner. "There's no magic formula for happiness. That's a truism. All you have to do is look at the fifty percent divorce rate to know there is no one answer for why people fall in and out of love. One couple whose traits are polar opposite of another's might be completely happy together, while another couple with those differences might be at each other's throats. There's no way to know."

"I was hoping you would tell me what I should do."

"Angela, I have seen you improve emotionally from your terrible ordeal, and in large measure I sense it's because of Shiloh."

"Well, you've helped too."

"Thank you. I hope I have. Think of me as an editor. I don't write the book, but I correct the author's errors and point him or her in the right direction. That's what I'm doing for you. You have to decide what your life would be like—with Shiloh... and without him. But the decision will be yours to make. I can't make it for you."

* * *

Doctor Albright left at the end of their session, and Angela remained in the study, thinking about everything the doctor had told her. After forty-five minutes, Shiloh knocked on the door. "Angela, are you okay?"

Angela said, "Can you come in for a minute. I'd like to talk to you."

Shiloh entered the room, uncertain what to expect. "What's the matter?" he asked.

"I'm nervous."

"About what?"

"About what I'm going to tell you."

"Don't be nervous. Just go ahead and tell me. What is it?"

"Nothing... I mean, I have a... I mean there is a problem... It may be just my problem... I don't know... Maybe it's not a problem." Angela was babbling.

"Whew," Shiloh said. He knew the best way to deal with something difficult was to face it head on. "Why not just tell me what's going on?"

She took a deep breath and blurted out, "It's about you and me. I talked with Doctor Albright and confessed to her that... well... I confessed I've... fallen in love with you."

Shiloh's head snapped back and he laughed out loud. "You confessed what?"

Angela was stunned and embarrassed. He was laughing at her. A rejection from Shiloh had been her biggest fear.

"I'm sorry. I didn't mean to... I shouldn't have told—"

Shiloh put his finger to her lips. "Shh. Listen to me, Angela. Do you remember I spoke separately with Doctor Albright the last time she was here?"

"Yes."

"I told her how I felt about you, but I was worried you didn't feel the same way or that I could upset you. She said I should tell you how I feel."

"That's exactly what she told me."

"Well, this is how I feel—I love you, too, Angela Foster."

* * *

Just after eleven, a pickup truck turned into the parking lot of the 7-Eleven store on Route 588. The driver parked off to the side, got out of his truck, and locked his doors. He waited until no one was around then walked into the desert toward the safe house under cover of a moonless sky. Fifteen minutes later, when he was at the rear of the house, he saw the shift cop on the patio having a smoke.

The driver dropped to the ground and watched. When the cop finished his smoke, he flipped his cigarette into the desert and went back into the house through the kitchen door.

The driver rose, put on a ski mask and took out his .45. He crept to the house and peeked through a side window to see the cop pour himself a cup of coffee.

Neither Shiloh nor Angela were visible—both were asleep in their bedrooms. The cop took his coffee into the living room and sat down on the sofa to read. He checked his watch. 11:30. The relief shift cop would be there in half an hour. The driver had to act quickly. He slowly opened the screen door to the kitchen. It creaked slightly. He held his breath. But the cop heard the sound. He drew his revolver and warily walked into the kitchen.

A shot rang out. The cop fell to the floor, wounded. Shiloh woke with a start and leaped out of bed. He grabbed his revolver from his bedside table, cracked open his bedroom door and saw the silhouette of the driver skulking toward him. "Angela, lock your door!" he shouted. "Don't come out!" Seconds later, he heard Angela's door latch.

Shiloh threw his bedroom door open and aimed his revolver at the man, but the man saw him and fired off two rounds first. Shiloh dropped to his haunches and returned fire. Neither man was hit, but the driver retreated and ran through the kitchen and out the screen door into the desert back to his pickup.

CHAPTER 50

Clay was awakened from a sound sleep by the harsh ring of his cell phone. He reached for it on his bedside table and saw the call was from Hope. It was 12:30. He imagined she was calling on her way home from work to whisper sweet good nights and say things that would make his night of sleep that much more pleasant. "Hi, sweetheart. What makes you—"

"Clay, help me!"

He threw the covers off and sat up on the side of the bed. "What's the matter?"

"I'm being followed."

"What?"

"There's a car following me. He's right behind me. I don't know what to do. Oh, my God, he turned on his flashers."

"Where are you?"

"On 14"

"Why are you out there?"

"25 is closed from an accident. I didn't have any choice."

"Hope, don't stop. Do not stop! Do you hear me?"

"He's closer now. I'm afraid it's that guy. But what if it's a cop?"

Clay suspected otherwise. "It's not a cop. Don't stop. Do you understand? Speed up. Try to make it to the city. Do not stop!"

"Oh, my God, he's trying to pull alongside me."

"Speed up! Don't let him catch up to you! Go faster!"

Suddenly he heard nothing.

"Hope! Hope! Are you okay?" he shouted repeatedly into the phone.

Nothing.

"Hope! Hope—"

"Clay, another car is driving toward me."

338

"Put your hazard lights on and flash your high beams, but don't stop!"

She didn't respond.

"Hope, talk to me!"

"Oh, thank God! The guy behind me slowed down. He's not behind me anymore. It looks like he pulled off the road. I think he stopped chasing me."

"Listen to me. I don't want you to slow down."

"Oh, Clay, I'm shaking. I think it's the same guy who killed my girls. He got so close I thought he was going to knock me off the road."

"You're gonna be okay."

Hope was sobbing into the phone. "What should I do?"

"Go to your condo. I'll meet you there. How far away are you?"

"I don't know—maybe ten minutes."

"Are there any other cars on the road?"

"A few. I see traffic building up ahead."

"If you're sure the guy has stopped following you, I want you to go straight to your condo and lock the door."

"There's no one behind me now."

"Good. Get to your condo and wait for me. I'll be right there. Do not open the door for anyone except me. Do you understand?"

"Okay, I won't."

"Even if you think it's a cop, don't open the door. Understand?"

"Yes."

Clay threw on some clothes and clipped his holstered service revolver onto his belt. He flew out the door, turned on his LED flashers, and raced off to Hope's. When he arrived, he spotted her BMW under a parking lot lamp and pulled up alongside it. He turned off his flashers and looked around the lot but didn't see anyone lurking. Hope's apartment was dark. He hurried up the steps, and when he reached her door, turned to scan the parking lot again but saw no one. He knocked.

"Who is it?"

He was elated to hear her voice. "It's me—Clay. Open up."

"Clay—"

"Yes, it's me. Open up."

The foyer light flicked on and the door swung open. Hope rushed into Clay's arms as he stepped into the foyer. She reached around him and pushed the door shut. "Hello, Detective Bryce." Her voice was calm and she nuzzled up to him.

Clay stepped back and held her by the elbows, bewildered by her behavior. "What's going on, Hope? Are you okay? You're acting strange."

"Aw, come on, Mr. Detective-man. Have a seat." She took him by the hand and walked him to the couch. "I have a surprise for you."

Clay was confused. "Was someone chasing you or not? Were you playing with me?"

"Hush up for a second, Clay. Now, come on. Sit down. I'll be right back."

"Hope, what the hell are you doing?"

"Stay right here. Promise?"

He sat down on the couch, still uncertain what to think.

She was insistent. "Promise?"

"Yeah, okay."

Hope went to her bedroom and sang out to him, "I've got a surprise."

Clay shook his head at her playfulness. On the one hand, he wasn't happy with her frantic call in the middle of the night, but on the other, he thought he knew how she was going to surprise him.

In a suggestive voice, she called out again, "I have something for you."

"Hope, it'd better be good after all this. You scared the hell out of me."

"Oh, it is. I know you'll agree."

Ten seconds later she reappeared in the living room wearing a black ski mask. She aimed a revolver directly at him with one hand, and held one of her cherished teddy bears in the other. Clay was speechless.

"Surprise!"

"What are you doing, Hope? This isn't funny. Don't point that gun at me." Clay had seen enough. He made a move to get up from the couch.

"Sit down!" Hope shouted. "I'll use this if you get up, and that's a promise."

Clay instinctively reached for his revolver.

She stopped him. "Pull out that gun and I'll have to shoot you." She glanced at her stuffed bear. "Right, Teddy? He should trust that I would shoot him, shouldn't he."

"Stop this shit, Hope. What's going on with you?"

She spoke first to her bear, then to Clay. "What's that, Teddy? Okay, that makes sense. Mr. Detective-man, Teddy wants you to do us a favor and pull your gun from your holster. Like right now. He said you should use only two fingers just like you see on TV. Got that?"

Clay didn't believe she was serious. "You are so funny. I'm not going to give you my weapon."

"Oh, yes you are. If you don't, I will have to kill you. Plain and simple. And then you'll never find out why I killed those girls from the Bend."

"You mean Emily and Carrie?"

"Ah huh. And Gwen. And Holly too."

Clay was incredulous. "But, why?"

"Well, Mr. Detective-man, after all your hard work, wouldn't it be a shame to never know why? Teddy thinks it would. That's why we need you to take your gun from your holster and put it on the floor."

Clay finally got it. He understood this was not a game. Something strange had gripped Hope. He heard it in her voice. She was angry, controlling, psychotic—and she spoke to a stuffed animal. He showed her his hand and slowly drew his gun out with his thumb and forefinger.

"Now put your gun on the floor and kick it over to me."

Clay did as he was told.

"Good boy, Mr. Detective-man. Now lean back and relax. Believe me—if you get up from that couch I will shoot you." She leaned the bear on the end table facing Clay. "Teddy, make sure he doesn't do anything stupid, okay?" She then reached down and picked up Clay's service revolver.

"Hope, you're wearing a ski mask and talking to a teddy bear."

"Yes, that's because Teddy's my best friend. I tell him all my secrets."

"So you were faking it on the phone about being chased by a cop car."

"Yes. I called from here. I was pretty good, huh?"

"I'll say. Very convincing."

She reached into her purse and pulled out another ski mask. She tossed it underhand to Clay. "Put this on when I tell you to."

Clay remembered Agent Stephenson's explanation why killers put ski masks on their victims. *She's going to rationalize she doesn't know me before she kills me.* He threw the mask onto the floor. "I'm not putting that on. You're planning to kill me, aren't you?"

"Yes."

"Why? I don't get why."

"Don't lie to me. You know why."

"Okay, then why?"

She peeled off her mask and placed it next to the teddy bear. "I realized that night at Le Chanticleer that you didn't love me, that you didn't have any intention of staying with me. You basically told me you were planning to leave me for Holly Paine, abandon me like all the other people in my life. Everyone ends up leaving me. It's so sad when people do that to other people."

"What are you talking about? Holly Paine? I wasn't going to leave you for her. How could I? She was already murdered. All I said was we shouldn't rush our relationship. That we should talk things out before I moved in with you. I never said I was going to leave you. I thought we had something special going on."

Blinking rapidly, she tilted her head first one way then the other. She waved her revolver recklessly toward Clay. "Everyone I've ever been close to in my life has left me. Even my adopted parents. Everyone. And then you planned to leave me too."

"You can't think that way. First off, your adopted parents didn't leave you on purpose. You said your mother died in an auto accident and your father died of a broken heart a year later."

"Oh, but they did leave me. Don't you see what I'm saying? I've been abandoned my whole life. Even the teddy bear my daddy gave me was taken from me."

"But, think about it. No one is going to take your bears away from you now."

Hope stared through Clay and echoed what he said. "No one is going to take my teddy bears away from me. Ever!"

Clay knew he had to play along if he was to get out of this alive. He had to stall her. Engage her. Find a window of opportunity that would allow him to reason through her psychosis. "How about this? How about I promise to never abandon you?"

"Too late Mr. Detective-man. It's too late. Fool me once, shame on you. Fool me twice, shame on me. John Grainger fooled me, oh, so many times, so I'm not going to let *you* fool me too."

"Is that what this is all about? You're pretending you're the serial killer so I'll move in with you? Come on. This isn't funny, Hope. Stop it, okay?" Again Clay started to get up from the couch. "I'll move in with you, if that's what you want."

"I said sit down!"

This was no prank. "You said you killed all those girls. Did you really?"

"Yes. Surprised?"

"But why?"

"You mean why did I kill all those whores from the Bend?"

Clay snapped back. "They weren't whores. You told me that yourself."

"Oh, I beg to differ. They were whores all right. It wasn't my fault, you know. I took care of them. I looked after them. I stood up for them. And what did they do? They turned around and stole the man I loved away from me."

"You mean John Grainger?"

"Yes. They… they tempted him and they had sex with him. I had to kill them so John would come back to me."

"You told me you didn't love John anymore. So you've been faking it the whole time you've been with me?"

"No, Mr. Detective-man," she cooed. "I wasn't faking it. I fell for you."

"Listen to me, Hope. I never said I was going to leave you. Not for Holly Paine—not for anyone. I just wanted to go slow."

"That's not how I remember it."

"It's my fault. I didn't do a good job explaining my feelings."

"Well, do you want to hear about those girls or not?"

"Yes. Of course I do."

"Okay. Where do you want me to start? How about with Emily Coburn? I told you I didn't remember her, but I lied. She was the first one to tempt John to stray from me, but I got even with her. I buried her in the desert. And the funny thing was, nobody even missed her. She just disappeared, and no one cared if she was alive or dead. That's what our world has come to. Isn't that sad, Teddy?"

Clay tried to reason with Hope. "But you know it wasn't Emily who tempted John—it was the other way around. He was the one who tried to have sex with her. She even filed a suit against him. John badgered her to have sex, but she wanted nothing to do with him."

Hope shrugged her shoulders. She was not contrite. "Yeah, I knew all about the harassment suit. Jason told me about it. But you have to understand, it really was Emily who tempted John—the way she strutted around him. He's a weak man when it comes to women. He couldn't help himself. I didn't blame him—I blamed her. She had to pay for leading him on. Period!"

"What about Carrie Kirkland?"

"Oh, she was something else, that little vixen. She was having sex with John and then she tried to blackmail him. He didn't know she was only sixteen. He really didn't. She looked and acted way older than that. I didn't know how old she was when I hired her. She even fooled Jason. Can you believe that? The head of HR and he was fooled too."

"What happened to Carrie?"

"Do you remember that argument your girlfriend Holly told you about—the one in the parking lot?"

"Yes, I remember, but I'll say it again, Holly was not my girlfriend."

"Yeah, whatever you say. So do you know who Carrie was arguing with?"

"Actually, I do. John."

"That's right. Afterward he called me and said he needed to see me. He came over here and told me what she said to him."

"Why would he call you? I thought you two weren't talking."

"Yes, but for some reason he trusted me."

"What did he tell you?"

"He said Carrie had sent him a note to meet her in the parking lot after her shift, and that's when she confessed she was only sixteen years old." Hope laughed. "Ha! Can you imagine how crazy John went? He told Carrie not to tell anyone. But the little whore said that if John didn't pay her to keep quiet, she was going to tell the police he had raped her."

"And?"

"And they argued. He told her he wasn't going to pay her anything, so she started to scream, and she yelled 'rape, rape.' John said he tried to quiet her but he couldn't. Finally, Jack Youngblood ran over to find out what was going on."

"So what then? John decided to pay her what she wanted if she left the Bend, right?"

"Yes, but he wanted me to give her the money."

"Why you?"

"I don't know. A year earlier, he had asked me to do the same for Emily, so I guess he thought he could trust me."

"Did he ask you to pay off Emily too?"

"Yes. He had to pay her or risk her suing him. I said I'd handle the money for him, but I knew I was going to make both those girls pay for what they did to him. They caused him to be unfaithful to me."

"Does John know you killed them?"

"No."

"He doesn't? You're telling me it wasn't his idea?"

"No, he had nothing to do with that. It was totally my idea."

"Has he said anything to you since we discovered they were buried in the desert?"

"No. Nothing. He's probably happy you found them."

"Why? So he wouldn't have to worry about the girls coming back and asking for more money?"

"Yes, probably."

"And what about Jack Youngblood? Did you kill him too? His death wasn't an accident, was it?"

"No, it wasn't." Hope became contrite. "I'm sorry. So sorry. Mr. Youngblood was such a nice man—a nice, nice man. He was just doing his job. But since he knew about Carrie... You know we didn't have any choice, did we Teddy?"

"So you ran him off the road?"

"Yes, I had to."

"And James Donovan?"

She arched her eyebrows but said nothing in response.

CHAPTER 51

The ringing of Hope's phone startled them both. Clay glanced at the phone on the end table and then at Hope to see what she would do. She took her eyes off him for a split second to reach for the phone and he leaped at her from the couch. But she reacted quickly, firing her .45. The shot grazed Clay's temple above his right ear, the impact knocking him to the floor. Blood trickled from his wound. Waving her revolver at Clay, she shouted, "Didn't I say I would shoot you if you got up?"

He reached for his wound, uncertain how serious it was.

"You'll live," she said, and answered the phone. "Hello ... What? ... God almighty! ... Where are you? ... Yes ... Now ... I said *now*!" When the conversation ended, she slammed the phone back on the table and ordered Clay back on the couch. "Don't try that again."

"Who was on the phone?"

"My inept partner."

Within seconds Clay heard a knock on the apartment door and a muffled voice from outside. "It's me."

Without taking her eyes off Clay, Hope opened the door a crack. "Come on in."

The man was dressed in a plaid shirt and blue jeans.

"So what happened?" she asked. "Do I have to do everything myself?"

"I didn't know the son of a bitch had a gun." The man ran his fingers through his hair. His eyes were hollow with dark rings under them. Years of drug use had taken their toll on this once good-looking man.

Clay recognized him immediately. "Well, I'll be damned. Jim Donovan in the flesh. You're almost unrecognizable with the beard and ponytail. You're not dead after all."

"Does it look like I'm dead?" Donovan sneered. He turned to Hope. "What happened to him? Why is he bleeding?"

She shrugged. "Mr. Detective-man came after me. I had to shoot him."

Clay noticed Donovan wore cowboy boots. "Nice boots. What did you do with the ones you were wearing when you pulled Angela Foster from her car?"

Donovan looked at his boots. "You like them? They're new. Hope bought them for me. We had to throw the other ones away."

"Because one had a broken heel?"

Donovan ignored Clay's comment and turned to Hope with impatience. "Come on, Hope, let's get this over with. What do you want me to do?"

Their conversation was interrupted by the ring of Clay's cell phone.

"I forgot to take his phone away from him. Let me have it Mr. Detective-man."

Clay made no effort to retrieve his phone from his jacket. It continued to ring.

"Now," she demanded, and took a step closer to him. She pointed the gun at his head. "You've got three seconds to give it to me. One. Two—" Clay pulled the phone from his pocket.

"Your caller's leaving a voice mail. Who is it, one of your girlfriends? Slide it here." She picked up the phone to see who had called. "Oh, it's your friend Shiloh. Let's hear what he has to say."

She waited for the voice mail alert to sound, then put the phone on speaker. They listened to Shiloh's message. "Detective Bryce, the kidnapper found us. He shot Officer Dunleavy, but Angela and I are okay. I know I'm not supposed to use the phone for any reason, but I called 9-1-1 for an ambulance. I scared the shooter away, but he might be back. What do you want us to do? Call me right away."

Hope said, "Well, Jim, that answers my question about what happened. Did anyone follow you here?"

"No. I made sure of that. You know I had no choice but to get the hell out of there."

"You couldn't finish the job I asked you to do?"

"I'm telling you, I'm lucky that sergeant kid didn't nail me."

Clay was shocked at the turn of events involving the safe house. "How did you know where Angela and Shiloh were staying?"

"You told me Angela needed ongoing psychological care. I tracked down the two psychologists at St. Vincent's and had Jim follow them every day until he figured out one of them was dropped off at a house on 588 three times a week."

Clay knew they were ready to kill him. He had to keep Hope talking. In the most casual tone he could muster, he said, "Jim did a lot for you, didn't he. I didn't realize you and he were friends."

"Yes, Jim and I have been friends for quite a while now," Hope explained, "—ever since John left me."

"I assume you were Hope's partner in all the murders, Jim. I was wondering what happened to you."

Donovan didn't respond.

"Jim's not a talker. He's a pretty quiet guy, aren't you, Jim? And, yes, Jim's been my partner. He would drive his pickup. Actually, it was kinda fun, wasn't it, Jim?"

Still no response from Donovan.

"We put a light on his truck, and he puts on a sheriff's badge to pretend he's a tribal cop. Teddy comes with us too. He likes riding in Jim's truck. He sits between us, and I explain to him what's happening because he can't see over the dashboard."

"Shiloh thought Jim was talking to someone when Angela was kidnapped. Was it you, Hope?"

"Yes."

"Okay, I'm beginning to understand. You wanted to get even with Emily and Carrie because they stole John from you. And you also killed Gwen Willington for the same reason."

Hope nodded solemnly. "Yes, Gwen too. I hated to kill her because she was so sweet. But everyone saw John acting like a puppy dog, drooling all over her. I was embarrassed to see him act like that. Everyone knew John was meant to be with me, *not with her*. It was common knowledge, wasn't it, Teddy?"

Donovan shrugged as if to say, "It's not my problem that she talks to a stuffed animal."

Clay continued to question Hope, waiting for an opening when he could wrest her gun from her. "What about Angela Foster?"

"Angela, that poor, naïve girl. John was trying to get her into bed too, but she wouldn't give him the time of day. I tried to get rid of Angela to protect John from himself. He never stops trying to sleep with every good-looking woman he meets. I have to get rid of all the temptations he faces."

"Jim, what do you gain by doing this for Hope?" Clay asked.

Again Hope answered for Donovan. "I can answer that, Clay. Money. Lots of it. I gave Jim the blackmail money that John gave me to give to Emily and Carrie." She smiled at Donovan. "But you've used most of it up, haven't you, Jim? We'll just have to get more from John, won't we, sweetie?"

Jim nodded, his sunken eyes darting back and forth between Clay and Hope.

"Tell me about Denver Stennet. He told me he went to Jim's apartment complex to look for Carrie the night she went missing. Was that a lie?"

"No, he was there."

"That night, Carrie told us it was Stennet who put together a plan to blackmail John. That no-good jerk was the one who made my John leave me. Can you imagine that?"

"What happened?"

"After we killed Carrie, we drove back to Jim's apartment. We were in the parking lot when we saw Stennet pounding on the door demanding to be let in. But the landlord wouldn't budge, so Stennet went back to his car and sat there a long while. We guessed he was waiting for Jim to show up. Or maybe Carrie. We didn't know. But one thing we understood— Stennet knew too much. We had to take care of him. So we followed him when he left the parking lot. Clay, you should have seen what happened. Jim rammed Stennet's truck into the ravine. It did cartwheels all the way down to the desert. It was like the demolition derby. Kinda fun to see, wasn't it, Jim?"

Donovan smiled and nodded.

Clay looked at Donovan. "Why did you move out of your apartment?"

Hope answered before Donovan could speak. "Because we knew the manager would be able to identify Carrie and Stennet. And if the police investigated, they would trace everything back to Jim. So he moved out the next day."

"You've been in hiding all this time? What about Stennet? He didn't die in that crash. What did you plan to do about him?"

Donovan finally spoke. "We didn't think we had to do anything."

Hope added, "We knew he wouldn't tell the police about Jim and me because he would have incriminated himself. After all, he was the mastermind behind the plan to have Carrie blackmail John."

"But then you ended up killing him anyway."

She answered, "That's correct, but not for a couple of years. We decided to have him confess to the killings and then commit suicide. We thought you were getting too close to learning the truth, Mr. Detective-man."

Clay was incredulous. How could this woman he cared so much about be a heartless killer? "Your suicide idea might have worked if it wasn't for the ketamine in Stennet's system. That's what made no sense. When the ME discovered the ketamine, we realized he hadn't committed suicide."

Hope nodded. "Is that what tipped you off—the ketamine? That was stupid on our part. We didn't know it could be found in his system."

Donovan was getting impatient. "Come on, Hope. What's done is done. Now, let's get this over with too."

Hope said, "Okay, sweetie. You have your ski mask?"

"Yeah. In my pocket."

"Put it on. We'll take care of Mr. Detective-man and bury him in the desert. She tilted her head toward Clay with a sad look. "I'm sorry, Clay. I really did like you. I still don't know why you would have left me for Holly. I had so much more to offer you." She then flashed a suggestive smile. "Didn't I?"

He forced a smile back at her. "Yes, you did, Hope. But I'll say it again, I had no interest in Holly—none whatsoever."

"Honest?"

"Yes. You are the only one I care for. In a million years I would never have been unfaithful to you the way John was."

"You're lying and I know it. Hey, Jim, Mr. Detective-man thinks I am so gullible. Isn't that a hoot?" She waited for Donovan to put on his ski mask. "He thinks he can charm me with all his lies."

Jim didn't care. He nodded impatiently.

"Okay, now, keep an eye on him," she said as she put her on own mask. "Let me have your gun."

"Why?"

"Just give me the damn gun, Jim."

CHAPTER 52

Jim handed his .45 to Hope. She set it on the table next to teddy, then exchanged her own .45 for Clay's service revolver and waved it at Clay.

"I don't have a ski mask on," he said, and with a wary eye toward Donovan, inched forward on the couch, coiling to spring at her. He wasn't going to be shot without a fight.

Bang!

Donovan staggered backward. "Why?"

His body shuddered violently before he fell heavily to the floor. Blood pooled around him. Hope had fired a bullet into his chest.

Clay shouted, "Why did you do that?"

Hope shrugged. "I asked him to do one thing on his own."

"How are you going to explain that to the police?"

"Um, let me think." She smiled and contorted her eyes and lips, lifting her forefinger to her chin. "Let's see. What shall I say to the police? Oh, I know. I'll tell them how Detective Bryce saved my life. How I was in my car, and how Jim chased me, and how I phoned you in a panic and you told me to go to my condo. And then when you got here, you found Jim holding me prisoner. Jim admitted he was the killer. And if it weren't for you, I'd be dead too. You shot him with your gun and saved my life. How's that sound?"

Clay knew the answer to his next question, but asked anyway. "How are you going to explain why you shot me?"

"Oh, I didn't shoot you. Jim did. Right, Teddy? Ha! First you shot Jim with your gun, but then, poor you." She set Clay's revolver back down and picked up Donovan's .45. "Jim shot you with his gun at the same time that you shot him dead. And, boohoo, you died too."

356

"So, Jim's going to be the bad guy in all this?"

"Why, yes, of course. He was always going to be the bad guy. I made sure of that."

"Like planting the gloves and ski masks in his stuff when he moved out of his apartment?"

"Yes. I knew if the police ever investigated Jim they would find that evidence. Pretty clever, eh?"

"Not clever—diabolical."

Hope flared with anger. She waved her gun at Clay again and said, "Don't ever use that word again. Do you understand?"

"Okay. I won't. Calm down. Calm down."

She took a deep breath, which seemed to calm her. You know what? You're going to be the hero in all this—a dead hero, but a hero nonetheless. Won't that be nice? I'll even go to your funeral and cry for you. Now, be a good boy and put on that ski mask."

Clay continued to stall. "But you haven't told me everything yet. You said you killed Holly. But I'm not sure why. Because you thought she was going to steal me away from you? Is that the reason, or was it because you thought John had been unfaithful with her? Which was it?"

She looked out into space trying to reason why she framed Grainger. "Oh, no. I remember now. I found out John was trying to take Teddy away from me, just like those mean foster parents did when I was a little girl." She curled her mouth, her lips quivering like a child about to cry.

"What makes you think he was trying to take Teddy? Did Teddy tell you that himself?"

Hope nodded repeatedly in puppet-like fashion.

"Yes, Teddy told me. That's how."

Clay was shocked at how paranoia had taken possession of the woman he thought he loved. Why hadn't he seen this before? Were John Grainger's comments about her jealousy and control a sign of her paranoia?

"And what did Teddy say to you?"

"That John tried to get him to leave me and go live with him."

"No kidding. He tried to get Teddy to leave you?"

"Yes, isn't that what I just said? He tried to tempt Teddy by telling him he had lots of games he could play at his house, and he would be able to go swimming in his pool, and he would buy Teddy a dog, and take him for walks and everything."

"What about John's clothes? Who took them—Denver Stennet?"

"No. I did. The night John had his party and there was all that commotion about Liza falling into the pool, I went to his closet and took a shirt and a pair of his trousers and threw them out the back window. Then, when I left the party, I got them and took them home with me."

"Why did you pretend it was Jason who called Desert Breeze to have Stennet fix John's bollard? What did Jason have to do with Stennet?"

"Nothing. I wanted you to think they were partners—that they were the killers. And Simon. I know you were beginning to suspect him too. You see, I figured if you had doubt about who had a reason to kill Holly, there was no way John would be arrested for her murder. I still love John, you know. I didn't really want him to go to prison for a crime he didn't commit."

"But you said you didn't love him anymore. That you loved me, and that you were getting even with him for trying to take Teddy away from you."

"I did? Oh, I guess I did. I don't know what to think. I would have loved you more if you hadn't taken up with Holly. You know, since we're being honest with each other, Mr. Detective-man, why can't you just tell me the truth about Holly?"

"For the hundredth time, I had no interest in her."

"Ah, you're still lying. Teddy told me you've been lying all along. He said you're no different than any other man. Men always have their eyes out for other women—younger, prettier, richer. Just like John always does. I know you're the same way. The only person who has never lied to me is Teddy. He's been my best friend forever, and he would *never* leave me for anyone else. He's the only person I can trust. I wish I could have said that about you."

"I'm not like that, Hope. I fell in love with you the very first time I laid eyes on you."

"Oh, if only I could believe you. Right, Teddy? We just can't believe him."

Clay finally saw an opening. He could use Hope's obsession with Teddy to distract her. "You *can* believe me. Ask Teddy. He'll tell you. After all, Teddy and I talked a lot whenever I was at your condo."

She turned her head toward the stuffed bear. "Is that true, Teddy?"

Clay answered, "Yes, it's true, Hope. We've become very good friends, Teddy and me. I'm surprised you didn't know that. I told Teddy you had asked me to move in with you, and that I was going to surprise you and tell you yes."

She looked toward her ever-vigilant teddy bear. "Teddy, why didn't you tell me that? What's that? Oh, is that right?" She turned back to Clay. "Ha! Teddy says you're lying again. Oh, my

God, don't you ever stop lying? Now pick up that mask and put it on."

"I'm not lying and I'm not putting on the mask. You're going to know who you're killing when you shoot me."

"I know who you are. Now put it on."

"I'll tell you what. If you put a mask on Teddy, I'll put one on too. He should be wearing a mask, you know."

"Teddy, he's right. You should have one too." She smiled at Clay. "He likes it when I put one on him. You do, don't you, sweetheart?"

Hope was transfixed with her teddy. "What did you say? I can't hear you." Without thinking, she set her .45 on the table to pick up the bear. She tilted her head to hear what her teddy was telling her, while shaking her head back and forth, trying to will away her psychotic haze.

Clay didn't hesitate. He leaped off the couch and threw himself at Hope, but she quickly snatched the gun from the table and turned it toward him. He grabbed her wrist with one hand and with the other tried to wrest the gun away, throwing her to the floor and quickly overpowering her. But she wouldn't let go of the gun. She bucked and clawed, screeching, "Get off me! Get off me!"

"Stop it, Hope! Stop it! Listen to me. Listen. Don't do this. Let me help you."

She shook her head violently. "Get off! Get off! You're just like everyone else."

"No, I'm not, Hope. I loved you. I wasn't going to leave you."

She didn't hear him. She was too mired in her paranoia, crying with heart-wrenching sobs, her chest heaving, her face contorted.

Clay couldn't bear to see her like this. "Hope, I loved you. Please, let me have the gun."

She wouldn't stop fighting.

A shot rang out.

Her body went limp.

"Oh, my God. No!" Clay eased the gun from her hand and knelt next to her. He brushed the hair from her face. "I loved you, Hope. I was never going to leave you."

She looked up at him and a tear rolled down her cheek.

EPILOGUE

Captain Ellsworth requested the serial killer task force meet for a final briefing. "Special Agent Stephenson, would you please discuss the psychology of abandonment and how that led to Hope Archer's motivation to kill the women of the Bend?"

"When a child is abandoned by its parents through death, adoption, whatever, the psychological effect the loss has on the child as he or she grows can sometimes be dramatic. That's particularly true if the child is shuffled from foster home to foster home without any hope of being adopted. Understand, the majority of adoptions work out just fine, but obviously Hope Archer's unfortunate childhood experiences led her to develop an overwhelming sense of unhappiness that negatively—and permanently—impacted her. She was never able to get over the perception that everyone she cared for would abandon her. As a result, she suffered so severely, she sought vengeance against those she felt were responsible for her losses. Again, I'm not suggesting Hope's condition is the norm, but it played the predominant role in her psychoses."

"What about her obsession with stuffed bears?" Chief Johnstone asked.

"Her first teddy bear—the one her father gave her—brought her some degree of comfort and security. But when it was taken away from her by an uncaring foster parent, she had nothing left to hold onto for comfort. It must have caused her incredible psychological pain. Even as she collected the bears, they did not fill her lifelong sense that people she cared for would abandon her, including the perception that Clay was going to leave her."

Clay struggled deeply with the realization that Hope was so tragically ill. How could he not have known? She was the only woman since his divorce who made him feel alive again. She was all he could think about. He knew he would have to get over her, but it would take time. Hope had survived her gunshot wound, but would spend the rest of her life in the Santa Fe Hospital for the Criminally Insane. "Hope trusted only her teddy bear. I've visited her, but she is heavily sedated and basically uncommunicative."

"Hank, what's the DA going to do about John Grainger? Those were serious charges against him," Ellsworth said.

"Our office agreed with Grainger's attorney that his client had been entrapped by Carrie Kirkland and Denver Stennet. The charge of criminal sexual misconduct against him has been dropped. But, as I understand it, because of his many dalliances with Indian Bend employees, Grainger lost his position there as Operations Vice President."

"He's been replaced by Simon Learner," Clay added. "And although it must be an awkward situation, Jason Alvarez continues as Director of HR reporting to Simon."

"Jacoby, what's going on with Shiloh and Angela?"

"Shiloh's returning to active duty. He wants to make the Army his career. But the two will be getting married before he heads back to Fort Hood—and Bret Colby's going to be the best man."

The End

ABOUT THE AUTHOR

Tony Spallone turned his long-time love of fiction writing from hobby to published novel in 2014. His first, *Murder at Breeze Canyon*, received high praise. *Murders in the High Desert* is Spallone's second book to be published. He and his wife Patti love the southwest, particularly New Mexico, the setting for both stories. He has a graduate degree in psychology, was an officer in the army, and has held various executive positions in business. Tony Spallone lives in Chester Springs, Pennsylvania. You can reach Spallone on his website www.tonyspallone.com.